CIRCLES IN THE STREAM

ALL THAT GLITTERS

CRY OF THE WOLF

AvALon

∼ Web Of Magic ∼

Omnibus Collection

Book 1–3

RACHEL ROBERTS

Seven Seas

AVALON: WEB OF MAGIC
OMNIBUS COLLECTION: BOOK 1-3

Published by Seven Seas Entertainment.

ISBN: 978-1-935934-29-5

Cover and interior art by Allison Strom

Interior book design by
Pauline Neuwirth, Neuwirth & Associates, Inc.
Printed in the United States of America

1 2 3 4 5 6 7 8 9 10

WOODS

OWL CREEK
BIRD SANCTUARY

EAGLE RIDGE

WOODS

WOODS

OWL CREEK

BAMBOO
FOREST

DEER
MEADOW

PORTAL
FIELD

MIRROR
LAKE

HIDDEN FALLS TRAIL

MAGIC GLADE

ROCKING
STONE

SWAN LAKE
TRAIL

HEDGE
MAZE

SWAN LAKE

TURTLE
BOG

ALTAKAWAY RIVER

WOLF RUN
PASS

WATER
GARDEN

ROSE
GARDENS

TOPIARY
GARDENS

ADRIANE'S
HOUSE

SCULPTURE
GARDENS

RAVENSWOOD
MANOR

MIST TRAIL

STONE WALL

MAIN GATE

PLAYING
FIELDS

MAIN ROAD

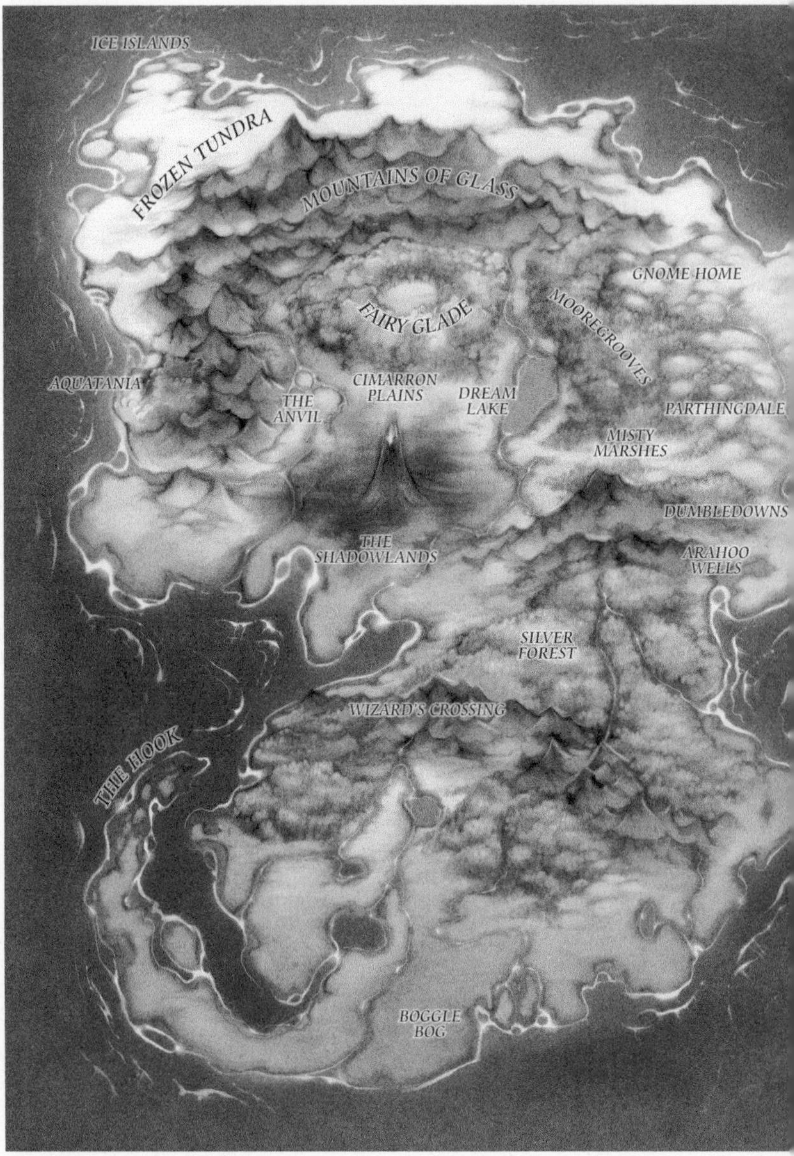

ICE ISLANDS

FROZEN TUNDRA

MOUNTAINS OF GLASS

GNOME HOME

FAIRY GLADE

MOORGROOVES

AQUATANIA

CIMARRON PLAINS

DREAM LAKE

PARTHINGDALE

THE ANVIL

MISTY MARSHES

DUMBLEDOWNS

THE SHADOWLANDS

ARAHOO WELLS

SILVER FOREST

WIZARD'S CROSSING

THE HOOK

BOGGLE BOG

CIRCLES IN THE STREAM

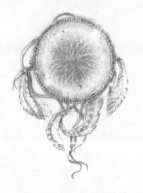

1

*T*HE BIG CAT crouched low in the tall grass. Dazed, she looked around the meadow and knew instantly she was no longer in the Shadowlands.

Sadness welled inside, threatening to devour any strength she had left. Her world in flames. Her family gone. She had escaped—and for what? To end it all here in a strange world, alone?

The wind picked up, hot and humid across the open field. If she could just reach the trees . . . she willed her legs to run, to keep going . . . but it was too late.

The creature shot from the sky, sweeping over her in a mass of wings, claws, and teeth. Desperate, the cat lunged into the forest of giant firs and stopped, breathing hard. The clean air cooled her seared lungs, but even that slight movement was agony. Her vision went in and out of focus. Trying to get her bearings, she realized she could only see from one eye. She had to move—find a safe place to hide.

A low growl rumbled into a twisted laugh. The creature towered over her. With a roar like thunder, it struck.

THUNDER ROCKED ACROSS the skies, sending the three dogs into fits of howling.

Twelve-year-old Emily Fletcher tried to calm them. "It's just a storm." But no matter what she did, they slunk low to the ground, growling and whimpering. Usually they were happy to play in the backyard with her—a daily break from their kennels at the Pet Palace. But this afternoon they ignored the ball Emily rolled out to them, pointing their noses instead toward the forested slopes in the distance.

Emily followed their gaze. Her eyes fell over the expanse of trees that met the playing fields and parkland that bordered her house. She had been in Stonehill, Pennsylvania for eight weeks, and although she'd been an avid hiker back home in Colorado, she'd not yet begun to explore these woods. For one thing, she had no friends—for another, she'd been way too busy. Helping her mom set up Stonehill Animal Hospital and the Pet Palace Animal Hotel had pretty much taken up all her

time. Not that Emily really minded. She loved animals—
had a magic touch with them, her mom always said—and
being busy kept her from being lonely. Sometimes she
barely remembered that her parents were now officially
divorced and she was thousands of miles from everything
and everyone she knew. Sometimes she remembered all
too well.

She ran a hand through her curly, auburn hair.
Animals can sense a drop in air pressure before people
can, she reminded herself. That must be why the dogs are
acting so strange.

Lightning flashed, splitting the sky with jagged forks.
Jellybean, the Harrison family's dalmatian, began to leap
up and down, barking. Pumpkin, Mrs. Stalling's little
white poodle, cowered, and Emily tensed in spite of
herself.

"Okay," she said, giving up. "Let's get inside."

The dogs barreled through the side door of the small
barn that Emily and her mother had converted into the
animal hotel. Emily herded the dogs into their kennels.
Biscuit, Mr. Franklin's golden retriever, walked forward,
turned backward to growl, then circled, moving forward
a few more steps before turning to growl again. Jellybean
threw himself at Emily and yelped loudly.

"What's wrong, guys?" Emily asked, gently pushing
Jellybean back into his kennel. "What's got into you?"

Biscuit pointed her nose up to the ceiling and howled.
In the back room, a cockatiel screamed.

Something else screamed.

Emily froze, stock-still. What was *that*? She waited, her ears straining. Behind her, the dogs were near panic.

It came again, the sound ripping through her like broken glass. Emily cried out. An animal was in trouble!

Instinctively she zoomed into crisis mode. She'd been around animals ever since she turned five, the year her mom, Dr. Carolyn Fletcher, first went into veterinary practice. Emily had assisted in several emergencies: a dog that'd been shot by a hunter, a cat hit by a car. She'd seen the blood and the bones and the suffering in the animals' eyes, and it never got any easier.

Emily ran out of the barn and into the main building that housed the clinic. Her mother would need her help! She raced into the foyer and slipped on the wet floor. She looked down and gasped. Blood. Lightning flashed, suddenly illuminating her reflection in the hallway mirror as if she were a ghost. She stood there, holding her breath.

Shouting from the emergency room made her turn.

She heard her mother yell, "Put it down here!" There were sounds of scuffling; men were shouting and an animal roared in defiance. Each scream tore through Emily, making her cringe. Still, she pushed her way inside—into pandemonium.

"Hold it still!" Carolyn ordered. Two policemen struggled to hold a wriggling tarp down on the operating table. A razor-clawed paw swept out from under the tarp, raking down a uniformed sleeve and breaking one man's grasp. The other man slammed the animal down hard.

"Emily, get the hypodermic!" Carolyn shouted over the animal's yowls.

Emily remained frozen and watched as her mother drew back the tarp. Carolyn's gasp stuck in her throat.

It was a cat. An enormous cat. And it was burned—badly. Only small patches of its leopard-spotted fur remained; everywhere else, the skin was oozing blood. One of the cat's eyes was swollen shut.

"Oh no, oh no," Emily thought she heard herself saying over and over.

"Emily! Move it!" The animal twisted in Carolyn's arms and took a mad swipe, ripping the sleeve of her tunic. Instinctively, she jerked back, grabbing her arm.

The cat struggled to stand, but its paws slipped in the pools of its own blood. Emily stared at the awful wounds. Burns everywhere—and, on one flank, a set of deep claw marks. But what mesmerized her was the green glow that seemed to emanate—shimmering, almost bubbling—from the burned flesh.

Didn't anyone else notice? Emily wondered.

"Emily!" her mom shouted. "I need your help, do you hear me?"

Emily looked up. Shaking, she fumbled around the supply cabinet for a hypodermic, trying to get it out of its wrapping. Somehow she managed to measure out the dose of tranquilizer her mother called out to her. The cat twisted hard, letting out an awful cry. The pain lanced into Emily's chest, making her scream. The needle fell to the floor.

The cat was up on its feet, snarling. It turned to face Emily. Glaring through its one good eye, it bared razor teeth and crouched to strike.

Sadness overwhelmed Emily, deep and empty like nothing she'd ever known.

As if in a dream, she slowly moved forward.

"Keep away from it!" one of the cops shouted.

The cat looked straight at her. A hard glint of steel flashed from its gold-green eyes and Emily felt a rush of feelings wash over her: rage, hate, pain, fear, and . . . something else . . . something Emily recognized instantly. Loss.

She stared at the cat. It's all right. You're with friends. We want to help you . . . Had she spoken out loud?

The cat's expression calmed, the feral glow fading from its eyes as its muscles relaxed. Emily looked up to see her mother pulling a needle from the cat's side. The animal slid to the table, fighting to keep eye contact with Emily.

Leaning her head in close, Emily heard a whisper, a single word . . . *"Home."*

A hand was on her shoulder, pulling her back. It was her mom, her grip firm but gentle.

"Thank you, officers. We've got everything under control now."

"You're sure you'll be okay, Doctor?" one of them asked.

"This is what we do," she replied, pulling on surgical gloves. "Where did you find this animal?"

The older of the two policemen shook his head. "We didn't find it. She did." He jerked his thumb toward the far corner of the room. "Out at the Ravenswood Preserve."

For the first time Emily noticed the dark-haired girl who stood watching, black eyes wide against tanned skin. Where had she come from?

Carolyn turned to the girl. "Any sign of what might have done this to her?"

"No." The girl's long dark hair fell over her face as she edged toward the door.

"You did the right thing, calling for help," Carolyn assured her.

"Yeah. . . . " The girl was out the door in a flash.

"Emily, get scrubbed. Andrea's gone for the day, so you're assisting. You know the burn drill: soak, clean, and cover." The officers had left, and her mom was all business now.

But Emily was frozen again. *Home.* She was sure she'd heard it. But *who* had said it?

"Emily!" Carolyn set down the steel trays. "What's the matter with you? Let's go! Now!"

Emily willed her legs to move. Her hip hit the side of the exam table, making it spin on its wheels. "I . . . can't . . . I . . . " she faltered.

"If you can't help, then get out!"

Carolyn was already dousing sterile bandages with

ice-cold alcohol and laying them over the worst of the burns. Emily looked from her mom to the cat, and then stumbled out of the room in a daze.

Tears streamed down her cheeks as she walked out onto the hospital's covered back porch. What had happened to her in there? She had *wanted* to help—she really had! How could she have frozen up like that, at a critical moment, with an animal's life on the line? Never before had she acted like that, so clumsy and powerless. She hated it!

She walked into the backyard, trying to calm her breathing. She caught a glimpse of the black-haired girl running across the fields toward the forest. Something ran alongside her. It looked like a big gray dog. Emily shook her head, thinking about those awful burns. What could have hurt an animal like that? And what kind of animal was it, anyway? It looked like a leopard—but leopards didn't live in the Pennsylvania woods . . . *out at the Ravenswood Preserve* . . . Is that where it came from? Suddenly Emily shivered as a strange feeling swept over her. It felt like something horrible was approaching . . . something evil . . .

"Boo!"

With a shriek, Emily wheeled around—and found herself staring into the laughing face of Kevin Deacon, the fifteen-year-old who worked part-time at the hospital, cleaning out cages and caring for the animals. "Kevin, you idiot! Don't ever do that again!"

Kevin just laughed some more.

"I'm not joking!" Emily turned away so he wouldn't see how upset she really was.

Kevin's mischievous smile faded. "I heard some awful noises a minute ago." He brushed a lock of sandy hair from his forehead. "Some animal hurt pretty bad, huh?"

He could be such a jerk sometimes, but Emily had to admit that he did care about animals. "Yeah."

"Your mom's a great vet."

"I should have—I mean, yeah." Just go away and leave me alone!

"I saw that girl running away as I rode up. What was *she* doing here?"

"She found the animal, a cat." Emily sniffed, calming down a little.

"That girl's really weird."

"What do you mean?" Emily asked.

"She lives in the woods! At the Ravenswood Preserve."

"She *lives* there? Wow." Emily's eyes widened.

"Yeah, well, if the town council has anything to say about it, Ravenswood is going to be shut down."

"Why?" Emily asked.

His blue eyes sparkled as he edged closer to her. "It's haunted."

Emily laughed. "Haunted? That is so juvenile."

He shrugged. "Hey, the place used to be amazing. Old Man Gardener collected all kinds of animals. We used to go there as kids, feed deer, peacocks, even monkeys.

Now no one goes there. They say a monster roams the woods . . ."

Emily snorted. "C'mon, Kevin, get a grip."

Kevin glanced back at the clinic. "Look, I don't know what happened to the cat in there—but from the screams and the look on your face, it's bad, right? It doesn't take a genius to figure out that it was probably attacked by the same . . . *thing* . . . that's already killed a couple of dogs."

In spite of herself, Emily shivered. "Why don't they just talk to that Gardener guy who owns the place?" she asked.

"He disappeared," Kevin whispered. "Just upped and went one day, vanished. Spooky, huh?"

"So who takes care of all the animals?"

"His caretaker, I guess. Some old woman. People say she's a witch."

"Kevin, stop it," Emily shook her head. "There are no such thing as witches." She was getting goose bumps.

"My friend Tyler saw a ghost about three weeks ago, right near the Rocking Stone."

"The what?"

"The Rocking Stone, it's been here forever. It's an Indian monument, like a lighthouse for ghosts."

Emily was trying not to let his ridiculous stories get to her.

"Something's in those woods," Kevin said slowly. "That place should be condemned."

"What would happen to the animals?" Emily asked.

But Kevin was already on his way into the clinic to begin his chores.

Emily looked out to the west, where the dark clouds had broken. The sun was setting behind the forest, sending up a fiery glow.

"I don't believe in witches, monsters, *or* ghosts! I'm not afraid." But somehow she was.

2

$\mathcal{E}$MILY FOUND HER mother in the lab, examining something under a microscope. At the sound of Emily's footsteps, Carolyn looked up, concerned.

Emily paused. "How is—?" She stared at her sneakers. She couldn't complete the question, afraid she'd already seen the answer on her mother's drawn face.

"She's alive," Carolyn told her. "Heavily sedated, but stable."

Emily burst into tears. "I'm so sorry!"

"Shh, okay, it's okay, sweetheart," Carolyn said, wrapping her arms around her daughter.

"I didn't help you . . . You needed me and I froze!" Fresh tears ran down her face.

"Honey, it was pretty intense," Carolyn reassured her.

Emily pushed away from her mother and squared her shoulders. "I need to see her."

"Okay."

Emily walked to the door of the recovery room and, after a moment's hesitation, opened it. Inside, the room was quiet, the shades drawn, the walls lit softly by a small lamp. The cat lay in a spacious cage. An intravenous needle was taped to her shoulder, connected by a tube to a bag that contained fluids and antibiotics. The cat was almost entirely wrapped in bandages. Her breathing was labored and shallow.

Emily knelt beside the cage. "You're hurt so bad," she said. "I'm sorry I didn't help. Please don't die . . . please."

As Emily spoke, the cat's breathing slowed and became more even. Its one good eye was halfway open and looking at her.

"I'm right here. I won't leave you," Emily promised.

The cat closed its eye and fell back asleep.

Carolyn walked into the room and knelt next to Emily. "She's sleeping. Breathing's regular. That's good."

Emily gave Carolyn a quick smile. She pointed to a patch of spotted fur on one of its rear paws. "What is she, a leopard?"

"I'm thinking maybe a margay, or some unusual kind of ocelot," Carolyn answered.

Emily stared at the cat. "What kind of animal could

have made these marks?" she asked, flashing on Kevin's "monsters."

"I might have guessed a bear," Carolyn mused, "but only black bears live around here—largely vegetarian and almost never aggressive. Of course, we don't know what other kinds of bears might live on that preserve." She shook her head. "But that still doesn't explain the burns . . . "

Faintly visible under the bandages, Emily noticed the green glow was still there.

"I've never seen anything like it," Carolyn continued. "The burns seem to spread out from the claw wounds . . . but the only way that could be is if . . . " She shook her head again. "If the claws were toxic somehow. Or—"

"What?" Emily asked.

Carolyn sighed. "The burns may not be accidental. They could have been inflicted by someone."

Emily gasped in horror. "What kind of a person would do that?"

"It may not be that. There may have been some toxic dumping in that preserve."

Emily's eyes widened. "What if other animals out there are in trouble? We have to help them!"

"Oh, no, you don't," her mom said sternly. "Don't even *think* about going into those woods until we find out what—or who—caused those wounds." She stood and straightened her lab coat. "I was preparing some skin samples to send to the university for analysis."

"I want to stay down here tonight, with her."

Carolyn frowned. Emily pressed on. "Burn victims benefit if they're surrounded by people who care about them."

Her mother smiled. "All right, I suppose it wouldn't hurt."

Emily smiled back.

THAT NIGHT, EMILY dragged her sleeping bag, a careful selection of stuffed animals, and two pillows into the clinic's recovery room and set herself up as close to the cage as she could.

"I brought you, Mr. Snuffles," she said softly, holding up the orange lion. "See, he's a cat, too."

The cat lay sleeping, breathing calmly. Emily opened the cage and placed Mr. Snuffles far to the side, careful not to touch the injured animal's bandages. Gently she stroked a patch of uncovered fur on her shoulder.

That's strange, she thought. The cat had two bumps, matching mounds that protruded behind each shoulder blade. They were hard but spongy, like cartilage.

"What are these?" she mused aloud. Could it be a fracture? No, her mom was too good a vet to miss anything like that. And the cat didn't even twitch when Emily touched the bumps. They must be something else, something normal for this cat.

She closed the cage and snuggled down with her other stuffed friends. She was happy to be doing something for the cat at last. She would watch her all night. But the cat seemed at peace now, and Emily found it harder and harder to keep her eyes open. Finally, she couldn't fight the exhaustion anymore. As her eyes closed, she imagined she heard a thin, distant voice.

"Thank you."

SUNLIGHT POURED INTO the room as Carolyn drew back the shades. "Good morning, Doc. Rise and shine!"

"Mornin'," Emily mumbled as she tried to untangle herself from her sleeping bag. Finally, she kicked the bag away and stuck her nose up to the cat's cage. To her great relief, the cat's sides were rising and falling with deep, smooth breaths. "She looks better."

"Breathing's stabilized," Carolyn confirmed, carefully laying her stethoscope on the cat's side. She checked the cat's pupils, then deftly inserted a thermometer. A few moments later she was shaking it back down with a smile. "You're absolutely right. No fever, and she definitely seems better." She smiled. "You've got the magic touch, Doc!"

Emily beamed. For just a moment, she let herself think she had helped heal the cat. But of course, she knew that was nonsense. Other than her simple presence, she'd done nothing. Still, she resolved to stay with the cat until it was really well again.

OVER THE NEXT few days, Emily remained at the cat's side, chatting quietly or reading to her, stroking the spots of unburned fur. Once the intravenous needle was removed, Emily took over feeding her soft food and liquid vitamins.

On the third afternoon, Emily was lying on her makeshift bed, skimming through her yearbook from last year. Her class would all be starting junior high. Everyone but her. Because she'd known that, she'd made sure to collect as many signatures as possible.

Friends 4ever, Alison, who played on her soccer team, had written.

2 good 2B 4-gotten. Laura had drawn a smiley face next to that, adding Good luck!

Wherever you go, there you are, her best bud, Taylor, had scrawled.

Emily looked around. Here I am. A stranger in a totally new place where school would be starting in about three weeks. She realized she was dreading it. Here, middle school *started* in sixth grade. By seventh, all the kids already knew each other.

If only her mom hadn't found this veterinary practice

to buy in Stonehill. If only her dad hadn't moved to Seattle, where his new wife's family lived. The only thing that hadn't changed was having to deal with animals in pain. And she wasn't even good at that.

Emily felt it before she looked up. The cat was watching her. Both eyes were open now, the injured one only halfway, but looking clear and bright behind still-swollen tissue. Emily felt a wave of happiness at seeing the cat awake. She dropped her book and scrambled to the open cage. "Hi, there."

The cat licked Emily's nose with a sandpaper tongue. Emily giggled. "Stop that, you silly!"

Trying to stretch, the cat licked tentatively at the edge of a bandage. The recovery process was clearly beginning, but, between patches of singed fur, her wounds looked ragged and ugly.

Emily's heart sank at the thought of this magnificent animal horribly scarred for the rest of its life. "You're going to be just fine," she promised. "Your fur will grow back as pretty as ever."

"Well, our patient's up and about, I see." Carolyn walked into the room and over to the cage.

Gentle as a kitten, the cat allowed Carolyn to inspect her wounds and bandages.

"Mom, what do you think those bumps are on her shoulders?" Emily asked.

"I don't notice anything abnormal, Doc," her mother

replied. "Her joints may be a bit swollen. Now, as for my other patient . . . "

"What other patient?"

Carolyn lifted Emily's chin and felt her forehead. She swiveled Emily's face this way and that, and stared into her eyes. "Hmmm, pale, needs exercise and sunshine. And I have just the cure." She left the room and returned almost immediately with a soccer ball and dog leash. "Take these and call me in two hours."

Emily opened her mouth to object.

"You've done an amazing job with her, but how much longer do you expect Kevin to handle your chores?"

Emily hesitated, taking one last look at the cat. The cat just yawned and curled up with Mr. Snuffles.

ARROWHEAD PARK LAY at the foot of the wooded mountains to the northwest of town. There were two baseball diamonds, a soccer field, and an extensive playground, but near the woods the land was left open.

Emily, Jellybean, Biscuit, and Pumpkin ran past the picnic grounds and into the meadow that lay before the deep woods. It was an ideal spot to let the dogs romp. Despite the heat, the day was beautiful. The recent storms had lifted the humidity, and hints of a breeze made the flowers shimmer in the sunlight. Emily had to admit that, on a day like this, Pennsylvania was almost as pretty as Colorado.

"Ladies and Jellybeans!" she called, tossing the soccer ball in the air. "It's time for . . . Doggie Soccer!" The dogs yelped excitedly and began jumping for the ball, running circles around Emily.

"Okay, okay, hold on," she laughed, kneeling down to unhook the dogs from the group leash. Jellybean jumped and entangled her arm. Biscuit had wrapped the leash around her back. Pumpkin was winding in and out of her legs. Emily tried to stand up but, instead, fell down tangled in leashes.

Laughter drifted over Emily as she lay in the grass like a mummy. She looked up to see three girls sitting on a picnic table.

"What a geek!" One, with long red hair, pointed.

Emily felt her face go red as she slowly shoved the dogs aside and unwrapped herself.

The girl in the middle, willowy, with a cap of curly blond hair, stared straight at Emily. "I think she lives over at Clueless Farms. She must have forgotten her pitchfork." That sent the first girl into a fit of laughter.

Emily slowly got up and dusted herself off. She shook auburn curls from her face.

The third girl, the one on the end, turned slowly. Clad in a pink tube top, khaki shorts, and pink sneakers, she wore her long blond hair loose under a studded baseball cap. She squinted. Emily tensed for another snide comment, but all the girl said was, "Hey, that's Pumpkin, Mrs. Stalling's poodle. Mrs. Stalling's gone to France."

"Cool. I'm going there next year," the first girl said

"I'm going to Brazil with my dad," the curly-haired girl replied.

The trio seemed to lose interest in Emily. She walked into the meadow after the dogs. Please don't let them be kids from my school, she thought. If that's what kids here are like. . . .

She gave the ball an angry kick and it went flying. Biscuit, Jellybean, and Pumpkin shot like rockets chasing down the ball.

The ball came rolling back to her and she gave it another sharp kick. It sailed through the air toward the edge of the woods—and bounced oddly off to the side.

"Garg!"

Emily was startled by the loud grunt. The dogs stopped and looked in the direction of the cry.

Emily ran over to see whom she'd hit. "Oh, my gosh, I'm so sorry. Are you—"

There was no one there. She looked around. Something dashed out between the trees, shaking its head and stumbling as it ran away into the woods. Emily blinked. It looked like . . . a ferret?

Bewildered, Emily didn't have time to react. Jellybean and Biscuit were after the creature in a flash, letting loose a chorus of barks. Pumpkin sat and wagged her tail.

"Hey! Wait!" Emily yelled. "Come back here!" But the dark forest seemed to swallow her cries.

She felt a weird chill come over her. She hesitated. She didn't believe Kevin's nonsense about haunted woods and scary monsters. Just the same, she felt a tingle along the back of her neck. But the dogs were her responsibility. She had no choice. She had to find them!

Emily attached the leash to Pumpkin's collar. "It'll take more than a few haunted trees to stop us," she said, faking a courage she didn't feel. The little poodle lunged forward eagerly, pulling Emily into the dark shade of the trees. "To the haunted woods!"

There was no turning back now.

3

*T*HE LAND SLOPED gradually uphill and, after awhile, Emily had to stop and catch her breath. She cautiously looked around. Nothing seemed remotely haunted about this forest. It was just trees, undergrowth, and lots of shade. Just like hiking in the Rockies back home—her *old* home, she corrected herself.

"We've got to find a trail." Her voice fell flat in the stillness of the woods.

As if in answer, Pumpkin pushed on straight through the underbrush.

Emily bent forward, with one arm held up as a shield. "Or we could go your way." Branches whipped at her legs and scratched her face, and then they were through and onto a narrow but well-worn path.

"Good job!" Emily exclaimed. "Pumpkin, are you part bloodhound?"

Pumpkin yapped and tugged at the leash. Emily allowed the poodle to pull her briskly up the path. Thick trees and lush plant growth surrounded her. It was hard to take Kevin's stories seriously as she breathed in the sweet smells of the forest—but it was also hard to forget the terrible burns on the cat and her mother's fears that someone might be in these woods, hurting animals. The cool air turned damp on her skin and she shivered.

She could no longer hear the other dogs barking. She hoped that didn't mean they'd caught the ferret. Or worse, that something had caught *them*.

"Come on," she told Pumpkin. "Find Biscuit and Jellybean."

Pumpkin followed the trail. On either side, the woods seemed to be getting darker and more ominous. Emily was straining to hear any signs of the runaway dogs. The rustle of leaves made her look around nervously. Light and shadows played in and out of the trees. Twisted overhanging branches seemed to reach out for her. The trail led around the side of a hill, curved to the left and then spilled out onto a dirt road. Emily slid down a sudden incline, piling right into Pumpkin. She looked up. A large stone arch with twin iron gates was in front of her. On either side of the arch stretched a tall stone wall. The gates were closed. Emily stared in dismay. The dogs could be anywhere. There was a sign on the wall next to the arch. She walked over to read it.

RAVENSWOOD WILDLIFE PRESERVE
Open 11 AM to Duh

Emily giggled as she realized that vines had grown over the last letters on the sign and arranged themselves to look like an "h." She pulled the vines aside and read again:

Open 11 AM to Dusk.
Please don't feed the animals,
and stay on the paths.
Garbage in, garbage out policy,
$200 fine for littering.

"Wow, this is it! The wildlife preserve!"

Emily glanced at her watch: 11:30 AM, but the gate was closed. Then she remembered what Kevin said about the old man disappearing. Maybe there *was* no one to keep the place open now. Except a caretaker who happened to be a witch!

"Rrrroof!"

The sound came from the other side of the wall. She grabbed the iron bars and jumped up on the gate, trying to peek farther into the estate. No sign of any dogs.

"Rrrouff!"

They must have gotten through somehow.

"Get back here!" she called sternly. But there was no response. She was starting to feel queasy. "Maybe we could find a way in somewhere else—"

Creeaaaakkk . . .

The sudden screech of metal on metal startled her as the heavy gate began to swing open. She hung on. "You have visitors," she said nervously.

She jumped off the gate onto the road on the other side. "Jellybean! Biscuit!" She really hoped they'd come bounding out of the woods so she wouldn't have to go in after them. But neither dog appeared.

Emily drew in a breath. What if whatever had mauled the cat was still here? Hadn't Kevin said a few neighborhood dogs that had wandered in had been—*no*! Emily shook her head. She was so not going there. She'd find the dogs. And they'd be fine.

There seemed to be two ways to go: the main road or a smaller path that led off to the left. "Which way?"

Pumpkin pulled her along the smaller path. Emily's heart began to beat faster.

The woods closed around the path, deeper and thicker. The air smelled of damp earth. She called again, "Biscuit! Jellybean!"

Emily thought she heard a few woofs in the distance, but she couldn't tell which direction they were coming from. She had a fleeting sense that something was following her. A soft rustling startled her. She turned to her right and thought she saw the strangest thing: a white mist snaking through the trees. A ghost? There was a loud squawk, and a flash of green and red and purple flew between the tree branches. Tropical birds, she thought, certainly not native to these woods. When she looked back, the mist was gone. Must have been a trick of the light, she told herself.

"Arff!"

Pumpkin pointed to the right. Emily saw a shadow move between the trees.

"Who's there?" she called out, her pulse pounding in her ears. This was getting really creepy. A rustling in the undergrowth startled her and she whirled around to see the back of a very large animal as it disappeared from view. What was *that*! A moose? No, stupid, there're no moose in Pennsylvania. Oh yeah, right, this is a wildlife preserve. Who knows what kind of animals are here? In fact, who even knew *she* was here? She was all alone in the *haunted* woods . . . Okay, she told herself, calm down, don't panic.

As she led Pumpkin down the other path, visions of "haunted woods" and the old witch who lived there sprang up as in those Grimm's fairy tales that had scared her when she was young. The hairs on the back of her neck stood up. Turning around, Emily saw the white mist again. It was moving through the trees straight toward her. "Oh, no . . . this is not good . . ."

She ran up a little rise, then stopped to look over her shoulder. The wavering white mist was still there, getting thicker and closer. She scooped up Pumpkin and started to walk faster—then she broke into a run.

Low-hanging branches caught at her clothes, scratching at her arms and legs. This was all too weird and crazy, Emily kept thinking. She was just letting herself be spooked by what Kevin had said. But the cat—the cat was real. She was starting to panic. She had trouble catching her breath, but she couldn't stop running.

"Help! Help!" she cried out, but her screams were swallowed by the dark and hungry forest. She was in deep woods now. She stumbled over tree roots, pushed through the undergrowth—turning her head, she saw the white mist right behind her. For a split second, Emily froze. She willed her legs to move, to run. But she'd only taken a few steps when she tripped over something and did a face plant into the ground.

There was a yelp and then she realized what she had fallen over—Jellybean! Her heart leaped. He was totally fine. Nothing had mauled him. A second later Biscuit came trotting up and licked her face. Relief flooded through her.

"Bad dogs!" She scolded them half-heartedly—and stopped.

There, under a natural archway formed by trees, was a wolf. Its fur was silver, fading to white. Its eyes, rimmed in charcoal, were warm gold. It sat perfectly still, staring back at Emily. Then it stood and turned to walk through the archway. Jellybean and Biscuit followed.

"Hey, wait!" Emily called. She probably should be scared, but she wasn't.

With Pumpkin close at her side, Emily walked through the archway. The wolf was nowhere in sight. But something else definitely was. Beyond the archway stood the largest boulder she had ever seen. She craned her neck to look at the stone tower, following it up to a jagged peak that pointed into the sky. It was so tall, she wondered why she hadn't noticed it looming up above the trees.

"Wow," Emily breathed. "It's the Rocking Stone." So Kevin was right about one thing, anyway. The rock was *amazing*. Lines of quartz glistened all around the sides, catching the sunlight. When she looked more closely, she could see markings that looked like graffiti.

"Look what you guys found!" she exclaimed to the dogs.

She stepped around the rock—and saw what it was hiding. A magnificent forest glade surrounded by a perfect circle of tall firs. In the glade's center, a lake shimmered like a sky-blue mirror, except where willows brushed the water with the tips of their flowing branches. At the far side, a rippling stream flowed into the forest and a small bridge arched across the water. Songbirds trilled in the treetops. Golden sunlight poured through the trees. This was the most beautiful place she'd ever seen!

"Ruff-chooo!" Pumpkin sneezed. She had stopped to sniff something.

Looking down, Emily saw a clump of incredible flowers: small, fuzzy puffs of every imaginable color!

She bent down and picked one of the flowers. It looked like a sparkly dandelion. She blew on it and tiny glittering tufts danced away on the breeze.

"I might have just discovered a whole new species. Genus: Emily," she laughed.

"Yipp!"

"Okay, okay. Genus: Pumpkin."

Emily felt like an explorer discovering a new world. Suddenly three animals stepped out of the trees. Emily stopped and held her breath. They looked like deer, but not like any deer she had ever seen. They had green striped fur and purple eyes. They bent their heads gracefully to drink from the lake, then looked up and scampered away. Emily shook her head. Deer aren't green! Must have been the sunlight reflected off the water. A bright red bird—could that really be a scarlet macaw?— flapped from a treetop to a lower branch, where it joined another bird, this one purple and orange. These creatures seemed so peaceful, so comfortable in their surroundings, not even bothered by the dogs. Surely there could be no dangerous predator around.

Slowly, so as not to startle the animals, Emily walked to a flat rock at the edge of the lake and sat down. She pulled off her sneakers and socks, stuck her feet in the

water, and splashed her toes lazily. Her reflection swirled in the water. It felt so refreshing, clean, and cold, like a mountain pool. She dashed some on her face, then flicked water at Biscuit. With a bark, Jellybean took a flying leap and landed in the pond, sending water cascading all around. Emily threw water at Pumpkin, who ran around barking happily.

And the water turned pink.

Emily stared. Bright colors—orange, purple, red— began to bubble up, sending soft circles out across the pool. The colors deepened, becoming darker and richer. Emily jerked her feet out of the water. Then she saw something under the surface, glowing.

Leaning over, she stuck her hand in the water, reaching . . . The tips of her fingers bumped against something small, cold, and hard in the wet clay. Her hand closed around the object and her stomach lurched. She felt as if she had just taken the first drop in Gigantor, the huge wooden roller coaster that used to terrify her.

There was a loud rustling in the forest. Terrified, Emily scrambled to her feet, looking around. The dogs pressed tightly against her legs, whimpering. What was happening?

Wind whipped across the glade, stirring up small eddies of dried leaves and dirt. Three, four, then six tiny whirlpools spiraled and twirled across the grass. One spun right by Emily's legs and, out of the corner of her eye, she thought she saw a figure. A figure made of twigs, dirt, and leaves? A sound buzzed from the swirling debris.

"Beeeeeeeeeeeeee . . ."

"What?"

"Bbeeeeeeewrrrrrrrrrrr . . . " Another mini-tornado twirled by, sending pebbles and bits of dirt flying. Squinting against the dust, Emily stood stock-still as a third little whirlwind spun crookedly by her leg.

"Beeeewaaarre . . . " it hummed.

The shrieking wind grew louder, scattering the figures across the glade. Tree limbs snapped and came crashing to the ground. Emily sank to her knees, wrapping her arms tightly around the dogs. Frantically she looked about for a place—any place—to hide. Then she saw it—and her heart stopped. A dark purple shape loomed up through the trees, making its way straight for her and the dogs. She whirled around and saw the ghostly mist flow between two trees and seep into the glade. It was about to envelop her, and there was nothing she could do. She was trapped. Her heart was in her throat; she couldn't breathe. The mist fell silently over Emily and the dogs, covering them in a soft blanket. The dogs shivered. She hugged them close, soundlessly willing them to keep quiet. Through the misty veil she saw a shadow move past. It looked like a giant dark purple bear. Emily didn't know why, but for a moment she wasn't frightened. She allowed herself to breathe.

BOOM!

The ground rocked. Something had fallen out of the sky! Something big. The earth around her trembled from the impact. The wind kicked up again, as if blasted by the beating of great wings. The air itself seemed to twist, a wobbling spiral that made Emily sick to her stomach. She sensed animal cries of terror, creatures frantically fleeing through the brush.

Emily didn't move. The thing that fell from the sky was some kind of animal. No, *creature*. She could feel it probing, searching for prey. Whatever it was, it was no bear; she was sure of that. It was bigger, more dangerous. It moved slowly around the glade, snorting and growling.

Emily huddled in the thick mist with the dogs tight against her. She was so frightened she could hardly think. The dogs were wriggling and starting to whine. Trembling, she pulled out the group leash and, one by one, hooked up each dog. "Shhhhh," she whispered. But she fumbled the last hook, and it closed with an audible *snap*!

The creature whirled and came straight toward them. Emily's heart pounded like a sledgehammer. Even through the misty veil, she could see the faint outlines of long, sharp claws, monstrous wings, and red-hot glowing eyes.

She could smell it, too, something rotten. She was going to gag. She closed her eyes as a blood-curdling roar made the dogs whimper. There was a beating of great wings, a rush of hot air—and the creature took off, disappearing into the sky.

Then all was quiet. Emily opened her eyes—and stared straight into the eyes of the silver wolf. They blazed with gold fire. She wanted to scream, but nothing came out.

"Do not be afraid." She heard no sound, and yet she understood the voice perfectly. *"You are safe for now."*

Emily blinked and shook her head. The dogs were staring at the wolf, amazingly calm, as if they, too, had heard the reassuring words.

A tightness in her arm made her realize she'd been clenching her fist all this time. She opened her hand and saw that the object she'd picked up from the water was in her palm. It was a small, rough, dark stone.

She looked back to the wolf, but it had disappeared again. What had just happened? What was that flying . . . *thing?*

Without another thought, she pulled on her shoes, grabbed the leash, and ran as fast as she could, back past the Rocking Stone, back the way she'd come. The dogs galloped ahead and she let them pull her along. Soon she was back at the dirt trail and followed it to the main road out of the preserve.

The farther she got from the woods, the more the whole thing felt like a dream. Ghosts weren't real. Wolves didn't talk. There were no rainbow flowers. And huge flying monsters? Was *that* what had attacked the cat? She shuddered.

Biting her lip, she sped up again, tugging on the leash. She was *not* going to think about any of this weirdness anymore. She was going to go straight home, where she belonged.

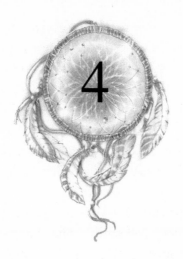

4

"*U*NABLE TO LOCATE server. Please check the server name and try again."

Shoot! Emily sat at her desk, staring at the computer screen.

As soon as she'd gotten home and cleaned herself up, she'd gone online, trying various search engines to track down information on the Ravenswood Wildlife Preserve. But either the links had the address wrong or the Web site no longer existed.

She couldn't ask her mom for help—she didn't want to explain about almost losing the dogs and going into the woods.

She thought of e-mailing her dad. He was a scientist. He'd know what to do. But what would she say? "Dear

Dad, having a terrific time here. Today I met a monster and a ghost and I discovered some new flower with rainbow seeds that light up like tiny fireworks . . ." Ha! Her dad would think she had moved to Transylvania, not Pennsylvania.

Okay, think . . . "If one thing doesn't work," he'd say, "then try another way." She typed in "Rocking Stone." A page of sites came back. "Indian Totems." She hit the hot link button.

The site was part of a Web ring dedicated to Native American legends and stories. She skimmed down the listing. There it was: "The Rocking Stone." A sacred monument called "Aluns," a Lenni-Lenape name which means "arrow." Such stones were believed to be landmarks used to locate doorways to the spirit world. . . .

She sat back. Those woods were haunted, all right. Kevin had not been wrong about that. *Something* was going on out there! But what had happened to her today was simply not possible. She had to have imagined it. Except she hadn't imagined the cat. Something evil had attacked it. And whatever it was, it was still out there.

"Emily . . ."

"Who are you?" She walked through silver-white fog. She had an impression that animals were hiding in the swirling mist, watching her.

A chorus of voices called her name. "Emily ... help us ..."
"I don't know how to help you!" she cried in frustration.
The mists swirled violently, streaked with waves of colors.
The voices were wiped away as razor claws ripped through
the misty curtain. The monster snarled, revealing a mouth
full of dripping fangs. Red-hot demon eyes fixed on her. It
knew she was helpless! With a roar it attacked—

Emily bolted up in bed as her eyes flew open, her mouth agape in a silent, choked-off scream. Her Pooh nightlight glowed softly near the door. She fought to calm her breathing. It was only a dream, it wasn't real ...

Something else was glowing in the room, and it wasn't coming from the nightlight. Emily quietly slipped from her bed and padded over to the pile of clothes she had thrown off earlier. She stared. The glow came from the pocket of her shorts. She reached inside. A pulsing blue-green washed over her face as she pulled out the stone she had found at the glade. It felt warm and reassuring in her hand, smooth and slick to the touch. Smooth? The stone she'd plucked from the pond had been rough!

Somehow most of the crusty layers had vanished. The stone was shiny and faceted in places. The blue-green surface was shot with clear, sparkly veins of purple. She turned it over and over. How could she not have noticed how pretty it was when she found it?

It felt ... magical.

"Ridiculous!" she snorted.

She sat holding the stone, looking at it for answers.

But no matter how hard she tried, she couldn't think of anything that didn't sound completely insane. Maybe it was radioactive, or part of a meteor, but it felt so . . . right. More strange things had happened to Emily today than in the whole rest of her life. She hated things she couldn't explain! *Everything* had a scientific explanation, didn't it? Okay, so what *had* really happened?

She knew what she had to do. Regardless of what might be in those woods, she was going back, back to that glade to find some answers for herself.

THE SUN HAD risen, but the dew still sparkled on the grass. It was going to be another beautiful day. Emily walked across the park and playing fields, her long shadow stretching ahead of her as she followed it westward. It fell to her right when she turned up the main road to the Ravenswood Wildlife Preserve. As she approached the iron gate, she hesitated.

What was she doing? Last time she'd *had* to go in there—she'd had no choice. This time she was going back on purpose—and she knew it might not be safe.

Emily was terrified. Had she actually seen a monster in those woods? She thought of the glowing stone. *Could* it be radioactive? Was someone doing experiments on the animals there?

She squared her shoulders. She was determined to

find that glade. She'd stick to clear trails. Any sign of trouble, she'd turn back immediately.

She swung the heavy iron gate open and passed through.

This time she followed the main road. There was no sign of the magical puff flowers. And no sign of the ghostly mist, either. The path turned into a pebble drive-way that sloped downward through an expansive lawn. And at the far end stood the imposing structure of an incredible mansion, nestled in the woods. As Emily approached, it rose up like an ancient castle complete with ivy-covered stone turrets. The main house was huge, and there were smaller buildings that could have been guesthouses or stables. Two large front windows seemed to watch her like dark eyes. She had the oddest feeling that the house itself was alive.

Yeah, right! Houses were *not* alive. A light flared from a second-story window. That was strange. Could Mr. Gardener have returned? Or maybe it was a witch with a big cauldron! Maybe she was a good witch, like Glinda. Or maybe she ate little children like in Hansel and Gretel. Stop it! Emily scolded herself. You're being silly. Those're fairy tales, kid stuff.

Then she heard the scream.

"Oweeeiiioo!"

What was *that*? Someone was in pain!

"Ooooweeeiooooo!"

Frantically Emily looked around. The high-pitched moan was coming from somewhere in the woods!

"Heeellp!"

Emily turned and ran in the direction of the voice. She zigzagged through the trees, making her way around thorny thickets and muddy hollows. The cries were nearer now and more distinct.

"Ow! Ow! Heeelllppp—gah!"

Emily crashed into a small clearing—and stopped, panting hard. Kneeling by a tree was a girl. She had her back toward Emily as if doubled over in pain. Long, shiny black hair fell over her dark T-shirt. She wore black jeans and hiking boots.

"Are you okay?" Emily gasped, out of breath.

The girl turned her head, fixing startled dark eyes on Emily. It was that strange girl who'd brought the wounded cat to the clinic. "What do you think you're doing here?" she demanded.

Emily moved back a step. "I . . . I . . . you called for help," she said, confused by the girl's hostility.

"I did not!" The girl was crouched over something. "This is private property. Get out of here!"

Emily wasn't about to be intimidated again. "And what gives *you* the right to be here?" she shot back.

"I *live* here," she said.

Emily tried to peer over the girl's shoulder. "What's that you've got there?"

"Nothing," she insisted, maneuvering her body between Emily and whatever she was hiding.

Emily edged closer.

"Go home!" the girl demanded, dark eyes flashing. "You don't belong here."

"Neither do I!" exclaimed a high-pitched voice. "And whatever I am, I'm certainly not nothing. Ow, my leg! Ow-ow-owwwie!!!"

Emily faked to the left, then twisted around to her right. Before the other girl knew it, Emily was past her.

She blinked, totally surprised. In front of her, a golden

ferret writhed in pain, his foot caught in a steel trap that was way too big for his elongated, furry body. "He needs help!" Emily exclaimed.

"That's what I was trying to do, genius," the girl replied.

Emily bent over to examine the ferret closer. His fur was mostly pale gold with wisps of brown; his feet, tail tip, and mask were darker brown.

"Watch out, he'll bite you," the girl warned.

Cautiously, Emily reached down to find a good grip on the trap.

"Owwie, owwwie . . . ow—Aghhh!!!!"

"Hold still a minute," she told the ferret. "I haven't done anything yet."

"Oh. Well, get on with it."

Emily's jaw dropped. She stared at the ferret. "It's . . . it can't be—but I think he's *talking*!"

"Score one for you," the girl replied.

Emily tried to pull apart the steel jaws, but she wasn't strong enough. The other girl reached out to help. Together, they pulled the trap open just enough for the creature to wiggle his foot free.

"Oh, that feels so gooooood! I could kiss you, but I'm not sure I even have lips!"

Emily's head whirled. This was impossible!

The ferret sat and examined his foot. "What in the world am I?" he asked, alarmed. "I look like some sort of *rodent*!" He stood and hobbled. "Aaahhh! How could they do this to me?" Then he looked up at Emily and his small eyes, set inside the brown mask, blinked. "Hey, aren't you the one who hit me on the head with that big rock?"

"It was a soccer ball," she corrected distractedly. Wait a minute! She was correcting a *ferret*!

"Is that some kind of formal greeting here? Beaning me on the head?"

"It was an accident."

"What kind of world is this? Everything hurts!" the ferret whined.

"What's he talking about?" the other girl asked. "You hit him?"

"No, I mean, yes, I—" Emily stopped suddenly. "But—but—that means . . ." She sat down hard on the ground. "If we can *both* hear him, then it must really—I mean, can it be talking?" She shook her head. "No way! Not possible!"

"Stop talking about me as if I'm not here," the ferret complained. He tried to walk on his wounded paw. "Owww!" He was obviously in pain.

That snapped Emily back to reality. "We've got to get him to my mom. She can fix up his leg."

"No way—I am staying right here. I am *not* going anywAahHH . . ." The ferret screamed and leaped onto Emily's leg, grabbing at her shirt with his claws. Emily turned. Her heart began to pound. A great silver wolf stepped out of the shadows and walked to the dark-haired girl's side. It sat down and cocked its head at Emily. It was the wolf from the glade.

"Hello, healer."

Emily was stunned. Was that the *wolf*'s voice in her mind?

"Help, it's a mistwolf!" yelled the terrified ferret.

The girl was patting the wolf. "You know this person?"

"We had an adventure," the wolf replied.

"What?" The girl sounded hurt.

"Thank you for . . . whatever you did," Emily stammered, trying to pull the panicked ferret off by his good leg. "I think you, uh, might've saved the dogs and me."

"How can *you* hear her?" the other girl demanded angrily.

"I don't know," Emily whispered. "I just can."

The dark-haired girl raised her hands in frustration. "What's going on around here?"

"Good question," Emily answered, shaken. What *was* going on in these woods? Some weirdness that made her think animals could talk?

The other girl turned and bent close to the wolf. "I don't like this. I thought you only talked to me."

"This is unlike you, warrior," the wolf said.

"But it's *our* secret," she pleaded.

"She is a healer," the wolf replied calmly.

Emily was a little shaken by the wolf's words.

"Gahh! Stay away from it! It's a mistwolf!" the ferret

screamed, poking his head out from behind Emily's arm.

"Stop whining, she's not going to eat you!" The dark-haired girl got to her feet, distracted from her anger and suspicion.

"*I will leave until later,*" the wolf told her. "*The little traveler needs time.*" Rising, the wolf wheeled about on her haunches and padded back into the woods.

"Smart wolf," Emily commented.

The other girl glared at her. "I don't know who you think you are, but these are *my* secrets."

"Whatever!" Emily felt like her circuits were over-loaded. She couldn't take any more of this bizarre input. "I'm taking this ferret back to the clinic."

"A ferret?!" The ferret was looking himself over in Emily's arms.

"Maybe my mom can figure out what it is," Emily continued.

"What do you mean, what it is?" The other girl moved closer.

Emily tried to stay calm. "Animals do not talk."

"Well, this one does. And all we need is your mom to tell everyone." The girl started pacing. She gazed in the direction where the wolf had disappeared, then looked pleadingly back to Emily. "People think this place is weird enough already!"

"You're just going to accept a ferret that talks?"

"Could you wait, at least?" the girl asked.

"For what?"

"Just wait, that's all . . . to tell your mother. Until we can figure out what all this is about."

Emily stared at the girl she had only just met. She could tell that the girl cared deeply for these woods—and for the animals that lived here.

"Well, my mom can set its leg anyway." Cradling the ferret gently in her arms, she started walking away.

"It'd be faster if you go the other way."

Emily stopped. "What?"

The raven-haired girl sighed. "Come on, you'll just get lost," she said, dusting off the seat of her black jeans.

"Fine!"

Emily followed the girl and soon they were on a narrow dirt track, heading out of the preserve. The ferret lay still in the crook of Emily's arm, muttering incoherently.

"I'm Emily Fletcher," Emily offered.

"Adriane Charday."

"Hi, Adriane. Nice to meet you again."

"Yeah," Adriane said half-heartedly. "Uh . . . same here."

". . . maybe it was the wrong portal," the ferret mumbled. "Maybe I should have gotten better directions . . . maybe I should have just stayed home!"

"I didn't know there were wolves in this part of the country," Emily tried again.

"This *is* a wildlife preserve, you know," Adriane snapped. She caught herself and calmed down. "Her name is Stormbringer. She's a mistwolf."

"Mistwolves! What have I gotten myself into?" the ferret whined.

"I've never heard of mistwolves," Emily said, trying to ignore the fact she was holding a talking ferret.

"Mistwolves are legendary, everyone's heard of them!" the ferret squirmed in Emily's arms.

"She's the last of her kind." Adriane said.

"How do you know that?"

"She told me," Adriane answered.

"That is so weird!"

"No weirder than the fact that *you* can hear her speak," Adriane retorted.

The girls looked at each other.

"Just what kinds of animals are on this preserve?" Emily asked incredulously.

"All kinds—supposedly. I haven't found any except for Storm . . . and the cat—and now this ferret."

"Adriane, I think the wolf saved me yesterday," Emily said in a soft voice. "I was about to be attacked by this . . . I don't know, animal-thing, I couldn't really see it clearly, but the wolf hid me in this mist . . . " she faltered. It still seemed so unbelievable.

"You think that thing attacked the cat?" Adriane asked.

"I . . . don't know."

Adriane took a deep breath. "Look, I'm sorry I was such a jerk. I didn't want to share this with anyone. I've only known Storm for a few weeks, she's *so* amazing . . ."

"I understand." Emily nodded. "Not that I've got any-one to tell," she added under her breath.

Adriane heard her anyway. "What do you mean?"

"We just moved to Stonehill, my mom and me. I don't have any friends here."

"I should have stayed in the Misty Moors . . . dumb Fairimental magic . . ." the ferret complained as the girls walked on.

"Noisy, isn't he?" Adriane commented.

"Adriane, animals *don't* talk!"

"Before I met Storm I would've said the same thing."

"I've got to find that portal!" the ferret yelled out.

"What?" both girls asked in unison.

"Something is not right! I have to get back home!" the ferret exclaimed.

"Where do you come from?"

The ferret narrowed his eyes and looked around suspi-ciously. "I'm not talking . . . not saying another word."

"Good," Adriane said.

"Not a peep," added the ferret.

"Fine," said Emily.

"A ferret . . ." the ferret moaned. "How revolting!"

"He must be delirious," Adriane said to Emily.

The girls made their way across the park grounds and into Emily's backyard. They entered the animal hospital through the back door.

The ferret looked around. "Wh-where am I?"

"At a place where we can take care of your leg," Emily said, depositing him on the examining table.

"I don't need to be taken care of," the ferret insisted. "I need to be changed out of this body! Gah! Wait till I get my hands on those Fairimentals!"

"Paws," Emily reminded him. "You have paws."

"What are Fairimentals?" Adriane asked.

"Uh-oh. Me and my big mouth," the ferret said, beginning to back away. He regarded them with fear in his eyes. "How do I know you're not the enemy?"

"The enemy? What enemy?" Adriane asked.

"We're friends," Emily assured him. She heard footsteps approaching the room. "Ssshhh," she said suddenly. "Don't say a word! Just let my mother set your leg. She's a doctor."

The ferret sighed. "All right, all right. Just make it snappy. I've got to find that portal—"

"Quiet!"

The door opened and Carolyn came in, her face drawn and pale. She smiled at Emily. "Hi, Doc, what do you have there?"

"What's wrong, Mom?" Emily asked. Her heart skipped a beat. "Oh, no! Not the cat?"

"No, a dog was found this morning near Arrowhead Park . . ."

"It didn't make it?" Emily asked.

Carolyn shook her head sadly. "Oh, hello again," she said, noticing Adriane. "Aren't you the girl who found the cat?"

Adriane nodded.

"She's doing fine, thanks to your quick thinking." Smiling, Emily's mom held out her hand. "I'm Carolyn Fletcher."

"Adriane Charday." Adriane shook her hand politely. "I found this ferret up on the preserve. Emily helped me free him from a trap."

"A trap!" Carolyn turned to Emily. "Didn't I did tell you to stay out of those woods? It's not safe up there!"

"I agree!" the ferret exclaimed.

Adriane clasped her hand over the ferret's mouth. "Shut up!"

"What?" Carolyn said.

"Uh, wassup? With his paw, I mean." Keeping a hand over the ferret's mouth, Adriane stretched him out lengthwise.

Carolyn gently felt up and down both rear paws. "This doesn't look bad," she said. "No breaks, not even much of a wound. Lucky for him it wasn't a big trap."

Emily bent over the ferret. She looked at him, then at Adriane. "What the . . . " She peered at his injured paw. The leg was sound and straight! "Must have been the other leg . . . " she muttered, turning him over in Carolyn's hands.

Emily stared in astonishment. The ferret was practically healed! She was about to tell her mother that not thirty minutes ago his leg had been broken, but she caught Adriane glaring at her. Emily remained silent.

"You can handle this, Doc," Carolyn said, walking toward the recovery room. "Just clean the wound and bandage it."

"Okay, Mom," Emily said.

Adriane grabbed the ferret close to her face. "Listen, you—keep your mouth shut in front of other people!"

"I will do no such thing!" he said, crossing his paws and looking away.

"Oh, yes, you will," Emily insisted. "You want to be taken away and examined by a billion doctors and scientists?"

"Well . . . I . . . "

"And probed and dissected?" Adriane added.

"Gak!"

Adriane handed the ferret to Emily as Carolyn walked back inside, drying her hands with a towel. Emily grabbed a bottle full of water and shoved it in the ferret's mouth, cradling him like a baby.

"Poor thing is thirsty," Adriane commented.

"Blurbbboo!"

"Completely dehydrated," Emily agreed.

"Foothpagg!"

Carolyn turned to Adriane. "So, Adriane, how is it that you were on the preserve?"

"My grandmother's the caretaker. I live with her there."

Emily gave Adriane a sharp glance. "Where are your parents?" she asked.

"Emily . . ." her mother said softly.

"I have parents." Adriane glared back at Emily. "They're artists, they travel a lot." She looked very uncomfortable.

Carolyn smiled. "Well, you're welcome here any time," she said.

"Mom?" Emily began. "That dog . . ." She faltered.

"What about it?" her mother prompted her.

"How did it . . . I mean, what killed it?"

Her mother sighed. "I'd have to say that whatever attacked the cat was the same thing that killed the dog." She headed for the door. "I've got to run to an appointment. I'll be home in time for dinner."

The moment Carolyn was out the door, Emily whirled on Adriane. "What's going on over there?"

"PhatooiIEE!" The ferret leaped to the table and scampered away. "What are you trying to do, drown me?"

"What are you talking about?"

"You live there, you must know something. Or your grandmother does."

"No, she doesn't!" Adriane was horrified.

"Hurt animals are being found in those woods!"

Adriane blinked back tears. "You think *we're* doing something to hurt the animals? My gran loves animals!" Adriane started to pace. She whirled around to face Emily. "You're as bad as everyone else in this stupid town!" She stalked toward to door. "I'm outta here."

Emily ran after her. "Wait!"

Adriane stood there, arms crossed over her chest, glowering.

Emily felt ashamed. "I'm sorry. I just get so *mad*! I *hate* seeing animals hurt."

"Me, too," Adriane said quietly.

"I shouldn't have accused your grandma, but have you ever asked her what's going on?"

"I can't talk to her." Adriane raised her arms in frustration. "She's always saying weird stuff about spirits and giving me herbal roots and yucky charms."

"Yucky charms? They're magically delicious!" Emily exclaimed.

The girls broke out laughing.

"Aaaagh!" The high-pitched scream made them jump. It came from the adjoining room. They ran in— and found the cat standing on the makeshift bed straddling the ferret and looking at him as if he were a tasty treat.

"Help!" the ferret screamed.

The cat looked up. Seeing Emily, she backed off and crouched, still eyeing the ferret, a low growl rumbling from her chest. The ferret rolled out from under the cat's paws and fell on the floor with a thud. "This beast thinks I'm a rodent!"

"Ferrets are not rodents, more like weasels," Emily informed the ferret.

"That's comforting!"

She walked over to the cat. "This mean ol' ferret scare you?" She brushed her hand over the cat's back. Most of the bandages had been removed but the terrible scars remained. The cat nudged Emily with her head, then rubbed against her. The growl turned into a purr that sounded like a lawnmower.

"Glad to see you're getting your normal appetite back," Emily told her with a smile.

"Don't tell me she talks, too!" Adriane exclaimed incredulously.

"Not exactly . . . I mean—this is so crazy! Animals *don't* talk!"

"Well, then," Adriane said, "what about him?" She jerked her thumb at the ferret, who was poking around the room, exploring curiously.

The ferret made his way to the side of a shiny metal cabinet. "Stupid thing thought I was a weasel." His reflection glared back at him and he shrieked.

"And what about Stormbringer?"

Emily's mind was whirling, trying to sort it all out. "I hear the wolf clearly—in my head. But the ferret actually talks out loud."

"What about the cat?" Adriane stroked the cat's head with gentle fingertips.

"She's . . . like faint static. I can just barely make out a word here and there." Emily shook her head. "But how can we hear them at all?"

"I started hearing Storm when I found this." Adriane rummaged in her pocket and pulled out a shiny stone. Shaped like a paw print, it was banded in gold, amber, and brown.

Emily's eyes went wide. "That is *so* weird."

"It's tigereye. I kind of like it," Adriane said defensively.

Emily reached into her pocket and pulled out her own gemstone. "No, I mean, look at this."

Adriane stared in amazement. "Where did you find that?"

"In this glade on the preserve. I saw some birds and some . . . weird deer."

"You saw animals there?" Adriane asked.

"Yeah," Emily said. She felt her pulse quicken at the memory of what had happened there. "Where did you find yours?" she asked.

"In the woods near a big field."

"I wonder if there are any more," Emily mused.

Adriane shrugged. "I don't know."

The sound of a loud purr distracted them. They looked over to see the ferret scratching the big cat under her chin. The cat's eyes were closed in pleasure.

"I'm really an elf, you know," the ferret was telling the cat.

The cat stretched and licked the ferret's head.

"Blah!"

"Emily, do you believe in magic?" Adriane asked.

Emily shook her head. "If you asked me that yesterday, I would have thought you were nuts. Now . . . I don't know."

The front door of the clinic banged open, and Emily heard Kevin's familiar, clomping stride coming down the hall toward them.

Instinctively, both girls stuffed their stones into their pockets. Emily went to the door and opened it. Kevin, holding a FedEx envelope, came into the room. "Hey, Em," he said.

Then he saw Adriane behind her. "Oh, hey," he said to her.

"Hey, yourself," she replied.

"Yeah, whatever," he said, waving the envelope at Emily. "This came for your mom."

Emily looked at it. The return address was the University of Pennsylvania. Curiosity got the better of her and she snatched the envelope. "She's not here right now. I'll give it to her later, okay?"

Kevin frowned, but after a glance at Adriane, decided not to object. "I've got some shelves to stock," he said, backing out of the room. "See you later."

"Yeah." Adriane looked down.

Emily stood there, holding the package.

"The other kids around here don't like me much," Adriane said after Kevin was gone. "I'm used to it, though."

"They're just being jerks."

"So what is it?" Adriane nodded at the envelope.

"Lab report on the skin samples from the cat," Emily explained. After a moment's hesitation, she opened the envelope and read the report. Its contents made her heart sink.

"Listen to this: 'Results of testing are inconclusive . . . traces of toxin . . . recommend extreme caution . . . The area should be quarantined until further testing by agents from the Centers for Disease Control.'"

Adriane gasped. "Quarantined? They can't do that! Me and Gran live there!" She grabbed Emily's arm. "You have to hide that letter!"

"But it was sent to my mom. I shouldn't even have opened it."

"Emily, if they shut down the preserve, we'll have to move," Adriane pleaded. "I've only been there six months, but it's my home now. I can't move again!"

Emily thought for a moment. "Okay, I'll keep the letter hidden—for now. But if this radiation, or whatever it is, is not coming from the preserve, then where is it coming from?"

"I don't know." Adriane sprang up. "I've got to go tell Gran what's going on. If they close down the preserve, who'll protect the animals?"

The question echoed in Emily's mind. "I'll come with you." She grabbed the ferret, who was busy examining his reflection. "I think we'd better take you with us, before somebody hears you talking."

"What's wrong with me talking?" he asked, sounding insulted.

"Around here," Emily told him, "ferrets don't talk."

"I am not a ferret. I am an elf."

"Yeah, and I'm Dr. Dolittle," Emily said.

"I'm an elf!" he insisted again. "My name is Ozymandias. You can call me Ozzie." He smiled a ferret smile.

Adriane stared at him. "We need to make a pact," she turned to Emily. "To keep all this secret—at least for now."

"Okay."

The two girls held out their hands. As they shook, a furry paw came down and sealed their pact.

6

$\mathcal{E}$MILY FOLLOWED ADRIANE across the park and over a small hill that put them right on the main road to Ravenswood Wildlife Preserve. Ozzie rode comfortably in Emily's backpack. His head poked out of the top, snout covered with crumbs from a power bar he'd found inside.

"Okay, Mr. Ozzie the Talking Ferret, spill it." Adriane smacked the side of the backpack.

"Spoof!" Ozzie spit out a mouthful of power bar. "What-what-what?"

"Where did you come from?" she asked.

"How did you get here?" Emily added, swinging the pack around to rest against her chest.

"How come you can talk?" Adriane demanded.

"Stop, you're making me dizzy! One minute I was there, then I fell through the portal to here. I'm an elf. Well, I *was* an elf. Now look at me. I'm a furry beast with paws and *fleas*!"

He tried to scratch his back. Emily reached into the pack and scratched it for him.

"A little to the right—ooooh, good one."

They passed through the iron gates of the preserve and headed down the main road.

"What's a portal?" Emily asked.

"It's a . . . you know . . . a portal," Ozzie said.

"No, we don't know," said Adriane.

"A doorway between worlds," Ozzie explained. "I fell through one and ended up here."

"And where did you come from Alice . . . Wonderland?" Adriane asked, rolling her dark eyes.

"Ozzie! And I came from *my* world!"

Adriane was starting to get impatient. "Listen, ferret face . . . " She leaned toward him.

"Gak!" Ozzie dove back into the pack.

Emily gave Adriane a stern look. "Does your world have a name?" she asked Ozzie.

"Aldenmor," Ozzie squeaked from inside the pack.

"What are Fairimentals?" Emily asked.

Ozzie popped his head back out. "Don't you know *anything*? They're magic—the really powerful stuff."

"What do the Fairimentals want?" Emily asked.

"They are looking for . . . something."

The girls stopped and both looked at the ferret. "What?"

"Mages," Ozzie whispered. "Magic users."

"Magic? You sure fell down the wrong rabbit hole, Alice." Adriane laughed and smacked the backpack again.

"It's Ozzie!"

The road ended at the circular drive in front of the manor house. Emily stared in awe at the old architectural monstrosity. Close up, it seemed spookier than ever, but at the same time, it looked inviting, full of secrets waiting to be revealed.

"You actually live here?" Emily walked over and peered in the sidelight windows that framed the enormous wooden front door. Ozzie clambered out of her backpack and leaped to the ground.

"No, we live in a cottage around the back," Adriane explained.

"I wonder what it's like inside," Emily murmured, burning with curiosity.

"Most of the place is locked up," Adriane told her. "But it has a ton of rooms and an old library up top."

"That sounds cool." Emily stepped back and looked at the huge brass door knocker. It was shaped like the head of a lion. "Kevin told me they used to have tours here."

"Yeah, that was a long time ago."

"So what do you think happened to Mr. Gardener?" Emily asked.

"I don't know. He just disappeared."

"I hope he ended up better than I did," Ozzie commented.

A sudden scuffling noise from inside the house made them jump.

"Maybe he's still inside," Emily said, uncertainly.

"No way," Adriane scoffed.

"Should we knock?" Emily pressed on the door—it was open. She glanced at Adriane with a look of surprise, then pushed the door in all the way. The hinges squealed softly.

The girls peered in. Ozzie craned his head around Emily's legs to get a look for himself. A wide hallway ran from the front door to an open foyer filled with couches, tables, and chairs. The girls were careful to leave the door open behind them. In silence, they edged forward into the foyer. Emily let out a loud breath.

"Wow! Look at this place!"

Paintings hung on the walls: animals in beautiful garden settings; the mansion itself, in all its early glory; gardens filled with deer, peacocks—even lions and tigers!

"These are amazing!" Emily stopped in front of a large painting of a man surrounded by three white tigers. "Who's that?" she asked.

Adriane glanced up. "That's Mr. Gardener."

Creeeaaakkk—thud!

The front door had closed. The girls whirled around as a figure stepped out from a column of dusty sunlight.

"I see you've made some new friends, Little Bird."

It was an old woman. She had dark wrinkled skin, and piercing dark eyes like Adriane's. A long white braid hung over her shoulder in sharp contrast to her forest green ankle-length dress. Her arms jingled with silver and turquoise bracelets.

"Gran, we were just looking for you," Adriane exclaimed. "This is Emily . . . and this is, um . . . "

Ozzie stood beside Emily, arms crossed, tapping one paw on the floor. He didn't say a word.

Gran bowed to him. "Welcome, Woodland Spirit," she said. Ozzie's eyes widened.

Then Gran turned and looked Emily up and down with a piercing gaze. "Come here, child. I don't bite."

Emily shuddered. Kevin had said this woman was a witch. She knew that had to be nonsense, but staring at the old woman now, she suddenly wasn't so sure. She glanced uncertainly at Adriane, who just rolled her eyes.

Gran reached out and touched Emily's cheek with gentle fingers. "You are a special one, child."

"Thank you . . . I think."

Gran chuckled. "It is good to see Little Bird with friends. My name is Nakoda, but you can call me Gran."

"These pictures . . . " Emily asked. "Do all those animals live here, on the preserve?"

"At one time or another," Gran replied. "I have been with Mr. Gardener for over forty-five years now."

"Where *is* Mr. Gardener?" Emily asked.

"Oh, I'm sure he's on important business."

"Something to do with animals?" Emily pressed.

"Most probably. He's quite the animal expert."

"My mom's a vet. We love animals."

"I can tell. Come, it so dusty here, why don't we go to our house."

The girls followed Gran out the front door. Emily leaned in to whisper to Adriane. "How come she calls you Little Bird?"

"It's my Indian name—she gave it to me. She's Bird Woman, so . . . I'm stuck with it, until I find my own." Adriane paused, looking uncomfortable.

Emily shrugged. "My mom calls me 'Doc.' I don't mind."

"Yeah, real cute. Hey, you don't have to stay if you don't want—it's okay."

"Are you kidding? This place is so cool!"

The caretaker's cottage was off to the left of the main house, down a cobblestone path and through a grove of pines. The cottage was more like a lodge, with dark wooden beams making geometric patterns against a white plaster background. The girls and Ozzie followed Gran down a narrow hallway into a cozy, old-fashioned kitchen in the back of the house. It was bright and cheery. Crystals hung in the windows, catching the sunlight and casting rainbows on the walls. Gran poured some lemonade for the girls.

"Please, sit, eat," she said, gesturing to the wooden dining table off to the side of the room.

The girls sat down and Ozzie sniffed around the table. Suddenly famished, Emily took a cookie from the serving plate on the table. It was moist and delicious. Ozzie grabbed two cookies and ran off with them. Adriane sat without eating.

"Gran, we have to talk," she said. "About the animals."

"I know," Gran replied.

"What's happening to them?" Emily asked, trying not to sound accusing.

Gran looked sad. "I don't know, Emily. This place has always been a safe haven for animals. But something has changed."

"Gran," Adriane said, "people are going to come and shut the place down. Maybe worse . . . "

"I know, Little Bird. The mayor's office called earlier, requesting my presence at a town meeting tomorrow night. Animals are being hurt, and people are frightened."

"But they can't shut Ravenswood down!" Adriane protested. "It's our home!"

"Yes, this is our home and Mr. Gardener's, and home to many animals," her grandmother agreed.

Adriane stood up, eyes sparking. "We have to fight this!"

"Ah, Little Bird, you are so full of fire. Sometimes patience is the road to follow."

"But we have to *do* something!" Adriane pleaded.

"Have faith, Little Bird," Gran said calmly.

Emily and Adriane exchanged glances. Then

Adriane seemed to come to some internal decision. She sat back down.

"Look, Gran," she said, pulling her stone out of her pocket. She held it out to show her grandmother.

"I found one, too," Emily said, holding out her stone.

Gran's eyebrows rose as she studied the stones. "Where did you get these?"

"We found them in the woods," Adriane told her.

"Keep these very safe," Gran said. "Crystals and gemstones are often charged with energy. They may hold strong magic."

The girls looked at each other.

"Magic?" Emily repeated.

Ozzie popped his head up by the side of the table.

"But the stones don't actually *do* anything." Emily turned to Adriane. "At least, mine doesn't."

"Sometimes that which seems to do nothing can have great effect," Gran explained. "A tiny pebble, thrown into a quiet pond, makes one ripple, then another, then a whole wave of ripples that spread in ever-growing circles."

"English please, Gran," Adriane said.

"There is much to learn about magic, Little Bird. Perhaps the obvious is not always the answer."

A furry paw stretched across the table, followed by a long furry body. "Delightmmphul," Ozzie mumbled, stuffing another cookie into his mouth.

The girls stared at the ferret. They stared down at their sparkling gems. They looked back at Ozzie.

"Whaaa?" Ozzie demanded around a mouthful of cookie. "Whaa I do?"

Gran didn't seem to notice. "I have work to do," she said, getting up. "You two—three—stay and eat." She walked out the kitchen door.

"I really like this house," Emily said after Gran had left the room.

Adriane jumped up. "Want to see my room?"

"Sure."

Emily got up and followed Adriane, leaving the ferret to his feast. "Don't eat too much," she called back to him. "You'll get a tummy ache."

"bUrrp," Ozzie replied.

Adriane's room was an explosion of color. Bright yellow paint peeked out in the spaces between the patchwork of posters on the walls; the ceiling was dark blue with constellations of glow-in-the-dark stars. Emily studied the posters. Rock bands, mountain climbers high above the clouds, motocross bikers careening down dirt trails, snow boarders shooting sprays of white snow. . . . She hardly knew Adriane, but she never would have pegged her for the type to have a room like this!

She turned around full circle, taking it all in. "It's fantastic!"

"Thanks." Adriane was much more animated in her own space. She leapt over the bed to rummage through the shelves by her stereo. "You like Smash Fish?" she asked over her shoulder.

"I've never eaten it. Any good?"

"Ha! It's a band. Here, listen to this." Crunching music blared out of two tower speakers. Two smaller satellite speakers hung from the opposite corners, creating a surround sound effect. The music was a little harsher than what Emily was used to, but it was catchy, with a strong melody. She noticed a red electric guitar leaning against a wall. "Is that yours?" she asked.

"Yup!" Adriane bounced over to the guitar and picked it up. "Sweet, huh?"

"I guess."

Adriane ran her hands over the polished red body. "A real Fender Strat!" She strummed across the strings. "I've got this cool practice amp, too," she said, indicating a small box on the floor. "Check it out!"

The girls laughed as Adriane rocked out with the music.

"What is that horrible sound?" Ozzie stood in the doorway, paws over his ears.

"It's rock 'n' roll, Ozzie," Adriane said. "Real magic!"

Ozzie's eyes widened. "Ah, so this is magic in your world. It's so noisy!"

Adriane turned down the volume on the stereo and set her guitar gently against the dresser.

"Ozzie," Emily said, "we don't *have* magic here."

"I knew I fell in the wrong portal." Ozzie jumped on the bed and flopped over a large pillow. "Ooh, I just want to go home."

"So tell us, what's the magic like where you come from?" Adriane asked.

Ozzie stretched over the pillow. "Well, there's not much left. That's why the Fairimentals sent me here. To get help."

"Why do they need help?" Emily asked.

"Our world is in danger," he said. "There's something called the Black Fire. It's poisoning everything."

"Including animals?" Adriane looked to Emily.

"I suppose so. I was told it's the result of horrible dark magic."

"Tell us more about Fairimentals," Emily prompted.

"They're forces of nature and they protect the good magic of Aldenmor. I'm no expert but all magic is fueled by nature—air, water, earth, and fire."

"Sounds confusing," Adriane said.

Ozzie sighed. "*You're* confused? The Fairimentals sent me to find three human mages who can help us, but there's no magic here and I haven't met any mages—only you." He flopped over on his back. "*And* I'm a ferret!"

For some reason, Emily flashed on the bizarre twirling bits of leaves and dirt she had seen in the glade. "What do Fairimentals look like?" she asked.

But Ozzie had fallen asleep. Emily sat back, leaning against the wall. Then she noticed several objects hanging over Adriane's bed. They were round wooden hoops, with a variety of colorful strings and cords threaded across them, like a spiderweb. Gemstones were woven amid the strands, and feathers hung from the bottom.

"What are those?" she asked Adriane.

"Dream catchers," Adriane told her. "Gran hung them. She says they're a web of protection. They're supposed to catch bad dreams and let the good ones in through the center hole. The energy of the gemstones strengthens the good dreams."

"Like a barrier between two worlds," Emily said in a hushed voice.

"Emily," Adriane said hesitantly. "What if Ozzie really does come from another world?"

"So now we're also supposed to believe in magical worlds, too!" Emily shook her head.

Adriane stared at her. "After what's happened here—after what you've seen—can you sit there and tell me it's not possible?"

"I don't know," Emily had to admit. "There's so much weird stuff going on, I don't know what's possible."

Adriane was silent. She gazed at the dream catchers. A slight smile played across her lips. "You know what might be cool?" Her jet-black eyes flashed. "What if we took the stones *we* found and weave them into . . . "

"Dream catchers?" Emily guessed, intrigued.

"Better. Power bracelets," Adriane responded.

Emily was into it. "Sorta like making our own web of . . ."

"Protection." They'd said it together.

A few minutes later, the girls sat cross-legged on the floor amid a pile of rawhide strips, satin, and lanyard. Adriane had the idea to combine the colored lanyard and black satin string, and Emily shared some knots she knew. It took some trial and error to find a way to hold their stones securely, but at last they each had a very cool new bracelet.

Adriane held her arm out and turned her wrist this way and that. "Not bad," she said admiringly.

Emily stood up and stretched her legs. Her gaze settled on a framed photograph of a handsome couple.

Adriane saw her looking and took the photograph down. "My mom and dad. They're artists. They do these 'performance art' and sculpture exhibits. Pretty weird, huh?"

"How come you live with your grandmother?" Emily asked.

Adriane shrugged. "They left to go on a world tour. So they dumped me here in a nice *stable* environment for a change. They say they're going to settle in upstate New York when they get back, but I've never been in the same school more than a year."

"My dad lives in Seattle. We e-mail each other a lot," Emily said.

"At least you talk to him. My parents send me postcards . . . sometimes."

Emily couldn't imagine being so out of touch with your own parents.

"So, you've been here six months, right?" Emily said, not wanting to intrude further. "That means you've been to school . . . "

"Middle school." Adriane snorted. "The way some kids act, you'd think it was Stonehill Academy."

"There must be some kids you like?" But Emily remembered the girls in the park.

Adriane shrugged. "Friends are overrated."

Emily blinked. "You can't mean that."

Adriane's silence told her she meant exactly that.

A pang of homesickness swept over Emily. She'd always had friends she totally connected with.

She turned around to face Adriane. "What do you think is going to happen at the meeting tomorrow night?"

"They'll probably kick me and Gran out of here." Adriane began to pace back and forth. "Then they're gonna send in the Army to kill all the animals. Then they'll cut down all the trees and make a golf course or something!"

Emily laughed, not knowing if Adriane was joking or not. "That's a bit extreme, don't you think?"

"You saw the letter. Quarantine! How extreme is that?"

"What can we do?" Emily asked, feeling a familiar wave of helplessness.

"If we can prove there really *are* rare animals here, they'd *have* to leave Ravenswood alone! That glade where you found your stone—do you think you could find that place again?" Adriane asked.

"It's right behind the Rocking Stone."

Adriane stopped. "There's nothing back there but woods."

"No, that's where I saw it. I was going back there when I ran into you and Ozzie."

"We need to find that glade! Can you get away tomorrow?" Adriane asked.

"As long as I get my chores done . . . which reminds me, I should get back. "

"What should we do about *him*?" Adriane jerked her thumb in the direction of the snoring ferret.

"I'll take him with me." Emily gently scooped the ferret up and deposited him in her backpack.

"Mommy, I don't want to ride the flobbin," Ozzie mumbled, sleepily.

Adriane shrugged. "Elves! Come on, I'll walk you and Alice up to the main road."

Outside, the western sky was awash with orange and purple, tingeing the forest with a magical glow. From out of nowhere, Stormbringer appeared by Adriane's side and joined the girls as they made their way along the road. The wolf was silent and Emily had to remind herself that Storm wasn't just Adriane's pet dog, jogging along beside them. When they reached the edge of the park grounds, the girls stopped.

"Okay, tomorrow we'll search the woods and see if we can find the animals," Adriane said.

"We're going to have to be really careful."

"I'm not afraid," Adriane boasted. "Are you?"

"I grew up hiking in the Colorado Mountains, where plenty of wild animals roam—I'm not afraid." Emily tried to sound as brave as she could.

"You know," Adriane said, "there's an Iroquois story that says if two people wear the same bracelet, it means they're linked, joined."

"Like . . . friends?" Emily smiled and raised her bracelet.

Adriane grimaced. Then a small smile escaped her lips. She held her braceleted arm next to Emily's. The two gems sparkled in the fading sun.

*T*HE NEXT MORNING, Emily was up early. She dressed quickly, pulling on shorts and an aqua T-shirt. Sliding on her hiking boots, she ran downstairs to check on the cat. Her remaining bandages looked clean and dry—no more seepage through the white gauze, no unnatural glow evident at all—and she actually ate all the canned food Emily gave her.

Emily went to the Pet Palace and fed the dogs, then returned to the house where she fetched Ozzie from her room. He was still sleeping on the big fluffy pillow she'd given him for a bed.

As she slipped him into her backpack, he opened his eyes. "Hey, what're you doing?"

"Rise and shine, we're off to see the wizard."

"Really? That's great news!"

Emily shook her head as she bounced down the stairs. "You are one wacky ferret."

"Thank you."

Carolyn was sitting in the kitchen eating a grapefruit and making notes in her scheduling book.

"Hey, Mom." Emily opened the refrigerator and grabbed the orange juice. "I'm going over to Adriane's, okay?"

"Chores done?"

Emily smiled. "Yup. And the cat's doing much better, too."

"That's great, Doc. But wouldn't it be better if Adriane came here?"

"Why?" Emily gulped down her juice while she waited for an English muffin to toast.

"I'm not happy about you going into those woods."

"Mom! Adriane lives in a house, not in the woods!" She left out the fact that once she was at Adriane's house, she was, technically, already in the woods. She lathered her breakfast with jam and handed a piece to Ozzie.

"Strawberry! Yumm!"

Carolyn looked over. Emily and Ozzie both smiled back.

EMILY MADE HER way across the park and up the road to the preserve. The morning air held a faint crispness that reminded her summer was fading. She sighed, thinking of what September would bring: more changes.

Ozzie was rummaging around in her backpack.

"Stop fidgeting," she told him.

"Where's the oatmeal ones?"

"They're in there."

Ozzie stuck his head out. "Can this wizard help us find the portal?"

"I was kidding about the wizard."

"Oh." Ozzie leaned out of the pack, clearly depressed. "I'll never get home, will I?"

"Maybe *we* can help you."

He perked up. "You'd help me?"

"Of course I would, and Adriane would, too"

"You know, if I have to be stuck here, I'm glad it's with you."

Emily smiled.

They found Adriane outside the cottage, brushing the mistwolf's coat to a shiny luster. Stormbringer's eyes were closed in pleasure, but she opened them when Emily and Ozzie arrived.

"Morning," Adriane said with a smile as she glided the

brush over the wolf's back. She had on hiking boots, a dark blue T-shirt, black jeans, and a baseball cap with the words NO FEAR embroidered on it.

"Hey!" Emily returned. She looked at the wolf. "Hi, Stormbringer!"

"Hello, healer. Hello, traveler," the wolf replied, nodding to Ozzie.

"Why do you call me 'healer?'" Emily asked.

"That is what you do."

"Just don't call me breakfast!" Ozzie scrambled down Emily's side to the ground.

"I have already eaten," the wolf assured him. She looked as if she were grinning. *"It was a—"*

"Gah! Don't tell me—I don't want to know!" Ozzie put his paws over his ears.

Adriane knelt and unrolled a large scroll. "Check this out. It's a map of the preserve. I took it off the wall in the foyer."

The girls spread the map on the ground and crouched over it. Ozzie joined them.

"It's old, but the basic layout of the preserve is still the same," Adriane said. "So . . . I say we start here up at the north quadrant and follow this trail. It winds down here to the Rocking Stone."

"I don't see the glade near the stone," Emily observed. "It's not on the map."

"I fell out in a big, open area," Ozzie offered, walking out onto the map to study it.

"Looking for the rabbit hole, Alice?" Adriane asked the ferret.

"I am not a rabbit." Ozzie looked himself over just to make sure.

"Do you have any idea how we can find it?" Emily asked him.

"I don't know, but it's magic. Magic attracts magic, I know that much," he replied.

"We don't have any magic," Emily reminded him.

"Gran said these stones hold magic." Adriane held up her wrist. Sunlight reflected off the gold and amber jewel.

Adriane rolled up the map, stood, and slung her olive-green backpack over her shoulder. "Let's move out!"

Emily followed Adriane across the wide lawn in back of the manor. A garden of hedges and flowers lay just beyond the green; the hedges were planted in geometric patterns with pathways in between, like a maze. Near the entrance stood a large stone fountain in the shape of a mermaid. She held a beautiful carved urn over her head and water poured from it to splash off her up-curved tail into the round basin below.

"This place is just so amazing," Emily breathed.

"C'mon, slowpokes!" Adriane had ducked through an opening in the trees at the edge of the lawn. Emily quickened her steps to catch up. They found themselves on a trail winding through a section of open woodlands. Narrow swaths of meadow separated clusters of trees and bushes. Stormbringer trotted on ahead, fading from view among the tall feathery grasses and wildflowers.

"I feel like I'm on a safari!" Emily exclaimed. The girls crossed a small stream and entered a section of forest thick with tall junipers and furs.

Suddenly Adriane stopped and looked around. "Hold up," she said.

Emily heard a rustling of leaves and the patter of approaching hoofbeats. "Over there!" She pointed through the trees.

The most amazing creatures came bounding through the woods. They looked like deer, but with long ears and green stripes like zebras.

"What *are* those?" Adriane whispered.

"They're like the animals I saw in the glade. Maybe some kind of zebra?" Emily guessed.

"Jeeran," Ozzie simply stated.

The girls looked at him.

"What?" Emily asked incredulously.

"Jeeran, herdbeasts found in the hills of the Moorgroves. I've seen lots of them. They're fast and jump really high."

"Don't tell me they come from your world, too?" Adriane asked.

"Okay."

"Okay, what?" Emily asked.

"Okay, I won't tell you," Ozzie replied.

"Wherever they came from, they're here now," Adriane laughed. "Come on, this is wild!"

The girls ran through the woods and came to a wide-open field, but the strange animals were too swift, and the field was empty. Adriane kicked the dirt.

"Look, there's the Rocking Stone!" Emily pointed to where the jagged peak rose above the trees in the distance.

Adriane pulled the map from her backpack and studied it. "We can pick up the trail on the other side."

They started across the open field. The tall grass brushed against their legs. The air smelled sweet as soft particles blew around them.

"Hey! Look at you—you're sparkling!" Adriane said.

Emily looked down at her arms and saw that they were, indeed, sparkling. Her legs looked like they were covered in tiny glittering lights. Then she saw them. "It's the rainbow flowers!" she exclaimed. All through the grassy expanse, they were sending tiny bursts of color into the air.

"That is *so* cool!" Adriane exclaimed, spinning around like a dancer.

"Your hair is all sparkly," Emily laughed. Rainbow twinkles were catching on Adriane's long, dark hair.

Ozzie hopped out of Emily's pack and started nosing around in the flowers. "Magic seeds. This is good, very good."

"What are you talking about, Jack?" Adriane asked him, grinning. "They're going to grow into beanstalks?"

"Jack?" Ozzie looked around. Then he nosed a flower again. "Can't you feel it? It's fairy magic!"

"These flowers were all over that glade," Emily said. "Right before . . . " Her voice trailed off. "Where's Storm?"

"Off somewhere. She has a mind of her own." Adriane was crouched low, studying something in the dirt. "There are animals around here somewhere," she announced.

"What did you find?" Ozzie nosed his way over to look. "BLAH! That's disgusting!"

"Quiet, Alice, it's just animal droppings."

There was a rustling in the grass. The three turned together. A jeeran was standing there watching them, not fifteen yards away. Soft green-striped fur rustled as it breathed. Big purple eyes blinked at the girls.

"Wow. I've never seen anything like that," Emily whispered.

"It's so amazing. What do we do? Like, hello we come in peace?" asked Adriane.

"Might work," Emily replied.

Emily started walking slowly towards the animal. The jeeran tensed but stood still as Emily approached. It stood as high as Emily's nose. She stepped closer, hand reaching out. Ever so slowly, her finger made contact with the animal's forehead and it blinked its eyes, pulling its head back to sniff her fingers. Emily smiled and ran her hand over the animal's mane. The fur felt so soft and silky. Emily broke out in a grin. She turned to face the others.

"It likes me."

Bang!

The sound of gunfire split the air. Ozzie screamed. The jeeran bolted.

"Guns!" Emily exclaimed. "Someone's shooting!"

"Over that hill!" Adriane pointed.

Ozzie dived into Emily's backpack. "They don't hunt ferrets in this world, do they?" he squeaked.

"They shouldn't be hunting here at all!" Adriane exclaimed angrily. She ran up the hill. Emily and Ozzie followed.

On the other side of the hill, three hunters were creeping across the grass. One of the men had his rifle raised. The other two were holding a huge net between them. They were moving slowly toward the most bizarre creature Emily had ever seen.

"What the—!" Ozzie scampered to Emily's shoulder to get a better look.

"Is *that* the monster?" Adriane asked.

"That's no monster!" Ozzie exclaimed. "I'd recognize that purple fur ball anywhere!"

As they watched, the hunters crept slowly toward the huge creature, but unlike other animals, this one didn't seem to have a sense of danger. It didn't move. It just sat.

Ozzie was getting more agitated. "That's Phelonius!" He dug his claws into Emily's scalp.

"Ouch! Calm down, Ozzie!" Emily pulled him off her head.

"We've got to help him!" Ozzie wriggled out of her arms and leaped to the ground.

The men were shaking their heads and gesturing toward each other. Then the man with the rifle pointed it at the sky. *Bang!* The creature still didn't move. The man lowered his gun and moved forward slowly.

"We can't let them capture Phel!" Ozzie insisted.

Emily looked at Adriane.

"I don't know, it's a talking ferret, maybe they're all crazy," Adriane offered.

"It's a creature of magic!" Ozzie yelled

"And it's not dangerous?" Adriane asked.

"Nooo!" Ozzie was very frazzled. "You've got to do something!" he urged the girls.

Emily nodded her head at Adriane. "All right."

Adriane straightened her shoulders. "Okay, I'll distract those hunters, while you and Alice see if you can move that . . . thing . . . out of here."

"Be careful," Emily said, crouching low in the tall grass.

"You, too." Adriane took a deep breath and confidently walked down the hill. "Hey!"

Startled, all three hunters whirled to face her.

"It's a kid!" one of them said. "Go on home, it's not safe around here."

Undaunted, Adriane continued until she was right

next to them. "This is a wildlife preserve," she said. "Didn't you see the signs? They say 'No hunting.'"

"Who are you?" the rifle-holder asked.

"I'm Adriane Charday. I live at Ravenswood Manor."

"We don't have to listen to a kid," one of the net-holding men said.

Their backs were to the creature—and to Emily. She seized the moment. "Let's go," she said to Ozzie. She dashed into the field and skidded to a stop right in front of the purple giant. Ozzie was running so fast he hit the creature's belly and bounced back off. The thing was enormous, easily eight feet tall. It sat motionless in the grass, surrounded by a ring of rainbow puff flowers. Deep purple fur shimmered in the sunlight. Emily stared in wonder. It looked sort of like a cross between a great bear and Humpty Dumpty. Its giant eyes were shut. A think line for a mouth ran across its face and it had no neck. Ozzie scrambled up the huge beast and looked into its face. "Phelonius! It's me! Ozymandius!"

The creature just sat, eyes closed, still as a statue.

"Maybe he's been tranquilized," Emily whispered.

"No, no," the ferret said quickly. "He can't be tranquilized. That's absurd!"

"You have no right bringing rifles onto private property!" Adriane yelled in the distance.

"This preserve has no right harboring killer grizzlies," one of the men countered.

"That's no grizzly! It's a rare . . . um, panda from

China . . . and it's worth a million dollars! If anything happens to it, you'd be responsible!"

"I don't care what it is, we're bringing it in!" the hunter threatened.

Emily studied the creature. She felt oddly drawn to him. She realized she should probably be scared—but she wasn't. She ran her hand over his smooth fur and felt a wave of calm wash over her. Light caught her eye, and she looked down to see her gem pulse a soft aqua blue. She took a deep breath.

"What are you?" she asked.

"He's a fairy creature." Ozzie had resorted to kicking the giant. "Wake up, you big thing!"

Looking past the creature, Emily saw that the field fell away into a shallow gully. "Maybe we can roll him down into that gully." She placed her hands on the creature and pushed. "Come on, Ozzie, help me!"

The creature put up no resistance as he started to tilt over. Despite his girth, he felt as light as air.

"What?" Ozzie cried. "That's ridiculous, you can't roll—aaaahhhhh!"

In a cloud of rainbow dust, the giant fur ball starting rolling down the hill, the shrieking ferret hanging on.

"What was that?" asked one of the hunters.

"If you harm that panda, you're all going to be in big trouble!" Adriane yelled.

"Get out of our way!"

The huge creature rolled to a stop in the gully, sitting

upright. Keeping her head down, Emily quickly crawled back to peer across the field. She saw the man with the rifle start to shove past Adriane.

Suddenly he stopped. "Hey, where did it go?"

Watching Adriane point to the trees in the direction opposite the gully, Emily noticed an opalescent glow at her friend's wrist. The section of woods that Adriane was pointing to rustled and shook, as if disturbed by something passing through.

"Look over there!" a hunter cried. "It's in those trees!"

The hunter with the rifle moved off in the direction of the sounds. "Come on!"

For a moment, Adriane looked stunned. Then she seemed to collect herself and yelled after them. "And stay off this property!"

8

*T*HE ENORMOUS CREATURE sat like a giant Buddha, unaffected by anything that had happened.

Adriane came sliding into the gully. "That was *so* weird!" she exclaimed breathlessly.

"How did you do that?" Emily asked, wide eyed.

"I don't know," Adriane said slowly. "I was so focused on doing something to distract the hunters. Then I saw the trees and reached for them . . . it was intense, it felt like I was pushing through water."

"I saw your stone glow," Emily said.

Adriane glanced at her bracelet. The paw shaped stone looked perfectly normal. "I pushed harder, in my head, and my stone flashed and then the trees across the field started to shake and move!"

Emily peered at her own gemstone. "Do you think these are really magic stones?"

"Memerrmeemee!"

Adriane looked around. "Where's Alice?"

"Ozzie!" Emily stood up quickly. "Where are you?"

"MmurrRRMMppphh!"

Emily circled the purple creature. "Ozzie?"

"Mm hmm . . . !"

She put her hands on the giant. His fur felt warm and soft. "Help me move him."

Adriane got up and pushed alongside Emily. Two gigantic eyes opened and blinked. They were deep reservoirs of calm and gentleness. He blinked again.

"Please, could you move just a little?" Emily tried. "Our friend seems to be caught under you."

The purple giant seemed to search Emily's face. She felt overwhelmed by a sadness so deep that tears welled in her eyes. But the feeling passed in a flash and her hands fell away from the creature's side as he lumbered to his feet.

"Gah!" Ozzie sputtered.

Emily reached down to peel Ozzie off the ground. "Are you all right?"

"No! I'm all flattened out!" The ferret shook dust off himself and kicked the big creature. "What are you trying to do, squish me?"

The huge beast just blinked down at Ozzie. Then silently, he turned and started to walk away.

"Hey, come back here!" Ozzie yelled. He ran and grabbed hold of the creature's leg, then scampered all the way up to his shoulder.

"We'd better follow him until we're sure those hunters are really gone," Emily said.

The girls ran to catch up as the purple giant entered the woods. He moved silently forward as if gliding on air, trailing a colorful wake of rainbow flowers behind him.

"So that's where the flowers are coming from!" Emily exclaimed.

"Phelonious, am I glad to see you! I thought I was sent to the wrong place!" Ozzie gestured wildly with his arms as he chattered into the great beast's ear. "I ended up in this strange body—what were those Fairimentals thinking? Look, I'm a weasel!!!" he wailed.

A flash of color moved through the trees behind them. Emily grabbed Adriane's arm. "Did you see that?"

"See what?" Adriane stopped to look. In the stillness, they heard rustling and the patter of hoofbeats. Suddenly a herd of jeeran burst through the brush, bounding through the trees.

Adriane whirled around. "Look, there's more!"

Behind the jeeran, a group of strange duck-like birds appeared. They were goofy-looking, with silver bills and webbed feet too big for their bodies. One of them waddled right up to Emily. It cocked its head up at her, but made no threatening moves.

"Hello," Emily said.

"Hello yourself," it responded. It spoke out loud, its rubbery beak moving weirdly to shape the words. "Are you a mage?"

"Mage? No, I'm a girl."

"A warlock, then?" it persisted.

"We're not warlocks," Adriane said.

The creature thought for a moment. "All right then." It waddled past them, herding the others along the trail of rainbow flowers left behind by the purple giant Ozzie called Phelonius.

Following the parade of animals, the girls made their way around a mass of dense thickets. Phelonius was entering the natural archway that led to the Rocking Stone.

"This is it!" Adriane exclaimed. "The glade must be on the other side!"

Emily hung back, suddenly overwhelmed by the reality of being back here again.

"C'mon!" Adriane called.

Reluctantly Emily followed, hoping the glade really *was* there. They skirted the immense boulder—and stopped.

"Wow." Adriane stopped, awestruck. "This is amazing!"

The glade was just as awesome as Emily remembered. The slender boughs of the weeping willows touched the pond, sending cascading ripples through the water's reflection of the sky. The ground was a flower-carpet of rainbow colors. Sparkling sunlight glinted off the turquoise wing of a bird perched on the arching bridge.

"Wow . . ." Adriane breathed, looking around. "I can't believe this was here and I never knew it."

Phelonius was settling his great bulk beside an enormous tree. Stormbringer padded out from the far trees and walked over to him, lowering her head, her ears, and her tail in a wolfish bow. Emily caught brief glimpses of animals huddled together.

The ferret raced over to the girls.

"Ozzie, what is he doing here?" Emily asked, looking at the purple creature.

"I don't know yet. He's not talking."

"An animal that *doesn't* talk—what a concept," Adriane remarked.

"Phel is not an animal," Ozzie said. "Come and say hello."

Emily and Adriane followed Ozzie over to Phel. The glade was still. A brightly colored bird darted over the water and zipped past. Emily blinked. It looked like a tiny dragon, with wings! It was gone before she could be sure. She looked around and felt surrounded by animals. They stood at the outskirts of the glade waiting—but for what?

"This is Emily and Adriane," Ozzie said. "They're girls, but they seem to have a talent for magic." He sat back, pleased with himself.

"Hello," Emily said shyly.

"Hi," Adriane said.

Phelonius blinked, and Emily felt a wave of warmth and love pour over her.

"What kind of creature is he exactly?" she asked Ozzie.

"Phel's a fairy creature, he's *made* of magic."

"How can that be?" Emily's rational mind wondered.

"We can touch him! We can see him!" She shook her head. "I don't know what to believe anymore."

"Prove it," Adriane said to Phel. "Show us magic."

The corners of Phel's thin mouth turned up into a smile. Tiny pinpoints of light sparkled across his fur. Then as if by some silent signal, dozens of animals began to emerge from the forest. Emily rubbed her eyes. "I think I'm seeing things," she whispered.

"Emily, that's . . . that's a . . . " Adriane stammered incredulously. "What is that?"

Before them stood a pony with resplendent wings of bright orange and yellow, like those of a butterfly. A dozen jeeran stepped forward, followed by a host of other creatures. Some had wings, some had scales, and one had the body of a cat and the head of a bird. Emily could not even begin to identify the others.

Then she caught her breath. A magnificent white owl with glowing turquoise eyes hobbled to a halt at her feet. Her heart, so full of wonder a moment ago, emptied with a dull ache. The owl's wings glowed a sickly green—just like the burns on the cat.

"My wings can't fly." Emily heard the words in her head as clearly as if they'd been spoken aloud.

"Emily!" Adriane was pointing to the animals.

Emily was taken aback by the tears that ran down Adriane's cheeks. She looked more closely at the other animals. "Oh, no!" she gasped.

"Oh, my." Even Ozzie seemed shocked.

The hind legs and back of one of the jeerans was a patchwork of raw abrasions, all colored with the faint green glow. It swayed slightly, as if just standing up was an effort. The winged pony's flank was slashed by a lightning strike-shaped burn. Some of the animals couldn't walk very well, and others were helping the wounded move along. The creature she'd met earlier was herding forward several others of its kind, all covered in the noxious glow.

Pain throbbed like hot coals as Emily felt the animals' misery—but she also sensed a spark of hope that flared in them upon seeing Phel. She gripped Adriane's hand.

A jeeran, its leg crisscrossed with greenish burns, approached Phelonius. Emily held her breath as the purple giant reached out toward the jeeran. Immense but gentle paws touched the animal's sides and legs. The jeeran shivered. Phel's fur shimmered. The brighter he shone, the fainter the green glow became. Then Phel's light faded and the horrible burns were gone!

"How did you do that?" Emily asked, astonished.

He removed his paws and released a cloud of rainbow sparkles that twinkled through the air. The jeeran bent a front leg in a bow to Phel, then danced away, its hooves kicking up dirt and grass.

Adriane turned to Emily, her face full of wonder as one by one the injured animals approached Phel. As he worked, more and more rainbow sparkles floated and danced over the glade. The air glittered. Rainbow puff flowers sprouted and blossomed. Emily's pain washed away like that of the healed animals, leaving in its place an incredible sense of hope and dreams . . . and magic.

Adriane had found Stormbringer herding animals forward and she ran to her friend. "How can this be happening?"

"Magic finds a way, warrior."

Emily looked down at the owl sitting near her. As gently as possible, she lifted it in her arms. Then she turned to Phel.

"I want to help," she said.

9

EMILY HELD THE owl as Phel's great paws stroked its wings. The jewel on her wrist pulsed with a bright blue light. She was concentrating so hard, she was barely aware of Adriane, Ozzie, Stormbringer, and the other animals watching. As the light from her stone mixed with Phel's warm glow, she could *feel* the poison leaving the owl's body, could *sense* its strength returning. Her heart leaped into flight. The owl opened its bright eyes and looked adoringly at Emily. She gently scratched its head and was thrilled to see a glimmer of turquoise and gold run through its feathers.

"There, is that better?" she asked.

"A mouse would be good."

"That was amazing, Emily," Adriane breathed.

Emily laughed as she brushed the soft feathers with her hand. Then she lowered the owl to the ground.

"Ariel likes you." The duck-thing was standing there watching.

"Thank you . . . I think. Her name is Ariel?"

"Yes."

"What's your name?" Emily asked.

"Ronif," it told her. "I'm a quiffle."

Emily blinked. "My name is Emily. These are my friends, Adriane, Ozzie, and Stormbringer." She pointed to each in turn.

The quiffle looked them over. "All right, then." He waddled away to tell the others.

"Come on, let's help them." Emily got up to carry one of the wounded quiffles to Phel. Adriane joined her.

The sun dropped low behind the trees, its golden rays cutting across the glade, but Emily hardly noticed, too busy holding and soothing the sick and wounded animals while Phel healed them. Adriane and Storm moved among the larger animals, helping them get to Phel.

At last no more animals came forward. Emily sat down, exhausted and exhilarated at the same time. She held the beautiful owl in her lap and gazed at the extraordinary collection of creatures gathered in the glade. They were all watching her. She sensed their joy at being healed, and yet they seemed nervous, darting glances into the woods and up toward the sky.

Adriane approached, half a dozen baby quiffles riding

in her pockets, and three more in her arms. Adriane plopped three into Emily's lap, then sat down carefully, so as not to disturb her passengers. Ariel let the tiny quiffles snuggle into her feathers; they cooed happily, and Emily laughed.

"Fantastic!" Ozzie said as he walked over.

"We didn't really do anything," Emily said. "Phel healed them all."

"Don't be so modest."

"Did you see your stone glowing?" Adriane asked. "Like mine did, when I made those trees move."

Emily checked her jewel. It wasn't glowing now. "Maybe the stones react to magic," she suggested.

"Very possible," Ozzie said. "Phel's flowers are seeding the whole place with magic, the stones could be absorbing it."

"Yeah, maybe they store the magic—like batteries— and let us use it," Adriane ventured.

"Could anyone use these, or . . . just us?" Emily wondered.

Adriane looked at Ozzie, eyes narrowed. "What else do you know that you haven't told us?"

"Those burns." Ozzie said, looking over at the animals. "It's the Black Fire. I had no idea it was this bad. And they're the ones that made it here. Who knows what's happened to the others left behind."

"No wonder they're all scared," Emily said. "Talk to them, Ozzie."

"Who, me?"

"Tell them everything's going to be all right," Emily prompted.

"Come on, Ali—Ozzie," Adriane said.

"Oh, all right." Ozzie got up and walked over to the animals. "Hello, I'm Ozymandius, er, Ozzie." The animals all perked up, eyes wide open, ears pricked forward. The ferret steeled himself and faced the crowd. "I am an elf."

"You don't look like an elf," Ronif the quiffle remarked.

"That's right, genius! I know I don't *look* like an elf!"

"Go on, Ozzie, you're doing great," Emily said encouragingly.

"I'm from Aldenmor, like you. I grew up in the village of Farthingdale, near the Moorgroves."

Sounds of recognition were heard from the animals.

"It's a secluded Elven place. Too secluded for me—I wanted to explore the world. If I had known any better I would've stayed home!" He surveyed the expectant faces and continued. "One day, I wandered out among the Moorgroves and got lost in the dark forests. Phel found me and brought me to the Fairy Glen, and I actually *met* Fairimentals!"

Murmurs of wonderment surged through the crowd.

Encouraged, Ozzie grew more animated, waving his paws and shuffling back and forth. "They knew I was coming, don't ask me how—who knows the ways of fairies? They told me Aldenmor was in great danger, that soon there would be no place safe."

An animal bugled agreement; Emily thought it was one of the jeerans.

"The Fairimentals are searching for an enchanted place, the source of all magic. They said they needed 'humans' to help. I was to find three mages. A healer—" He paused and looked directly at Emily. "A warrior—" He looked at Adriane. "And a blazing star."

Eyes wide, Emily glanced at Adriane. "Blazing star?" she whispered, perplexed. Adriane shrugged.

Ozzie continued. "I didn't have the faintest idea what they meant, but it's not every day a Fairimental asks for your help. So I followed their directions and somehow ended up getting tossed through some portal and into this world—stuck in the body of a ferret! I don't really know much else. It's kind of fuzzy," he said apologetically. "My giant-sized brain's been compressed to the size of a peanut!"

Ronif stepped forward. "The Fairimentals were right. The Black Fire is destroying our world, poisoning us. If we hadn't found our way here, and if you and the great fairy creature hadn't helped us, we would have died."

"What is Black Fire?" Emily asked.

Ronif turned to her. "It rains from the sky and seeps through the ground, burning all that it touches."

Emily turned to Adriane. "My mom was right," she said. "It's some kind of toxin, or radiation, maybe."

"Now we are refugees here in this strange land," a winged pony said.

"Some of us have left families behind." The speaker was one of the quiffles. The others voiced their agreement. The baby quiffles buried their heads in Emily's arms and started to cry.

Another winged horse stepped forward. "We pegasi know of legends." It looked directly at the two girls. "Old legends say that once, long ago, animals and humans worked together to make magic."

Emily looked down at her stone. *Mage . . . healer . . . magic. . . .* The words ran round and round in her head.

Ozzie spoke up again. "If the legends say that animals and humans once worked together, then that's what we are going to do again." He pointed to Emily and Adriane. "The important thing now is that you have friends here. Somehow, we'll figure it all out together."

The animals signaled their approval with bleats and neighs, barks and hisses, quacks and hoots.

"Go, Ozzie!" Adriane cheered.

The sniffling quiffles stared up at Ozzie.

"Hey now, I may be a weasel, but I can still dance!" Ozzie shuffled an elf dance in front of the quiffles. "Look, the wigjig!"

He leaped into the air, twisted, and landed with his arms outstretched—and fell over backward. The quiffles giggled.

"What I wouldn't give for feet," Ozzie mumbled into the dirt.

Suddenly the ground beside him swirled and he jumped back. The animals looked at one another. Emily and Adriane stared as four small pools of dirt and twigs rose from the ground, spinning into tiny whirlpools.

"Fairimentals . . ." someone in the crowd said reverently. Everyone fell silent as the whirlpools danced toward the girls.

Emily and Adriane stood quickly as the whirlpools buzzed around their legs.

"*Sankk uuuu . . .*" The voice seemed to come from the closest whirlpool, and Emily turned to follow it.

"*Frrrrienndss . . .*" came the voice of another.

"*Ssssssssrrrrrr . . .*" another said in a swirling frenzy. It burst apart, twigs and leaves flying.

The first whirlpool spun by even faster. "*Serrrrrrrrrrecch . . .*"

"Search. Search for what?" asked Emily, listening hard.

"*Hommmmm . . .*"

"*Hommmmmm . . .*"

"*Hommmmm . . .*" the third cyclone added its tiny voice in a harmonic chorus as the three spun together, weaving in and out and around the girls.

"Please, can't you tell us more?" Emily had bent over to make sure they could hear her.

One tiny tornado spun wildly by her. *"Weecannnottt-sttaaayherrrr . . ."*

"Er . . . I don't mean to be rude, but before you go, you think you could, mmm, like, change me back?" Ozzie whispered.

"Uucannnnottgoobackk . . ."

The whirlpools were wavering, starting to fall apart, as if the strength it took to communicate was too much for them.

"Please, don't go! Where is home?" Emily was close to tears.

The whirlpools spun faster, trying to hold together for one last message. But with a whisper they blew apart and became the wind.

"Nooo!" Emily cried.

"Emily . . ." Adriane said in a hushed tone.

There on the ground before them, a word was etched in the dirt:

AVALON

"Thanks a lot!" Ozzie was jumping up and down.

Avalon.

Emily stared at the word as a cool breeze blew it to dust. What did it mean?

The animals moved about restlessly. Somehow they understood what the Fairimentals were saying: that there was no going back. They were refugees without a home. An unspoken sadness spread through the glade.

"What about the monster?" a little quiffle asked in a tiny voice. A perceptible chill swept through the crowd.

"Why does this dark creature hunt us down?" asked a blue rabbit-like animal.

"It's out there somewhere, waiting," a pegasus said ominously.

Phel stepped forward and the crowd parted to let him through. Pinpoints of light sparkled from his shimmering purple fur and a shower of stars gently cascaded over the glade. A sense of calm spread through the animals.

Emily rose and went to Phel. She put her arms around him as far as she could reach and held him close. He made a soft noise. Adriane joined Emily. The little quiffles giggled, and the girls laughed. Slowly others crept up to snuggle in. Emily and Adriane were soon buried in warm animals.

"You, too, Alice." Adriane reached out and pulled Ozzie in.

"Gah!"

For that moment, surrounded by the giant arms and warm magic of Phel, no one was afraid.

STARS WINKED IN a velvet sky as Adriane walked Emily down the road out of the preserve.

"Well, we found the animals," Adriane said at last.

"We sure did." Emily agreed.

"So, what's your analysis of the situation, Doc?" Adriane asked lightly. But she looked tense.

"Well, most of what we know is still pretty vague." Emily felt better analyzing the facts. "But one thing seems sure: these animals have come from another world, and that world is being poisoned by something terrible."

"Go on."

Emily took a deep breath. "Okay, now some kind of doorway between worlds has opened—a portal as Ozzie calls it—and the hurt animals are making their way here, where it's safe."

"But how safe?" Adriane asked.

"And the Fairimentals want us to find something . . . a place," Emily continued.

"Avalon. The home of magic."

"Adriane, Ozzie said the Fairimentals need three mages . . ."

Adriane looked at her, waiting.

"If we *are* two of them . . . who's the third?"

"I don't know anything about mages," Adriane said with a shrug. "But I do know we *can't* let Ravenswood be destroyed. Those animals have nowhere else to go!"

"You're right. We have to do something."

"We will." Adriane held up her bracelet, and the striped jewel sparkled in the moonlight.

Emily lifted up her own gem. "Together," she said. A spark flashed between the two stones—a connection forged between friends, a bond that would last forever.

Adriane turned and walked back up the road to the preserve. Emily looked out over the parklands at the warm lights of her house.

Avalon. The word drifted through her mind like a soft breeze as she walked home.

10

*T*HE STONEHILL TOWN Hall was a two-story red-brick building right on Main Street, across from a nicely tended park with a playground and lots of benches and trees. Carolyn parked their green Explorer while Emily searched the crowded parking lot for Adriane and Gran. Then she heard the sputtering of an old pickup truck and looked over to see Gran barreling into a parking space. The ancient engine protested, shuddered, and came to rest.

"Hey!" Adriane jumped out to greet Emily.

"Hey," Emily returned. "Mom, this is Adriane's grand-mother."

"Please call me Nakoda," Gran said warmly.

Carolyn held out her hand. "I'm Carolyn Fletcher."

Gran smiled. "It is my pleasure. Emily is a special child."

"She'll do." Carolyn smiled back.

The town hall was jammed. Mayor Davies was up on the podium, listening to people argue back and forth about the Ravenswood Preserve. They were convinced some dangerous predator was killing innocent animals.

Why couldn't these people see how important Ravenswood was? Emily thought. Suddenly her wrist began to itch like crazy. She checked her bracelet. Her stone was pulsing light! Quickly, she pulled down the sleeve of her sweater to cover it. But she had the strangest sensation that someone was watching her. She looked around the room and her eyes met the bright blue eyes of the blond girl whose friends had teased her at Arrowhead Park.

"Who's that?" Emily asked Adriane in a whisper.

Adriane scowled, "Kara Davies, the mayor's daughter."

"You don't like her much," Emily surmised.

"Who wears pink sweaters and perfectly matched pink sandals? She's such a Barbie!" Adriane crossed her arms over her chest and glared daggers at Kara—and suddenly the jewel on her bracelet sparked. Startled, Adriane covered her wrist

The blond girl's eyes narrowed.

"We think it was a bear!" one of the men Adriane had confronted on the preserve called out. "Almost had it, too."

"And?" the mayor prompted.

"It got away," the hunter scowled. "But we'll get it!"

Emily stiffened. "They're talking about Phel," she whispered to Adriane. But she couldn't dare tell anyone about Phel, that he was magic! How could she explain that he'd *healed* the animals?

The crowd was buzzing. "Place should be closed . . . Wild animals near our town—it's too dangerous!" People were clearly upset.

Mrs. Beasley Windor, a very vocal member of the town council, stood up. "Let's just cut to the chase here." Her beady eyes and sharp nose made her look like a hawk. "We can't have dangerous animals running around like a jungle. Ravenswood has a history, but I say it *is* history!"

"The animals need a place to live also!" Emily said more loudly than she'd intended.

"Yeah, they have rights, too!" Adriane echoed.

"Excuse me! Since when do *children* have a voice in town matters?" Mrs. Windor said condescendingly. "Especially those involving public safety!"

"Mrs. Windor, please," the mayor said. "We still need proof of these accusations."

"Oh, really." She walked forward and slapped a letter onto the lectern in front of the mayor. "Why don't you read this, Mayor?" She gave Carolyn and the girls a snide look. "It's a copy of a letter sent to Dr. Carolyn Fletcher from the University of Pennsylvania."

"Uh-oh, this is bad," Adriane said to Emily.

Carolyn glanced at Emily. Emily tried to smile but felt her lips lock into a grimace.

The mayor quickly read the letter. "Well, this settles it then. Health officials from the Centers for Disease Control will be here in two days, so if we can't find a solution to this problem, they will give us one."

"You got that right." Mrs. Windor was smiling. "The place should be shut down and the land properly developed!" she repeated to a chorus of agreements.

"Okay, folks, let's take a break and cool down," the mayor said. "Mrs. Charday, may I speak to you for a minute? You, too, Dr. Fletcher."

Carolyn and Gran rose. Adriane and Emily started to follow, but Carolyn stopped them. "You two wait outside. You think you can do that without creating a town incident?"

Emily knew better than to argue with her mother when she used that tone.

Mortified, the girls left the building and walked over to the park. Except for their moods, the summer night was perfect—low humidity, a cool breeze, and a golden waxing moon.

Adriane kicked at a small rock. "Now what?"

"My mom's gonna kill me about that letter!" Emily wailed. "I wish we had done something else!"

"Shhh, wait, someone's coming," Adriane hissed.

In the orangey glow of a street lamp, Emily saw pink

sandals. She and Adriane stared as Kara Davies strolled up to them.

"What?" the blonde girl asked. "Is there gum in my teeth?"

"What do you want?" Adriane asked rudely.

Kara didn't seem fazed. "It's a free country. I can walk here if I want to." She looked at Emily. "Almost didn't recognize you without a pile of dogs."

Emily reddened. "I'm Emily Fletcher."

"I'm Kara Davies—"

"We know who you are," Adriane interrupted.

"So, I know who you are, too," Kara replied, not missing a beat.

"Great, now what do you want?" Adriane shot back.

"Nothing . . . I just thought you could tell me what store in the mall carries those bracelets."

"You can't buy them," Adriane told her with obvious satisfaction.

"I can *buy* anything I want." Kara dismissed Adriane with a flick of her hand.

"Well, you can't *buy* these!" Adriane held up her arm and shook the bracelet in front of Kara's face. The stone blazed to life with a fierce golden fire. Startled, Adriane quickly pulled her wrist behind her back.

Kara's bright blue eyes were as wide as saucers. "Wow! How'd you make it glow like that? Batteries?" she guessed.

Adriane looked at Emily. Neither girl replied.

Kara tried a new ploy. "Maybe I can help you and your wild animals, if you give me one of your bracelets," she offered slyly.

"No way!" said Adriane.

"Wait a minute," Emily said. "Maybe Kara *can* help us. If we show her where we got these, maybe she could convince her father to help . . . *all* the animals." She looked meaningfully at Adriane.

"Daddy always listens to me," Kara boasted. "But first you have to take me to the store where you got those."

"Read my lips," Adriane stated. "No *way!*"

"Adriane, maybe Kara can find her own stone," Emily suggested.

"Sure, I'm a power shopper," Kara smiled, showing perfect teeth. "And you can just tell me where in the mall, you wouldn't even have to go with me."

"Oh, of course, it would be just horrible being seen with us," Adriane said.

"I just meant it might be easier," Kara replied, as if she were speaking to a three-year-old. She twirled the ends of her long blonde hair.

Emily nudged Adriane.

"Okay," Adriane agreed. "But we have to take you there."

"And you have to promise that whatever we show you, you'll keep secret," Emily added.

"Of course," Kara dropped her voice to a whisper. "I understand how important it is to keep cool about fashion. Pretty soon everyone would have one."

"Geez! That's not the point!" Adriane burst out.

Kara gave a well practiced 'Like what's with her?' look.

"So, you promise?" Emily prompted.

Kara was getting impatient. "Yes, yes, fine."

"Emily!" Emily looked up to see her mother calling her from the steps of the town hall. Gran stood beside her. Others were leaving the building. Evidently the meeting was over.

"Coming!" Emily called back. She turned to Kara. "Tomorrow at noon, meet us out by the baseball diamond in the playing fields and we'll take you into the woods."

"You found those in the woods? How disgusting! Forget it!"

Adriane shrugged. "Okay, fine, we'll do it without you."

"Wait, lemme see those again." Kara grabbed for Emily's wrist.

Brilliant turquoise light flared from the blue-green gem. Kara jumped back. It was so fast it might have been a trick of the light. This time it was Emily who was shocked by the vivid flare of her jewel.

Kara stared with her mouth open. "Okay, noon," she said.

AS THEY DROVE home, Carolyn filled Emily in on her conversation with Gran and the Mayor. Too many people were worried about dangerous predators, and even the mayor had to admit an interest in the money a new development would bring the community.

"The university analysis presents more immediate problems," Carolyn gave Emily a look.

Emily sank into her seat. "I shouldn't have hidden it. That was pretty dumb, huh?"

"Yes, it was. Especially since the mayor's office faxed me a copy only a few hours later." She glanced at Emily. "Since you read it, you know they detected an unidentified toxin and they recommended quarantine."

"But they can't do that!"

"Health officials will be here in a few days. Unless we can show them the place is safe, it may have to be shut down."

Emily softly rubbed the jewel under her sweatshirt sleeve. She and Adriane *had* to figure out how to help Phelonius and the animals. Time was running out.

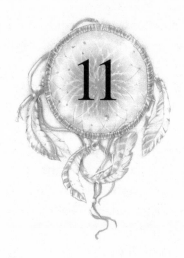

11

*I*T WAS A quarter to noon when Emily left her house. With the Pet Palace population slowly dwindling as vacations ended, her chores were taking less time. She thought hard as she crossed the picnic grounds and headed over to the baseball fields. The townspeople were wrong—Phel was no monster! But they were also more right than they knew—something evil was in those woods and it was stalking all kinds of animals. How could they fight *that*? How—

"How is this supposed to work?"

Emily looked up to find Kara standing on home plate. The blond girl wore a silver silk jacket over a pink T-shirt that said ROCK STAR in fake silver gems. Light green shorts and strappy sandals completed the outfit.

"Oh, hi." Emily said. In her concern for the animals, she had almost forgotten about Kara.

"What are we supposed to do?" Kara demanded. "Just wander around in the woods? It's creepy—and dangerous. Do we have a treasure map or something?" Her steely gaze bore into Emily.

"How 'bout we just saddle up and follow the old Injun trail?" Adriane had come up from the other direction.

"Do you *always* wear black?" Kara remarked, taking in Adriane's black jeans, black T-shirt, and black hiking boots with clear disdain.

"Just until they invent a darker color," Adriane retorted. She tossed her long black hair over her shoulder. "Let's go."

"Where are we going, exactly?" Kara asked.

"You're about to get the grand tour of the Ravenswood Wildlife Preserve," Adriane told her. "We show you around and then take you home. That's it." She turned and walked back up toward the road. "And no lectures."

"Hey!" Kara ran to catch up. "What about those stones?"

"If you find one, we'll throw you a party," Adriane said.

"What's with her?" Kara asked Emily.

"She's worried about the animals that live in the preserve," Emily told her. "And if the place is closed down, she and Gran will have to move."

"Why don't you and *Gran* just move into a normal house?" Kara pressed.

Adriane stopped and faced Kara. "Look, just stay behind us and try not to say anything too stupid, *please!*"

"You know, you should really try a little bran in your diet."

"Someone shoot me now!" Adriane strode quickly up the path.

Emily and Kara hurried to keep up with Adriane as she forged into the woods. The sun poured golden beams through the overhead branches and cool breezes blew the leaves, creating shifting patterns of light and shadow across the forest floor.

Kara had only one thing on her mind. "So, what do I look for? Minerals? Quartz crystals? I have a book on gems in my backpack." She slung off her leather pack and began digging in it.

"You do? That's really cool." Emily was impressed. Adriane moved on ahead, not wanting any part of the conversation.

"Here, look." Kara pulled out a small, fat book. "See? *Identifying Minerals and Gems*. It's grouped by structure, composition, and luster. The structure is the shape, composition is the purity of the stone, and luster is color."

"Wow." It struck Emily that Kara might not be as shallow as she seemed. She might even be pretty smart.

"Here's the really precious stones, emeralds, sapphires—and my favorite—diamonds!" Kara said. "We can look up your stone in here, too."

Emily held up her wrist as Kara flipped through the pages, trying to find a match. "We made our own bands," she commented self-consciously. "It was Adriane's idea."

Kara barely glanced up. "Not bad. I have some silver chains that'll look much better. I'll get you one."

"I love silver, thanks," Emily said.

"Here, looks like aventurine." Kara pointed to the page. "Properties include protection and healing."

Emily's hazel eyes widened. What a coincidence that she, of all people, should pick up a healing stone! Sunlight reflected off the stone, sending shimmers of color through it.

Kara was mesmerized. She softly touched the jewel. Blinding shafts of blue and green light flared from the stone.

Both girls screamed and Emily jerked her hand back.

Adriane wheeled around and ran back. "What happened?"

"I don't know, my stone, it just—" Emily began.

"That was so awesome!" Kara exclaimed. "I've never seen anything like that!"

"What did you do?" Adriane asked Kara accusingly.

"Easy, Godzilla, I didn't do anything. Her stone just lit up like a sparkler."

Adriane glared. Kara beamed.

Adriane turned to Emily. "Are you okay?"

"I'm fine." Emily answered. The gem, in its woven bracelet, was now back to normal. "That was so weird."

"I have the perfect silver chain for *my* jewel," Kara went on excitedly.

Adriane ignored her. "We're coming up to the topiary gardens. Over there." She pointed to a garden of living sculptures. There was a lion, a giraffe, and an elephant, even a dinosaur all carefully carved out of magnificent foliage. "The topiary gardens are one of the most amazing gardens on the estate."

"Oooh, look!" Kara bent over and picked up a sparkly stone. She studied it, scrunched her nose, then tossed it away. "What'd you say?"

"Never mind."

As they walked into the garden, even Kara seemed impressed with the carefully sculptured hedges. "Wow, tree animals! Cool!"

Adriane continued. "First designed in 1920, each of the hedge sculptures is supposed to represent an animal that was on the preserve at that time."

"I thought we were in a 'no lectures' zone," Kara commented.

"Oh, yeah." Adriane and Kara actually smiled at each other.

"And another thing," Kara continued, "these hedge sculptures can't possibly represent the animals that were on the preserve."

"What do you mean?" Adriane asked.

"Hellloo! That's a unicorn, and that's . . . like, a dinosaur! I'm pretty sure the hedge-a-saurus has been extinct for like a billion years."

"Maybe they represent animals that were just visiting," Emily said.

"Oookay." Kara skipped ahead through the tall hedges. Out of the topiary gardens, the lawn sloped downward. Kara stopped as Ravenswood Manor loomed ahead like a gigantic haunted house nestled in the woods. "Are you related to the Adams Family?" Kara quipped.

"Very funny," Adriane replied. "You've never seen Ravenswood Manor?"

"Just in some old pictures."

"They used to have tours here," Emily said.

"Big business on Halloween, I bet," Kara remarked.

Adriane just rolled her eyes. "Come on, we'll go out past the manor. I'll show you the gardens out back."

"What about my stone?"

"We said you *might* find one," Adriane said.

Kara crossed her arms and pouted.

"We *could* look around a bit more," Emily suggested.

"All right!" Adriane led them to the side of the manor and onto another path. They were soon in deep woods and the air was cool and damp. Above, the boughs seemed woven together into a solid canopy of green.

Something rustled in the trees.

"What was that?" Kara whispered nervously.

"Just animals," Emily reassured her. "They won't hurt you."

"This is creepy. It's like they're following us."

"They probably never saw anything like *you* before," Adriane said sarcastically.

"On any other day, I might take that as a compliment." Kara studied the ground around her. She gingerly picked up rocks and pebbles, compared them to pictures in her book, and placed some neatly in her backpack.

"Remind me again why she's here," Adriane grumbled to Emily.

"To convince her father to keep the preserve safe."

"Ugh, bugs!" Kara announced behind them. "And I bet there's poison ivy all over here."

"Just keep looking for stones," Adriane shot back over her shoulder. "They could be anywhere."

She leaned in toward Emily again. "And what about the CDC?" she continued. "How are we gonna get through that inspection?"

"I don't know," Emily admitted.

"I don't think they have a listing for 'Black Fire.'"

Over the next hour, Kara amassed a small collection of stones. But none of them glowed, no matter what she did. After a while, she sat down, picked out the nicest stone, and held it tightly in one hand.

Emily noticed and nudged Adriane. The two girls watched, trying not to laugh, as Kara bent over the stone, wrinkle-browed and frowning, a look of intense concentration on her face. Realizing she was being observed, she glared icily at the other girls.

"What are you doing?" Adriane asked incredulously.

"Resting—what's it to you?" Kara got up and tossed the stone away in disgust.

"One of the stones you find is bound to be special," Emily consoled her.

Kara upended her backpack, pouring the stones on the ground. "None of these are any good!"

"Face it, Barbie," Adriane said, "the magic doesn't like you."

Kara jumped to her feet, slinging her empty pack over her shoulder. "That's it! Look, I am Kara Davies, and you are a couple of weirdos. If you think for a minute I'm going any farther into these woods in my brand-new sandals, you're as crazy as you look! I am turning around right now and going to the mall, where normal people go!" She stalked off angrily.

"Now what?" Emily asked. "We can't let her wander around the woods alone."

"She'll be completely lost in about, oh, fifteen seconds," Adriane said.

"Aaahhh!" Kara's scream cut through the forest.

"Correction: ten," Adriane said. "Come on."

Emily and Adriane cut back in the direction of Kara's voice. They found her off the main trail, on a smaller path, looking down into a ravine.

"What now? Did you see a bee?" Adriane taunted.

Kara pointed to a gully ahead of her. "What's that?"

Emily looked—and her breath caught in her throat. With a cry, she slid down the incline.

"Emily, wait!" Adriane cried. But all of Emily's senses were focused on the wounded creature that lay there, half buried under debris. Carefully, she cleared away the branches and wet leaves. As if in a dream, she saw her stone pulsing wildly with blue light. She felt light-headed.

"Ariel!" she cried.

The owl lay in the gully, her body torn and bruised almost beyond recognition. One wing was mangled and bent at an impossible angle. A sickly green glowed in spots on the owl's body. Carefully, Emily felt the owl's chest to see if she was breathing. She was alive—just barely.

"Ugh! That's disgusting!" Kara said, peering down.

"I need something to carry her in!" Emily called up.

"Leave it, it's dead," Kara said. "Aahh—hey!"

Adriane was pulling Kara's silk jacket off her shoulders.

"What are you doing? That's a DK!" Kara protested.

Throwing it down to Emily, Adriane said, "If either of us had a jacket, believe me, we wouldn't want yours."

Emily gently wrapped the owl in Kara's jacket, then carefully carried her up out of the ravine.

"Is she all right?" Adriane asked.

"No. We have to get her to Phel—quickly."

"What about *her*?" Adriane nodded in Kara's direction.

Kara stood, silently fuming.

Emily's only concern was the owl. "Ariel's going to die if we don't get her to Phel right now!"

"Let's go. This way." Ignoring Kara, Adriane started down the small path. Emily followed, cradling Ariel in her arms. When Kara realized she was being left behind, she ran to catch up.

"Where are you going?" she demanded.

Adriane whirled around. "We need to get this animal to where she can be healed!"

"She's hurt bad," Emily said softly.

"Well, lucky I found her, huh?" Kara said. Then she paused. "What's a Phel?"

"Look, just remember your promise," Adriane said sharply. "You tell no one about what we show you."

"I knew it! A secret place you weren't telling me about!" Kara's eyes sparkled.

"I'm serious! Promise!" Adriane insisted.

"Okay, okay, I promise," Kara said.

Emily hurried along the trail, Adriane at her side. Kara was falling behind, her sandals no match for the logs and rocks that littered the forest floor.

They entered the archway of trees and rounded the Rocking Stone as a voice called out, "There you are! Did you bring any food? Oh no, what's happened?"

Kara caught up a moment later, looking up at the immense boulder. She stepped past it into the glade and her eyes opened wide. "Wow!" She looked from the lovely willow trees to the clear crystal waters of the pond. Flowers bloomed everywhere and rainbow sparkles drifted lightly in the air.

"Ozzie, where's Phel?" Emily was frantic.

"Probably out spreading magic seeds," Ozzie replied.

Out of the corner of her eye, Emily could see Kara approaching. Clearly, the blond girl intended to meet whomever Emily was talking to. "Hello, I'm—" Kara began. Then she stopped, puzzled, and looked around.

"Who's that?" Ozzie asked.

Kara peered at the brown-and-gold ferret, then back at Emily. "Who said that?" she asked. When no one answered, she shook her head, confused. "What is this place?"

"Just another garden," Adriane said.

"Oh really! Well, I've never seen flowers like these!"

"Phel, where are you? Phel?" Emily was beginning to panic as she paced around the glade, cradling the owl.

"Phel, phel, phel . . . " Kara looked about. "What is a Phel, and where can I find a jewel—hey!" Ozzie was standing in front of her. "Get away, you . . . rat!"

Ozzie rose on his rear legs and crossed his arms. "Who you calling a rat?"

"Aaahhh, it's talking!"

Kara started to back away. She turned to her left and saw a winged horse! A green-striped deer watched her. Everywhere she looked, another bizarre animal appeared.

Kara whirled around—and came face to face with a huge purple creature. Two gigantic eyes stared at her

"A purple bear!" she shrieked, backing away.

"He is not a bear," Adriane said calmly.

In spite of her fear for Ariel, Emily couldn't help noticing the interest the animals were showing in Kara.

"Who are . . . what are all these . . . these . . . *things?*" Kara stammered.

Phel reached forward with huge paws.

Kara grabbed Adriane. "Stay away from me, you bear!"

"Let go of me! He won't hurt you!" Adriane said.

Panicked, Kara looked up at the giant creature. Phel spread his arms wide. The air seemed to swirl—and something formed between his huge paws. It looked like a circle in the air. Phel spread his paws apart, and the circle widened, revealing . . . *stars.* Pinpoints of light were strung out along what looked like a web—almost like a giant, three-dimensional dream catcher.

"It's a fairy map!"

Kara's head jerked around. The ferret jumped up and down next to Phel. More animals were gathering around, watching.

Phel suddenly released the web of stars and it floated over Kara, gently cascading down like a starry rain. She was covered with sparkling dots of light as the web encircled her.

Kara screamed at the top of her lungs, swinging her backpack to bat away the strands of stars. She jumped as if covered in ants, waving her arms and kicking her legs. The magical image tore apart in swirls and vanished.

"Kara, are you all right?" Emily called out.

"The map! It's all gone!" Ozzie sat on the grass, moaning, his head in his paws.

Kara slung her backpack over her shoulder. "I'm getting out of here right now! Keep your dumb stones. I can buy better ones at the mall!" She turned and stormed out past the Rocking Stone.

Adriane turned to Emily. "So much for her helping us."

"Get me out of here!" Kara screamed from behind the rock. "I'm freaking out!"

"Adriane, you'd better take her back," Emily said nervously. "I'll help Phel with Ariel."

Adriane grimaced. "I'll be back as soon as I can." She headed out. "Keep your shorts on," she yelled to Kara.

"You didn't tell me you had bears here—and whatever else you're hiding!" Kara shouted.

As their voices faded into the distance, Emily walked over to Phel. He was sitting by one of the trees. As she lay the owl before him, she realized he was different now: weaker. His color wasn't as vibrant, he seemed duller, with a tinge of gray . . . and no rainbow flowers bloomed about his feet.

"Please, you can help, can't you?" she asked, gazing up at his eyes.

Phelonius looked from the owl to Emily. A tear ran down his cheek. She could feel Phel's pain, a deep sadness, and it hit her—he did not have the magic left to heal the owl.

Emily felt the familiar sting of helplessness well up inside. Suddenly her hands were covered by Phel's large paws. Her stone began to glow softly with pale blue light. Phel moved Emily's hands over the owl.

She recoiled, instantly knowing what Phel wanted from her.

"I can't," said Emily, tears spilling from her eyes. "I'm not a *real* healer. I couldn't even help that poor cat!"

As Phel pulled his paws away, Emily blinked back the tears. Her gem had been transformed! It was now a polished, crystalline blossom glistening with rainbow sparkles. It looked exactly like one of Phel's magic puff flowers.

Emily held her breath. She hardly noticed when Phel guided her hands back to the owl, holding them steady as she touched the snowy feathers.

She gasped.

Her stone pulsed faster, beating along with her heart. Suddenly she felt the owl's heartbeat, out of sync with her own, weaker. Phel closed his eyes and Emily concentrated. She *willed* the owl's heart to beat with hers.

Slowly the wounded owl stirred. Emily felt something pushing against her, a sense of weakness, of pain. But she couldn't break its grip. She felt the owl slipping away. "No! Stay with me!"

The feeling of loss engulfed her, threatening to pull her into a dark abyss of despair. She'd lost so much

already—her dad, her friends, her home. Then she thought of the cat, how she had failed when she needed her most.

"No!" Emily cried out. She reached deep inside. All her emotions seemed to rise up at once and the jewel erupted with jagged blue light. It swirled around her wrist, spreading up and down to cover her arm and her hand. Concentrating hard, she willed the light to flow over the owl. Focus . . . focus on the heartbeat. Pulse . . . pulse . . . pulse . . . steady, strong . . . And then she *felt* the owl's heartbeat lock with her own. The jewel and both hearts began to beat as one. Steady, strong . . . The light faded . . . The owl stirred and opened her eyes.

Emily threw herself into Phel's arms, crying and laughing at the same time.

"I can't believe it. We did it!" she said through her tears.

"I think that counts as magic," Ozzie commented.

12

"**Y**OU SHOULD HAVE seen Ozzie, he was so impressed. He was bragging to all the animals how *he* discovered you, a real healer!" Adriane laughed.

Emily was on the phone in her room, listening to her friend. She had run right home with Ariel. Even if the owl seemed healed, she wasn't taking any chances. Only after her mom gave the owl a clean bill of health did Emily relax.

"I only helped Phel, and it was pretty scary," Emily said, not wanting to talk about *how* scared it made her feel. "How did you do with Kara?"

Adriane snorted. "She blabbered the whole way back about how Ravenswood should be fenced off and locked up tight."

"Well, we had no choice, we had to take her to the glade." Emily said.

"Yeah . . . " Adriane's voice trailed off.

"What's the matter?" Emily prompted.

"That thing Phel did to Kara—" Adriane started.

"What was it?"

"Ozzie said it was a gift from the Fairimentals, a fairy map."

"A map? Of what?" Emily asked.

"Maybe where the animals came from?"

"Or where they're supposed to go." Emily remembered the word left in the dirt: AVALON.

"Something is going on here, Emily, and you and I are the only ones who know," Adriane said.

"And Kara," Emily reminded her.

"Yeah." Adriane paused. "We have to do something before Barbie opens her big mouth."

"Like what?"

"I think we should go and try to talk to the mayor ourselves."

"I don't know."

"We can say we're returning her jacket," Adriane suggested.

"I guess we can try," Emily said.

"Good. Meet me tomorrow. Ten sharp at town hall."

THAT NIGHT, EMILY couldn't sleep. She pictured Phel, alone in the woods. Well, not really alone. She had to laugh when she thought about Ozzie, insisting on staying with the big creature to protect him. Poor Ozzie, so far from his home, and the other animals, scared and lost in a strange world. Emily realized she was talking about creatures out of some dream, as if the old legends about the woods were turning real. Had magical animals been here before? Had humans and animals really worked together in the past? What was a fairy map, and why had Phel given it to Kara . . . and not her? She felt a pang of jealousy. Not the first time someone was jealous of Kara, that was for sure.

Whatever was going on, one thing was certain. Her life had changed forever, and not just because she wasn't in Colorado anymore. Emily stared at the wondrous jewel in her hand. A stone of healing and she had found it . . . or had it found her? She clutched it tightly, as if it really could give her some measure of protection from her doubts and fears. What had happened today with Ariel terrified her. A door had been opened that she didn't want to—*couldn't*—enter.

"There is no going back." Wasn't that what one of the Fairimentals had said? Was she ready to go forward? And where would that path lead? Emily sighed. Ozzie had

told Adriane that Phel's fairy map was a gift to Kara. She looked at her jewel. Was this *her* gift?

Quietly, she left her room and ran down to the Pet Palace.

The cat was wide awake, pacing back and forth. She had been moved to the Pet Palace, since she no longer needed constant care and attention. Emily sensed the cat's restlessness.

Emily walked over and sat down next to her. Moonlight drifted through the window, bathing them both in pale silver light. They stared into each other's eyes.

Emily held up her gemstone and ran it over the cat's mottled and sparse patches of fur. She moved it gently over the odd bumps on the animal's shoulders, trying to think healing thoughts. The stone sparkled softly in the moonlight. She visualized the scars vanishing, the mottled tufts turning to lustrous fur; she closed her eyes tight and concentrated. She opened them and—nothing. The cat looked exactly the same. She lifted her head and licked Emily on the nose.

Maybe healing Ariel had drained the crystal, or she needed Phelonius to guide her. "This is crazy! I can't do this!"

The cat stared at her.

"I'm sorry . . . I don't know what else to do." Emily broke down and hugged the cat, sobbing into her neck.

The cat pulled away and turned to pick up something from her bed. When she turned back to Emily, she was holding an orange stuffed lion. Emily took Mr. Snuffles from the cat's mouth. She could swear the cat was smiling at her.

"Taking and giving completes our circle. It's time to let go."

Emily stared at the cat. Maybe she had helped her heal after all. There *was* something more she could do for her, she realized. She reached out to pet her one last time. "We each have to find our own path," she said. Then she went to open the door to the outside.

Moonlight danced in the doorway. A cool breeze ruffled Emily's curls.

"Have faith, healer. The magic is with you, now and forever."

Without a backward glance, the cat walked out into the night. Slowly Emily closed the door and hugged Mr. Snuffles.

13

*T*HE SKY WAS overcast as Emily navigated her bike into the bike rack by the town hall. The parking lot was full. There seemed to be an unusual amount of activity this morning. It seemed like everyone was rushing about.

"Something's up." Adriane was already at the front steps, waiting for her. "Come on."

Together, the girls walked into the building and crossed the lobby to a desk where a stocky woman with big hair sat fielding phone calls.

"We'd like to talk to the mayor, please," Adriane announced.

"I'm afraid that's not possible," the big-haired lady replied.

"Why not?" Adriane asked.

"First of all, he's not here. Second of all, he's not here."

"We can wait."

"Suit yourself," Ms. Big Hair said.

"What's going on around here, anyway?" Emily asked.

"Haven't you heard? They caught the monster of Ravenswood."

Emily's face went ashen.

"What?" Adriane leaned forward.

A fireman shuffled through to drop some papers on the front desk.

"Who caught what?" Adriane pressed.

"It was a bear," the fireman said. "Can you believe it? A big *purple* bear."

"About time," Ms. Big Hair said. "If you ask me, that place should be shut down. Just stand over there if you want to wait—" By the time she looked up, the girls were gone.

KARA SAT SUNNING in a lawn chair in her backyard. She had everything perfectly laid out within arm's reach: a bowl of chips and trail mix, ice-cold lemonade, suntan oils, and her iPod. Rose-tinted shades covered her eyes and headphones covered her ears. She didn't see Emily and Adriane until they were practically standing right over her.

"Hey, you're blocking my sun!" she complained.

"Where is he?" Emily demanded.

Kara pointed to her headphones. "Can't hear you. Come back next century."

"You told them where he was!" Adriane accused. "You promised you wouldn't tell and you did! How could you?"

Kara sat up and removed her headphones. "Take it easy, Pocahontas. It's not hard to find a twenty-story rock. They're getting a court order to bulldoze the whole place anyway. So go find somewhere else to play."

"Ooohhhhh!" Adriane's eyes flashed with rage.

"Kara, you saw what's going on out there." Emily said, trying to be reasonable. "You saw all those animals."

"I don't know what I saw," Kara replied, clearly uneasy. "All I remember is the monster."

"He's not a monster, he's our friend," Emily told her.

"That figures."

"That's it!" Adriane advanced on Kara, her hands balled into fists. Bright gold fire suddenly flared from Adriane's bracelet.

Kara's jaw dropped. "How did you do that?"

Adriane stared at her gemstone. The stone pulsed with light. "I didn't do anything," she said, more to Emily than to Kara.

Emily turned slowly to Kara. "Maybe *you* did something."

Kara tried, but she couldn't hide her astonishment. "Yeah, right," she scoffed.

Emily held up her wrist. Both Kara and Adriane stared at the incredible crystalline flower that flickered with rainbow sparkles in the sunlight.

"Emily, your stone, it's . . ." Adriane started.

"Amazing!" Kara finished.

"Phel did it." Emily said.

"The purple bear gave you that?" Kara asked, her eyes wide. Emily moved the jewel closer to her. The stone flashed a bright burst of blue. Emily backed away and the stone cooled.

"You're making it do that," Kara said, eyes glued to the startling gem.

"No," Emily said. "You are. In the woods yesterday, Phel tried to give *you* something—a gift,"

"And you ruined it!" Adriane put in.

Kara bit her lip. "And why would it give *me* a gift?"

"I think, for some reason, you are part of this," Emily told her.

"Part . . . of . . . what?" Kara asked slowly.

Emily looked to Adriane.

"Phelonius is magic, just like these stones," Adriane explained.

Kara shook her head. "That's the most ridiculous thing . . . I ev—" She stopped as Stormbringer and Ozzie walked out from behind the rose garden.

"Aaahhhh!" Kara shrieked, knocking over the bowl of chips as she shrank back from the silver wolf. "Keep that thing away from me!"

Storm stood still and looked into Kara's eyes. The girl was mesmerized.

"Do not be afraid."

Startled, Kara looked around. "What? Who said that?"

"The magic is strong with you."

Ozzie looked up at Kara, studying her.

"There's no such thing as magic," Kara said.

"How do you explain *him?*" Adriane pointed to Ozzie.

Kara turned to Ozzie. The ferret was holding the bowl of trail mix in his paws. "These are delicious! Can I have some juice?" he asked her.

"Plenty of toys do that stuff," Kara said uncertainly.

"Come on, Emily, we don't need her." Adriane turned away, pulling Emily with her.

Emily faced Kara and held up her bracelet again. "Kara, Phel gave us his magic and now he needs our help. Are you in or out?" Emily asked.

Kara's eyes sparkled at the jewel. She focused back on Emily and looked over at Adriane, at the wolf and the ferret, all waiting for her. She scrunched her nose as if making an important decision. "They took it to a warehouse at Miller's Point Industrial Park."

14

"LIFE IS CHANGE," Emily's father had told her. "Be ready and excited." Somehow, she was neither. With Ozzie on her lap, she was seated next to Adriane on the Stonehill town bus, headed toward Miller Point Industrial Park. It had been Kara's idea to take the bus. The blond girl was sitting a few rows in front of them, listening to Earl the bus driver drone on about how the mayor should improve the bus lanes. Ozzie's brown nose pressed against the window as he watched the farmlands sweep by.

Emily turned to Adriane "Do you think this is crazy?"

"Not any crazier than running around the woods with a dangerous predator loose," Adriane answered with a wry smile.

"It's not crazy to help our friend," Ozzie said.

"Why can't the Fairimentals stay with us, Ozzie?" Emily asked.

"Their magic is bound to another world," Ozzie explained. "They can't survive here for long."

"Like Phel." Emily had to face the truth. Phel had limited time here.

"I don't think he was supposed to use so much of his magic to heal those animals," Ozzie said.

"What *is* he supposed to do?" Adriane asked.

"Seed your world with magic."

"Then why did he heal those animals?" Emily asked.

"I think he did it for you, Emily." The ferret was staring at her. "You are the healer." He turned to Adriane. "And you are the warrior."

"We're twelve-year-old kids!" Adriane reminded him.

"I know, but the Fairimentals came to you," Ozzie replied. "And you've heard Storm. I thought mistwolves were dangerous, but I was wrong. Storm carries memories of her kind that go back centuries. She knows the Fairimentals sent me to find three mages."

Adriane laughed. "Great. If we're two, who's the third?"

Ozzie looked to the front of the bus where a bored Kara sat.

Adriane flushed. "Oh no! Do *not* even go there!"

"She's trying, Adriane," Emily said. "Let's give her a chance."

Adriane looked out the window. "Forget it."

"I could be wrong, of course," Ozzie said. "Being a ferret wasn't part of the plan."

"Maybe they disguised you," Emily suggested.

"An elf in Stonehill—that *would* get people talking," Adriane added.

"But why did they choose me? I wasn't magical as an elf, and I'm not special now," Ozzie said with a hint of defeat. "I just want to go home."

"Ozzie, whatever reason you're here, I'm glad that you are," Emily said.

Adriane looked at Ozzie. "Me, too."

Ozzie smiled a ferret smile.

The bus pulled into the wide parking lot of Miller's Point. The industrial park covered about a square mile of buildings and landscaped parks. Behind the office buildings, on the far side of the park, was a row of warehouses.

"All right, we're here," Kara announced.

"A real Girl Scout," Adriane muttered.

"Where is he, Kara?" Emily asked.

"In one of those warehouses out back, until some UFO team or something comes to get it," Kara told them.

"But which one?"

"I don't know," Kara replied.

"I just hope we got here in time," Adriane said.

"If it wasn't for me, you would still be walking and would have shown up in about two weeks!" Kara fumed.

"All right, Kara," Emily intervened. "You were right, it *was* a good idea to catch the bus. Let's go."

The girls made their way along a mosaic pathway between the two main office buildings. They emerged on the other side onto an open green lawn with a small man-made lake, its water reflecting the orange and gold of the setting sun. A family of ducks quacked greetings as the girls passed. Ozzie rode in Emily's backpack as they marched down the road toward the semicircle of warehouses.

"How are we going to get back after we find him?" Emily looked around.

"We'll figure something out," Adriane said. She didn't sound too sure, either.

"Well, I have some magic of my own," Kara smirked.

"Oh?" Adriane's eyebrows rose.

"Yeah. It's called a cell phone." Kara held up her little flip phone.

Emily stopped suddenly. "Trouble."

Adriane and Kara stopped and looked where Emily was pointing. Up around the bend was a guard gate blocking the entrance to the warehouse section of the park. It was manned by security officers.

"Well, I guess this ends our little rescue expedition," Kara stated.

"No way," Adriane said.

A jeep was approaching the gate from one of the warehouses.

"Then we'll just walk through and tell the guards we're here to pick up the purple bear," Kara snickered.

"Good idea." Adriane closed her eyes. Concentrating hard, she formed an image and locked it in her mind. "Stormbringer," she whispered.

Adriane's jewel pulsed with white-gold light.

Kara couldn't hide her amazement.

A cloud of mist appeared and the great silver wolf materialized. Stormbringer walked forward to greet the girls.

"I heard your call, warrior."

"Can you help us get past that gate without being seen?"

The wolf shimmered as if radiating waves of heat. She seemed to expand, and then she was only soft gray-white mist.

Kara's eyes were wide with disbelief.

"Stay close together," the mistwolf's voice said.

"Hey, watch it!" Kara protested as Adriane pushed her up against Emily.

The mist slowly settled around them.

Slowly they made their way up to the main gate. Two guards sat in the gatehouse watching monitors, while a third paced outside.

"My ear itches," Kara complained under the veil of mist.

A small paw reached out and scratched Kara's ear.

"Eeeek!"

"Ssshhh!" Emily repeated urgently.

The jeep drove up and the gate began to swing open.

Adriane tensed. "Ready?"

The jeep drove past and the gate began to close.

"Go!" Adriane gave Kara a push. They shuffled forward, trying to stay together. Emily looked out through the curtain of mist. It was working! The guards didn't even notice them—

Ringggg . . . ringggg . . .

The pacing guard stopped and pulled his cell phone from its holster. He held it to his ear, then shook it.

Ringggg . . . ringggg . . .

"What *is* that?" Adriane whispered in a panic.

"Hello?" Kara said into her phone.

"*Ssshhh!* Keep moving!" Emily said.

The guard was looking around, obviously puzzled.

"Oh, hi, Heather!" Kara covered the end of the phone. "It's Heather," she whispered to the girls.

Adriane pushed Kara forward as the gate swung closed behind them. "Go, go, go!"

"Ooo, really? I love pink. How does it look?"

Adriane grabbed the phone from Kara's hand as they turned into an alley between the first two warehouses.

"This call is, like, *so* over!" she said into the phone and hit the OFF button.

"That was, like, *so* rude!" Kara objected.

The mist lifted, and the wolf reappeared.

"Ha! They didn't even see us!" Kara exclaimed. "Very cool."

Adriane turned to Storm. "Can you find Phel?"

The wolf sniffed the air and took off at a trot. The girls

and Ozzie followed. They passed several warehouses, and then Stormbringer led them into a dark alley. They were completely in shadows—the sun was almost gone.

Adriane raced up the steps to a door in the side of the building and tried it. "It's locked!" she exclaimed.

A dog barked and a faint light flashed out beyond the end of the alley.

"What do we do now?" Kara said.

"What about that window?" Emily pointed to a small window partway up the side of the warehouse.

"No one can fit in there," Kara said.

"I can," said Ozzie.

"Okay, let's get him up there." Adriane turned to Kara. "Bend over."

"No *way!*"

Emily looked back as a light flashed off the warehouse wall. "Kara, this is no time for arguments."

Kara, muttering angrily, knelt on the ground. Emily climbed up on her back.

"Owww," the blonde girl complained under the additional weight of Adriane, who hoisted herself up on top of Emily. "Why do I have to be on the bottom?"

"If we fall, you won't get hurt," Adriane explained, deftly balancing herself below the window ledge.

"Oh, good idea," Kara agreed. She wriggled to adjust her position, and Adriane wobbled.

"Stay still!" Adriane balanced herself. "Ozzie, get up here!"

The ferret scampered over Kara and Emily and up into Adriane's arms. She hoisted him up and tried to push him onto the windowsill, but it was still too far. She swung her arm back and flung Ozzie up into the air—but the movement of her arm pulled her over. "Whoaaaah!"

Ozzie went flying as she came toppling down onto Emily and Kara.

They looked up. Ozzie was dangling from the window sill by his front paws. They watched as he hoisted himself up and squeezed through the narrow opening of the window.

Emily grinned. "He made it."

There was a crash, followed by a boom.

The girls rushed to the door and waited. They heard the scampering of little feet across the floor, a few bumps, some thuds, and assorted *args* and *doofs*. Then silence.

Emily looked at the other girls. "Ozzie, are you all right?"

"Yes."

"What are you doing?" Adriane asked.

"I can't reach the door release," Ozzie's muffled voice replied.

"Why don't you use your magic charms?" Kara asked sarcastically.

Adriane turned to Emily. "Let's see if we can lift him."

"You think?" Emily looked doubtfully at her bracelet.

"Like when I made those trees move."

Kara raised her eyebrows.

"Okay, what do I do?" Emily asked.

"Concentrate really hard," Adriane said. "Picture Ozzie floating up to the lock."

Emily held her gem close to Adriane's, closed her eyes, and concentrated as hard as she could.

"Ooh!" Ozzie exclaimed from behind the closed door.

"What's happening?" Adriane asked.

"I'm on my tiptoes! Try harder!" Ozzie called back.

Flashlight beams bounced around the entrance to the alley.

"Hurry, the guards are coming!" Kara pushed at their shoulders.

"Stop it, I can't concentrate!" Adriane shot back.

"Anyone there?" a guard called out.

"Oh, hurry it *up*!" Kara pushed harder at the girls.

A flashlight beam swept the alley.

"Would you quit shoving?" Adriane snapped, turning back to Kara.

Kara's hand slipped off Adriane's shoulder and landed on the two jewels. The stones exploded with a flash of light.

"Whoooooaahhhhh!"

THUMP!

CRASH!

Something inside slammed against the ceiling and came crashing back to the floor. ". . . Ooooh!" Ozzie's voice sounded wobbly.

"Sorry," Kara said, pulling her hand back.

"A little more subtle," Emily suggested.

Kara lightly touched the stones. They pulsed with bright light as Emily and Adriane concentrated on floating Ozzie up to the doorknob.

"Upseee!" Ozzie was up.

The latch clicked open and the girls tumbled inside. Storm padded in behind them.

"We did it!" Emily exclaimed. Looking around the dark room, she held up her jewel and willed it to shine. She smiled as a pale blue light spilled over the entryway. Adriane added a soft golden glow.

Three darkened hallways ran off in separate directions.

"This is nuts!" Kara shook her head. "We're breaking and entering *and* using illegal magic stuff!"

"Magic is not illegal," Adriane shot back.

"I bet it is, too! How come like the President doesn't have this?"

"Sshhh, quiet!" Emily ordered. "Can you two please stop arguing for two minutes! Let's just find Phel and get out of here."

Storm sniffed and headed down the middle hallway. Kara and Adriane moved to follow at the same time and found themselves wedged in the doorway.

"You first, Princess." Adriane bowed to Kara.

"Oh no, after you," Kara said, bowing back.

"No, no, I insist." Adriane swept her arm toward the hall.

"Just come *on*!" Emily barged her way past the others and strode ahead.

The hallway led to what looked like a large storage area. In the dim light, Emily could make out a ramp up to a loading dock on the far side; the large, sliding garage door was shut. So, that's how they got him in here, she thought.

"Phel!" Emily called out in a whisper. "Are you in here?"

Something massive moved in the darkness.

Emily sidestepped, keeping close to the wall.

"Well, is it in here or—" Kara stepped forward, screamed, and disappeared.

"What happened?" Adriane moved in behind Emily.

Emily and Adriane inched forward. In front of them was a huge pit. Their glowing jewels cut swathes of weird light across the wide space. Phel lay on his back on the floor—with Kara standing on his belly.

"Hey, look what I found," she said.

Two gigantic eyes opened, blinked, then stared up at the startled girls.

"Phel! Are you all right?" Emily noticed the steps and quickly made her way down.

"Did you find himmmaahhhh . . ." Ozzie bolted into the room, his momentum taking him right over the edge of the drop. He bounced up Phel's belly and looked into a giant eye. "Phel! Thank goodness!"

Phel reached out giant paws and engulfed the ferret.

"Gaaaaooof!" was all Ozzie could say.

Adriane pointed toward the loading dock door. "We can get him out that way!"

Emily gently touched Phelonius. She could sense his weakness. She pushed the fear back. "We have to get you out of here."

Together, the three girls got Phel up and onto his feet. He was frighteningly light for something so enormous. Holding Ozzie under one arm, he shuffled along as they pushed and pulled him up the ramp toward the loading dock.

Adriane started hitting every button she could find to open the big door.

"Doesn't this place, like, have any alarms?" Kara asked.

With a loud *whhirr*, the door started to open. A horn blasted through the night. It rose to a crescendo, then started again. A second horn blared across the compound, followed by a third.

"Does that answer your question?" Adriane said.

"Let's go!" Emily ordered.

They pushed Phel out the door and down the exit ramp. Spotlights flared, flooding the compound.

"What are we going to do?" Kara screamed.

Everywhere they turned, searchlights skimmed the ground, trying to trap them in bright light. Men were yelling and dogs were barking.

"Stay where you are!" a loud voice shouted over a megaphone.

"We are in such major trouble!" Kara wailed.

"Hurry, come on, Phel, we have to run!" Emily pleaded, trying to push him to move faster.

"This is all your fault!" screamed Kara. "You forced me to come here! I'm going to be grounded for, like, five years!"

"You were the one who got him caught in the first place!" Adriane shot back.

"Stop it! *Stop it!*" Emily shouted. Her gem exploded, sending shafts of blue light shooting into the night. Spotlights burst to pieces and went dark. Sirens blared in the distance.

Stormbringer's frightening growl made the girls turn. The wolf was crouched and poised to attack. Three black guard dogs, barking wildly and baring vicious teeth, were running straight for them.

Adriane raised her stone.

"No!" Emily grabbed Adriane's arm. "We can't hurt them!"

The girls huddled together, shaking, against Phel's side.

"Hey, you! Ever seen a talking ferret?"

The dogs skidded to a halt, turned, and sprang up the loading dock ramp. A small furry creature leaped onto the rope pulley above the ramp, out of range of their snapping teeth.

"Ozzie!" Emily screamed.

Phel blinked great, sad eyes.

Kara shoved herself forward. "Security!" she called. "I'm Kara Dav—mmph!"

Adriane clapped her hand over Kara's mouth. "Are you crazy?" she hissed.

Phel's huge arms came down around the girls.

"To be here with you two? Yes!" Suddenly Kara looked down.

Her feet were no longer on the ground.

Phel was rising up into the air.

Kara screamed.

"Hold on!" Adriane grabbed onto Phel's fur.

"Ozzie!" Emily cried, struggling to break free of Phel's grasp.

The dogs barked and jumped, trying to grab the ferret from the swinging rope.

Storm shimmered into mist and snaked past the dogs. They looked in confusion at the mist.

Ozzie swung the rope over the dogs and jumped. He skidded down the ramp and ran for his life. The dogs barked and bounded after him.

"Wait for me!" Ozzie burst down the alley, inches in front of the snapping jaws of a black Doberman.

Emily slid down Phel's leg. Adriane reached down and grabbed onto Emily's right arm. Emily extended her left arm, reaching down . . .

"Hurry, Ozzie!" Adriane yelled.

The dogs would have him in seconds.

Emily slid right to the edge of Phel's giant foot.

"Emily!" Kara shrieked.

"I got her." Adriane had hold of Emily's leg.

Emily stretched her arm out, fingers clasping . . .

"Jump, Ozzie!" she yelled.

Ozzie closed his eyes and leaped. Emily caught his paw and pulled him into her arms. Below, guards and dogs grew smaller and smaller as Phel rose above the industrial park and drifted into the night.

THE SKY WAS ablaze with the orange-golden light of the full moon. Phelonius glided silently on his back, like a great sky whale, high above the countryside.

"Don't you ever do something like that again!" Emily squeezed the ferret in a hug and handed him to Adriane.

"That was the bravest thing I've ever seen." She hugged him, too. "You're okay, Ozzie."

Ozzie opened his arms and reached for Kara.

She scrunched her nose at him. "Nice job, ferret." With a quick glance to make sure Emily and Adriane weren't watching, she kissed Ozzie. "You ever tell anyone I kissed a ferret, I'll have you stuffed!"

Ozzie winked. "Our secret."

The girls and Ozzie sat on Phel's belly, looking out in total amazement. No one knew what to say. They were flying—being carried through the sky by a creature made of magic! Below, the streetlights and houses of Stonehill looked like exquisite toys.

"Hey!" Kara exclaimed suddenly, leaning over to the

side. "I didn't know the Feltners had a pool! And they never invited me over!" She sat back, crossed her arms, and pouted.

Emily and Adriane exchanged glances and started to laugh. After a minute, Kara began to laugh with them. Howls of laughter spilled into the night as they glided peacefully over the treetops, leaving the lights of the town to fade in the distance.

Behind them a dark winged shadow rose above the orange-gold moon. It closed in for the kill.

15

*P*HEL DRIFTED ON a sea of clouds. Kara raised her arms, her long hair furling in the breeze like a golden flag. Adriane searched the dark forests that appeared and disappeared between the low clouds.

Emily was studying Phel. He had been so weak back at the warehouse. How much magic was he using to fly? What would happen if he ran out? Would he come apart like those whirlwinds of dirt and twigs? She peered anxiously over his side.

"We have to get him home," Ozzie told her, seeing the worry on her face.

"How, Ozzie?" she asked.

"We have to find that portal and open it."

"How much longer does he have?"

Ozzie looked down. His silence was answer enough.

Kara was hanging over Phel's side. "Look. An arrow."

"That's not an arrow, that's the Rocking Stone," Adriane scoffed.

Kara shrugged. "Looks like an arrow," she repeated.

Emily narrowed her eyes. Kara was right: from this height, the ancient stone looked like a skinny finger reaching out . . . or pointing.

"Aluns," Emily said.

Adriane and Kara looked at her.

"Aluns," she repeated. "It's a Lenni-Lenape word meaning arrow. I found it on the Web. The Rocking Stone is supposed to point to a spirit door, a gateway—"

"Or . . . a portal," Ozzie said.

All four looked down.

"It looks like it's pointing to that clearing!" Adriane exclaimed.

"The glade?" Emily asked.

"No. Just beyond, to the left."

Out of nowhere, a dark shape swept past, sending Phel careening to the right.

"What was *that*?" Adriane asked nervously.

"I don't want to find out. Hurry, Phel!" Emily called out.

Phel turned towards the Rocking Stone and swooped into dense clouds.

For a moment a shadow was visible against a cloud. Something huge, with gigantic wings.

"Over there." Kara pointed.

Emily and Adriane looked, but it was gone.

They peered around anxiously.

"Hurry, Phel!" Emily called.

The clouds swept past, then parted like a curtain. The monster hung in the sky before them. Phel was on a collision course with two red-hot demon eyes and rows of razor teeth. The monster roared thunder and Black Fire erupted from its mouth to explode against Phel's shoulders. Kara screamed as Phel dropped like a rock, billowing green and black flames.

Wind whipped Emily's hair into her face. "Phel!" Her jewel flared blue and bathed Phel in a blanket of light, extinguishing the flames.

Phel dove low and pulled up in a sweeping arc, careening toward the trees at an alarming speed.

"Left!" Adriane yelled, leaning hard.

"Right!" Kara shrieked, pulling in the opposite direction.

The girls flattened themselves against Phel's body as he swept up and over the forest canopy. Branches and leaves scraped his back.

"We're going to crash!" Kara yelled.

"Adriane!" Emily shouted.

She reached across Kara to clasp Adriane's hand. Sparkles ran across Kara's body and the stones glowed bright. "We need to slow Phel down!"

"I got it," Adriane closed her eyes.

Brilliant rainbow light arced from the gems and spread

into a canopy above them. A parachute! Emily gripped Adriane's hand as Phel's descent slowed.

"Hold on!" Adriane yelled.

Kara put her head down and closed her eyes. Emily and Adriane held the rainbow tight. Ozzie wedged himself under the girls.

Phel soared past the Rocking Stone. With a final effort, he skirted the treetops and went down, bouncing hard on the ground. Emily's teeth ground together with the jolt. The rainbow burst apart, leaving a sparkling trail as Phel's body dug a long, shallow furrow in the grass. He came to a stop at the edge of the field.

Adriane was sprawled sideways across Phel's chest. Kara was hanging upside down, halfway down his side. Ozzie was stuck under Phel's paw.

Emily rolled over and hit the ground. "Are you all right?" She helped Adriane and Kara slide down. Ozzie jumped up to examine Phel.

"Thank you for flying Air Phel." Kara rubbed her head.

"Help him up," Emily told them.

Together they pushed Phelonius to a sitting position. The back of his head and shoulders was glowing with the evil green poison. It was eating away at him, spreading down his back. Parts of him were becoming transparent.

"Emily, you have to help him!" Ozzie pleaded.

Phel opened his eyes and looked at Emily.

"Tell me what to do!" she begged.

Phel's paw was blinking in and out.

Emily raised her stone and concentrated. The gem flashed blue light as she pushed hard with every ounce of will she had. She felt the dark power of the Black Fire. It was overwhelming, threatening to crush her.

"Help me!" Emily felt her face grow wet from sweat and tears.

Adriane raised her stone. It glowed hot white-gold.

"Kara!" Adriane yelled.

Kara stood between them and touched both stones. Golden fire swirled up her arm from Adriane's gem. Kara closed her eyes. Her long blonde hair flared as the magic passed through her, down her other arm, and flowed into Emily's stone. Blue and gold magic collided as green light flashed from Emily's wrist and streamed out to cover Phel. She felt her heart beating too fast; she was afraid it would explode as she fell into darkness . . . and then she felt another heartbeat, Adriane's, strong, pure . . . and Kara's, steady, certain . . . and Ozzie's, solid, true, pulling her back. Phel began to glow blue and gold, matching the stones. And the darkness fell away.

The light faded. Phel blinked his eyes. The green poison was gone.

But he was still fading in and out. Emily's throat tightened and she fought back tears. They had stopped the poison, but it was too late. She had failed again, and now she was losing Phelonius.

"What *was* that thing?" Adriane asked.

"A manticore," Ozzie said. "It's bad, real bad."

"What does it want from us?" Kara asked.

"Manticores track magic," Ozzie said.

"Why didn't it get Phel before?" Kara asked.

"Maybe Phel's magic was protecting him, hiding him," Ozzie explained.

"Phel doesn't have any more magic!" Emily cried.

"But you do," Ozzie said.

The treetops swayed, blown by a sudden wind.

"Hey, what time is it, anyway?" Kara asked in a rush. "I've got a ten o'clock curfew. I gotta go—"

"We need you, Kara," Emily told her.

"You do?" Kara asked.

"We do?" Adriane echoed.

"Every time she's near these stones, they go crazy!"

"What do we do now?" Kara asked.

"We have to send Phel home, back through the portal," Emily said.

"How are we going to do that?" Kara asked.

"Hey! Come back here!" Ozzie yelled.

The girls turned to see Phel slowly lumbering across the field. A few rainbow-puff flowers popped up behind him—but they withered and collapsed into dust.

The fairy creature's skin was translucent, a ghostly haze in the moonlight. His body seemed to be drifting apart, like Stormbringer turning into mist.

"What's he doing?" asked Adriane.

"Trying to make magic. But he's too weak." Ozzie answered.

"Our stones, concentrate on helping Phel," Emily said.

Emily and Adriane stood next to Kara and held their bracelets in the air. The jewels began to glow as Phel raised his arms. An electrical burst of wild magic leaped from the stones, startling the girls. Phel swirled the strands of blue and gold magic in the air. He wove the magic into a circular shape, a web, with a bright silver glow in the center. The shape became a three-dimensional ball that floated in the air in front of him.

Ozzie jumped up and down. "The fairy map!"

The glowing orb grew brighter and brighter. Phel collapsed to the ground, growing dimmer and dimmer. The twinkling web floated like a glittering beach ball over to the girls. Emily tried to grab it, but it danced away. Adriane jumped for it, but it eluded her grasp. It settled over Kara.

"Take it, Kara!" Adriane said.

"Come on, Kara, take it," Emily pleaded.

Ozzie sniffed the air. Something smelled foul . . .

Pinpoints of light reflected over Kara's face as she reached out . . .

A blast of wind tore it from her grasp.

The manticore landed with a ground-shaking *crunch* that rumbled like thunder across the field. Even hunched over, it was massive. It slowly turned its head, and slit demon eyes bore straight into the girls. Adriane's mouth froze open. All the color drained from Kara's face. The monster towered over them. The lower part of its body looked like a lion, the upper part resembled a bizarre ape beast with arms muscled like steel cords. Its head was grotesque, with long dripping teeth in a blood-red mouth. Its eyes flared red fire. Gigantic wings unfurled behind its back as it roared. The sound was deafening.

There was nowhere to run.

Embracing the ball of stars, its horrible mouth moved grotesquely as it spoke. "Mine!"

"How could I have been so stupid!" Ozzie cried. "It was after the fairy map."

"If that's what you want, then leave us alone!" Adriane shouted.

"What I want is not your concern, human," it replied, its mouth twisting into a sickening smile. "The fairy creature is dying. It was just a matter of time before it gave up the map."

Emily felt heat at her wrist. The jewel on her bracelet was still pulsing, blazing with light. Adriane felt it too: her stone was also glowing.

The monster stared suspiciously at the gems and growled low in its throat. "My mistress will never allow humans to control magic. Give me those stones!" it roared.

"I would highly recommend you do what it says," Ozzie piped up nervously from behind the girls.

"Fine, let it have them," Emily said. She tried to take off her bracelet but couldn't. "It's stuck!" The more she tried to move it, the more solidly it seemed to cling to her wrist.

"Emily, I can't move mine," Adriane said, panic rising in her voice.

"Me, either!"

"Hurry, give it the stones!" Ozzie was hopping up and down.

The monster reached forward with hands the size of chairs and claws glowing with green poison.

Adriane was desperately pulling and twisting at her bracelet. "It—won't—come—off!"

"Give it that stupid stone!" Kara shrieked. She reached to yank it from Adriane's wrist and the tigerseye stone exploded with golden fire. Jagged lightning pierced the ground in front of them. The girls stared at the smoking fissure.

The monster stepped back, red eyes flashing danger-ously. Then it leaped at the girls.

Something flashed past them and slammed into the creature with a sickening *thud!*

"Storm!" Adriane cried.

The monster staggered as the great wolf snarled and lunged for its throat. Grabbing the wolf, the beast twisted her head back, trying to rip it from her neck. The ball of stars floated in the air and bounced lightly away.

Adriane lunged forward.

"Adriane, no!" Emily grabbed Adriane and pulled her back.

Stormbringer's teeth raked through the monster's arm as she leaped free to rip at its leg, trying to unbalance it. The manticore whirled and knocked the wolf to the ground, pinning her under a massive foot. With a roar, it smashed a razor-clawed fist into her. Stormbringer's howl echoed into the night as she burst apart in a haze of mist and vanished.

"Storm!" Tears steaming down her face, Adriane screamed and tried to pull out of Emily's grasp.

"No!" Emily cried.

She and Adriane struggled and the two bracelets crashed together. Fire erupted from the stones and blinding wild magic flew out in all directions at once. A bolt blasted into a tree, splitting it in two. The monster bellowed with fury.

Kara clutched at Adriane and Emily as magic fire streamed from the jewels, arcing into the night sky.

"Try and hold it!" Adriane called out.

"I can't!" Emily screamed.

"Stay together! All of us!" Adriane ordered.

Kara hung on to Adriane and Emily as sparks of power raced over her to fuel the magic fire. Adriane and Emily swung the stream of fire like a bat. It came around hard, smacking the manticore, knocking it across the field.

The creature curled in upon itself and fell to the ground.

Wild lightning zigzagged erratically all around them.

"I can't control it!" Emily yelled.

The air wrenched. The ground twisted. The sky cracked . . .

And the portal opened.

It was an immense empty space hanging in the air just off the ground. Trying to see through it was like trying to see through a thick fog. They could just make out a web of glowing lines, stars winking in complex patterns.

"You did it!" Ozzie shouted.

"Wow!" Kara looked into the endless expanse of the magic web.

"Hurry, get Phel up!" Ozzie was pushing at Phel's side.

The girls rushed over and gently helped Phel to his feet. He was so light they had a hard time grabbing onto him.

"Hold on, Phel! Please!" Emily called. "You're almost home!"

The web of stars twisted into a sparkling tunnel. They pushed Phel toward it. He floated into the portal and was gone.

Emily and Ozzie looked at each other. "Go, Ozzie, take care of him."

Ozzie faced the doorway that would take him home. The twisting tunnel was already getting smaller. He looked back at the girls.

"Go, Ozzie!" Emily yelled. "Before the portal closes again!"

Ozzie leaped after Phel—and vanished.

"We love you," Emily called.

A rush of hot wind whipped the girls' hair and clothes. They clutched one another in terror as the manticore returned and swooped in to land beside the portal. Phel's twinkling ball of stars was cradled in its huge, clawed hands.

The girls backed away.

The creature held up the sparkling ball. "I will be rewarded for this prize. Though I did enjoy the hunt, and the animals were amusing sport." It grinned wickedly then turned red-hot eyes on Emily. Emily shrank back from the intense gaze and her gem flickered with dark purple.

"You have deceived yourself." The red eyes were hypnotic, and Emily felt herself falling back into those familiar feelings of despair. "Magic cannot change what you really are. You are weak and helpless and doomed to failure."

"No!" Emily cried out. She held up her gemstone. "I am a healer!"

Adriane raised her stone in the air. Kara stood between them, outstretched hands touching each of the jewels. Diamond-white blazed through her body to join the growing glow of blue-green and sun-gold.

"And no one messes with our friends!" Emily shouted as the magic built into an inferno of unearthly fire.

Fear flashed in the monster's eyes.

Blinding light streamed out of the gemstones and hammered into the manticore. Still clutching the fairy

map, it fell backward into the portal. The mist closed over it.

The twisting tunnel vanished as the web of stars glowed brighter and began to expand, spreading like an immense spiderweb over the entire field. The more it spread, the thinner it became . . . until nothing was left but a bright star hanging in the air where the portal had been. It twinkled—and winked out.

The clearing was still and quiet. Stormbringer came padding across the grass. Adriane ran to her, hugging the wolf and burying her face in the thick fur.

Exhausted, Emily sank to the ground, covering her face.

"Ozzie did it. He got home. That's all he ever wanted," she said quietly.

"He was one brave ferret," Adriane said.

"And kinda cute, too," Kara added.

"I'm going to miss him so much," Emily cried.

"Gee, you'd think I was already dead."

The girls whirled around. The ferret was standing right behind them.

"Ozzie!" Emily got up and ran to the ferret, picking him off the ground in a sweeping hug. "What happened?" she asked. "We thought you went home."

"And miss all this excitement? With all the trouble you get into, who's going to look after you three?"

"But I thought you wanted to go home," Emily said.

"I did, and here I am." Ozzie smiled.

"We lost the fairy map," Adriane said.

Ozzie shrugged. "Together we'll find another way."

"But what if the monster comes back?" Kara asked.

"It got what it wanted. But the Fairimentals also got something *they* wanted."

All three girls looked at him. "What?"

"You."

16

"WELCOME TO THE Ravenswood Wildlife Preserve," Gran said politely. The group gathered on the great lawn behind the manor had been oohing and ahhing over the expansive gardens, with their beautiful fountains and sculptures. Everyone turned expectantly to Gran. The entire town council was there.

"Mrs. Charday, on behalf of the town council, I'd like to thank you for inviting us to this remarkable place," Mayor Davies said formally. Beasley Windor scowled, looking around as if she expected a wild animal to jump out of a bush. "And, of course, our appreciation goes to Dr. Allison from the Centers for Disease Control in Atlanta."

Standing next to Emily's mom, the CDC health official waved. He was a tall, handsome man. Emily and

Adriane stood next to Gran. Kara was not there. Since the bizarre events two weeks earlier, they hadn't seen her or heard a peep out of her.

"The Ravenswood Preserve has been a safe haven for animals for over a hundred years," Gran said. "My granddaughter, Adriane, and her friend, Emily, will take you on the tour. Hiking is a bit difficult for me," she added with a small smile.

"That's our cue," Adriane whispered as they stepped forward. "Hi, everyone. If you'll all follow me, we'll begin the tour out back here on the great lawn."

The group followed the girls across the lawn to the maze garden.

On the other side of some hedges, a family of deer watched them.

"Ooh, deer," one of the women said.

"Can we pet them?" another asked.

"Yes, they're very tame." Adriane handed around some small bags of animal feed.

The group looked to Dr. Allison.

"It's quite all right," the CDC official assured them. "These deer are perfectly healthy and native to these woods."

The crowd gathered round to pet and feed the deer.

Mrs. Windor stood to the side, remarking loudly about how easily these lawns could be transformed into the back nine holes of a golf course. Fellow councilman Sid Stewart nodded enthusiastically.

Ronif popped his head out of a hedge behind Emily. "How's it going?" the quiffle asked.

Emily pushed the quiffle's head back down in the bush. "What are you doing? You're supposed to be waiting with the others!"

"Everyone wants to know what's happening," said the bush.

"Fine! Now get back and make sure the others stay put," Emily whispered.

The quiffle skirted away through the bush. One of the branches poked Beasley Windor's behind. Startled, she scowled.

Emily giggled as the group followed Adriane into a sculpture-filled water garden where peacocks strolled between the fountains, displaying their resplendent feathers. Everyone oohed and ahhhed, and Emily began to think they could really win them over.

"Oh, look!" someone cried. Heads turned skyward.

An incredible owl was perched atop a tall fountain. Emily winked, and Ariel winked back. Spreading her magnificent wings, the owl took off. She glided in slow, perfect circles over the heads of the amazed group and came to land on Emily's arm.

"How'd I doo?"

"Just wonderful!" Emily kissed the owl's head and smiled at the astonished onlookers.

"Well, Miss Fletcher, you certainly have a way with these animals," the mayor said.

Emily beamed. "Her name is Ariel. She's a snow owl, very rare." Ariel looked at the humans with huge, sparkling eyes.

The group looked to the CDC official. He laughed and gave a thumbs-up. Everyone crowded around Emily for a chance to pet the owl.

On the way back to the manor house the group buzzed with excitement. Beasley Windor was loudly suggesting the perfect place for the club house when she stopped in mid-sentence.

In the middle of the lawn, a large silver wolf sat staring at her with golden eyes.

Beasley Windor pointed. "Aha! See? A dangerous animal!"

Adriane walked over and patted the wolf. "Please don't be frightened," she told the crowd. "I'd like you all to meet Stormbringer. She lives with us here at the preserve. We take care of her, but she really takes care of us." She smiled.

"Incredible!" someone said.

"I never knew such creatures lived out here," another commented.

"She's very friendly and loves children." Adriane ruffled the wolf's fur.

All heads turned to Dr. Allison. He walked up and patted the great wolf. "Certainly seems healthy," he declared. "And obviously very well people-trained."

Storm stood admirably still, allowing everyone to pet and admire her.

Adriane hugged her. "I love you. You're the best!" she whispered.

"I'd rather be running with you through the forests."

"Fantastic!" Mayor Davies exclaimed, taking in a deep breath of the crisp late summer air. "I'd forgotten how invigorating being out here felt!"

"That's all well and good," Mrs. Beasley stated, "but what about the woods? How do we know it's truly safe out there?"

"There have been no attacks in the last two weeks," the mayor responded. "No reports of anything unusual, and Dr. Allison has personally checked these animals."

Carolyn stepped forward. "I've seen no sign of anything that would be cause for shutting down this preserve."

Dr. Allison spoke up. "Frankly, I haven't seen a trace of disease or toxins. Of course, something like that could still be lurking—"

"You see?" Mrs. Beasley interrupted triumphantly.

"Excuse me," the CDC man continued firmly. "Dr. Fletcher and I both agree that it could have been a diseased animal responsible for the attacks, but I've found no evidence of anything here that might pose a danger to public health. My recommendation would be to watch and wait. If anything further is detected, Dr. Fletcher will contact me, but for now I'd say you have a one-of-a-kind treasure that the whole town should be proud of. As far as the CDC is concerned, Ravenswood Wildlife Preserve gets a clean bill of health!"

"Yes!" Emily burst out as she and Adriane high-fived.

"Thank you, Dr. Allison." Beasley Windor stepped forward. "We're all very relieved at your report. However, the issue still remains. These animals can live anywhere. What the town needs is income, not animals. We need to put this to a vote, and *I* vote for the redevelopment of this land into the Stonehill Golf Course and Country Club!"

"She has a point," Sid Stewart said.

Emily's heart sank. "Oh, no!"

"I knew it!" Adriane kicked a stone. "Nothing ever works out!"

"Aww, you girls break a nail?"

They turned around to find Kara standing there.

"Kara!" Emily said.

"Oh, of course, you had to come and cast your vote for the country club," Adriane said snidely.

"Well, if we get one, I know I won't be seeing *you* there!" Kara shot back

Adriane fumed. Kara fumed right back at her.

"Mrs. Windor," Mayor Davies said. "Before we vote, I have a proposition for Mrs. Charday."

Everyone looked at the mayor. He pointed to Kara. "My daughter, Kara, has suggested we open the preserve for tours, to give people a chance to see this beautiful place and learn about the animals—just like it was years ago."

"Not a bad idea," someone said.

Emily and Adriane looked at Kara

"I told you I could talk Daddy into anything," Kara said nonchalantly.

"What do you say, Mrs. Charday?" the mayor asked.

Gran, standing with crossed arms, shook her head. She started to say no but stopped herself when she looked at Emily, Adriane, and Kara. Her expression relaxed and her eyes twinkled. "On one condition."

"Name it," the mayor asked warily.

"We'll allow the estate to be opened to the public in exchange for the town's support and protection of the preserve and its inhabitants."

"Agreed," the mayor said.

"*And,*" Gran continued, "you will allow us to apply for official federal landmark and wildlife sanctuary status."

"That's two conditions, but I think that will fly." The mayor smiled.

"Wow," Emily said.

Mayor Davies stepped forward. "All in favor of trying out the preserve as our new town project, say 'aye.'"

A resounding chorus of ayes came from the crowd.

"All those not in favor, say 'nay.'"

Everyone looked to Beasley Windor. Her mouth flapped opened and closed, but she kept silent.

"Done!" The mayor turned to Gran, a smile on his face and his hand extended. "I think we have a deal."

Gran shook his hand.

Emily's heart did a flip. "Adriane! Landmark status! That means no one can ever shut this place down again." She turned to Kara. "Kara, I can't believe it! You are amazing!"

"Yeah . . . that's great, Kara." Adriane looked down at her boots.

"Yes, it is. Excuse me." Kara went to join her father.

"Congratulations." Mrs. Windor had moved in front of Emily and Adriane.

"Thank you," Emily said.

Mrs. Windor bent in close. "Your little show-and-tell didn't fool me, missy! Something is going on out here and I'm going to find out what!" She turned and stormed away.

Mayor Davies had his arm around Kara's shoulders. "I'd like to officially appoint Kara as the mayor's liaison to the new Ravenswood Preservation Society!"

Emily and Adriane looked at each other. The *what?*

The council members applauded and Kara beamed.

"Thank you," Kara said, flashing her dazzling smile over the crowd. "I have lots of ideas, starting with our first fund-raising party."

"Marvelous!" exclaimed a councilwoman. The crowd buzzed around Kara.

Emily's mind was racing. "We could set up a Web site," she spoke up, "so people all over could learn about the preserve—and about wildlife conservation."

"A Web site! Excellent!" The mayor's smile was growing wider.

"We'd certainly link to it from the Chamber of Commerce Web site," a council member added. "It would be a real tourist attraction!"

Adriane dragged Emily away from the crowd. "Are you crazy! What are you talking about: Web sites! How're we going to do that? How are we going to learn about . . . all this?" She held up her stone.

"What do you think of our nifty club?" Kara bounded over. "Of course, I'll be president."

"Club?! This isn't the Girl Scouts!" Adriane burst out.

"Adriane, think," Emily said. "It's the perfect setup to learn about the magic."

Adriane was still mad. "You don't even have a stone," she reminded Kara.

Kara stared at the girls' jewels. "Oh, yeah, and another thing . . ."

"What now?" Adriane asked.

"I need my own jewel."

"It's a good start," the mayor was saying to the others. He waved his arm over to Emily, Adriane, and Kara. "And we've got a great team here to supervise."

"And it has to be big and sparkly like a diamond." Kara smiled a dazzling smile at Adriane.

"Why don't I just get out the magic carpet and we'll fly around and find one?" Adriane suggested sarcastically.

"You got one? I need that, too."

Emily had to laugh. Kara and Adriane were from such different worlds. If they could ever work things out, they might actually make a great team.

She looked across at the woods. She thought about how far she had come from that girl left behind 2,500 miles across the country, and what she had lost along the way. But Emily realized she had also found something. She was a healer and healers found hope.

There was so much to learn, a future so full of possibilities. Maybe Kara could find a magic stone of her own. Maybe Ozzie could find a way back into his real body. She looked at Adriane, so full of fire. A "warrior." Maybe she would find her true path.

The mystery of the web and the fairy map danced across her mind. What roads would it take her down? She thought of Phel and hoped he was safe. Maybe it was possible there existed a place where dreams came true. A place of magic where all creatures were safe. Was *that* what Avalon was?

She looked at her jewel. A soft aqua glow pulsed briefly. She smiled and looked back at her friends. Emily was no longer afraid of her future. Wherever it may lead, she knew she wouldn't be going there alone.

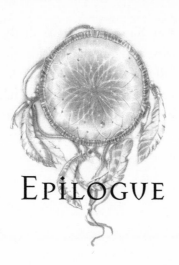

EPILOGUE

*T*HE CAT WATCHED from the trees. Emily's magic had helped her more than the girl knew. Of course, Emily had a sense of the magic only, not real knowledge yet. But that was okay, because the cat didn't belong with her. She belonged with the other one.

The cat purred and licked her paw. She and the other animals were in Ravenswood, away from the poison that was spreading across their own land. And they'd found the ones who would help them: the healer, the warrior, and the blazing star. There was hope for her world after all.

Still, they were not safe. The manticore would likely be back and more like it would come, creatures just as evil, just as dangerous . . . or worse. The Dark Sorceress would never stop. She would drain all the magic from Aldenmor, Earth, and all the worlds throughout the magic web . . . all the way to Avalon itself.

The cat was suddenly tired. Her eyes felt heavy. They closed . . . with the knowledge that it was all just beginning.

ALL THAT GLITTERS

1

KARA DAVIES' ROOM was a disaster of epic proportions. Discarded clothes lay everywhere. Jeans and sweaters smothered the bed. The white lace canopy above groaned under th---e weight of tops, blouses, and T-shirts. Capris, shorts, and leggings were piled so high up the window seat, they blocked the view of the sunset sky. Even the desk was buried under clothes. The only thing visible was the flickering screen of a pink laptop computer.

Tomorrow was the first day of seventh grade. Everything had to be perfect. Especially her outfit.

"It's gone!" Kara wailed.

"You haven't even worn it yet," a disembodied voice squeaked from beside the bed. Kara flipped a blue blazer off her bedside table, revealing a speakerphone. "Did you do a shopping bag check?"

"Tiff, I've looked everywhere!"

The laptop screen started scrolling messages from her buds in the chatroom.

credhed: emergency—kara crisis
beachbunny: just heard! Could it b more horrible 0.o
goodgollymolly: kstar, r u serious?

Kara ran her fingers across the keypad.

kstar: it's GONE! I can't find it NEwhere!!! :(

There was only one thing to do now.

"Mom!"

Mrs. Davies entered the room, concerned. "Kara, honey, what's wrong?"

"Mom, I can't find the Bisou sweater, the new pink one we bought!"

"I'm sure it's here somewhere. Did you look in the—" Mrs. Davies turned to stare at the empty closet.

"Whoa! Looks like The Gap exploded in here." Kyle, Kara's one-year-older brother, walked in, waving an ice-cream bar.

Kara whirled on him. "Kyle, did you take my new sweater?"

"Get real," Kyle laughed.

"I'll look downstairs, hon," Mrs. Davies said. "You'd better start cleaning up," she added on her way out.

"Hi, Kyle," said Tiffany from the phone speaker.

"Hi yourself."

"Kyle! If you drip anything in here, you're a memory!"

"Kara, here's the fax from the town council." Her father, the mayor of their town, walked in, casually dressed in running pants and a sweatshirt.

"Dad! I have a *real* crisis! I can't deal with that right now."

Mayor Davies gingerly stepped over some stuffed animals, victims of the fashion fallout. "It's the information for the Ravenswood Preserve website."

Kara groaned. Ever since she'd convinced her dad to let her and those girls she'd met a few weeks ago, Emily and Adriane, launch the Ravenswood Wildlife Preservation Society, she'd been regretting it. Together, the girls had convinced the town council that the old wildlife preserve was safe from dangerous animals, and that reopening it could benefit the town. They had even promised to set up an info-packed website all about conservation and endangered animals. Sure, it had seemed important at the time, but that was then. This was now, and now Kara needed to get ready. This was *seventh* grade.

"I'm sure you and your friends will want to get going on this," her father continued. "And you've got to *please* keep Mrs. Windor off my back. She's still lobbying to turn the preserve into a country club, so if you want to keep Ravenswood, give me something."

> **beachbunny:** What's going on at Ravenswood?
> **goodgollymoll:** Kara's gonna be protecting purple bears with her new friends
> **credhed:** what new friends? :(

Tiffany, Heather, and Molly were her buds, but she could hardly tell them why she was part of the Ravenswood team. Not even her own dear daddy *really* knew why she had to get along with Adriane Charday and Emily Fletcher. And, if she told any of them, they would never believe her.

A new IM chirped on the computer screen outside the chatroom.

> **docdolittle:** Hey Kara, whats up?

Kara glanced at the IM and nudged Kyle aside, flicking her fingers over the keypad.

> **kstar:** what
> **docdolittle:** did you get the info on the council website :)
> **kstar:** Ya, but I'm busy with my friends now, g2g

Kara closed out Emily's IM. Her friends (her *real* friends that she'd known since *forever*, she reminded herself) were waiting.

"What about the missing sweater?" Tiff asked over the phone.

"I'll think of something. Oh, and don't forget the barbecue here Saturday."

"Cool. Okay, see you tomorrow." There was a loud click from the speakerphone as Tiffany hung up.

beachbunny: l8rz
credhed: cu k
goodgollymolly: Good luck :)

"All right, *out!*" she ordered Kyle.

"Marcus and Joey are coming over Saturday, too," Kyle managed to get in before being pushed out the door.

"No way! Girls' night only! *Dad!*"

The mayor shrugged his shoulders. "Just remember, the Ravenswood project was your idea, Princess, so I'm counting on you."

"Okay, Daddy." Kara pouted as the door closed, then turned and kicked a pile of clothes into her closet. She was starting to hate Ravenswood. It was supposed to be a chance for her to shine (to host fund-raising parties and lead tours through amazing gardens—not *work!* But what she really hated was walking around with that big secret she had spent the last few weeks *not* blabbing about.

Magic.

Genuine magic that only the three of them could work. Well, just Adriane and Emily. They had found the most awesome gemstones that controlled the magic.

Emily had healed sick animals and Adriane had done all kinds of tricks and made friends with a magical wolf named Stormbringer. Kara didn't have her own jewel, but every time she got near their stones, the magic got stronger, as if she were supercharged. Just think what will happen when I get my own magic jewel! Kara smiled. She deserved to have the best jewel and the best magic. Maybe she'd even find the best magical animal, too. After all, that was what they were really doing at Ravenswood—helping magical animals.

Kara sighed and focused on the task at hand: clean up. She'd have to settle for option two for her first-day-of-school outfit. The lost sweater would turn up somewhere.

2

*T*HE UNICORN STOOD *in the woodland meadow. His deep golden eyes were wary but unafraid. Wildflowers blanketed the field in bright colors as Kara walked toward the magnificent creature. The unicorn raised his glimmering crystal horn, filling the meadow with flashes of brilliant light.*

Kara circled the great creature. He was breathtakingly beautiful. She ran a hand over his lustrous white hide; it felt soft as silk and shimmered gently. Breathing slowly, the unicorn lowered his head as Kara came around to look into his eyes.

His voice suddenly filled her head.

"I am for the blazing star."

She was special. If anyone were to ride a unicorn, of course it would be her.

With a leap, she was on his back.

The unicorn took off, racing across the open field. Confident, Kara leaned forward into the creature's steady gallop, feeling herself one with the animal, just as she had been taught at riding school. But this was no ordinary animal. This was the most magical of all creatures. The unicorn raced through the meadow and leaped. Instantly a portal opened—a circle of swirling stars hanging in the air before them—and the unicorn swept through.

Kara was bathed in diamond light as endless loops woven together in intricate patterns revealed itself before her: the magic web that connected worlds. Together Kara and the unicorn ran, faster . . . faster . . . streaking across the infinite web of magic.

"Come to me . . ." *Another voice, distant yet commanding, cut through her mind like steel.*

The unicorn raced along the web like white fire.

She was a golden girl, adored by all. She was a goddess, born to be with such a magnificent creature.

"You will be mine . . ."

She was a princess of magic . . . No! She was a . . . queen!

" . . . or everything you love will die!"

The unicorn stumbled. Kara flew headlong, golden hair tangling as she tossed and turned. A dark-robed figure watched, indifferent, as Kara fell, a shooting star fading into darkness.

Kara's eyes sprang open. It was pitch-black. Her heart pounded. For a second she couldn't move, then realized she was completely tangled in her bed sheets. She wriggled and kicked them off, ripping her pink satin sleep mask from her eyes.

At first she thought that the cold had awakened her, since the hairs along her arms and the back of her neck were standing up. But the room was humid, too warm for comfort. Blearily, she pushed her hair out of her face and looked around.

Pale moonlight glazed the room, glowing softly through the curtains as they wavered in the breeze. The air-conditioning must have gone out, she thought, burrowing back into her pillow. But then there wouldn't be a breeze, would there? As her brain fought its way to sense, she sat up.

The far window was wide open.

Puzzled, Kara stumbled over to shut the window. Had she forgotten before? She'd been pretty tired . . . She stopped short. The window screen was gone. She peered out into the darkness, but nothing moved, no sound broke the stillness. The screen must have fallen off somehow, she thought. Then she saw something on the ledge below her window: splotches of glowing, green muck, dripping into the gutter.

That's disgusting! How dare some big bird drop a surprise on their roof!

She closed the window with a bang and locked it. Shaken, she climbed back into bed, adjusted her sleep mask, and went back to sleep.

In the dark, beyond the window, two piercing green eyes stared back at her, then winked out.

3

F ACT OF LIFE: Some people complain about school. Go figure.

Not Kara. School was the best place to wear the newest clothes, catch the latest buzz, and see all her buds. School-work was like a game—and she wasn't bad at it. Not that she was a brainiac—not her style at all. She was a people person and knew how to use that skill to her best advantage. Nobody expected her to be an A student, and with every-body ready to help her if she needed it, what could be easier?

"Who'd you get for homeroom?" Molly shouted over the chaos in the hallway, brushing her dark hair as kids swirled around them, looking for lockers and classrooms.

"Heather and I got Mrs. Fitch, can you believe it?" Kara beamed.

"Oooh, you're so lucky! I got Ms. Scalise."

"See you at lunch—and, nice dress," Kara told Molly.

"You like it? Thanks." Molly looked grateful. "You look excellent, as usual. Hey, you find that sweater?"

"Not yet, it's a mystery." Kara flashed on the glowing green slime. But that was too spooky. She was in the real world now, her world. She tucked her white linen shirt more securely into her aqua-blue capris.

Smiling, Kara sauntered over to her new locker. Opening her backpack, she set up her command post. She positioned a mirror at eye level and a stickup light above, hung a brush from the side hook, and pasted an air freshener up in the top compartment. Books got stashed where they wouldn't get in the way.

"Perfect!" she said, slinging the backpack with her laptop and supplies over her shoulder.

Heather came flouncing down the hall. "Kara, come on! Everything okay?"

Kara nodded approvingly at the way Heather's white cashmere sweater complemented her long red hair. "Let's go."

Homeroom was a sunny classroom on the second floor. Kara picked a desk by the window. Heather sat right behind her, easy for Kara to swing around and chat.

Mrs. Fitch welcomed everyone and droned on about class assignments and homework. Kara's gaze kept wandering out the window. She had been so busy getting ready this morning, she'd forgotten to mention the missing screen to her father. *Glowing, green, dripping* . . . Thoughts of what had happened to her just a few weeks ago tumbled through her mind. At Ravenswood Preserve, creatures not of this world had arrived through a magical doorway—a portal. Some were cute, like the talking ferret named Ozzie. Some were mysterious, like the giant wolf, Storm, who could evaporate into mist. Some were dangerous, horrible, and scary, like the manticore that had terrorized the town for weeks. She tried to block those images and concentrate on where she was, in the real world, but she knew *they* were real, also. As real as the "purple bear," Phel. Everyone thought the bear had escaped, but she knew better. She, Emily, and Adriane had helped the creature return home—wherever that was. She also knew it wasn't really a bear—it was magic, just like the jewels Adriane and Emily found, jewels she didn't have . . . yet! They had used magic to open the portal, and Phel had gone home. She imagined herself leaping through the portal atop the most beautiful magical animal of all: a snow-white unicorn with a diamond-bright, sparkly horn. Riding together along stands of gold, friends forever. But that was a dream. Something had torn away her screen, and that was real. What if another monster had come to Ravenswood again? She felt goose bumps shiver over her shoulders.

Something moved outside the window. Just twenty feet away, a huge animal was half hidden in the branches of a maple tree. Kara froze. Suddenly she felt a connection, almost like an electrical shock, as if this creature knew her, knew she would be right here, right now. It turned its head. Cold green eyes zeroed in on her.

Someone screamed.

Kara looked around and realized it was her. The classroom was silent. Surprised faces were staring at her.

This can't be happening!

Heather's mouth hung open in a shocked grin; others were snickering.

"Miss Davies? Is everything all right?" Mrs. Fitch looked concerned.

Kara pointed to the tree outside the window. "That big cat," she said meekly. "It's staring at me."

Half the class got up and ran to the window to look. Mrs. Fitch looked out also, but there was nothing there.

"I don't see a cat," the teacher said.

"Maybe it's the *purple bear*," someone mocked.

The room exploded in laughter.

Kara felt her ears burning.

"All right! That's enough. There's nothing more to see. Take your seats. You, too, Miss Davies."

Kara hunkered down in her seat, fuming at the snickers and stares.

"That was, like, *so* weird!" Heather whispered behind her as Mrs. Fitch handed out a sheaf of papers to pass to the back.

Kara felt shaken and frightened. There had been a cat, but how could any cat be that big? What was it doing in the tree? Was it following her? What could it want? She tried to get a grip, but only thought of one thing: Ravenswood.

THE REST OF the morning went by in a blur. By the time she and Heather were cafeteria-bound, Kara felt somewhat better.

Molly and Tiffany were already waiting outside at their usual table, right under a shady tree. Carrying her tray over to them, Kara took a deep breath. Okay, chill. Maybe word hadn't spread about her bizarre disruption in homeroom.

"Been a rough morning. Kara had like a major *freakout* in homeroom," Heather announced as soon as she sat down.

"We heard," Molly said between mouthfuls of salad.

"Everyone's heard!" Tiffany added.

Guess the buzz stream's working just fine, Kara thought.

"So, what happened?" Molly asked.

"Yeah, Kara, what's up with that?" Tiffany prodded loudly.

"Quiet! Nothing. Just keep it down, you want the whole school to hear?"

"Hey, Kara, heard you saw another purple bear!" Joey Micetti stopped by the table with a tray of food, on his way to join his friends. Kara glanced around to see her brother and his buddies elbowing one another at the next table. The usual crew, Adam and . . . oh, great, that cute Marcus.

The boys were all snickering.

"This is so humiliating," Molly said, biting into her burger.

Kara sat silently.

"Go back to Pluto, Joey, with the other alien slugs!" Heather yelled.

"Maybe that's where the bear came from, outer space!" Joey taunted.

"Shows what you know. It was a big cat," Heather corrected him.

Kara wanted to disappear.

"Ooooh, a cat, that's a good one," Adam howled. "Kyle, your sister will do anything to get attention."

This day was quickly turning into a disaster. Kara was almost in tears, her face hot, mind racing. Breathe! It can't possibly get any worse.

"If she saw something, it was real!" Tiffany exclaimed.

"Suuurrre it was." Joey laughed. "Next thing you know, monsters are gonna be falling out of the sky!"

Crash!

A fur-covered thing landed in the middle of the picnic table. Food and drinks went flying. Kara and her friends screamed and jumped back as their uninvited visitor shook salad dressing off one back paw and straightened up.

"Whoa!" Joey fell over backward, startled. The other boys sprang from their table. Kids ran over to see what all the excitement was about, forming a ring around Kara's table and the creature that stood there.

4

IT WAS BIG, the size of a leopard. Spotted fur grew in random patches. Its body was crisscrossed with ugly scars. Dangerous eyes flashed across the crowd—and settled on Kara. She shrieked and tried to dodge behind Molly who squealed, pushed Kara away, and ran behind the tree. The big cat looked at them from under lowered brows, wild and glowering, and stalked down the table toward Kara.

Everyone panicked, yelling in confusion and excitement.

"What *is* that thing?"

"Ewwwww, it's disgusting!"

"Oh, man, that thing is wicked!"

"Someone *do* something!"

"Here, kitty, kitty." Adam was holding out his half-eaten burger, trying to lure the cat away.

"Don't feed it, you moron!" yelled Tiffany.

Kara froze, trembling, caught in the fierce glare of icy green cat eyes. Tiffany and Heather edged away from the table, but the cat didn't even glance at them. It made a noise halfway between a meow and a croak, looking right at Kara.

"Kara, run!" Tiffany cried.

But she couldn't.

The cat held Kara's gaze, its eyes searching. And suddenly Kara felt a sadness so intense she almost burst into tears.

A carton of milk splattered across the cat's back. She whirled, baring gleaming white fangs.

Joey closed in, waving a large stick. "Here, kitty!" The cat dug its front claws into the wooden table with an audible crunch. Scraggy fur stood straight up on end, making her look even bigger and scarier. The cat arched its back, bared gleaming fangs, and growled.

"Uh . . . good kitty." Joey backed off uncertainly.

The cat hissed ferociously—then lunged at him.

Joey leaped back, tripping over his own feet. "Help! Get it off!" he cried.

Gold light suddenly flared in the crowd.

"Stop it!" A tall, thin girl with long black hair stood between Joey and the cat. Adriane. Her eyes flashed with fury, daring anyone to make a move. No one did.

"Just back away," she said evenly. "She won't hurt you."

"Let me through!" Another girl pushed her way in. She had long, curly auburn hair pulled back in a ponytail. Emily. She ran right over to the animal, completely unafraid.

"Are you all right?" she asked softly, rubbing her hand gently over the cat's back, wiping away the dripping milk.

The cat looked at Emily and allowed the girl to check her over.

"Is she okay?" Adriane asked over her shoulder.

"I think so," Emily answered.

Adriane turned to Kara. "What did you do?"

Everyone stared at Kara.

"It's that creepy girl who lives in the woods, Adriane something," Kara heard Tiffany tell Heather.

"The other one is Emily Fletcher," Heather responded. "Her mom's the vet."

Kara gaped in disbelief. This was too much. How dare Adriane take that tone with her! Right in front of everybody!

Blue light sparkled as Emily's bracelet slid down to her wrist. Quickly she shoved her hand into her pocket, hiding her rainbow gemstone. "It's okay, Adriane," Emily said. She explained to everyone, "The cat lives at Ravenswood Preserve."

"What's it doing here?" Molly called out.

"It could bite somebody!" Kyle added.

Joey pushed forward. "Look at it. It's got rabies or something."

"She does not have rabies and you stay away from her!" Adriane was instantly in his face, fists balling at her sides.

Joey stepped back, embarrassed.

Kara noticed the tigereye gem at Adriane's wrist pulsing with gold light.

Adriane looked at Kara, then at her bracelet, and backed away. "She must have wandered down here, that's all."

"And Kara found her," Emily added.

"I didn't find your cat, it found me," Kara firmly told Emily.

Emily eyed Kara with interest.

"Ahh!" Molly shrieked and ran behind Kara. "It's in the tree!"

While they'd been arguing, the cat had leaped from the picnic table up into the big tree. Nimbly leaping from branch to branch, she found a way into the next tree, over the school fence, and into the woods beyond. Emily called after her, but the cat had disappeared.

As kids returned to their tables, Emily turned to Kara. "We have work to do this weekend."

Tiffany, Heather, and Molly shot Kara a look.

Emily noticed and quickly added, "We're setting up the Ravenswood Wildlife Preservation Society. It's like an independent school project."

"Kara, you're going to be working with *them*?" Molly asked, right in front of Emily and Adriane.

"In the woods?" Tiffany added, her face contorted in disgust.

"I can't believe you'd want to have anything to do with that," Heather scoffed.

"Well, it was all Kara's idea, actually. She's president," Adriane informed them with a smirk.

The girls all looked at Kara again. She gave Adriane a fierce glower, but she really felt like diving under the table.

Luckily the bell rang for afternoon classes. As kids hustled their trays to the disposal stations, the buzz was loud and clear: this was the coolest first day of school *ever*!

"We'll see you on Saturday," Emily said as they started to head back inside.

"I thought you were seeing *us* Saturday," Molly pouted. "Shopping and then the barbecue."

Kara hushed her friend, but she saw that Emily had heard. "Look, I promised my dad I would . . . look after things for him."

"It's so creepy!" Tiffany exclaimed.

"I'll be back in plenty of time for the barbecue," Kara assured them. "Just come over at six."

Kara led Molly inside. She sensed Heather and Tiffany softly whispering behind her back. Her ears burned.

This was not going at all like she had planned. How could she tell her friends what was really going on at Ravenswood? If they only knew how incredible those jewels were, what you could *do* with them. She sighed. At least she didn't look like a complete lunatic—the cat was real. But why was it stalking her? She hoped all this weirdness was over, but she had a bad feeling it was just getting started.

5

O N SATURDAY, THE air tingled with the scent of pine and moss as Kara walked up the road that led to Ravenswood Preserve.

Heather, Tiffany, and Molly had made it clear they totally disapproved of her plans to work with Emily and Adriane. Kara felt irritated. How'd she end up in the middle of her best friends and ... well ... *them?*

Okay, so Emily and Adriane were the only other two human beings on Earth who knew that the magic was real. But at school, they were so ... unpopular. Hanging with them could make *her* unpopular as well—right? Yet the adventure they had shared still played across her mind, a fairy tale with magic and magical creatures.

Well, there's room for only one princess in this fairy

tale. If she was going to be president of the Ravenswood Wildlife Preservation Society, she would have to get her own magic jewel—and soon! She'd make it up to Moll, Tiff, and Heather tonight.

Emily and Adriane were waiting for her as she approached the twin iron gates of the Ravenswood Preserve entrance.

"How are you doing, Kara?" Emily asked.

"Terrific," Kara answered sarcastically.

The tall gates creaked as Adriane pushed them open.

"So, what do we do first?" Kara adjusted her leather backpack and followed them up the gravel road.

"Adriane's gran said there's a computer in the library," Emily explained. "We thought we'd see if we can find it. We know the preserve used to have a website."

"Fine," Kara answered. "Let's just do this. I have a party to get ready for."

"We wouldn't want to keep you from your *friends*." Adriane tossed her long black hair over her shoulder and glared at Kara. Kara glared back as the girls made their way toward the manor house. The woods were quiet and peaceful in the warm afternoon sunlight. That lasted about three seconds.

"You should've told us right away the cat was on school grounds!" Adriane said angrily.

"Oh, now I'm supposed to report to you?" Kara was really getting annoyed. "Who put you in charge, anyway?"

"You gonna turn around and have the cat hunted down, too?"

Kara stopped and crossed her arms.

Emily quickly inserted herself between the two. "Adriane, Kara didn't know Phel wasn't a monster."

"Don't take her side, you always do that!" Adriane accused Emily.

Kara was fuming. "You got the preserve back! You and *Gran* have a place to live, as quaint as that is. What is your problem?"

"You are!" Adriane didn't skip a beat. "We don't hear anything from you for two weeks and then you waltz right in as if nothing has happened."

"So what? I've been busy."

"But something *has* happened, hasn't it, Kara?" Emily asked softly.

Kara shook her head. "Look, let's just get the site online so I can tell my dad it's done, and you can go play all you want with your—"

Adriane narrowed her eyes. "Our what?"

"Never mind," Kara said, turning away behind her curtain of golden hair.

"Go ahead, let's get this out." Adriane moved around to face Kara. "You can't stand the fact that we have magic jewels and you don't!"

"Adriane—" Emily touched her friend's arm.

"No!" Adriane continued, shaking Emily's hand off. "I

don't have to take this attitude from Miss Perfect, with her perfect clothes and her perfect friends!"

"Now that you mention it, I *don't* have a jewel," Kara shot back. "I have school now, and . . . things to do."

"So do we!" Adriane stepped back and assumed a fighting stance. Kara tensed.

Adriane spun in a balanced martial arts move. She swung her arm and a ribbon of golden light spiraled from the tigereye gem at her wrist. She whipped the stream of light into a golden ring. The dark-haired girl gracefully moved her arms, and the ring settled around Kara. Adriane resumed her stance, neat and slick. Magic sparkles danced around Kara and winked out.

Kara's mouth hung open as twinkly sparks tickled her skin.

"We've been busy, too," Adriane said, and turned away to continue down the road.

A cloud of mist swirled out from between the trees. The mist seemed to fold in on itself and grow darker, then vanished as Stormbringer appeared. The great silver-gray wolf padded over to Kara.

"We've been waiting for you, Kara."

The sound of the wolf's voice in her head was startling. "You . . . you have?" Kara looked into gentle, golden wolf eyes.

"The animals want to thank you for securing this home."

"They do?" Kara asked, looking at Emily.

"They're all anxious to see you, Kara," Emily told her.

"They are?" Kara looked at Adriane.

Adriane gave Kara a curt nod.

"We've also mapped a tour route of the preserve for you to show your dad and the town council," Emily said.

"Our *special* animal friends will hide in the glade when the tours are scheduled," Adriane continued.

"Wait till you see, Kara, it's so cool!" Emily's eyes sparkled.

Suddenly Kara felt as if she'd been left behind. What had happened here in the two weeks since she convinced her father to let the girls work at the preserve?

They rounded a bend and entered the grand circular driveway in front of Ravenswood Manor. With its towers and stained glass, the amazing old building looked like a castle. Ivy crawled up the stone walls to reach gargoyles perched under the eaves. Kara thought it looked haunted.

"What about the manor?" she asked. "Will that be part of the tour?"

"We haven't explored much of it yet," Emily responded.

"The garden tours and website should keep the council off our backs till we figure out how much of the manor we want to include," Adriane added.

Kara was actually starting to get excited. Emily and Adriane were really taking this seriously.

"Come on." Emily laughed as she walked around the cobblestone path that skirted the manor. "Ozzie's with the animals out back."

Kara and Adriane followed, glaring at each other.

"Show-off!"

"Barbie!"

"Come on, hurry!" Emily shouted, running out onto the manicured sea of grass that was the great lawn behind the manor. Kara was surprised by a cacophony of neighing, bleating, hooting, and other less identifiable sounds. Before her stood a herd of animals.

"All right, everyone. Calm down." A gold-and-brown ferret paced back and forth in front of the crowd like a small furry general.

The animals surged forward, bounding over the ferret.

"GaHoonk!" came his muffled response.

Incredible animals surrounded Kara; butterfly-winged horses, green-and-purple-striped deer with long, floppy ears, silver duck-like things, and others even more outrageous. Kara felt giddy.

"I am Ronif," one of the silver duck-things announced—quiffles, Emily had said they were called. "Emily and Adriane told us how you helped to give us a home here."

"Stories will be passed down to generations of quiffles," another quiffle proclaimed.

"The town allowed the preserve to stay open," Kara said modestly. "I really didn't do much."

"You helped fight off the manticore!" a winged pony said.

The animals cheered.

The ferret came bounding over. "Welcome back, Kara. Your friends missed you."

"I don't know about that, Ozzie," Kara said, bending down to speak to him. "Things seem to be going fine here without me."

"Nonsense. It's been much too boring." The ferret smiled.

Kara grinned, though she was a little embarrassed to be talking to a ferret. Well, not really a ferret, she reminded herself—he claimed to be an elf trapped in a ferret body, but Kara had her doubts. Would an embattled world of magic really send a *ferret* to find help against the forces of evil?

Emily stepped forward. "Okay, everyone, roll call!"

With quacks, neighs, and a hoot, the animals quickly fell into a line, shoulder to shoulder across the lawn. A large, white snow owl glided gracefully out of the sky to land on Emily's arm. Turquoise and lavender glistened in her wing feathers.

"I'm here."

"Thank you, Ariel," Emily said. "You remember Ariel," she said to Kara.

Kara gave the magnificent owl a little wave.

Emily took out a notebook and began to check off her list. "Pegasi?"

"We're here," a winged pony announced.

"Thank you, Balthazar. We have four pegasi," she said so seriously that Kara almost laughed.

"Quiffles?"

"All here," Ronif announced. Adriane scooped up four

baby quiffles, and immediately the other little ones tried to leap up into her arms. She fell over in the grass laughing, covered in quiffle kisses.

"There are six adults and twelve babies." Emily checked them off, then looked around. "Where're the jeeran, Ozzie?"

"Running in the field," Ozzie said, a little annoyed. "They can't stand still for more than two minutes!"

Kara looked across the lawn and saw the tail end of a green-and-purple-striped deer soaring over a hedge.

"We also have seventeen jeeran," Emily commented proudly, as if she were talking about normal deer, not some magical creatures from another world! She looked back at her list. "Brimbees?" she called out briskly.

"Here!" came a light, breathy voice.

Kara stared at what looked like big blue rabbits with iridescent dark blue spots.

Emily nodded. "Okay, that's everyone."

A small golden-winged creature about the size of a bat zipped up between the brimbees and hovered. It gave a squeak, its jeweled eyes dancing brightly.

"Who are you?" Emily asked, looking over her list.

"Skookee!" The bird-thing buzzed around Kara's head, picking at her long hair.

"Hey!" Kara ducked, swatting it away.

Ariel eyed the little flier with a hungry hoot.

The gold bird-thing gave a loud squawk, zipped off, and vanished.

"What was that?" Kara asked, brushing her hair back into place.

"I don't know." Emily re-checked her call sheet. "Anyone come through this morning?"

"Not on my watch!" Ozzie answered stoutly.

"Ozzie, this is a sanctuary," Adriane reminded him.

A large shape slunk behind the pegasi. Kara caught the glint of green eyes.

The big cat watched her, casually turned, and walked away.

"And, of course, the cat," Emily said. "She comes and goes, but she sure seems to be interested in you," Emily commented.

"I'll say!" Kara blurted out. "The school's going to be talking about it for weeks!"

"Yeah, so will the town council," Adriane said, depositing the baby quiffles back with the adults. "Including that horrible Mrs. Windor," she added with a shudder. "She's been against Ravenswood from the start. If she hears about a wild animal showing up at school, our wildlife preserve, and my home, are as good as gone."

6

KARA FOLLOWED THE other girls through a back door into the manor. Inside, a short set of steps led to the first floor. Wide hallways lined with paintings opened onto bright sitting rooms filled with plush furniture.

"Wait till you see the library, come on!" Emily said, as she propelled Kara up a steep staircase, down a hallway, and into a room straight out of the nineteenth century.

"Wow!" Kara breathed.

They were inside a gigantic round library, illuminated in golden radiance. Kara stared up at a vast domed ceiling. Zodiac figures with twinkling stars inset were painted on it in fine gold. Below the dome hung a complicated mobile of suns and planets, shiny discs of metal on long arms.

Large oval windows overlooked the great lawn and beautiful gardens out back. Across the parquet floor, a ladder was mounted on a track that ran around the perimeter of the room, allowing access to shelves high above. Books were crammed everywhere.

Kara walked over to look at a drawing taped to the wall. It was a map of the preserve. All of the gardens were noted, and dotted lines crisscrossed the area, carefully avoiding the special glade that lay hidden behind the ancient monument known as the Rocking Stone.

"Why does that garden have an X on it?" Kara asked, pointing to a section of the map.

"Some of the gardens are overgrown since we can't maintain everything ourselves," Adriane replied. "That one is the hedge maze. Gran said you can get lost in there for days, so it's off-limits for tours."

"Well, this library alone is worth a tour," Kara said, turning around to take in the amazing room.

"No way," Adriane countered. "We don't know what special stuff is hidden in here."

Kara shrugged. "Fine, let's just get the website online."

"I've been working on some ideas on how to organize it." Emily indicated the notebooks lying open on the desk.

"I can get Kyle and Joey to set something up," Kara said, looking over Emily's papers. "They live for this stuff."

"Are you nuts?" Adriane burst out. "We're not bringing those loudmouths in here. We can figure it out ourselves."

"Okaaay, if you say so," Kara said. "How about a blog?"

"We can't go blogging this all over the place," Adriane argued. "A website is more secure."

"The original website went down two years ago," Emily said.

"Just about when Mr. Gardener disappeared," Adriane noted.

Henry Gardener, the owner of Ravenswood, had mysteriously vanished, leaving the preserve under the care of Adriane's grandmother.

"It would be a lot easier if we could find Mr. Gardener's computer," Emily continued. "Maybe we can use his files to set up the site."

"Probably buried under all this stuff." Kara gestured at globes, telescopes, dragon-shaped chess pieces and compasses littering a wide mahogany table.

"Let's see the instructions from the council."

"Here." Kara opened her backpack and handed the fax to Emily.

"We should list all the animals: numbers, physical descriptions, habits and habitats, patterns—"

"Oh, really? You gonna add dwimbees?" Kara asked.

"Brimbees," Emily corrected.

"Yeah, those, too."

"Let's check for wi-fi," Adriane suggested.

"With what?" Kara asked, waving her arms around. "I don't see a computer here, do you?"

Adriane and Emily looked at her.

"What? Oh, no! You're not using my laptop."

"Come on, Kara, just to get us started," Emily said.

"I see how it works," Kara huffed. "You only want me for my stuff. Fine!" She pulled the pink laptop out of her backpack and opened it.

Emily booted up, opened the browser, and typed the town council's web address. "We have a connection."

The computer whirred, buzzed . . . and crashed.

"Great!" Kara yelled.

"That's strange," Emily mused as she rebooted. "We lost the council server."

"The line live?" Adriane asked.

An IM pinged onscreen.

beachbunny: Hey kstar—dance class was awesome :0) can't believe u missed it
goodgollymolly: Kstar who's gone be at the bbq? :)

Kara pushed past Emily's shoulder and flicked her fingers across the keypad.

kstar: not home, still working, just be there at 6
beachbunny: not home? U still at that creepy preserve with those creepy girls?

Kara felt her face flush.

kstar: g2g l8rz

She turned off the IMs.

"Thanks for giving up your precious time for us *creeps*!" Adriane seethed behind her.

"I didn't say that," Kara said meekly, stepping away.

"You can't judge Kara by her friends," Emily chided.

"She may be your friend, but she's not mine!" Adriane glared.

Kara was shocked.

"Kara, Adriane didn't mean that," Emily said.

"There wouldn't even *be* a club without me," Kara burst out.

"This is not a club!" Adriane yelled back.

Kara pressed on. "You like the fact that you have a magic jewel and I don't. And if I never find one, that would suit you just fine, wouldn't it?"

"Nobody's trying to keep you from finding a stone," Emily assured her.

"You want my stuff, fine. But don't expect me to stand around and be insulted." With that she turned and stormed to the far side of the room.

"Give her some space," Emily said, turning back to the laptop.

"I'd like to give her outer space," Adriane replied.

Kara pushed through the door, slammed it behind her, and stomped down the stairs. How dare they treat her that way? Especially when she was giving up a Saturday with her friends to be with them!

A feeling of righteous indignation swept over her as she walked outside and crossed the stone terrace behind the manor. She stopped to look up at the library windows, checking to see if Emily and Adriane were watching. But the big oval windows only reflected the sunny sky.

"They can keep their magical stuff," she grumbled. "Magic doesn't like me anyway!"

Kara marched straight across the lawn toward a row of giant hedges. She didn't notice the swarm of colorful creatures diving from the skies to follow her.

7

BEING OUTSIDE HELPED clear her head. Kara took a deep breath and looked back at the expanse of the great lawn. What a perfect place for the first fund-raising event. Now *that* was something she could handle! She imagined medieval torches encircling the magnificent gardens with the rocking sounds of Sampleton Malls blasting from the stage! She giggled. And Kara, the princess of the ball, in the most rad leather-and-silk gown, dancing the night away with the most handsome prince. Adriane can stay home and be the wicked stepsister she thought with a laugh and twirled past the rose gardens.

Such beautiful roses. She bent to admire a striking patch of China reds and rugosas. An amazing flower caught her eye. It looked like a dandelion, except the seeds were bright rainbow sparkles. It reminded her of Emily's magic jewel. *Zip!* Something buzzed past her ear.

"Koook."

"Hey! Watch it!" It was one of those bird-things, a blue one. Up close it didn't look like a bird, it looked more like a . . . a . . . tiny dragon! It hovered above the rainbow flower, dipped its small front paws in the seeds, and grabbed them. With a squeak it flew away, trailing rainbow sparkles behind it. Kara stood still as another one came out of nowhere. It hovered in front of her. This one was purple. It definitely looked like a miniature flying dragon, with jeweled eyes that reflected glints of light. A dragon . . . fly. Kara was pleased with the wordplay. A dragonfly!

"Scrook?"

"Shoo," Kara replied.

"Screeek!" The purple dragonfly swirled around Kara's head, picking at her hair. Kara waved it away, and it zipped over to another flower, grabbed clawfuls of seeds, and took off.

Kara was curious. Why were the little dragons taking the seeds? To spread them somewhere else? Bet Emily and Adriane don't know about his, she thought gleefully. She looked at her watch: 4:00. Time to collect her stuff and head home. Her friends were coming over at six.

She turned to go back to the manor, but the roses and brambles seemed to have gotten all tangled up behind her. She tried to push through. Ouch! The thorns were sharp.

Kara cut through an opening in the hedges and started down an overgrown path walled in on either side by towering hedgerows.

The path came to a dead end at the head of a T: she could go right or left. It looked like some kind of giant maze, she realized. *Gran said you could get lost in the hedge maze for days, so it's off-limits for tours . . .* Yeah, right, who would be so stupid to . . . well, getting lost in a hedge maze was just stupid.

Kara looked around. The hedgerows loomed above her, blocking the view of the manor.

"Hey! Hello? Ozzie? Storm? Someone? I'm . . . lost!" Where were all the animals now that she needed help? She kicked her sneaker along the gravel and a small cloud of rainbow seeds sparkled up into the air. Probably dropped by those pesky dragonflies. The cloud of seeds trailed to the right, so Kara followed. She walked into a wide circle with trails leading off in at least a dozen different directions.

There was a soft rustle in the hedge. She caught a glimpse of an animal rounding a corner.

"Hey, Dwimbee!" Kara ran around the corner and gasped. The big cat sat in the middle of the path, her green eyes gazing at Kara.

The cat yawned, then stood and strolled deeper into the maze, glancing over her shoulder.

She expected Kara to follow?! How dumb did that cat think she was?

The cat turned and blinked at her.

"I'm coming, keep your fur on!" Kara grumbled and crunched along, dire thoughts of rock'n'roll princesses who wander away from the party and get lost forever in enchanted hedgerows playing in her head.

The cat moved purposefully through the twisting green corridors.

Then she turned a corner—and walked out of the maze.

"Thank goodness! I thought we were going to be stuck in there forever!"

The cat was threading her way into a patch of deep woods.

"Hey, kitty! Wait for me." She set off into the trees, hurrying to keep the cat in sight. Deep, dense forest now surrounded her. But at least she was on a path, muddy and narrow, but definitely a trail.

"Kitty, where are you?" she called.

She saw the cat entering a wall of giant firs. Kara scrambled after her, looking up in awe at the trees, their green boughs covering the sky. She emerged into a wide-open clearing in the woods. A stream bubbled by, running into a large pond. Fir trees circled the glade protectively, and on the far side, the immense boulder called the Rocking Stone stretched its rocky finger way up into the skies.

Finally, a landmark she recognized! Beyond the Rocking Stone was a path that would take her back to the manor house. It was a moment before she realized where she really was—at the *secret* glade, where Emily had found her magic healing stone.

Kara headed for the pond. There, in the shade of weeping willow trees, something sparkled in the crystal-clear water. She knelt down to look closer. Stones, dozens of beautiful stones! She reached into the water and scooped up a handful; they were rough and unpolished, but flecked with crystal. Woot! A ton of *magic stones*! She held up a tiny green one and closed her eyes, concentrating on making the stone light up the way Emily's and Adriane's could. Nothing happened. She tossed it away and tried again with a yellow one, then a blue one. Nothing.

These didn't feel magical at all! Then again, how do you know if a stone is magical or not? The feeling that maybe she just didn't have what it took to make magic came over her. She had helped Adriane and Emily with magic, but the key word was "helped."

She looked up to see the cat sitting next to her. The animal's green eyes were magnetic, filled with deep empathy. Once again, Kara was shaken by the intensity of the feeling. The cat nodded toward a rock by the edge of the water. Kara scampered over and looked behind it.

Half submerged in the shallows was the most beautiful crystal Kara had ever seen. It was teardrop-shaped and scalloped like an ornate shell. She reached down and picked it up. Smooth and polished, it gleamed diamond bright, reflecting light in all directions. She stood up and held the stone tight.

Instantly, warmth pulsed up Kara's arm! It seemed to lodge in her heart and her eyes and her brain. The gem flashed, sending rainbows around the clearing. Magic! Kara jumped for sheer joy, shrieking with the wonder of it. She waved her arm in a circle and brilliant twinkles spiraled from the gem.

"I can't believe it," she cried. A magic jewel! A stone, her own stone, and the most beautiful one of all!

She danced over to the cat. "Thank you, thank you so much!"

It was as if she'd turned on a faucet of magic. Multicolored bubbles streamed everywhere, popping and bouncing around her. Kara spun in a circle, stretching her arms out, trailing ribbons of light from her jewel.

"Look at meeeeee!" she sang. "I have magic!"

"Sreeeeeeep!"

"Whooooooohoooo!" Kara cried.

"WOooOOooh . . ."

"Yeeheep!"

"Yeah, that's meeee—"

"Keekeee!"

Kara whirled to a stop. Wait a minute!

Five dragonflies were singing and dancing with her, ecstatically whirling and twirling in the air. Dozens more rocketed about, bursting out of bubbles of color. They thronged around her, chirping and flashing!

This was magic and it was better than she could ever

have imagined. No wonder Emily and Adriane were so in love with it!

"Can you believe this? The others'll absolutely die!" Adriane's tigereye and Emily's rainbow jewel were cool, but just wait until they saw *this* stone!

"It makes an impressive display."

"Oh, doesn't it? I can feel it, it's the most mag . . . gi . . . cal . . ." Kara slowly turned back to the cat. "What?"

"It suits you."

A look of suspicion crossed Kara's face. "You can talk?"

"Most humans have a hard time hearing without some magical assistance," the cat told her. She began to groom her mottled patches of fur.

"Say that again," Kara commanded.

"I am not a trained performer," the cat said mildly, sweeping her big, rough tongue across her shoulder.

"Sorry. It's just kinda unbelievable."

A golden dragonfly settled on Kara's shoulder and grinned up at her.

"Beat it, Goldie." Kara flicked it away. It vanished in a burst of color.

"I am glad you are pleased," the cat replied, standing up.

"Oh, yes! I'm going to . . . to *magic* myself right back to the manor!"

The cat turned. *"How do you plan to accomplish that?"*

Kara blushed, then made up her mind to try. How hard could it be? She held out her gleaming stone. "Mirror,

mirror . . ." No, that wouldn't work for transportation. Kara realized with surprise that she didn't have any actual idea how to work the gem. Her mind raced through possibilities. Abracadabra seemed a little risky. Twinkle, twinkle? No, that didn't seem like a good bet, either.

The cat came back a few steps. *"Start small,"* she suggested.

How did Adriane and Emily work their stones? They hadn't said anything about rhyming or spells. They just pictured something in their minds and focused on it.

Kara clutched the beautiful stone as hard as she could, squinched her eyes closed, and pictured herself rising off the ground . . .

Nothing happened.

Darn! She tried again, picturing herself as accurately as she could: lustrous blond hair, creamy skin, dewy red lips—no, she'd sworn off lip gloss long ago, make that pale pink lips—rising up, inch by inch, sparkling blue eyes still closed . . .

Her feet left the ground! She actually felt the magic pulling her into the air! She also felt little pinpricks through her shirt, along her skin, and even in her hair. She opened her eyes a crack and gasped. Dozens of little dragonflies were tugging her upward, their tiny wings beating furiously.

Her eyes flew open and she tumbled to earth—from a height of about five inches. "Hey!" Kara shouted, swatting away the pesky little things. Well, it took Adriane two weeks to figure out that trick with her stone. Just takes practice. This is going to be a blast!

"I have been watching the little dragons collecting magic seeds," the cat said. *"Those seeds compress into crystals. But the one you found doesn't feel new. It's too strong."*

"I knew it! Maybe there're more like this one," Kara said, running to the pond and searching among the pebbles in the water. The cat gave a sniff and started up the hill. "Oh, c'mon," Kara whined. But the cat kept going. "Okay, be that way."

She sat sifting through the stones as the dragonflies happily buzzed about. "Shoo, go away!"

Grabbing a few more stones, she examined them and tossed them away. The sound of gently running water echoed through the peaceful forest glen. She noticed the dragonflies had vanished. Everything was quiet except for the sounds of splashing.

Swish, swish . . .

Kara felt the oddest tingling sensation and realized the jewel was getting warm in her hand. She held it up to examine it. The stone pulsed with light, like a heartbeat. Flashes bounced off the water, sending an ashen glow into the trees beyond. The glade now seemed surreal. Suddenly she didn't feel so good. Her stomach twisted and she felt light-headed.

Swish swish . . .

There it was again. Something splashing in the water. Kara turned and saw a ragged old woman crouched by the side of the lake, dipping something into the crystal-clear water. Her face was turned away as she scrubbed in clean, swift strokes. *Swish, swish . . .* Looked like she was cleaning an article of clothing.

Was she a homeless person? What was she doing out here?

Uneasily, Kara got to her feet and approached her. The woman's whole outfit was rags, splotched and nasty. Slimy green weeds hung from her arms and legs. Yuck!

"Excuse me, are you . . . uh . . . all right?" she asked tentatively.

The ragged figure scraped the cloth up and down a rock. *Swish, swish . . .*

Kara felt dizzy. The trees were starting to sway around her. Fighting the queasiness, she looked closer. Greasy, stringy hair hung down, covering the old woman's face. Her long dress was ripped in shreds, revealing patches of pockmarked . . . *green skin!* With long, gnarly green fingers, the tattered old crone spread the cloth on the rock— it was pink.

Kara's world crumbled. Fear shot down her spine. It was her sweater! The pink sweater she had lost!

She froze, gasping for air.

The old woman turned to Kara. The . . . creature . . . had a woman's face, but its skin was green and covered with horrible sores. Blood-red eyes were set deep at odd angles to a—there was no nose, just a ragged hole where a nose should have been. The creature's mouth twisted as a hiss

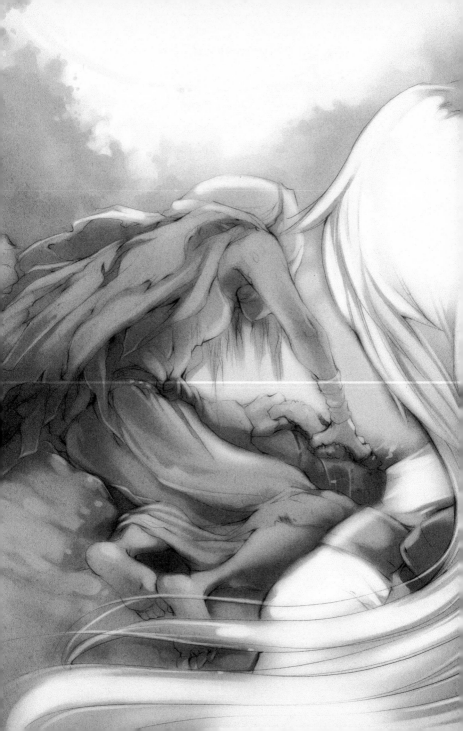

escaped through thin blue lips. The mouth contorted open, the hiss building into a howl. Kara's hands flew over her ears and she screamed. The creature lurched, monstrous in her fury, clawing her way toward Kara.

8

EVERYTHING SEEMED TO slip into slow motion as Kara whirled around, slid on the muddy bank, and tumbled backward. One of her sneakers went flying. With dripping green claws, the ragged apparition reached for her. Something big flew at Kara and she scrambled sideways in the mud. She turned to see the cat standing between her and the ghoulish creature.

With a snarl, the cat bared fearsome fangs.

The monster howled incoherently, reaching and clawing.

Kara leaped to her feet and ran. "Ow, ow, ouch!" she shrieked as her sock-covered foot came down on sharp rocks. She gripped her gem and focused. Quick! A new pair of Nikes with shock soles! But no footwear materialized.

"Use your magic!" The cat's voice was in her head.

"I'm trying!" Kara yelled back.

Think! Do what Adriane did. Kara concentrated. Left, right, arms together, swing tight . . . She pinwheeled her arms, whipping the crystal around, and landed on one knee, jewel pointed toward the monster. Tiny sparkles fizzled from the tip. Kara frowned. That cheer routine killed at the home game.

"Kara?"

"Over that way!"

Voices were approaching from beyond the trees. A moment later the animals came charging into the glade. In the lead was Balthazar the pegasus with Ozzie standing on his back.

"What is it?" a quiffle yelled.

"Another monster!" a brimbee cried in terror as the creature lurched toward Kara.

Ozzie jumped onto the pegasus's head. "Kara, are you all right?"

"No!" Kara ran to the animals, shaking with fear. "That thing is after me!"

A cloud of swirling mist swept by and Stormbringer appeared. The great wolf bared teeth and growled low. Stormbringer and the cat closed ranks in front of Kara, blocking the advance of the creature.

Huddled in tattered rags, the horrid thing hissed, "Givesss me jewel!"

"No way!" Kara yelled. "I found it and it's mine!"

"You found a jewel?" Ozzie asked.

"Yes, look. Isn't it awesome?" She held up the crystal and felt it flare to life, sending energy prickling through her hand and up and down her arm. "It's working!" she cried.

"Quickly, gather round!" Ozzie ordered. The pegasi crowded behind Kara; brimbees and the larger quiffles pressed in close. Storm and the cat stood on each side. The jewel blazed with light.

Suddenly, dozens of colored bubbles popped above them. Dragonflies zipped out, diving and twirling. Screeching, the ragged ghoul swatted them with gnarled fingers. A bright golden dragonfly spiraled down. Piping, frantic screams cut off as it hit the water and vanished.

"Goldie!" Kara shouted in fear and anger. With her free hand she clutched the cat and the jewel exploded with fierce power.

Kara screamed as diamond fire shot straight up into the sky so unbearably bright she could see it even through her closed eyelids.

The monster hissed and backed away. Kara's arms ached as she desperately fought to control the stream of magic. It was like trying to direct a tidal wave. The stream twisted back and forth like a fiery snake, knocking Kara to the ground as it dissipated over the glade.

She opened her eyes to see a ferret face staring at her, very concerned. Other animals surrounded her.

"What happened?" Kara asked.

"Storm sensed strong magic, then we heard screaming," Ozzie said. "We followed Storm and then we clobbered the monster!"

Kara got unsteadily to her feet and realized the creature had vanished. "Wow! My magic jewel totally evaporated the monster!"

The animals had helped her, Kara realized. They had supercharged her jewel, just like she always made Emily's and Adriane's gems go crazy!

"What *was* that thing?" she asked.

"It looked like a banshee," Balthazar replied.

"A what?"

"A cursed fairy creature. But this one was worse. It was poisoned by the Black Fire."

"Well . . . what's it doing here?"

"I don't know."

Kara walked over and picked up her pink sweater. It was burned through with ragged holes. She flashed on the glowing green slime outside her bedroom window. That *thing*, that banshee had been in her room! "What was it doing with my sweater?"

"Banshees practice strange magic," Balthazar mused. "Their spells often include articles of clothing so they can track their victim."

"Victim?" Kara repeated.

She looked at the jewel, now cool in her hand. She was nobody's victim. Now she had her *own* magic jewel! Grabbing her sneaker, Kara followed the group down the trail back to the manor. She looked over her shoulder for the cat, but she was nowhere to be seen.

9

"HEY!" KARA BOUNDED into the library with Ozzie, the quiffles, Ronif and Rasha, and Balthazar.

Emily was examining a pile of books while Adriane rummaged through a collection of odd devices scattered about a tabletop.

Emily gasped and jumped to her feet. "What happened to you?"

Even Adriane was astonished when she turned to look at Kara.

Kara was covered in mud. Her shirt was torn, her shoelaces were undone, and her pink sneakers were caked with dirt. Her golden hair was wet, slick against her head, and full of grass and twigs.

"What do you mean?" she asked, beaming with joy.

"Are you all right?" Emily walked toward Kara, her rainbow jewel pulsing softly with turquoise light.

"Never been better." Kara rocked back and forth, arms behind her back, hiding her secret for as long as she could.

Emily looked at the animals. "What happened?"

"You should have seen it!" Ozzie blurted out.

"Seen what?" Emily asked.

"Unbelievable!" Ronif exclaimed.

"We all helped," Rasha stated.

"The cat helped, too," Kara added with a smirk. "I talked to her."

"You what?" Adriane walked over, amber light pulsing from her tigereye.

"That's right," Kara said proudly, sliding sideways under the planetarium mobile. The clockwork mechanism suddenly came to life, comets and stars revolving and interweaving in a complex cosmic dance. Emily's eyes widened at the sudden movement. Balthazar ducked to avoid the swinging pendulum.

"Just what I said, I talked to the cat—oh, and I got attacked by a monster," Kara added. A comet swung by on an arc, following her. A shiny planet swept by, catching Ronif and whisking the startled quiffle into the air.

"The manticore is back?" Emily asked, shocked.

"Nooope, guess again," Kara said coyly.

"Oh, my." Ozzie stood on a table to study the intricate mechanism of the moving mobile. He tried to grab Ronif as the quiffle came swinging by, but a moon caught the ferret, swinging him into orbit. "Dooooohooo!"

Adriane was losing her patience, rubbing at the pulsing stone on her wrist. "If it wasn't the manticore, what was it?"

"It was a homeless monster thingy from the magic world!" Kara declared.

"A what?"

279

"Yeah, and it was washing my pink sweater."

"Thank goodness you were there!" Adriane confirmed. "We can't have monsters running around the preserve washing clothes."

"Well, you weren't even there, Miss Kung Fu show-off," Kara gloated.

"It was a fairy creature," Balthazar said, sidestepping as Ozzie and Ronif swung by on the moving planetarium. "A banshee, but horribly mutated, poisoned by Black Fire."

"Oh, no! How did you fight it?" Emily asked.

"Hmmm, well, let me see . . . with my amazing personality? No . . . my striking good looks? No . . . my cutting-edge yet tasteful fashion sense?"

"Would you stop fooling around!" Adriane yelled.

"Maybeeeee . . . I used . . . *this!*" Kara whipped out the jewel from behind her back. It flashed like a diamond in the light, casting rainbow sparkles across the room.

Emily and Adriane stared openmouthed.

"A magic stone!" Adriane exclaimed.

"Where did you find it?" Emily asked.

"In the glade, where you found yours." Kara stopped herself from saying, and it's bigger, better—no, the *best* magic jewel ever! She swung her arm around, trailing glitter from the jewel's tip. The clockwork planetarium sped up like a carnival ride.

"Help!" Ronif and Ozzie wailed.

"Kara! That jewel activated the mobile!" Emily exclaimed.

"Stop flashing that thing around!" Adriane said, jumping up and down, trying to grab Ozzie and Ronif as they swung by.

"I'm going to turn my room pink and stick Kyle in a tree and give all my friends new iPods."

"Wise choice of magical powers," Adriane cracked as she pulled Ronif and Ozzie down.

"Kara, stop using your jewel. It's doing something to mine!" Emily held up her wrist to show her gem shifting through rainbow colors.

"Has it changed?" Adriane asked Kara.

"What do you mean?"

"I mean, both Emily's and mine were rough stones when we first found them. They became polished and even changed shape after we started using them."

Kara shrugged. "Mine doesn't have to change. It's perfect the way it is."

"It's very powerful. We all saw it," Ozzie said.

"And it could be dangerous," Emily cautioned.

"I am going to do the best magic, ever! It's too big for my wrist, sooooo . . . I'm going to make a necklace!"

"Kara, I don't think you should use it until we figure out how it works," Adriane said.

"It works great!" Kara skipped around the room, drawing shapes in the air with magic sparkles. Her jewel flared brightly, briefly outlining sections of the walls. Faint images flashed as Kara danced by, as if her magic was an X-ray machine illuminating shapes behind the oak paneling.

"There's something behind there." Adriane pointed.

Emily noticed it also. "If Mr. Gardener's computer is hidden, maybe we can find it if we all use our jewels together."

"Okeydokey." Kara liked this game, now that she was a real player.

The girls stood together in the center of the library.

Emily held up her rainbow jewel.

Adriane held up her tigereye.

Kara raised her jewel between them.

"Concentrate on a computer," Adriane said.

Blue-green and golden light flared from Emily's and Adriane's gems. They all clasped their free hands together.

Instantly the magic flowed into Kara's jewel and silver-white light burst from its tip so intensely that all three girls recoiled. The magic stream slammed into the pink laptop, launching it across the room.

Kara shrieked, dropping the other girls' hands. The magic fell away as Kara ran over to check out her laptop.

"Wrong computer," Adriane stated.

"Magic works better when we help," Balthazar offered.

The pegasus, two quiffles, and Ozzie moved in to surround the three girls.

"Okay, everyone. Let's try it again," Emily said.

Standing in the center of the library, once again the three girls clasped hands and held their jewels in the air. The animals closed their eyes. Magic flared from Emily's and Adriane's gems and flowed into Kara's stone, sending diamond beams bouncing around the room.

The library lit up like a small city. Sections of wall glowed, revealing secret doors and hiding places, gadgets whirred and clicked, and the clockwork planets and suns zipped around their orbits.

"Concentrate on a computer!" Emily called out.

"And don't think pink," Adriane said to Kara.

Magic swirled around the room, twisting and blending into a single ribbon of turquoise, gold, and diamond-white. Suddenly the magic crashed into a section of wall, making it light up from within. A large panel slid to the side, revealing a giant screen.

"Look! Widescreen TV!" Kara exclaimed.

The golden light of the domed ceiling flashed and blinked out, casting the room in darkness except for the cool, soft glow of the screen.

"Enough!" Adriane ordered.

The girls dropped hands and let their stones cool.

Suddenly points of light, brilliant and dazzling, flashed overhead. The girls and the animals looked up in awe as a giant star map twinkled across the domed ceiling. Then they heard a voice.

"Welcome to the magic web."

10

"*I*T'S HIM!" EMILY gasped.

"Him who?" Kara asked.

"Mr. Gardener," Adriane said, amazed. "He owns Ravenswood. He disappeared about two years ago."

Ozzie, Ronif, Rasha, and Balthazar looked curiously at the man smiling at them from the large screen set back in the wall. He had long, gray hair and wore small, round glasses over keen blue eyes.

"What's he doing in there?" Kara wondered.

"Mr. Gardener, is that really you?" Adriane asked the image on the screen.

But no answer came. The kind face just kept smiling.

"It's a video file or something," Kara said.

Emily noticed a tray under the screen. She touched it and a keyboard slid out. "Look!"

She hit the ENTER button. The bright star map across the domed ceiling dimmed and was replaced by the golden luminescence.

"Whoever has found this station, the magic is with you," the image of Gardener announced. "I am sorry I am not here to greet you in person, for you must have many questions."

"I'll say." Kara crossed her arms.

"There is a portal, a gateway, in Ravenswood that leads to a world called Aldenmor. Sealed for centuries, it has recently opened, signaling that the time of magic has come full circle and three mages would soon be arriving."

His face faded, and the screen filled with sparkling lines like a Spirograph, lights marking various points along the grids.

Then Gardener's voice continued. "There is a web that connects many worlds, including Earth. Magic flows along this web to where it is needed. But there are very few places left that hold true magic, and over the years, the web has grown weak. If we are to save the web, we need to renew the magic from its very source, a hidden place called Avalon."

Fairimentals had come to the three girls and left them a message scrawled in the earth: Avalon. It was at the center of the whole magical mystery the girls had embarked upon.

"I have gone to seek great magic to aid you on your quest. If you are viewing this message, then I have not yet returned to begin your training. I cannot say if I have fallen to dark forces, but I can tell you this: be careful, young mages. Nary a corner of the web does not lie in some danger from a fearsome enemy. She is a magic master, twisted in her selfish desire to horde magic and use it for herself."

The image of Gardener paused, his eyes focused on them.

"This is your time, young mages. I have faith you will find what you need to fulfill your destiny. Good luck to you."

The face of Henry Gardener faded, replaced by a blank screen.

"What was that all about?" Kara asked, incredulous.

"Mr. Gardener's last message before he left," Emily ventured.

Ozzie scratched his chin. "Something is wrong. Gardener was expecting mages, not monsters."

"What exactly is a mage?" Adriane asked.

"A magic user," replied Balthazar.

"So Gardener was supposed to teach us about all this magic stuff," Kara huffed. "Thanks a lot for the help!"

"Now he's gone and he left us with nothing!" Adriane said angrily.

"What am I?" Ozzie leaped upon the keyboard. "Chopped barleycorn?"

"Of course not!" Emily kissed his furry head. "You're perfect."

"Well . . . I . . ." Ozzie swooned and sat backward upon the keys and a cursor appeared onscreen. It was a dream-catcher icon with jewels positioned top, bottom, left, and right, like the points of a compass.

"Whoa!" Ozzie scrambled to his seat as assorted icons appeared: animals, jewels, and one of Ravenswood Manor.

Emily moved the cursor around over the icons. One by one, different images of Ravenswood appeared: pictures and text about the wildlife preserve and rare animals that had lived there at one time or another.

"It must be the original Ravenswood files!" Emily exclaimed.

"Wow, so cool! Look at all this stuff on it," Adriane said.

"Good job, ferret." Kara looked at her watch. "Now how do we link it to the town council?'

Emily turned to the others. "Mr. Gardener went to a lot of trouble to keep this a secret. What if we had two sites?" she suggested. "We set up the Ravenswood Preserve site as our homepage for tour information and list the an-imals we *can* show on the tour, like Ariel and the other birds, Storm, peacocks, deer—but we also make a second level, our own password-encoded site."

"I like it, a secret site," Adriane said, smiling. "A website about magic—a magic web."

"Cute." Kara rolled her eyes. "You gonna design a space station too while you're at it?"

"Well, we can at least get our homepage up," Emily said. "But I don't think we should link it until we check out everything on here. You heard the message: we have to be careful."

"Agreed," Adriane said.

Kara frowned. "That could take . . . hours!" Again she looked at her watch: 5:30. "I'm late!" she cried. "I've got to get to my—"

The girls and animals all looked at her.

"—party," she finished sheepishly.

"So go," Adriane told her.

"Listen, Kara," Emily began. "It's okay. We know you have your friends, but we're your friends, too."

"Yeah . . ." Kara didn't look convinced.

"What I'm saying is, we share something, the three of us. Nobody else can know."

"What she's saying is, don't do anything stupid with that jewel!" Adriane cut to the chase.

"I get it." Kara was packing up her things. "No magic."

"Right. No magic until we can figure it out together. It's too dangerous," Emily said.

"Okay, I hear you!" Kara ran out the library door.

11

THE DAVIES'S LARGE Tudor house sat on meticulously landscaped grounds overlooking the Chitakaway River.

Kara raced up the driveway and burst into the kitchen with fifteen minutes to spare. A note from her mom was on the table.

"Nate and Alvin's delivery just left. Everything's ready out back. I'm meeting your father at the club. We'll be home around ten. Call us on the cell if you need us."

"Eek, I stink!" Kara took the stairs two at a time and rocketed to the bathroom for a quick shower.

A few minutes later, she dashed into her closet, scattering clothes every which way. She hopped back out, pulling on crisp new jeans and a bright green cami.

Gathering her hair back in a ponytail, she thought about what had just happened at Ravenswood—probably the most amazing thing that had ever happened to anybody on the planet! A banshee had come after her, but her animal friends had protected her. Best of all, she'd found magic.

She rummaged in her jewelry drawer and emerged with a silver chain necklace. She flipped open the locket clasp, removed the old star drops, and attached her new gem. She secured the chain around her neck.

"Perfect!"

"It is nice."

"Oh, yes," Kara agreed, looking admiringly in the mirror. "It's so . . . *what?*" She whirled around to see the enormous cat lounging among the pillows at the top of her bed. "How did you get in here?"

The cat looked coolly at Kara. *"Would've been easier if you'd left the window open."*

"You can't stay here. My mom practically freaked when I had a hamster! You're so much . . ." Kara stopped, at a loss for words. All she could think of was *worse*.

"Bigger?" A huge paw stretched, extending razor claws as a mouth full of sharp teeth yawned.

Kara nudged the cat over as she sat down to slip into a pair of slides. "Were you outside my window the other night?"

"You had another visitor as well," the cat replied.

"I can't believe that thing was in here." Kara shivered.

"I could stay and keep an eye on things, if that's okay with you."

Kara suddenly felt a little shy. "Okay with me." She ran her hand over the cat's scruffy-looking fur. "What's your name?"

"Lyra," the cat replied, eyes half closed as Kara scratched the corded muscles on her neck.

"That's pretty," Kara said, sounding surprised. "I'm Kara."

The cat yawned and lay back in the pillows.

The doorbell sounded.

Kara jumped, stopped quickly to check herself in the mirror again, then eyed Lyra. "Just stay here!" she ordered, and closed the door as she ran downstairs.

It was a perfect September evening with gentle breezes under clear skies. The table was set on the patio, overlooking a marble fountain in the garden behind the house. Candles flickered in lamps set around the yard. Tall pitchers of lemonade stood on the buffet table surrounded by plates of barbecued burgers and hot dogs, chips, salads, pickles, fruits, coleslaw, and baked beans.

Kara's friends were already in a party mood as she led them through the kitchen and into the backyard.

"Wait till we show you these rockin' routines," Tiffany told her.

Heather giggled. "You should have seen Tiff!"

"Girl, it's called rhythm, and I have got the moves!" Tiffany danced across the patio as the others laughed.

Kara smiled. Finally she could just relax and enjoy herself.

"How'd it go with you?" Molly asked.

"Yeah, tell us everything," Heather ordered, pouring some lemonade.

"Details, girl!" Tiffany shimmied by.

"Oh, you know, soooo boring." Kara twirled a strand of her blond ponytail in her fingers. "We have to research in this old library for the website."

Heather laughed. "Research?"

"Library? Sounds serious." Tiffany put her hand on Kara's forehead. "Hmm, geeky influence with a touch of dweeb," she diagnosed.

"Needs some time with her homegirls," Heather prescribed.

"And not with the beasts of the forests," Molly added, crunching into a celery stick.

"Well, there are no wild beasts around here," Kara said, firmly setting the record straight.

"Yo, yo, wass*up*!" Joey called out as Kyle and his friends spilled out onto the flagstone patio.

"Stand aside, ladies, the crew is here to bring it home," Marcus announced, placing a huge boom box on the floor.

"On second thought, I could be wrong." Kara rolled her eyes.

The girls laughed.

"Feeding time at the zoo! Let's eat!" Kyle started piling a plate with food.

"Sweet! We got some spread going on here." Joey grabbed a plate and started a first pass through the buffet.

"Hey, Kara, where are your superhero friends?" Marcus asked, filling his plate beside her.

"Huh?"

"The daring duo of the animal world!" Joey called out.

"They're not my . . . friends." Kara flushed. "I'm just working with them on the Ravenswood project for Dad."

"Joey was hoping Adriane would be here," Kyle teased.

"I was not," Joey said, his face going bright red.

"Dude, you said you like her." Kyle winked at Marcus.

"How could anyone like her?" Tiffany asked Kara. "She's so crude."

"She's okay," Kara said, more annoyed than she was willing to let on.

Tiffany stared at her as if she had grown an extra head. "What?"

"Well, Adriane only has her grandmother, and they're trying to get the preserve all fixed up."

"Exactly. *So* pathetic, right?" Tiffany said.

Kara flushed, twirling her jewel in her fingers. Adriane wasn't her friend, but the girl certainly wasn't pathetic. She was just . . . different.

"Kara, where did you get that?" Heather noticed her necklace.

"Oh, I found it . . . lying around."

Molly and Tiffany moved in to study the dazzling teardrop jewel that hung from Kara's neck.

"You always have the best accessories," Tiff said admiringly.

"It's true." Kara beamed.

"Who's for seconds?" Kyle asked, moving back to the buffet.

"The human disposal has spoken!" Kara announced. Everybody crowded around the buffet table, chattering and laughing, piling plates high.

Kara smiled. Just perfect—

"Peeep."

Something whizzed by the table and flew into the garden. It was a burger. A flying burger? Had she done that? She looked down at her jewel, but it wasn't sparkling any more than usual.

Just then a dragonfly zipped down the middle of the table, purple wings shining in the candlelight. It dodged among the plates and scooped up a couple of cherry tomatoes out of the salad bowl.

Kara's eyes bulged. Play it cool, maybe nobody will notice . . .

"Ahhhh!" screamed Heather. "What's that?"

No such luck.

"A huge flying bug!" Tiffany ducked and Molly choked. Joey leaped over to smack it away.

"Scroook!"

He smacked two tomatoes instead, splattering Tiffany and Heather.

"Hey!" Heather cried.

"Ohhh, gross!" Kyle and Marcus howled with laughter.

Okay, it's okay, Kara repeated to herself. Stay calm, everything's fine . . .

There was silence.

Everyone was looking at Kara. The girls had their mouths open. The boys were sputtering, desperately holding in their laughs.

"What?" Kara said, annoyed.

"Kara," Molly began.

"You have . . ." Tiffany continued.

Kara felt a tug on her scalp.

" . . . a big . . ." Heather stammered.

" . . . *bug* on your head!" Kyle fell over in a fit of laughter.

Something was entangled in her ponytail. Please let it be a bug, she thought. She worked her fingers through the long blond strands and something struggled frantically. "Ouch!" she yelped, as she felt a tiny stab against her scalp.

"Pweeek!"

"Kara, are you all right?" Molly asked.

"Fine, fine, it's nothing," Kara said, hopping backwards holding a fistful of hair.

She pulled a dragonfly free—a blue one.

"Skachooo!" It coughed a spark of flame and darted off into the twilight.

"Did you see that?" Molly asked, her eyes wide.

"The biggest firefly I ever saw!" Joey exclaimed. "It's like a jungle out here!"

"Kara, you sure you didn't bring your work home from the preserve?" Kyle asked.

"Very funny," Kara mumbled. "There are no wild animals around here!"

Out of the corner of her eye, she caught a large shape slinking around the buffet table. "Who wants another hot dog?" Kara grabbed a tray, quickly moving to block the view.

"I'll take one," Joey said.

Kara tossed a hot dog toward him. "What are you doing! I told you to stay put!" she whispered to Lyra, who crouched in the shadows to the side of the brick hearth.

The hot dog floated by her head. Kara reached out and grabbed it.

"Poooo!"

"Give me that!" She tugged back and forth with a red dragonfly.

"Where's my dog?" Joey asked behind her.

Kara yanked the hot dog hard and turned quickly. The dragonfly careened backward.

"Here!" She put the half eaten hot dog on Joey's plate. He walked away, puzzled.

Lyra growled low in her throat. *Something is here.*

"Thanks for the update! These dragonflies are ruining everything!"

"No, something else. It's fading in and out, fighting to stay here."

"What?" Kara looked around frantically. "Something bad?"

"No, but they've come for you." The cat slid back into the shadows.

"Hey, who's for dessert?" Kyle yelled out.

"Ice-cream sundaes, burnin'!" Joey whooped.

Is this dinner over yet? Stay calm! Everything's fine.

Drip . . .

"Hey! Something dripped on my head!" Joey said.

"Is it raining?" Tiffany asked.

Drip, drip . . .

Kara felt droplets on her face. She looked up. Not a cloud in sight.

Drip, drip, drip . . . Water was spritzing everywhere.

"Look, the fountain's screwy!" Marcus pointed.

Everyone stared at the fountain. Bursts of water were spurting from it, shooting straight into the evening air and spraying in all directions.

Kara ran across the lawn, looking around frantically.

"Web runner . . ." A tiny voice blew past like a breeze.

"Huh?" Kara looked at the tall Roman fountain, watching water spurt out over the tiered ledges. Droplets fell into the bowl like rain.

The drops swirled, shimmering as if they were trying to take shape. Kara looked closer. Twinkling and flowing, the drops merged. Kara's eyes widened. It was a tiny figure formed out of water with waves of long, crystal-blue hair. The figure shimmered, struggling to hold its form.

"The jewel . . ." The tiny figure's voice rippled across the water. Kara wasn't even sure she had heard it.

Kara leaned in closer. "What did you say?"

"Do not use the jewel . . ." The figure quivered, flowing in and out of its watery form.

"Why not?"

"It is . . . a trap."

"Kara, what are you doing?" Molly called out.

Kara whirled around and sat in the fountain, splattering the figure to droplets. "Nothing."

"You're sitting in the water!" Heather exclaimed.

The boys laughed.

"Uh, just checking the pressure. Be right there!" She jumped up and glanced back in the water. "What do you mean a trap?" she whispered.

Small geysers bubbled from the surface as two watery figures swirled to life.

"She knows you possess the jewel . . ."

"Who knows?" Kara could feel desperation from the tiny figures as they began to lose form.

"The bringer of Black Fire . . ."

"The Dark Sorceress . . ."

"Dark Sorceress? That doesn't sound good."

"Use it with care . . ."

"To your own heart be true . . ."

"Use the jewel, don't use the jewel! You're totally confusing me! Should I use it or not?"

"Kara, your ice cream's getting cold!" Kyle yelled.

Kara looked over at her friends. "Be right there!"

When she looked back, the figures were gone. The fountain was calm, water gently cascading down the marble as if nothing had happened.

12

KARA FELT RELIEVED when the party finally wound down. Kyle and his friends went to Joey's to check out some new video game, and not long after that, Molly's mom arrived to pick up the girls.

Kara cleaned up quickly, then headed to the sunroom for a nice hot soak in the Jacuzzi.

The glass-walled extension had been built onto the side of the house. The air was moist and heavy with the scent of flowers, trees bearing ripening fruit, and the hot steam of the Jacuzzi.

Kara was worn out. Thank goodness her mom had left the Jacuzzi heater on. She turned on the timer for the jets. Instantly the water in the large sunken tub began to churn and bubble. This is too bizarre, Kara thought as she changed into her bathing suit in the screened-off dressing area. The cat, and then the dragonflies . . . and what exactly were those watery things? What were they trying to say to me? And why me?

Fingers of steam crept into the dressing area, covering everything in soft mist. Kara stood before the mirror to admire herself. She turned the jewel around in her hands, studying its sparkling surfaces. Whatever was going on, it had something to do with this. She examined the jewel closely. Flecks of pure diamond radiated from the delicately scalloped shape. It was exquisite.

Yet something about it looked familiar. The shape. Where had she seen such an incredible crystalline form before?

It was hypnotic, sparkling with brilliance, yet below the surface, Kara could feel tremendous power pulsing like a mighty river.

Gingerly, she felt for the magic, letting her senses reach out. Prickling energy ran up and down her arms and through her hair. Kara felt light-headed as magic surged through the very core of her being. It was like nothing she had ever felt before—strange, wild, and wonderful!

She realized she was breathing too fast as the force crested like a tidal wave. Suddenly she was terrified of losing control. She frantically willed it to stop. Electricity pulsed through her body, trailing off her fingertips like faint static.

Just imagine what would happen if she *really* let the power go! Awesome!

"Mirror, mirror, on the wall, is this the coolest jewel of them all?"

A dull spark flashed in the misted glass. Kara wiped away the steam and regarded her reflection. Something wasn't quite right. Age lines creased out from her eyes, a streak of white parted her blond hair like a lightning bolt. Her skin looked cool, alabaster like a porcelain doll—had her summer tan faded already? And her eyes . . . Kara looked closer. Shivers ran up and down her spine. They weren't human. They were the slitted eyes of an animal!

Kara blinked. And her own adorable face looked back through clouds of mist.

Oh, boy, I really need to soak!

She removed her necklace and placed it on the dressing table, then padded over to the sunken tub and eased into the hot water. *Oh, heaven!* It felt wonderful. Bubbles, bubbles, lost in the bubbles. Steam circled up and enveloped her, so warm, so soothing, so nice . . .

Kara lay back and dunked her head.

Under water, bubbles churned around her, all thoughts of magic floating away . . .

The timer shut off, abruptly bringing the water to a dead calm.

Kara resurfaced, head and toes pointing out of the still water.

A single drop emerged from the jet, swirling with colors as it rose in the water. Kara watched through half-closed eyes, totally relaxed, as fluid shapes spread around her.

The drop enlarged, swelling like a balloon. The surface colors took on shapes, oily smears on water. Slimy colors turned muddy brown and green as long, stringy hair fanned from the bubble.

Kara held up a finger. Thick slime, like pond scum, dripped into the water. Her eyes flew open. She was lying in putrid green-and-brown water. In front of her, the banshee hissed as its foul head surfaced.

13

*T*HE MONSTER EXPLODED out of the slimy water. Kara screamed and scrambled from the sunken tub, splashing water everywhere. The ragged creature began to slosh its way—not toward Kara, but to the dressing table. The jewel! The banshee was after her magic jewel! Outside, Lyra scratched wildly at the closed glass door.

Kara ran around the tub but slipped on the wet tiles. Flailing about, she grabbed a towel hanging on the rack.

"Help—*oohhf!*"

The towel rack broke and Kara tumbled into the silk screen, falling forward and collapsing to the floor. She whirled and kicked the whole mass of screen, towels, and bathing suits at the banshee. The creature wailed, batting aside the debris. Kara got to her feet and lunged for the jewel. Behind her, the banshee fought free and lurched forward. It snatched at the mat under Kara's feet, sending her flying into a citrus tree. Sobbing, Kara watched in horror as the tree came crashing down against the dressing table in a rain of dirt, leaves, and tiny oranges. Her magic jewel careened across the tile floor toward the drain in the center of the room. It caught in the grate, sparkling like a diamond.

Outstretched ragged fingers reached for the stone.

Now or never!

Kara dove headfirst toward the jewel—and jerked to a stop.

The banshee had Kara's hair caught in its grip. Kara was wrenched upward. She reached desperately for the jewel but was yanked back again. Her hair was beginning to sizzle, burning under the banshee's acid touch. Kara screamed, inhaling the sickening smell of singed hair. She pulled away sharply. But she lost her footing and slipped again, crashing against the washstand.

Through her tears, Kara watched the creature's clawed, twisted hand reach out . . .

Suddenly the jewel rose into the air.

"KeeKee!"

"Goldie!" Kara exclaimed. Eyes red with fury, the banshee howled as it grabbed for the stone. But the jewel floated just out of its grasp.

Four more dragonflies popped into the room in bursts of light.

"Skeepooot!"

The banshee swatted at them, trying to get at the jewel.

"Here, over here! Good dragonflies!" Kara called out.

Goldie swooped toward Kara, the jewel wobbling in her tiny claws. She dropped it into Kara's outstretched hand.

Kara spun to face the banshee, holding the jewel out in front of her. "Stay back!" she screamed. She didn't know what to do. Should she use it, or not?

The banshee lumbered forward with sloppy wet steps and reached out.

Kara held the stone and concentrated on driving the creature back.

Astonishment and terror chased across the hideous face. The banshee's red eyes filled with despair, and the creature fell back, covering its face with clawed hands.

Kara threw her arms theatrically into the air and called on the power of the stone. *Make lightning smite the banshee into a million, million pieces!*

"Go away, scary thing!" she shouted wildly.

Power rushed through her like a freight train, sending circles of light swirling around her body.

The banshee cowered before the blazing magic.

Kara laughed triumphantly. Nobody was going to take her jewel. The creature began shrinking, falling in on itself, its rags spreading out across the tiled floor into a puddle of slime. Clawed fingers reached out in a desperate plea.

"You doom us all . . ."

Kara watched, amazed, as matted hair swirled around in clumps. With a final gurgle, the thing turned to green slime and vanished down the drain.

14

"*A*ND DON'T COME back!" Kara wiped her hands together.

A strange light gleamed behind her.

She slowly turned.

The mirror's surface swirled, as if filled with mist. Cold animal eyes glinted, distant and cruel—then faded. Kara's own wide blue eyes stared back from the cool reflective glass.

A trick of the light?

Kara looked closer at the disheveled blond hair sticking out over her ears.

What?

Carefully, she touched the back of her head and felt the short, stiff ends.

She whirled around and looked over her shoulder. An entire section of her hair was gone, singed off by the banshee. It was as if a mad barber had run a lawn mower up her neck and onto the back of her head.

"My hair!" Kara burst into tears.

Lyra was carefully picking her way through the wreckage. *"Hair isn't important."*

"Maybe not to you!" Kara wailed.

The cat regarded her with deep, calm eyes.

"What am I going to do?" Tears spilled down Kara's cheeks.

"It will grow back," said Lyra.

"I can't wait that long," Kara cried, her voice trembling. "What do I tell my parents and everybody in school? I can't tell them about that thing, I can't tell them about the jewel, and I can't tell them about *you!*"

She sniffled, trying to control herself. "I've got to fix this on my own."

"How?" Lyra asked suspiciously.

"Magic," Kara answered. "And you're going to help me!"

The cat cocked her head.

Kara clutched the gemstone in one hand and put her other on the back of her head. "Stand still and help me make magic."

"All right," the cat answered, moving next to her. *"Breathe calmly, and we'll focus together."*

Kara took a deep breath.

Hair! It must, *must* grow, she thought. She closed her

eyes tight and concentrated with all her might on how much she needed this to happen, right now.

Grow!

Kara pressed closer to Lyra. The gem grew warm and she thought she could feel a faint tingling on her scalp. And then her hand, clutching the cropped hair, dropped toward her shoulder. Her eyes flew open.

Yes! Her hair was definitely growing!

"*Is it working?*" Lyra asked.

"You tell me."

Puzzled, the cat looked into the mirror. Not only was Kara's hair growing, but the fur all over the cat's body was growing as well. Lustrous spotted fur now covered the bald and scarred patches.

"Look at you!" Kara said in delight.

Lyra's body was bushy with new fur. "*This is not funny.*"

"Skeehee!"

"Leeloo!"

The dragonflies somersaulted happily.

Kara pulled her hand away and twirled around, hair flying out in a golden cascade. She hugged Lyra, laughing with sheer relief.

"Oh, thank goodness!" she cried. "I'll have to get a trim, but at least I won't be going back to school looking diseased." She pulled a pink scrunchie around her hair.

Lyra examined herself in the mirror. "*I think we might have grown enough hair.*"

Kara felt her scrunchie drop lower . . . down her neck

. . . past her shoulders . . . Her hair was growing faster and faster. "Stop! Stop, please!" she yelled at her stone.

Nothing stopped. The scrunchie dropped toward her waist. Lyra was beginning to look like a woolly mammoth. "I take it back," Kara cried. "Reverse the magic!"

But the scrunchie didn't stop dropping as her hair reached her feet. "What do we do?" Kara sobbed.

"This was your idea. Make it stop," Lyra said.

Kara closed her eyes and concentrated, waving the jewel all around, but the hair kept growing. "I can't."

The dragonflies darted this way and that, lifting up long golden strands.

Kara began to cry again as waves of hair piled onto the floor.

"Stop crying, we have enough water already!" Lyra looked like a walking shaggy carpet.

"I have to call Emily," Kara finally decided. "We need help and fast!"

She stepped over mountains of hair, grabbed the phone from the wall, and punched in Emily's number.

"Hello?"

"Uh, hello," Kara squeaked.

"Kara, are you all right?" Emily instantly sensed that something was wrong.

"No!"

"What happened?"

"Can you come over here, like, right now?"

"You used the jewel!" Emily accused.

"Just get over here and hurry! I'm in the sunroom out back."

"Okay, hang on, I'll call Adriane. We'll be right there." Emily hung up.

With a grunt, Kara twisted the new hair, using four scrunchies to keep it together. It was a thick cable now, bumping along on the floor behind her. The big furry cat lumbered over.

Kara couldn't help laughing. "You look like Cousin It!"

"Who?" Lyra asked.

"Pheeheee!"

"Hoohaa . . ."

"Oooohoo!"

Four dragonflies landed on Kara's arms and lap. A purple one sat on Lyra, scratching the cat's back. Lyra closed her eyes and flopped down next to Kara.

"How did you get in here, anyway?" Kara asked Lyra as she petted the mini dragon's head.

"Up there," Lyra said, opening one eye and cocking her head skyward.

Kara looked up. The sunroom skylight was open. This cat was very agile!

She brushed Lyra's long, silky fur coat. "Nice coloring, it's beautiful."

"I didn't think it would ever grow back."

"So what happened to you, I mean, your fur?"

"I was burned trying to escape," Lyra told her.

"Escape from where?"

"A place called the Shadowlands." Her fur bristled.

"What were you doing there?" Kara stroked her fur back down.

"There was a raid in my forest. Hunters took us to a powerful sorceress."

Kara's eyes widened. She suddenly flashed on what the magic water things had told her about the Dark Sorceress. Shivering, Kara snuggled closer.

"We were brought to a dungeon and locked in with other animals. The sorceress was stealing our magic. I was the only one in our group who escaped. I tried to save my sisters, but I couldn't."

"That's the saddest thing I ever heard!" Kara burst into tears again, sobbing into the cat's silken side.

"Boohoop . . ."

"Aaahhhooooh . . ."

The dragonflies were crying all over Kara and Lyra.

"Do not cry for me." Lyra gazed into Kara's eyes. *"There is enough sadness in my world."*

Kara sniffled. "Do you think they're all right, your sisters?"

"I don't know. I was chased by the manticore and hardly remember falling through the portal into this world. Adriane found me, and Emily helped me to heal. When I discovered the other animals had been burned by the Black Fire, too, I realized I could not fight the sorceress and her dark creatures myself."

"Like the manticore and these banshees?"

"Oooo!"

"Skweek!"

Kara stroked the agitated dragonflies.

"*The banshees have also suffered at the hands of this sorceress. She would destroy our whole world to get what she wants.*"

"What does she want?"

"*Magic.*"

"I thought I wanted magic." Kara buried her head in the cat's still-growing fur. "I'm just stupid! Look what I did!"

"*Things are not always what they seem.*"

"They're not?"

"*You must look beyond what your eyes see, and what your fingers touch. Magic always starts from the heart, Kara.*"

"Do you think I'll ever learn how to make good magic?" Kara asked shyly.

"*Yes, I do. A true heart makes true magic.*"

Kara looked into Lyra's warm green eyes and smiled.

There was a knock on the glass door. "Kara, are you in there? It's Emily."

"Yes! We're in here!" Kara jumped up, sending the dragonflies flapping away. Deep piles of hair tangled around her ankles as she ran to open the door.

Emily and Adriane walked into the sunroom, mouths agape.

"FoooF!" Ozzie foofed, disappearing into the golden froth.

"What happened in here?" Adriane asked, surveying the hair-filled disaster area.

"We told you not to use that jewel!" Emily sounded really mad.

Kara burst into tears. "I *had* to," she sobbed, and she told them all about Lyra, the dragonflies, the barbecue, the water thingies, the banshee attack, and—worst of all—her hair.

"Talk about a bad hair day," Adriane said, looking with interest at the blue dragonfly that had landed on her shoulder.

"You have to help me!" Kara wailed. "My parents will be home soon!"

Waves of blond hair lapped halfway up the glass walls.

Four dragonflies hovered and chattered at one another, examining a moving lump of hair.

"Go away, you pests!" Ozzie called, his voice muffled.

"They helped me," Kara explained. "That's Barney, Goldie, Blaze, and Fred."

"You *named* them?" Adriane said, half smiling as she scratched blue Fred's head.

"Well, yeah . . . So?"

"Keekee!" A red one hovered in front of Kara and spit out a burst of color. "Oh, and that's Fiona."

"OooO!" Fiona dashed off.

"Look at *you!*" Emily picked her way over to the shaggy cat. Lyra rubbed against Emily's side. "Incredible! I tried to make her fur grow back and couldn't do it . . ." For a moment she faltered, but then she smiled. "This is wonderful, Kara!" Emily gave Lyra a hug.

"Kara, what did you do?" Adriane asked. "You just ordered it to grow?"

"Yes," she replied, shame-faced.

"Well, let's just cut it," Adriane proposed.

Emily shook her head. "We need to reverse this grow-spell, like, right now." She fished around in the hair for Ozzie and hoisted him up. "Suggestions?"

"*Ptui!* I think Adriane's jewel would be the most effective, since she and Storm have been practicing together." He turned to Adriane. "Can you call Storm?"

Adriane closed her eyes. Instantly, a ribbon of mist snaked through the door and Stormbringer materialized at her side.

"Looks like a hairy situation." The wolf's golden eyes sparkled.

Sproing! Two scrunchies snapped at once and blond hair spilled out, billowing around the room. Kara looked down in horror.

"Okay, Rapunzel, let's do it," Adriane said. "Picture your hair the way you want it.

The three girls stood together with Lyra, Storm, and Ozzie. The dragonflies swooped and danced all around them. Kara clutched her jewel and imagined her hair beautiful again, the most beautiful hair ever!

"Hair today, gone tomorrow," Adriane chuckled. Her striped golden stone brightened as she held up her wrist.

Kara's jewel blazed to life with bright light. "It's working!"

Suddenly more dragonflies popped into the room, filling it with color and motion. They swooped, picking up strands of hair, weaving it around the girls and their magic.

Kara concentrated super hard, feeling the power rush from her toes to her fingertips. The dragonflies themselves glimmered, their bright colors blending with the glow from the gems until the light was so intense that all three girls had to shut their eyes.

There was a burst of brilliance. Then the glow faded.

They all opened their eyes.

Kara just gaped. Festoons of hair were strung from the window and from the light fixtures, hooked over the skylight, and tangled on the trees.

And the hair wasn't blond—wasn't *just* blond—anymore. It was streaked with every color of the rainbow. Green, red, blue, purple, aqua, and pink glistened along the strands.

"Well, it seems to have stopped growing," Adriane announced.

"What do we do now?" Kara sputtered. "You can't leave me like this!"

"You're right," Adriane agreed. She opened a drawer and held up a pair of scissors. "Ready?"

Kara was speechless. She turned away and closed her eyes. "Not too short, okay?"

As Emily grabbed a big handful of brightly colored hair, Adriane started cutting. The dragonflies snatched up

wads of loose hair, weaving and braiding in graceful motions, then flying out through the skylight, trailing glittering rainbow strands behind them.

"What do you think?" Emily finally asked, trimming the last bits of hair out of Kara's eyes.

Kara cautiously faced the mirror. Her hair fell just past her shoulders, like before, but it was still streaked with every color imaginable—blue, red, green, yellow, purple . . ."Oh, man . . ." she breathed.

"It's unique," Adriane said, appraising Kara's new do. "Definitely you."

"I have rainbow hair!" Kara exclaimed, horrified.

"You're welcome," Adriane said.

"What am I going to tell everyone?" Kara wailed. "You have to fix it!"

"Kara, we can't keep messing around with magic until we know what we're doing," Emily said. "I think we're lucky we did what we did."

The dragonflies were dragging the last unattached scraps of multicolored hair up through the skylight.

"Just tell everyone you got some new highlights," Adriane suggested.

"From where!" Kara screamed. "The circus?"

"You'll think of something," Emily said. "But no more magic! Okay?"

"Yeah, okay," Kara said glumly. Keeping a magic jewel secret was one thing, rainbow hair was something else.

She watched as Adriane, Ozzie, Emily, and Storm left the sunroom. She turned to see Lyra gazing at her. Her fur was perfectly restored; thick and gorgeous and just the right length.

"Well, at least one of us got it right," Kara said.

"Thank you."

"For what?"

"For helping me."

"I didn't do anything except make a total mess."

The cat licked her shoulder and walked out the door, lustrous fur shining in the moonlight.

Kara sighed. She had wanted magic and she sure had gotten it. At least it wasn't a complete disaster. She had helped Lyra. Kara had to smile. Somehow that seemed to make everything better.

15

KARA CAREFULLY CHECKED herself in her locker mirror. Her hair was tucked neatly under a pink beret. Cute, she thought. Too bad I'll have to wear it till like . . . *forever!*

"Kara, come *on*, we're late!"

Kara turned to see Molly charging toward her. "Assembly, remember? Everyone's there already."

"Oh, yeah, I forgot. Let's go, Mol." Kara adjusted her blue blazer, linked arms with Molly, and headed down the hall. She could get lost in the crowd for a while. Perfect.

The auditorium was filled to capacity. Kids were yelling, tossing balls of paper, hip-hopping in their seats, and creating general assembly mayhem.

"Kara, Molly, over here!" Tiffany waved from where she and Heather had saved two seats. "Hey, cute hat," she said, reaching out to touch the beret as Kara slid in next to her.

Kara jerked away.

"What's up with you?" Tiffany laughed.

"Oh, it's . . . new," Kara said quickly.

"This sure beats homeroom, huh?" Heather commented, leaning across Tiffany.

"Look at Marsha Luff's dress, do you believe it?" Tiffany murmured.

"What about Lori Eller's hair!" Heather squealed.

At least it's only two colors. Kara sat back, eyes darting back and forth.

Feedback squawked from the stage.

"Okay then," Principal Edwards said, poking the microphone. "Settle down, everyone."

The general mayhem settled to a quieter general mayhem, a few giggles and laughs cutting through.

"On behalf of the school board, I'd like to welcome you all to a new year at Stonehill Middle School. We have our first pep rally tomorrow afternoon, the Harvest Ball dance next month, and the best football team ever, right, Coach?"

Coach Berman raised his arms in triumph as a bunch of boys cheered from the back of the auditorium.

"Stonehill rocks!" someone yelled.

Kara started to relax as Mr. Edwards continued his welcome-to-school speech. Okay, this is working. No one will notice me—

BOOK 2: ALL THAT GLITTERS

A *pop* sounded under her seat.

Heather and Tiffany looked at her.

"S'cuse me," Kara said, patting her tummy.

"Pook?"

"Go away!" Kara whispered, dropping her books on the floor.

"Splaaa . . ." Fiona disappeared in a burst of red.

"Along with sports, we also pride ourselves on academics and community service," Mr. Edwards was saying.

Pop! Pop! Pop!

Kara look around. Oh, no, those little—where were they?

"We have some terrific school projects planned for this year," the principal continued, "and some of our students are getting involved in community projects, building leadership and responsibility, working to help our town, demonstrating qualities we can all be proud of."

"Woohoot!" Blaze hung down from the front of Kara's beret. She shoved him inside and adjusted the hat, smiling as Tiffany gave her a quick look.

"The mayor has commissioned a group of students to work on something we can all share in, the Ravenswood Wildlife Preservation Society." Principal Edwards beamed.

What?

"Keekee, play!" Barney pulled at Kara's finger. He was sitting in her lap.

She squashed the purple pest into the pocket of her jacket.

The principal was looking around the auditorium for someone.

Oh, no! Kara shrank down in her seat. Do *not* go there!

"And the town council has appointed Kara Davies president of the Ravenswood project."

Kara slid farther down into her seat as whistles and laughter went up from the crowd.

"Kara, come up." The principal beckoned. "I know this is unscheduled, but we're so proud of the example you're setting for the entire student body. Come on up and tell us about the great work you'll be doing."

"No, thank you," Kara squeaked.

"Kara!" Tiffany laughed. "Get up there!"

"I, like, *so* do not want to go up there!"

But her friends were already pushing her from her seat. This has got to be a bad dream, no, a horrible nightmare, she thought, walking onto the stage.

"Thank you, Mr. Edwards."

"Weekoook."

Kara pulled down hard on her hat.

"So tell us, Kara, are you excited to be president of the new organization?"

"Huh? Oh, yeah, it's good to help animals." What a lame-o, she thought, mortified.

"Uh-huh . . ." The principal was looking at her expectantly.

"We hope to open the preserve again soon and teach

people about conservation and protecting wildlife, and we have our own web—'Skooo'—too." Kara slapped her pocket.

Startled, Mr. Edwards glanced at her. "Excellent. Let's have a hand for a fine example of one of Stonehill's most promising young people."

Kara sent her best smile into the audience.

"Kookoo!"

Kara slapped her head—and felt hair. Out of the corner of her eye something moved. Kara watched in horror as her pink beret slowly inched across the stage floor. She shot out her foot and pinned it down.

"KaAsplaaP!"

The auditorium fell silent. Heather, Molly, and Tiffany sat with mouths agape.

Uh-oh.

Kara's hair unfurled like a bright neon rainbow flag.

She felt the hot flush run from her shoulders to her face as the auditorium suddenly erupted in hoots, jeers, and hollers.

Kara stood in the middle of the stage, alone, her world falling apart.

"Ms. Davies!" the principal said in shock. "What is the meaning of this outrageous display?"

Kara felt two inches tall. She was being reprimanded by the principal in front of the entire school. This was it, her life was over. She'd be the laughingstock of the school forever.

"It's symbolic!" someone yelled from the middle of the auditorium.

All eyes turned to the girl who had stood up. It was Emily.

Kara froze. This was much worse than any monster she had faced.

"Beg pardon, young lady?" the principal asked Emily.

"Kara is symbolizing the true meaning of the Ravenswood Wildlife Preservation Society, a rainbow coalition of all species working together. We live in one world, so everyone should work together to save the animals and our planet."

The principal looked at Kara expectantly.

She nodded quickly, smile frozen in place.

"Ms. Davies!"

Kara flinched.

"Fabulous!" He beamed. "Truly inspired! What a wonderful symbolic message to the world!"

Kara took over, instincts kicking in. "Thank you, thank you. Let's all work together to make our world a better place." She raised her fist in the air. "Animals are people, too!"

The crowd went crazy, cheering and clapping, as Kara left the stage, the envy of everyone.

Mr. Edwards was scratching his head but smiling. "Thank you, and welcome to another school year."

With assembly over, everyone bolted for the doors.

Molly, Tiffany, and Heather came running through the crowd as kids pressed in to look at Kara's amazing hair.

"Oh, Kara, it's gorgeous!"

"Kara, that is the coolest thing ever!"

Emily and Adriane stood in the hall, waiting to one side as the students spilled out. Kara was all smiles, grinning ear to ear.

Pushing past the crowd, Kara crossed over to Emily. "That was incredible, what you just did," she whispered.

Emily smiled. "That's what friends are for."

16

$\mathcal{A}$T LUNCHTIME, KARA walked through the cafeteria to cheers and waves.

"Kara, over here!" Tiffany, Heather, and Molly had saved prime spots under the shade of a sprawling oak. Kyle, Marcus, and Joey sat nearby with trays overflowing with spaghetti.

A quick scan of the area revealed no sign of those pesky dragonflies and no wild animal sightings. Kara crossed the lawn to join her friends, her rainbow-bright hair flowing in the wind.

"Kara, you are something else!" Marcus said.

"Yeah, no wonder the place was a mess last night," Kyle snickered. "Mom and Dad yelled at me, but I told them it was all your fault."

"Thanks, you're a pal," Kara said, sitting down.

"Why didn't you say something?" Tiffany asked.

"Spill it, girl, how'd you do it?" Heather studied Kara's hair.

"There must be a hundred colors!" Molly exclaimed.

Kara noticed Emily and Adriane coming out of the cafeteria, balancing trays and surveying the crowded tables.

"Well, I had some help." Kara waved. "Emily! Over here!" She ignored the look Heather and Tiffany gave each other.

Emily tapped Adriane and nodded in Kara's direction. They walked over, Adriane scowling behind Emily.

Heather frowned. "Do we have to sit with them?"

Kara ignored her.

"No wonder you wanted to end the barbecue early," Tiffany said. "You were planning this all along!"

"Believe me, no one was as surprised as I was," Kara replied.

Molly slid over to make room for Emily. "I just love what you did with Kara's hair. It's so original. Could you do mine, too?"

"It wouldn't be original then, would it?" Adriane smirked as she took a seat beside Emily.

Once again, Kara found herself in the middle: Emily and Adriane on one side, Tiffany, Heather, and Molly on the other. Well, this is interesting, she mused. No nuclear explosions . . . yet.

"Oh, I don't care." Molly smiled. "I think it's so rad!"

"Actually, it was Adriane who did my hair." Kara glanced at Adriane and held out a hank of multicolored hair for everybody to admire again.

Tiffany and Heather looked shocked. "What?"

"Who'd a thunk under all that black is a fashion designer!" Kyle called out.

"I'm not big on fashion," Adriane said quietly.

"That's for sure," Heather said out of the corner of her mouth.

Adriane glowered, putting her hands on the table. Her loose lanyard bracelet slid down her wrist to reveal her tigereye jewel. It flashed with bright gold light.

Heather's eyes widened. "How did it do that?"

"They react to light," Emily said quickly. Trying to distract attention from Adriane's jewel, she showed them her own rainbow jewel in its simple woven bracelet.

"You have one, too?" Molly gazed in awe at Emily's bright stone. "Where can we get them?"

"These jewels are totally unique," Kara explained, twirling her own on her silver necklace. "You can't get one."

"*They* have one!" Tiffany huffed.

"All part of our plan to get attention for the preserve," Emily told them.

"Can we come and check it out, too?" Molly asked excitedly.

"And get our own light-up jewels?" Heather echoed.

"*No!* Uh . . . I mean—" Adriane flushed.

"Of course you can visit the preserve," Emily said. "But we have a lot of work to do there first."

As Kara listened, she couldn't help but be struck by the realization that her friends—Heather, Tiffany, and Molly—only days ago were totally making fun of the preserve. And now, they were, like, all over it, all because they wanted "light-up" jewels. That is so shallow, Kara thought. And she knew she'd been exactly the same way. Or maybe she still *was* exactly the same way.

"The whole point is helping animals," Emily said.

"Just wait till you hear about the big fund-raising party," Kara told them. "We're going to have music, just like Live Aid!"

"Excellent! We're in on that!" Heather's eyes lit up.

Marcus glanced over. "Yeah, like who?"

"Well . . . Linny Lewis or Sampleton Malls, maybe."

"Choke! That is so lame!" Joey sauntered over, brushing back a lock of dark hair from his face. "What about Toad Force?"

"Or Smash Fish," Adriane put in.

Joey looked at her in surprise. "Yeah, all right!"

Kara almost laughed. Had Adriane actually blushed? She looked again, but Adriane was studying her tray as the boys moved off, heading back inside.

"Hey, rainbow girl!" Kyle called over his shoulder. "Press is here!"

Two eighth graders approached, carrying cameras and notepads. "Can we get a picture for the Stonehill Journal?"

"Cool. Sure." Kara stood and fluffed her hair, fanning out the bright colors.

"Right. Outstanding hair," the older girl said, snapping a picture.

"Thank you, it's symbolic."

The girl with the camera stepped forward. "How about a group picture?"

"Come on girls, photo op," Kara said, pulling Emily and Adriane over to her.

Side by side they stood, three together, Kara in the middle, rainbow hair flaring behind her. She put an arm around each girl and actually felt a connection, the bond of Ravenswood—and magic.

TO: Daddy1@townhall.hill.net
RE: RWPS update
Hey Daddy,
Guess who? It's me! We're getting our picture in the paper, Emily, Adriane and me for the Ravenswood Wildlife Preservation Society, isn't that cool? I know you will be so proud. Oh, and don't freak out when you see my hair, it's symbolic. I'll explain later. That's where we are on the RWPS for now.

Kara sat in study hall, laptop open in front of her. But her eyes kept wandering toward the window in search of unidentified flying animals. Ravenswood was on the map now whether she liked it or not. Everyone knew about it. But wasn't that the point? Wasn't that why the town council had allowed the girls to keep the preserve open and get the website up?

Of course it was, and she was doing a fantastic job. Even Emily and Adriane had to admit it. So why couldn't they just fit in with her group? Why did she have to do this juggling act? No matter what she did, it seemed someone got hurt. And that made her feel . . . awful.

Emily was sweet and pretty sharp. Kara was growing to like her more and more, and after that amazing save this morning, she owed Emily big time. And Kara got the feeling Emily wouldn't hold it over her, wouldn't expect anything in return except to be treated with respect and an open mind. Is that what made a real friend?

But Adriane—Kara and that girl would never get along, end of story. They were just too different, they had nothing in common. Kara twisted the sparkling jewel in her hand. Except this: magic.

Kara sighed and went back to her e-mail. Funny—the words looked wrong. She rubbed her eyes. The letters seemed weird. She looked closer. Words were stretching and starting to move around the screen. How bizarre!

Suddenly she felt her stone pulsing like a heartbeat.

The words on the screen were stretching, shifting around like pieces of a puzzle.

I

The letter turned red and started to melt down the screen.

know

Words from her e-mail were fading . . .

who

. . . leaving only a few that turned red.

you

The last words remained . . .

are

. . . dripping like blood.

I know who you are.

Fear crept up her spine. She shivered, quickly hitting keys to try to clear the screen. Nothing worked. Who was sending this?

Blood-red letters melted down the screen around two hard, cold eyes that stared at Kara. They were magnetic and vicious—half-human, half-animal. Kara froze. It was the same evil face she'd seen in the mirror.

The animal-woman pointed a finger and the laptop screen seemed to stretch, bulging outward. Kara's stomach knotted in fear as a sharp silver claw pushed through the screen, reaching for her.

She gasped and slammed the laptop closed.

I know who you are.

17

"THAT'S *IT*!" KARA stormed into the Ravenswood Manor library. Emily and Adriane were sitting before the computer screen, scrolling through information. Balthazar, Ozzie, and Ronif peered over the girls' shoulders.

"Something is in my computer," Kara announced angrily.

They all turned to stare at Kara.

"Your computer?" Emily echoed.

Kara dumped her backpack on a table, pulled out her pink laptop, and handed it to Emily. "Look!" she said. "Please."

Emily flipped open the laptop and turned it on. Adriane came around to watch. Kara backed away, nervously twirling a strand of purple hair in her fingers.

"Oh, no!" Adriane exclaimed in horror.

Kara jumped back. "Be careful! I told you!"

Adriane turned the computer toward Kara. The screen displayed her desktop with the new Linny Lewis wallpaper she had made.

"Linny Lewis is after you?" Adriane laughed.

"*No!* Lemme see that!" Kara marched over to look.

To her relief, the screen was perfectly normal. "Something weird is going on around here," she said.

"You mean weirder than normal?" Adriane asked.

"Yeeaaah . . ." Kara said, looking into the faces of a talking ferret, two quiffles, and a pegasus.

"Maybe your computer has a virus," Emily ventured.

Kara shook her head. "Someone left a message."

"What message?"

"It said, 'I know who you are.'" Kara shivered. "How creepy is that?"

"Maybe it read the Stonehill Journal," Adriane cracked.

"Oh, very funny! And if she did, she'd know who *you* are, too! But it's all happening to me!"

"She?" Balthazar asked.

"I think so. She had these weird eyes." Kara twisted her gem in her hand.

"That jewel," Adriane said. "It's been nothing but trouble!"

Kara glared at her.

"Kara," Emily said, "ever since you found it, these creatures have been after you, right?"

Kara swallowed. "Um . . . sorta . . . maybe."

"Maybe what?" Adriane asked.

"The night *before* I found this jewel, one of those banshees was in my room. It took my pink sweater. Why did it do that?"

Emily turned back to the computer screen. "We've found some files that Mr. Gardener left." She clicked on a book-shaped icon. A heading in an old-fashioned scroll spread across the top of the page. "Creatures of Magic." Below was a list of names, each accompanied by a picture.

Emily scrolled down. Some of the creatures they recognized: jeerans, pegasi . . .

"There's quiffles!" Ronif exclaimed.

The creatures became darker, more bizarre, some hideously ugly and monstrous.

"Eww, creep me out!" Kara made a face.

"Any of these look familiar?" Emily asked.

"No."

"There's a manticore," Ozzie pointed out. The terrifying winged demon looked out from the screen. Even though it was only a picture, its razor teeth and blood-red eyes sent chills up and down Kara's spine as she recalled facing the real thing only weeks before.

"Wait, open that one," she instructed.

Emily clicked on the thumbnail and the screen filled with an image of the ragged creature Kara recognized from the glade and the sunroom.

"That's *it*," Kara said, backing away. "Only it doesn't have that green stuff."

"You mean Black Fire," Balthazar nodded.

"The ones we saw looked badly poisoned," Ronif confirmed.

"Banshees," Emily read. "Creatures of fairy that have been cursed. They have long, streaming hair and ragged clothes. Eyes are fiery red from constant weeping. Banshees cry because they foretell darkness and pain."

"Like messengers of bad news?" Adriane asked.

"They were monsters, not messengers," Kara said.

"There are a lot of poor creatures on Aldenmor that wander the Shadowlands," Balthazar said. "Hideous and twisted by dark magic."

"What's the Shadowlands?" Emily asked.

"A place on Aldenmor. It used to be beautiful forests and meadows until the witch destroyed it."

"It's where Black Fire comes from," Kara informed them.

They all looked at Kara.

"Lyra told me. She was there. She was captured by hunters and brought to this castle where this . . . person was torturing animals."

"That's terrible!" Emily cried, outraged.

"Lyra escaped, but her sisters didn't." Kara felt the cat's sadness, connected to it somehow.

"We know of this Dark Sorceress," Balthazar shuddered.

"A terrible witch who hunts animals," Ronif added.

"Lyra said she's stealing magic from the animals," Kara continued.

"Trying to force animals to make magic," Ozzie grimaced. "It's a complete perversion of the magic. Horrible!"

"But we know *our* magic is stronger with our animal friends," Emily reasoned.

"And the legends that say humans and animals once worked together to make strong magic," Balthazar agreed.

"Well, now the animals have defenders to protect them!" Adriane punched her fist into her palm for emphasis.

"That's right!" Ozzie sprang to his feet. "Let's go!"

"Ozzie." Emily caught his tale and pulled the agitated ferret back. "We don't know what we're up against yet."

"But I'm not an animal," Kara argued. "Why is this sorceress after me? And she can't have my jewel!"

"Why would she want your jewel and not ours?" Adriane asked.

"Cause mine's better," Kara quipped, then added, "I don't know, but she's not getting it and neither are those banshees."

Adriane pointed back to the computer monitor. "According to this, 'Banshees foretell dark magic and the fate of those who are touched by evil.'"

"How do they do that?" Emily asked.

Adriane read on. "They wash an article of clothing of the one who is tainted."

Kara felt the blood rush from her face. "It was washing my sweater. What am I going to do? I'm tainted!" she wailed. "Do I smell bad?"

"Kara, don't you think there's something odd about your jewel?" Emily asked.

"What do you mean?"

"What did it look like when you first found it?" Adriane asked Kara.

"Just like this." Kara held out the dazzling gem.

"Ours changed as we used them, as if they became tuned to us."

"That would make sense," Ozzie added. "Magic jewels are tuned to a specific person. Only they can use it."

"Well, mine got here all powerful and ready to go. So what?" Kara clutched the stone close. "Just takes some time to learn to work it right." But she knew she had none of the control Emily and Adriane had over their magic.

"Kara, maybe that jewel is not for you," Emily said slowly.

"How do you know when a jewel is really for you?" Kara held up the magic stone. Bright facets cast sparkles across her face.

"You just know, Kara," Adriane replied. "It's like they reflect a part of who we are."

"Well, those banshees aren't after *your* jewel, they're after . . . mine." Kara realized what she was saying. Her jewel was different. But how? What part of her did it reflect? Did the banshees know *she* would be the one to find this jewel? Was she tainted with dark magic?

"If this sorceress is hunting animals, she may want the jewel to trap an animal," Balthazar suggested.

"Oh, no!" Kara's mouth opened in horror. "Do you think she's after Lyra?"

"Kara, this isn't just your problem," Emily said.

"We're in this together," Adriane agreed.

"That's right, we all are," Ozzie said, waving a paw to include the other animals.

"So what do we do?" Kara asked.

"Whoever is after that jewel will come back for it." Adriane looked at the others. "We'll just have to be ready to deal with it."

"So I'm supposed to wait around like a sitting quiffle?" Kara complained. "No offense," she said to Ronif.

"Those water creatures told you the jewel is a trap, right?" Emily said.

"Yeah . . . but they were confusing me and I sat on one."

"We think they were Fairimentals, like the ones that came to us made of earth and twigs," Emily explained.

"Kara," Ozzie said. "The Fairimentals sent me to find three human mages, a healer, a warrior, and a blazing star."

"So?"

"So . . . we don't know what a blazing star is . . ."

"What's your point?"

"Maybe you're not the one . . ." Ozzie said cautiously. "The blazing star."

Kara was speechless. How could she *not* be the blazing star? She found the most fabulous jewel! Had she only found it by accident?

"But Ozzie," Emily said. "Kara makes magic happen stronger when she's around us."

"So do we," Ronif pointed out.

"What, so now I'm like a magical animal?" Kara scoffed.

Ozzie tapped his chin thoughtfully. "Kara obviously conducts magic, like the animals do, so maybe the jewel is a test."

"A test? Why are they testing me and not Emily and Adriane?"

"Maybe they're being tested in different ways. But this time the Fairimentals came to you. We don't know what a blazing star is. But three mages are needed to help Aldenmor and the animals."

"I want this to be mine so bad!" Kara admitted, holding the crystal tightly. But even if it only attracts bad magic?

"I'll ask Storm to watch out for you," Adriane offered.

"All the animals are on the look-out for anything unusual," Ozzie put in.

"So, are we all agreed?" Emily asked.

Adriane and the animals nodded.

"All right," Emily said. "In the meantime, we continue to sort out this website information and separate what we want to hide."

"Mr. Gardener left us a lot of stuff here," Adriane said.

"Yeah, and look what happened to him," Kara moaned.

"We don't know what's happened to him," Adriane pointed out.

"Exactly!" Kara grabbed her backpack and laptop. "Okay, I can't believe I'm saying this, but I'm going home to do homework. Maybe it will take my mind off this crazy stuff."

"Okay, but no more magic," Emily cautioned.

"Yes, Mother."

"Anything happens, you call us, right?" Adriane prompted.

"Yes, Father."

Adriane narrowed her eyes, then smiled. Kara smiled back, and suddenly everyone broke out laughing. Kara tried to hold the good feelings close, a shield to push back her fears. But inside she could not help but think about what the banshees foretold: dark things were coming. How were they supposed to fight a sorceress destroying an entire world when they barely understood their magic?

Ozzie had been sent from Aldenmor to find three mages. The healer, which Emily had proven herself to be, the warrior, who could only be Adriane, and a blazing star. She was undoubtedly a star: smart, cute, the center of attention, impeccably groomed—but was that enough? She couldn't ignore the awful feeling that something wasn't right. That she might not be good enough. But one thing had become crystal clear. Kara wanted this more than anything in her whole life. And she always got what she wanted.

18

THE REST OF the week went by in double Kara time as she dove into a whirlwind of school and social activities. It was almost as if things were . . . normal. Well, as normal as they can be when your hair is a hundred different colors and then some.

On Saturday morning, Mrs. Davies dropped Kara at the Stonehill Galleria Mall. The enormous glass-and-chrome complex might have been daunting to some, but not to Kara. Huge skylights capped the ceilings and mirrored hallways ran past stores, all leading to the coin-scattered fountains and immense food court in the central atrium. She cruised the main floor past Eddie Bauer, Foot Locker, Hot Topic, Sharper Image, and The Gap. Chic fall fashions decked the window displays and SALE signs beckoned. Maybe later, she thought, when her hair would-n't clash with everything she tried on.

The food court was packed; some cooking show was giving product demonstrations and handing out free samples. Heading up the escalator, she spotted Heather and Molly going into Banana Republic. "Hey, homegirls! See anything good?" she called out cheerfully.

Molly waved back. "Just starting here. Then looping the place."

"Where's Tiff?"

Heather pointed to Tiffany, who held up a black three-quarter sleeve wrap top. Kara gave her a thumbs-up. Thrilled, Tiffany dove back into the racks.

"Meet us at the food court, K!" Heather called.

"Okay!" Kara rounded the second-floor escalator and headed up to the third floor.

The Clip Joint was in the corner, full of mirrors, funky chemical smells, and cool gray light from skylights that reflected an overcast sky. Lightning flashed, buried in the clouds. A few raindrops spattered on the glass, but inside it was warm and dry. Customers draped in gray chatted and leafed through magazines as hairdressers in black T-shirts and pants combed and cut and colored and coiffed.

Kara walked up to the receptionist, a girl with spiky black hair. "Hi, I'm Kara Davies. I have an appointment."

"Great hair! How did you get those highlights so bright?"

"It was a mixture of things," Kara replied. "But I want my original color back."

"Angela," the girl yelled to the back of the shop, "rainbow girl is here!"

A young woman with short blond hair came bustling across the room. "Come on back." Angela led Kara to a sink and sat her down. "Just relax, we'll get this water nice and warm," she said, wrapping a towel around Kara's neck and turning on the water. "I'll be just a minute."

"Okay." Kara sat with her back to the sink, looking at her rainbow reflections in the mirrors. Her hair was pretty amazing, she had to admit. Maybe I should keep it, she thought with a giggle.

A drop of water hit her in the face.

Kara glanced over into the sink.

"Web runner," whispered a familiar high-pitched voice. A tiny liquid figure swirled out of the steamy water. Another Fairimental. It was only inches high, its voice almost lost in the noise of the shop. Kara looked around. No one was paying any attention.

"Are you a Fairimental?" Kara whispered.

"I am water . . ."

Kara could see that the figure was struggling to hold its shape. She felt the great exertion and powerful magic it took for the Fairimental to come here.

"Look, what do I do with this jewel?" Kara asked quickly. "I can't make it work right."

"Some things are yours only for a short time," the watermental gurgled.

Oh no! Had Ozzie been right after all? Maybe she wasn't the blazing star.

"Beware, the Dark Sorceress is coming . . ."

Kara shuddered. "Is Lyra in danger?"

"She wants *you* . . ."

"I don't understand." Kara bit her lip. "What does she want from me?"

"Your magic."

Kara quickly glanced around the shop. Everything seemed normal. No one had noticed her talking to the sink. When she looked back, the Fairimental was gone. My magic? The water thingy said *my* magic. Her jewel hung around her neck, pulsing with diamond light.

"You sure you want to bleach this color out?" Angela said, returning to the sink.

Kara covered the jewel with her hands. "Yes."

Angela adjusted the chair, leaning Kara back over the shiny black sink.

"Never seen anything like it," Angela admitted, lathering up the hair. Kara forced herself to relax as Angela rinsed out the shampoo and worked in the conditioner. "We need this to set for a few minutes," she told Kara. "Back in a sec."

Kara moved her neck into a more comfortable position and felt her jewel warm in her hand. *My* magic. Through half-closed eyes, she gazed at the mirror across from her.

Images of the shop flickered on the glass, dim and unreal in the cool, stark light. The glass began to shiver as ripples spread and the surface seemed to fall away. A gossamer spider's web of lines interlaced and stretched back, reaching to infinity. Cool. Must be reflecting from the toy store across the hall, she thought. A small light moved along the grid, arcing its way toward Kara.

She stared as the spot of light took form, expanding into an image: a magnificent white horse with a long, flowing mane and tail, streaking like a comet across the web. Something flashed. A crystalline horn sparkled on the horse's forehead—just like the jewel she grasped so tightly in her hand. A unicorn! The majestic creature was something out of a dream—her dream.

Swish, swish . . .

Kara felt cold air rush over her.

"I'm sorry, but you can't come in here." The receptionist was trying to keep a ragged old lady from shuffling into the salon. The tattered thing was hunched over, face hidden under a long shawl.

Swish, swish . . .

Kara jerked up. "Oh, no!" This can't be happening! Not here!

"Please, you have to leave immediately," the receptionist said to the hunched creature. Outside the doors, Kara saw *another* banshee shambling toward the salon.

She jumped to her feet. "Storm!" she hissed. "Where are you?"

She frantically searched the salon. Where was that stupid wolf when she really needed her!

"Are you all right?" It took a second for Kara to realize the voice in her head was Lyra's.

"Lyra! They're *here*! In the mall! Where are you?" she whispered urgently.

"Nearby."

Kara moved to the front window, looking for the cat. "You can't come in here. People will freak out!"

SPLAT!

A third banshee smashed into the window. Its hideous face pressed to the glass, eyes red from weeping, empty dark openings where its nose and mouth should have been.

Kara leaped back. What do I do? I have to do something!

Her jewel raged like fire against her chest.

Darting past the trio of banshees, Kara ran out of the salon and skidded into the hallway of the mall. In the mirrored wall, her hair was wild, glued together with gobs of drying conditioner and sticking out in all directions. Something moved inside the mirror. The unicorn rose up on his hind legs, shook his mane, and leaped away. Kara ran after him, the banshees shuffling behind.

Kara rushed toward the open circle of the mall's center hub. Looking over the railing of the atrium from three stories up, she saw the food court spread out below, full of people.

Swish, swish . . .

Swish, swish . . .

Kara turned. Five banshees were closing in from both sides of the hub. She backed into the railing, trapped.

Something darted through the crowd below. An animal, big and spotted like a leopard. Lyra!

"I'm up here!" Kara screamed out to the cat.

"Hey, Kara!" someone called.

Kara looked down to see Molly, Tiffany, Heather, Joey, and Marcus at one of the tables.

"Hair looks much better!" Joey called out. They all laughed.

The big cat was headed right down the center of the food court. No, Lyra! You can't be here!

A wail made Kara turn. A banshee reached for her. Kara screamed, kicking it away.

A terrifying roar split the air. Lyra leaped up on a table, scattering food and drinks. She leaped to another, trying to reach the escalators. Pandemonium erupted as people ran screaming, trying to get out of the way of the ferocious beast.

"Help!"

"A leopard loose in the mall!"

"Call security!"

"Over here!" Kara yelled, waving to Lyra.

Thunder rocked across the atrium as lightning lit the skylights overhead.

Kara whirled—right into the face of another gruesome, grasping banshee. Burning claws sank into Kara's arm. The jewel flashed searing bright, instantly bathing Kara's arm in white light. She screamed and tried to twist away, but another banshee was at her back, filling the air with a foul, rancid sewer stink. Kara choked and tried to cover her face. A green hand was clawing at her necklace, trying to rip the silver chain from her neck.

Kara struggled to pull away and grabbed the railing. Below, police officers were entering the food court, walkie-talkies in hand as they rushed through the crowd. The view vanished as Kara lost her footing and went down, slamming into the hard floor. Her breath was knocked from her chest; she couldn't scream. Banshees clawed at her hair, her clothes, her flesh.

With a roar, Lyra crashed into the banshees, knocking them off Kara. The big cat stood crouched, teeth bared, growling dangerously at the creatures.

Kara stumbled to her feet. "Help! Help!"

"Up there!" someone yelled.

"The leopard!"

"It's got Kara!" Molly yelled.

"Oh, Kara!" Tiffany cried in panic.

Police rushed up the escalators. "Don't make any sudden moves!" they ordered.

Kara turned back. Lyra growled ferociously at the banshees, trying to keep them away. The officers thought the cat was attacking *her*!

"We have to get out of here!" she told Lyra urgently.

Lyra hissed. *"Go while I hold them off."*

The cat swiped at the banshees with a massive paw and they stumbled back.

Kara dashed around the circle all the way to the other side of the atrium. Security guards were trying to contain the crowds of curious shoppers below. The police moved cautiously toward the big cat, guns drawn.

"No!" Kara screamed. "Don't hurt her!"

Slowly fanning out, officers closed around the cat, trapping her against the balcony railing. Lyra snarled. She was surrounded.

"Kara!"

"Lyra!"

The cat crouched low and snarled. With a roar, she leaped.

The police scattered. One was too slow. Lyra's huge paws clipped his shoulder, sending him flying backward. A shot rang out, echoing like thunder across the cavernous atrium.

Kara watched in horror as Lyra soared into open air— she was trying to jump from one side of the atrium to another, a space of several hundred feet! The cat wasn't even halfway across when she lost momentum. She was going to plummet three stories with nothing to break her fall but the hard floor below!

Suddenly two iridescent golden wings fanned open from the cat's back! Lyra flew across the wide-open space and crashed to the floor by Kara's feet. The magical wings shimmered, folded close, and vanished. Sobbing uncontrollably, Kara buried her face in Lyra's thick coat.

"We have to move," Lyra urged. *"Now would be a good time."*

Kara looked up to see the astonished police running around the circle toward them. She jerked back sharply. "Oh no!" Her hands were full of blood. Lyra's blood.

Out of the corner of her eye, she saw something move. The unicorn! It was leaping from mirror to mirror, running toward an emergency exit at the end of the hall.

"I have to get you to Emily!"

Lyra stumbled to her feet and lurched forward. Kara helped the cat stay upright as they staggered down the hall. Reaching the door, Kara slammed into the security bar. The door flew open and a piercing alarm began to wail.

Kara and Lyra tumbled down two flights of steps and burst into another hallway.

"There! That side door!" Kara pointed. She urged Lyra forward, moving down the mirrored hall. Kara looked over her shoulder. No sign of any police. They were going to make it!

Thunder boomed and the lights dimmed. Kara saw herself reflected in the darkened mirror. Suddenly the reflection twisted, her face becoming strange and sneering. It was not her own image at all, but that of an older woman with silver-blond hair and the hypnotic, slitted eyes of an animal.

"I know who you are," the Dark Sorceress said, her voice smooth as velvet.

Kara was mesmerized. Every fiber of her being screamed at her to run, but she couldn't move. *I know who you are.* The message on her computer screen!

"You are right to be afraid." The animal-woman's words seemed to float through the air. "The banshees have foretold darkness will befall you."

"Call them off!" Kara cried. Her own voice sounded desperate to her ears, childish and high.

"Only magic can keep you safe," the sorceress continued. "But you need to make it truly yours."

"You mean with this?" Kara held up the jewel.

"Use it . . . and bring me what I seek."

"I won't let you take Lyra!"

"That pathetic beast is useless to me. You know what I want."

The sorceress jerked her finger upward, and the jewel around Kara's neck flew into the air. The chain tightened, biting into the back of her neck.

Smiling in triumph, the sorceress pointed.

Kara slowly turned. The unicorn stood in the mirror behind her. His eyes blazed with fury and desperation. The sorceress was hunting the unicorn all along. Yet there he was. Kara's heart felt like it would break as she realized using the jewel must have summoned him.

"You can take what you want. Or are you too afraid to use the jewel?" The sorceress twisted her hand, pulling the jewel closer, making Kara cry out in pain.

Her feet slid across the floor as she tried to pull away. "Lyra . . ."

The cat lay sprawled on the floor, blood pooling under her belly.

"You do not need anyone."

"Who are you?" Kara gasped.

"Don't you recognize me, dear?" the sorceress spoke. So cool, so casual, the words held no threat, no pain, just truth. "I am you."

Kara's eyes widened.

"You want magic. I can give it to you." The sorceress's eyes blazed, and for the first time, Kara tasted the full power of the jewel—it was overwhelming.

The hallway tilted at a dizzying angle. Diamond fire burst up her legs, twisting like snakes around her arms, rocketing into her brain and into the very depths of her heart. Power rushed through her like a tornado threatening to take her off the face of the earth. Stars exploded behind her eyes as magic crackled like lightning across the mirrors.

She couldn't stop it, she didn't want to stop it. With this jewel, she could do anything her heart desired and it was all hers!

The Dark Sorceress laughed, her animal eyes blazing as she reached a long silver claw though the glass.

With a sudden blast of white light, Kara was back in the hallway. Breathless, she turned to face the unicorn.

Pure and selfless, the creature was giving his magic to her, fighting to pull her back from the sorceress's grasp. Kara clung to the unicorn's magic like a shield. She felt caught between forces she could barely comprehend. But she knew that if she succumbed to the Dark Sorceress, the unicorn would fall with her.

The jewel flared around her neck. "I am not you!" Kara cried at the sorceress. She threw her hands in front of her and the power blasted outward, every ounce of it directed at the wicked face in the mirror.

Magic exploded in the hallway, shattering the glass. Shock waves ricocheted like gunfire as silver shards flew everywhere. Kara scarcely noticed as she pulled Lyra to the door.

"Hang on, please!" Kara kicked open the exit door and dragged Lyra into a driveway behind the mall. Black clouds swirled above while a cold, damp wind whipped through the parking lot. Thunder ripped across the sky and rain began to fall.

Kara hunched over Lyra's fallen body. Rain splattered her face, mixing with her tears. "Help me! Someone help me!"

"I am here," a voice said, clean and pure as the rain.

Kara turned. The unicorn stood on the pavement not four feet away. The creature was magnificent: tall, lean, and muscular, with a lustrous white satin hide and long silky mane and tail curling in the wind. A scalloped crystalline horn protruded from its forehead, glistening with faint rainbow colors.

"Please," Kara sobbed, trying to lift the heavy cat. "I have to help my friend."

"We must ride . . ." the musical voice echoed strong and certain inside Kara's mind.

The unicorn knelt before her. Kara stared, openmouthed, as she realized the creature had come to help her.

Gasping, she pulled and pushed and managed to hoist Lyra's limp body across the unicorn's neck. The great magical beast rose, standing tall and strong, his horn glowing like a crystal beacon pointing defiantly at the darkened sky.

Gripping a handful of silky mane, Kara leaped up on the unicorn's back. With a snort and a nod of its head, the unicorn bolted. Across the pavement of the parking lot and into fields beyond they ran. Kara could no longer make out features of the landscape that flew by in a blur. Faster and faster, they galloped across the open meadow—then, with a great leap, they vanished, burning across the sky like a blazing star.

19

KARA STOOD ON a beach, watching waves rolling lazily upon the warm sands. Thick mist obscured something hidden on the horizon. Roiling clouds sparkled like distant lightning. Under a dawning sky, the wind became whispers, as dozens of willowy wraithlike figures surrounded her. Draped in delicate, flowing robes of gossamer, they had enormous eyes, exotic in the half-light. Sparkling emerald hair cascaded over faces with beautiful pale skin, smooth and flawless, untouched by age and time.

Surely she was dreaming.

"Is she the one?"

Kara heard them talking, studying her. She sensed warmth, but something else, too. Expectation? Excitement?

"The unicorn came to her!"

The wraiths swirled around her.

"She wields the jewel!"

One of them glided close to Kara, impossibly beautiful and flowing with light. Kara's fear seemed to melt away.

"Where am I?" she asked.

"You are safe here, child."

Another wraith floated around her. "The jewel you hold is the most powerful of magic. It has been lost to us for hundreds of years."

"Many have suffered trying to retrieve this jewel."

"You can't take this." Kara clutched the jewel. "I need it."

"Do you think you are ready to wield its magic?"

Kara flashed on Lyra's bleeding body somewhere at the edge of her mind. "My friend is hurt, dying because of me." She felt her cheeks wet with tears.

The wraith fluttered. "Sometimes magic brings loss."

The first wraith faced Kara. "Close your eyes, child."

Kara closed her eyes. A soft breeze dried her tears.

"Now open them."

Kara blinked and looked out at the gleaming ocean. The strange glowing mist still hid whatever lay underneath.

"Do you see any difference?"

"No," Kara said, confused.

The wraith sighed, a sound like the wind crying.

"Only those who truly understand the magic can find Avalon."

"Where is Avalon? How do we get there?"

"There are fairy maps to guide the blazing star."

Kara's heart sank. Phel had tried to give her a fairy map, and she had destroyed it. "I ruined everything, didn't I?"

"Everything changes," the first wraith said. "Changing all the time. It is the way of magic. There is always another chance to make a difference."

"I have to help my friend," Kara pleaded. "Please, let me keep the jewel."

"Go now. And when you are ready, you will find your way back to us."

"Kara!" As they sang out her name, chills coursed through her body.

"Kara . . ."

The figures swirled around her, blazing into bright ribbons of light.

"Kara, are you all right?"

Grass tickled her nose as she opened her eyes. She was lying in an open field at Ravenswood. The dark sky was filled with menacing clouds. Slowly, shapes came into focus. Ozzie was looking down at her, concerned and frightened. Adriane was touching her shoulder, her face grim.

"What happened?" Kara asked, struggling to sit up. She grasped the jewel still hanging around her neck and let out a sigh of relief.

"Storm brought us here," Adriane told her.

Kara's breath caught in her throat. "Lyra!"

"Emily's trying to heal her," Ozzie said worriedly. "But we need your help."

Across the field, Emily leaned over the still body of the cat. Ronif, Rasha, Balthazar, and some of the other animals stood nearby. Kara got to her feet and rushed to Emily's side. "Can you heal her?"

Lyra lay in the grass, her beautiful fur caked with blood.

"She's not responding to my magic." Emily wiped at her eyes, red from tears. "I couldn't help her when she was burned, either."

"Yes you did, Emily!" Kara gripped Emily's shoulders, making the girl look at her. "You healed Ozzie, you healed Ariel, you even healed Phel! You kept Lyra from dying. You can do it again."

"But I had Phel's magic to help me," Emily cried.

"And now you've got ours!" Kara held up her jewel, radiant in her hand. She called to the animals, "We need your help."

"Hurry everyone, gather 'round!" Ozzie ran about, herding the animals closer.

"Tell us what to do, Emily," Adriane pleaded.

"Concentrate as hard as you can on giving her strength."

The cat's sides barely rose and fell with her shallow breaths.

Kara tried to visualize pushing her own energy into

Lyra, reviving her, healing her. Light from her jewel began to pulse between her fingers.

Ronif suddenly looked past the huddled group. "We have company."

A dozen banshees surrounded them. Rain pasted their filthy rags to their sickly glowing bodies.

"Keep focused on Lyra!" Kara ordered.

With piercing wails, the banshees began to close in on them, arms outstretched, grasping. The weeping cries broke the animals' concentration, and Lyra's breathing grew ragged and weaker.

"What do we do?" Rasha asked.

"There's too many of them!" Ozzie looked around frantically.

"You have to keep them away!' Emily exclaimed. "We need time!"

Adriane sprang to her feet. "We'll hold them back. Storm!"

"I am here." The mistwolf materialized from the shadows, golden eyes shining.

The banshees shambled forward, weeping madly. Facing the creatures, Adriane and Storm stood side by side. Arms crossed in front of her, the warrior assumed a fighting stance. Storm's eyes blazed, matching the gold light that flashed from Adriane's gem.

"Stay with me, Storm." Adriane swung her arm, streaming arcs of bright magic. She whirled around, spinning the light into a ring. Storm crouched low, teeth bared, as Adriane turned faster, building ring upon ring of magic. Faster and faster she spun, surrounded by expanding loops of golden fire.

Kara bent over Lyra and grasped Emily's hand. White diamond sparkles burst from Kara's jewel, running up and down her arms like electricity. With a wave, the magic leaped into Emily's jewel.

"Focus on her heartbeat. Keep it strong," Emily instructed. Green-blue light from her rainbow gem began to pulse in a steady rhythm.

Kara's jewel fell into sync with Emily's, flashing with the beat of their hearts.

"That's it," Emily said.

Magic streamed out of Emily's jewel, enveloping the cat in a cocoon of glowing rainbow light.

Suddenly the light shifted as if it were being pulled away. "I can't hold it!" Emily cried. The magic flew apart, spreading wildly out across the field.

Kara felt Lyra's pulse drop. "Don't let her go, Emily!"

"Hurry," Ozzie urged, watching the banshees approach.

Kara saw Adriane spinning like a top. Black hair whirling around her, Adriane began to rise into the air. She flipped into a somersault and sent the glowing rings of magic flying outward. Waves of light crashed into the banshees, knocking them back with the force of the blow. The warrior whipped golden fire into a huge ring about her head. Then with a snap of her wrist, the ring soared over the banshees and floated down around them. The warrior pulled tight, trying to keep the banshees away from Kara. Suddenly the golden magic burst apart, splintering across the open field.

The banshees scrambled forward again, reaching madly for Kara.

Power exploded from Kara's jewel, blasting diamond fire around the field. Magic zigzagged like wild lightning. Suddenly, ground trembled; the air twisted and ripped open. Amazed, the girls and animals looked into the looming maw of the portal.

20

"THE PORTAL'S OPENED!" Ozzie screamed.

Glistening strands sparkled behind the thick, swirling mist that covered the portal. Wind whipped at the girls as they backed away.

The banshees staggered backward, covering their faces.

In a shimmering green flash, a black-cloaked figure took form and stepped out of the portal. Long, slender fingers drew back the hood, revealing green animal eyes and cool, porcelain skin framed by silvery hair slashed by a bolt of lighting.

It was her—the woman in the mirror. The Dark Sorceress.

"So, it has come to pass," the sorceress sneered. "Three new mages. Clumsy and inept, yet you wield magic."

Kara's blood turned to ice. She saw the animals shrinking away from the evil apparition.

The figure looked past Kara and regarded the banshees, who cowered on the ground in fear. "Persistent, I'll give you that much," she told them. She turned cold animal eyes to Kara. Her voice was soft as silk and sharp as a razor. "They've been after the jewel for some time. How interesting that you should find it, don't you think?"

"Plesszze," a hideous voice crackled. It was a banshee. It looked at Kara. "Help uszz."

"Why don't you just take it, if that's what you want?" Kara asked the sorceress.

"I can't use it," the sorceress said softly, hypnotic eyes locked on Kara's. "It was meant for you."

Kara hesitated. *Was* the jewel meant for her? It had to be! After everything that had happened, she still held it in her hand. And the power, the magic—it felt glorious!

"You know your magic is the strongest, your jewel the most powerful. Don't deny what is yours. Use the magic and fulfill your destiny."

"Kara, don't listen to her," Ozzie implored. "You heard the Fairimentals. The jewel is a trap!"

The sorceress eyed the ferret and laughed. "What a cruel joke the Fairimentals have played on you. An elf in the shape of a . . . puny rat. Do you even remember who you are anymore?"

Ozzie backed away uncertainly.

"Don't use the jewel!" Adriane called out.

"I know what you want," the sorceress urged softly. "With this magic, no one can stop you. No one can tell you what to do. Use the jewel and make it yours forever."

Kara felt the words echo in her mind, taking hold.

"Kara, no!" Emily cried.

Adriane whipped her wrist and sent a bolt of magic arcing through the air. The Dark Sorceress raised her hand and the magic splintered into sparks, raining back over the girls and animals.

With a savage snarl, Stormbringer attacked. But the great wolf passed through the cloaked body as if the sorceress were a ghost. Storm danced away, snapping.

The sorceress stared at Adriane, eyes flashing with rage. "You bond with a mistwolf!" Her blood-red lips twisted with scorn. "Bonds can be broken." She turned back to the terrified banshees. "Useless creatures." She looked at Kara. "Now you may destroy them."

Kara steeled herself. This was why she wanted to have magic. Now she wouldn't have to worry about the banshees anymore. She could stop *anyone* who got in her way.

Kara raised the jewel, then stopped. "What do you want from me?"

"You must fulfill your destiny, as the banshees foretold."

A destiny of *dark* magic, Kara realized.

"You want me to use my jewel to call the unicorn," Kara said. "You want his magic."

The sorceress smiled, revealing sharp fangs. "You know how it feels to want magic, don't you?"

Kara faltered. The Dark Sorceress was right. Magic was everything she wanted.

"Prove yourself." The sorceress's eyes blazed with an inhuman glow as she pulled the final strings of the trap. "Call the unicorn," she instructed calmly. "He cannot resist your magic."

My magic. Kara tightened her grip on the jewel.

What should she do?

A banshee reached forward, clawed hand outstretched, sadness burned forever in crying eyes. "You must not take his magic."

Kara studied the ghastly face. But hideous as it was, the creature wept as if its heart was truly broken.

Some things are yours only for a short time.

Kara looked from the banshees to her friends, then at the beautiful glowing gem. "What if I never find another magic jewel? I want this to be mine!"

"Then you are truly like her!" wailed the banshee. "As it has been foretold."

To your own heart be true.

There is always another chance to make a difference.

The sorceress smiled so cruelly it made Kara sick. This was not how magic was supposed to work. How could she keep the jewel when each time she used it, it would bring her closer to being something so evil? How could she face herself? How could she face her friends?

The truth burned through Kara as powerful as any

magical force: even if she *never* found another one, this stone was not hers to keep. She was not the blazing star.

Kara lowered her hand. "You really think I'm like you?"

She felt for the clasp on her locket. The crystal hung quiet, cool, as she removed the stone—and gave it to the nearest banshee.

"No!" The sorceress's face contorted with fury. "You stupid child!"

Backing away, the banshee hissed and wrapped her clawed hands around the glowing jewel.

Kara whirled on the sorceress. "You don't know who I am."

Brilliant light streamed up into the sky, raining down over the banshees. Kara watched in amazement as the creatures began to change, their horrible faces and dirty rags transforming. The vile green glow dissolved and flowed away, revealing beautiful wraith-maidens who shone with clean, pure magic. The same wraiths Kara had just seen in her vision.

The image of the Dark Sorceress shuddered and warped, becoming transparent.

"Your magic is nothing without me to guide you," the sorceress hissed as she continued to fade. "Your precious animals will never be safe, here or on Aldenmor."

The spectral image twisted into mist and vanished.

The wraiths swirled around the girls with a sound like bells.

"We are free."

"Free of the evil spell."

"How do we stop that thing from coming back?" Adriane asked.

"You must construct a web of protection before the portal closes."

"How?" Emily asked.

Pop! pop! pop! pop! pop!

Dozens of rainbow bubbles appeared, dragonflies popping out all over, each one trailing streams of something behind them.

"What are they holding?" Emily asked.

"My hair!" Kara exclaimed.

The dragonflies zipped into the field, long strands of Kara's rainbow hair held in their mouths and paws. Fiona and Blaze darted past Kara with a dip and a wave, and Barney flapped by, glimmering lilac. The dragonflies lit the air with their shimmering eyes and an occasional tiny burst of fire. A little gold one buzzed in front of Kara's face, trailing a long strand of rainbow hair. "Keekee!"

"Goldie!" she exclaimed. "Can you build a web?"

Goldie chattered with perfect assurance and then flittered straight up above Kara's head, coughing out a fiery rallying cry. The busy little fliers tugged trailing streamers behind them like wisps of starlight, gossamer thin and glittering with raindrops. They flew off in different directions, warbling dragonfly calls and pulling the strands. Soon they had woven strands into a rainbow web.

"It's working!" Kara shouted.

"Use your jewels to power the web," the wraith said.

All around the girls, the animals gathered: quiffles, pegasi, brimbees, and jeeran. Emily and Adriane held up their jewels. The dragonflies fluttered in the air, holding the web in place over the portal.

Kara stood between her friends, arms outstretched. She reached out and touched Emily and Adriane's hands. Even without a jewel of her own, sparkling diamond light raced through her body and into the other girls' stones. This time, the magic felt right, made by a true heart and true friends.

As power poured into the strands, the dragonflies glowed more brightly, their jeweled eyes glistening like sequins. The rainbow colors of the web shimmered, and the droplets of water caught in its net sparkled like diamonds, reflecting the stars that twinkled behind in the darkness of the portal. The net stretched outward, then snapped tightly into place, perfectly woven with one hole in the center.

"Look at that!" Ozzie exclaimed.

"It looks like a—" Adriane started.

"—dreamcatcher," Emily finished.

The dragonflies had woven the strands of Kara's rainbow hair into a dreamcatcher.

"Only those who use good magic may pass through," the wraith said.

The wraiths swirled into the portal, their delicate bodies shining. As their pure magic touched the dreamcatcher, its rainbow strands flashed, strengthening the protection spell.

The portal swirled and vanished, leaving a blanket of light rain falling upon the forest. The wraiths were gone and the field was quiet.

Kara started to walk to her friends. Everyone stared, awestruck, at something behind her.

"What?" she asked in alarm.

The unicorn stood in the field, white as the purest snow. He bowed his head, horn sparkling with colors.

Kara approached the beautiful creature. "She wanted you all along, didn't she?"

"Yes."

Yet despite the risk, he had come to her. She hugged his neck, crying softly into his lustrous, smooth hide.

"I wanted your magic, too," she said, feeling an emptiness in her heart so vast, she felt she might cry forever.

"You have saved the fairy wraiths and helped all these animals."

"Now I have nothing," Kara sniffled.

"It is time for the magic to be renewed," the unicorn said. *"You are the blazing star."*

Kara's eyes widened. With a touch as soft as a kiss, the pain was gone. She lifted her head. "Will I see you again?"

"Yes. Go to your friends. They need you now."

Diamond light flared from the unicorn's horn. The magical creature reared back on his hind legs, magnificent and free. In a flash of light, he vanished.

Kara turned back to Emily, Adriane, and the animals. In the center of the group sat Lyra, green eyes flashing.

"Are you all right?" Kara ran over to the big cat.

"*Seems so.*" Lyra rubbed her head against Kara's cheek.

Emily smiled. "She's a little weak, but she'll be just fine."

"I was so scared." Kara hugged Lyra tight. "I thought I'd lost you."

"*You saved the unicorn,*" Lyra said. "*The most powerful of all magical creatures.*"

"Yeah, and I lost all my magic."

"*Not quite.*" The big cat gazed at Kara, waiting.

"Hey! I can still talk to you!" Kara exclaimed. "Even without the jewel!"

The cat looked at her, warmth and love in her eyes. "*Is that okay?*"

"Yes, it's okay!" Kara turned to her friends and shouted with joy. "I can still talk to her!"

Emily, Adriane, and the animals all smiled back.

"You did an amazing thing, Kara, giving your jewel to those fairy creatures," Ozzie said.

But Kara knew how close she had come to taking the unicorn's magic. The temptation to keep the jewel had nearly blinded her, but she had made her choice. She would choose to work with her friends and protect all magical creatures. Even without the jewel, she was the blazing star. Whatever magic she had was inside her, something no one could take away.

21

KARA SAT BACK in the soft leather chair, her laptop open beside her, feet propped up on an ornate footstool that stood on carved animal paws. She was in a pleasant sun-drenched sitting room overlooking the great lawn of Ravenswood Manor.

Kara shook out her restored blond hair. She was feeling better. For the first time in days, nobody was trying to kill her. She had been frantic about not showing up at home Saturday after that incident at the mall. But no one noticed. Her parents had been at the country club all day. Kara was in the clear. No one yelled, and she wasn't grounded. Another amazing magical moment. The only one upset was Kyle when he found out he'd missed all the action at the mall.

goodgollymolly: u ditched us at the mall
kstar: sry about that, I had to make sure the cat got
back to ravenswood safely
credhead: the whole mall shut down lol

Kara winced. The cat showing up at school was one
thing, having it run around the mall being chased by police was totally different. Even if the gunshot was accidental, the town council was not going to be happy, especially
Mrs. Windor, who would use this as more ammunition to
try to close down the preserve. The website just *had* to
work!

Emily and Adriane had spent the last two days detail-
ing the site. Now that they had the old Ravenswood files
as their base, the work went much faster. The data for the
public access section of the site was finished and ready.
They had an explanation of the RWPS, its mission to protect and educate about wildlife and endangered species,
plus directions to Stonehill and Ravenswood. Emily was
working on adding a section of pet tips and a list of animals on the tour.

Then there was the second, password-encoded level.
They had begun to add a compilation of everything they
had learned so far about magic. Combining that with files
already on the system, it was quite a collection, from
sketches of the duck-like quiffles that Adriane had drawn,
to a catalog of magic jewels and animals, and pictures of

beautiful dreamcatchers, like the one that now protected the portal.

> **goodgollymolly:** u don't care about us anymore :(
> **beachbunny:** what do you see in them?
> **credhead:** it's not like they give good parties and they're pretty far down the food chain as far as clothes go
> **kstar:** so they don't know clothes, that's not everything

There was silence. All IMs ceased ringing. Maybe she had gone too far with that one. But she was sure now of one thing.

> **kstar:** Ravenswood is really important to me. U know, credhead's got singing lessons, ggmolly's helping her mom with catering, bbunny has dance class, pretty soon we'll be trying out for all sorts of stuff. Does that mean we stop being friends?
> **goodgollymolly:** no :)

"Kara, we're almost ready!" Adriane shouted down the hall.

Kara closed down her IMs with an unaccustomed feeling. Was there anyone who really understood her?

The door pushed open and Lyra walked into the sitting

room. Her spotted fur shone in the sunlight streaming through the big windows.

"Where have you been?" Kara asked, annoyed.

Lyra stretched hugely. *"I thought you would like some space."*

"I don't need space." Kara glanced at the cat and back to the screen. "I like company."

"Really? I hadn't noticed." The big cat padded over and plumped down next to Kara's chair.

Kara sighed and gently scratched Lyra's neck. "It's just I always have all this stuff going on, school, friends, parties, and shopping. Before, I didn't have to choose, I was like a passenger in a car." She looked at the cat. "But now, this time . . . I'm driving the car." She pouted. "I don't know how to drive. I'm too young."

"Maybe you are too young," Lyra agreed. The big cat gazed evenly at the blond-haired girl. *"But you made a good choice, and I have faith that you will make more good choices."*

Kara smiled and gestured to her backpack sitting on the floor. "You like cat food?"

Lyra sniffed. *"Then again I could be wrong."*

"Kara, come on!" Adriane called out.

"Okay!" Kara called back. She shut down her laptop, picked up her backpack, and ran down the hall.

In the library, Adriane and Emily sat at the console looking at the RWPS homepage. Storm was stretched out by the window soaking up the sun. Ozzie, Balthazar,

Ronif, and Rasha were examining the screen, comparing it to a printout propped up beside them.

"So, we're, like, live?" Kara asked, laying her backpack on the table.

Emily smiled. "As soon as we connect to the council's server."

"That's great. What about the second level?"

"All we have to do is enter our password, and we'll have access," Adriane said.

"Anyone else who knows the password will be able to access us, too," Emily added.

They all looked at the keypad.

"Okay, are we ready?" Emily asked excitedly.

"Not quite," Kara said, standing beside the table.

Emily and Adriane looked at her.

"Before we open the site to the world . . ." The girls and animals studied her curiously. " . . . While this is still ours, at least for the next few minutes . . . I just wanted to . . . I mean, I thought we could—oh, never mind." Kara opened her backpack, pulled out a small box tied with a pink ribbon, and handed it to Emily. "This is for you."

Emily's eyes went wide. Adriane gave the gift a quick glance.

"Is it my birthday already?" Emily giggled.

"Go on, just open it," Kara instructed.

Emily untied the pretty ribbon, opened the box, and lifted out a sparkling silver bracelet. "Kara . . . it's beautiful!"

"Yeah, the clasp will hold your jewel securely around your wrist, see?" Kara helped Emily remove the jewel from its woven setting, attach it to the silver clasp, and lock the bracelet.

Emily held her arm up. The bracelet and jewel were a dazzling combination. "I love it, Kara. Thank you," she said, beaming.

Kara smiled, then looked at Adriane who quickly turned away as Kara reached in her backpack and held out another box.

"I can't take your gift," Adriane said, eyes downcast.

"Yes, you can, and you will!" Kara ordered. "If you're going to keep doing all that fancy jumping and flying stuff, how do you expect your jewel to stay in place, huh?"

Adriane's mouth twitched in a smile.

"Take it . . . please." Kara held out the box. "I want you to have it."

Adriane slowly took the box from Kara. She opened it and held up an exquisite black wristband inlaid with turquoise.

"This is too much . . ." Adriane gasped.

"You like it?"

"I . . . yeah, I do."

"You're welcome." Kara smiled at her.

Adriane smiled back.

"How could one ferret be so right?" Ozzie burst out. "I think I might cry!"

All three girls looked at the ferret.

"I've found all three mages, the healer, the warrior, and the blazing star! How great am I?"

They all laughed, bound together by the magic they shared and the friendship they were learning to trust.

"Okay! Let's get this club happening!" Kara exclaimed.

Emily sat at the console and connected to the council server.

Adriane stood next to Kara. "Remember when I told you the magic didn't like you?"

"Vaguely."

"I was wrong," Adriane admitted.

Kara arched an eyebrow. "Even though I gave it back?"

"It likes you *because* you gave it back," Adriane said.

Kara and Adriane smiled at each other. Emily couldn't help but smile, too, as the connection was made.

"Congratulations, ladies and gents!" Emily announced. "The RWPS homepage is live. I think it would only be fitting that our esteemed president be the one to officially open the magic web." She grinned at Kara. "Would you do the honors, please?"

Kara smiled at her friends and typed in the password that would announce to the world they had arrived: Avalon.

WELCOME TO
RAVENSWOOD WILDLIFE PRESERVE
Open 11 A.M. to dusk

Please stay on the paths and don't feed the animals. Take only pictures and leave only footprints.

Here, we are all explorers and students of nature. We all have a role in protecting our natural world and every creature that lives there. If we care for the earth, these special friends and wild places will be preserved and available for our families and future generations to enjoy.

THE RAVENSWOOD WILDLIFE PRESERVATION SOCIETY CREED:

- Respect our planet and all life forms we share with it.
- Preserve endangered and threatened animals and their habitats.
- Protect wild animals and wild places.
- Save all wonders of the living natural world.
- Value the wilderness and the wild things that live there.

CRY OF THE WOLF

1

SUNLIGHT FLASHED THROUGH the trees as the dark-haired girl ran, plunging wildly into the woods. Yellow, orange, and red leaves crunched under her boots as she dashed past towering maples, cherries, and ash. It had recently rained, and the woods smelled clean and crisp.

"Follow my voice."

Adriane Charday heard the words in her mind as clearly as if they had been spoken aloud. Listening closely, she turned toward an outcropping of rocks and leaped over a downed log, running hard, breathing steadily.

"You're getting cold."

Adriane turned sharply left, her long, jet-black hair blowing in her face. "We'll see about that."

With a quick sweep of her wrist, she cut her gemstone through the air. It sparkled gold from its setting in her black-and-turquoise bracelet, and Adriane smiled, confident she was on the right trail.

It had been a month since she and Emily and Kara had learned about the magic web: the network of magical energy that connected Earth to other worlds. They had discovered a portal to a world called Aldenmor and learned of the Dark Sorceress, her attempts to capture magical animals, and of the horrible Black Fire poison. At first, both monsters and animals from Aldenmor had come through the portal—right into the Ravenswood Wildlife Preserve, where Adriane lived with her grandmother. The animals all spoke of Ravenswood as a legendary sanctuary of magic and it had to be protected. With the help of some pesky little creatures called dragonflies, the three girls had woven a magical dreamcatcher over the portal, hoping it would let good things through while keeping evil creatures out.

But with magic you just never knew. The dragonflies didn't seem to need a portal at all—they just popped in and out of nowhere. Banshees that had stalked Kara had been able to move through water, and had even attacked her in the Jacuzzi. One thing was sure: magic was unpredictable. They had to expect the unexpected.

The discovery that magic was real was the most monumental thing that had ever happened to the girls. What was even more astounding was that each of them seemed to have a part to play in a larger puzzle, a mysterious destiny that required each girl's own unique talents as mages, human users of magic. Elemental beings were trying to protect the good magic of Aldenmor. They were called Fairimentals and according to some ancient prophecy they needed a healer, a warrior, and a blazing star to do . . . something. What that something was exactly, the girls didn't know. Neither did their magical animal friends. But whatever it was, it involved finding a mysterious hidden place, the home of all magic: Avalon.

Emily, the healer, spent a lot of time with the magical animals that had made Ravenswood their new home. When she wasn't with them or helping out at the Pet Palace, she was in Ravenswood Manor's incredible library, cataloging information about wildlife, both earthly and magical. More and more, too, she had emails to answer, as curious people began to surf their way to the Ravenswood blogs the girls had set up.

Kara, the blazing star, was President of the Ravenswood Preservation Society. She spent half her time setting up tour schedules, planning fund-raising parties, and reporting on their progress to her father, the mayor. The other half she spent making sure the town council never found out about the magical animals hidden at Ravenswood. Not all the members of the town council wanted a wildlife tourist attraction outside of their town, and Kara had to keep them reassured about their decision to keep the preserve open with the girls working there as guides.

Adriane felt it was essential to learn all she could about the magic she shared with her wolf friend. Her name was Stormbringer and she was a mistwolf, a creature of great magic. Storm had called Adriane "warrior" from the first moment they had met and the girl spent every spare moment practicing, experimenting, pushing herself further and faster, obsessed with embracing her new abilities, scared she could lose them.

She took a deep breath of crisp autumn air and lengthened her strides, stretching into the run. She and Storm had been playing this new game of hide-and-seek for about two weeks now, experimenting with the magic of her tiger's eye gem called the wolf stone. Each time Storm moved farther away, testing the limits of their connection. How far could they go from each other before the connection was lost? So far, they hadn't reached the limit—if there was one.

Through the trees, Adriane caught a trail of mist vanishing over a rise. She made a sharp right, and then sprinted up the hill, trying not to slip on the moss.

Brow furrowed, she concentrated on her stone and was rewarded with a quick image in her mind of Storm. The big silver-and-white wolf was just on the other side. With a grin, she crested the top, and leaped.

"Adriane!" Storm's voice cut through her mind. *"Watch out for that—"*

The image of the wolf vanished as Adriane flew through trails of fog with a startled cry.

"Oof!"

Her shoulder knocked into something hard and she landed in a pile of sticky leaves and twigs. Facedown.

Storm was loping toward her, tongue lolling.

"—tree," she finished.

The tree's oversized leaves had been holding rainwater—until Adriane had bumped into it. She glared up through her now sopping-wet bangs. "Thanks for the heads up."

"Are you all right?"

"I was concentrating so hard on seeing you, I didn't see what was right in front of me."

The wolf seemed to be laughing. *"You must learn to see the tree through the forest."*

Adriane spit out a piece of leaf. "That's forest for the trees." She sat up, picking matted leaves from her face and hair. "Oh, look at me!"

"Wait a minute," Storm commented. *"I think you missed a spot."* Her tongue flashed out, licking a bit of leftover leaf from Adriane's chin.

"Cut it out!"

The wolf's golden eyes danced with mischief. *"Hold it. Here's another one."*

Adriane squealed as Storm planted her big paws on the

girl's chest, knocking her flat onto her back, her tongue slobbering over every inch of her face.

"Forget it, that doesn't help!"

Storm lowered her head and pulled back.

Giggling, Adriane dug her fingers into the thick fur at the wolf's neck, then gave a heave and flopped her over. Together, girl and wolf rolled across the hill, then lay still, side by side, panting.

Adriane's down vest was now covered in leaves. Storm's coat had twigs sticking out of it.

"You look ridiculous," Adriane said, giving the wolf's stomach a thump.

"A mistwolf never looks ridiculous," Storm informed her. She rolled over onto her back and stuck her legs in the air, twisting from side to side in an attempt to dislodge the debris from her coat. *"Mistwolves are dignified and fierce."*

And alone, Adriane thought suddenly, her smile fading. There were no other mistwolves. Storm was the last of her kind.

Was it fate, or destiny, or just some haphazard random coincidence that she had met Storm? Maybe she'd just been lucky.

She sat and gazed at the forest spread out below. The autumn colors rippled like wildfire, blazing under the noon sun. Storm sat down beside her. Draping an arm over the wolf's back, Adriane pointed to a clearing in the forest off to the west. "See there by the Rivanna

River?" she asked. "That field is where I first found my stone, and you."

She looked at the beautiful amber-and-gold stone, the same color as the oak leaves that gently spiraled around them. She didn't know where the stone had come from; she knew only that finding it had made her feel special, as if it had been put there just for her. In her hands, the rough stone had transformed into a smooth, polished jewel in the shape of a wolf's paw, and a bond was made, forged like iron between a lone wolf and a lonely girl.

Taking a deep breath of crisp fall air, she leaned against Storm, comforted by the solid strength and furry warmth of the wolf. It occurred to her that just as the mistwolf's solid form could evaporate into mist, so could this luck disappear. Wasn't that what always happened? She felt the familiar knot of fear in her stomach starting to build.

Adriane remembered when she first arrived at Ravenswood, not even a whole year ago. She hadn't wanted to live with her strange grandmother in a weird house. She didn't want to have anything to do with Stonehill, Pennsylvania, at all.

This is *not* my home, Adriane had thought. And no one can make me say it is!

She'd been all over the world and had lived in all kinds of places because her parents were famous artists. Some people might think that was glamorous. It wasn't. It was lonely. Always moving from place to place. Never feeling she belonged.

She frowned. They hadn't even come with her—they had just dropped her off with a grandmother she barely knew and flew off again to who-knew-where. They sent postcards . . . sometimes.

"Do you want to talk about it?" the wolf asked.

Adriane made a face. "No."

"That probably means you should."

"What are you, my counselor or something?"

Storm didn't answer, and Adriane continued to lean against her, listening to the wolf's heartbeat, feeling the way Storm's chest moved in and out with each breath.

"My parents stuck me here, and I won't even see them till next summer," she said quietly into the wolf's soft fur. "They don't want me." There it was—she'd finally said the thing that had been a hard, hot ball of pain ever since she'd come to Stonehill.

Her parents didn't want her.

Like Storm, she was alone.

"You're feeling sorry for yourself again, aren't you?" Storm asked. *"You get this funny look on your face."*

"I do not." Adriane sat up.

Her long, dark hair fell over a scowling face. She knew she was acting like a grumpy two-year-old, gearing up to throw a tantrum. She tried to calm herself. "How come my closest friend in the world has four feet?"

Storm gave a strange bark that Adriane recognized as wolfish laughter. *"You're just incredibly lucky."*

Adriane grinned. "Did I miss out on the 'plays well with other humans' gene or something?"

Storm touched her cool nose to Adriane's cheek. *"I was without a pack until I met you."*

"What happened to the mistwolves, Storm?"

"They vanished. I have some memories from Aldenmor, but I feel like I have always been here, connected to the forests of Ravenswood."

"Don't you want to find out?"

"Our paths have led to each other. And together we will find the answers we seek."

"I can't even find you without a magic stone."

"You are my packmate. You will always find me."

"How can I be sure?"

Storm's warm golden eyes turned to look into Adriane's dark ones. *"Our bond is sure. Hold it tight and never let go."*

"I won't, Storm. Not ever." She hugged the wolf, burying her face in the soft silver fur. "It's everything."

"You must trust in your gifts."

"Sometimes you sound just like a human grown-up," Adriane said.

"There's no need to be insulting," Storm replied.

Adriane snorted. Storm had been right, as usual. Talking about the things that bothered her always helped, even if it didn't really solve them.

"Life is moving all around us." Storm jumped up, dissolved into mist, and vanished. *"Don't get left behind!"* Her voice seemed to hang in the air where she had been sitting only a moment before.

Adriane leaped to her feet and went after her friend, more determined than ever to be strong. Maybe in the process she'd discover something all her own. A place where she truly belonged.

2

WHERE WAS THAT wolf hiding? Adriane skidded to a stop at the edge of a large clearing. The size of a football field and ringed by magnificent oaks and pines, the field rustled with the wispy sigh of meadow grass and wildflowers.

This was the field where they'd discovered the portal, hidden by magic they could not yet control. Closing her eyes and concentrating hard, she held up her braceleted arm and moved slowly in a circle, scanning the trees, thinking not of the jewel itself but of what she wanted it to help her do. Focus on Storm, her friend.

The wolf stone sparked to life with an amber glow.

The sharp image of crystal-blue water flashed in Adriane's mind. Mirror Lake.

"I've got you," she called out, laughing.

"Then come and get me." The wolf's voice filled her mind.

Adriane stepped into the field, focusing on Storm's image—

—Flash—

The wolf stone flared with light as the forest faded around her.

Holding up her wrist, Adriane spun in a circle. "Storm, I'm going to find you," she called out.

Trees swept past her field of vision in a blur—

—Flash—

She felt the soft padding of paws hitting the hard earth in long strides.

Adriane pushed hard, closing her eyes, and the wolf stone blazed with light—

—Flash—

The sudden smell of damp wood filled her nose; the leaves beneath her feet felt cool and damp.

Feeling the magical connection grow, Adriane willed herself with all her might to find her friend—

—it was as if a door suddenly flew open.

She opened her eyes and every detail of the forest came into sharp focus. Adriane staggered, overwhelmed with sights and sounds, tastes and smells, sensations unlike anything she had ever experienced. It was as if she no longer was in her own body. She was low to the ground, mighty muscles corded and taut, ready to leap and run with the strength of a wolf.

She *was* a wolf, running free, the wolfsong filling her heart with a power she had never dreamed possible.

"Storm!" she cried out.

Two wild hearts beat as one, a hunter without prey, a warrior without purpose, a lone wolf without a family, never to hear the yelps of pups, the last of her kind.

Caught in a whirlwind of feelings she could not control, Adriane threw back her head and howled. The sound tore from her throat, feral and wild, echoing through the forests and beyond.

Before her, the portal in the field swirled open. How could it have opened? The sparkling dreamcatcher hung in front of the portal, floating in the air before a spinning tunnel of stars.

From somewhere across the astral planes, the wolfsong answered her call.

Head lowered, Adriane turned and saw a mistwolf shimmer into existence. A huge black wolf stood in the field. He raised his black-ruffed head and howled.

Could this really be *another* mistwolf? Was Storm not the last of her kind?

Adriane ran toward him. "Who are you?" she called out.

The wolf backed away, the fur of his ruff standing out threateningly. Fiery golden eyes narrowed and stared as she approached.

"I am Moonshadow, pack leader of the mistwolves. Who dares to call the wolf pack?" The wolf's lip curled, revealing long, sharp teeth.

Adriane stopped short. "I am packmate to a mistwolf."

The wolf snarled, then tensed, ready to strike. *"Humans do not belong with mistwolves."*

As if possessed, Adriane snarled back, an inhuman cry. Her stone flashed golden fire on her wrist and she instinctively leaped for the wolf.

Silver mist flashed in front of her and Storm appeared, teeth bared.

The two wolves faced each other.

"Stand aside, the human has challenged me," the strange mistwolf called.

Storm glared fiercely at the other wolf. *"She is my packmate. Her fight is my fight."*

"You belong with us," the pack leader said, a strange sadness to his tone.

"You cannot be real. There are no others."

The giant black wolf threw back his head and howled. Behind him, dozens of mistwolves appeared from the portal. Blue, black, white, silver, golden, female, male, and pup, they stood looking at Storm. Suddenly, they lifted their heads and howled as one.

Storm answered. And the wolfsong filled the field.

Adriane wanted to feel it, to share it with her friend. She threw her head back and howled with them. The wolves suddenly fell silent and faced the girl.

Adriane stifled her howl, self-consciously aware that she was not a part of the pack.

"This is a time of peril for all mistwolves," the pack leader said to Storm. *"You must run with us now."*

Adriane's world began to crumble. She understood the joy that filled Storm's heart and the white-hot fear that filled her own.

Storm locked eyes with her. *"I must follow the call of the wolfsong."*

Adriane lowered her head.

"Be strong, warrior."

Adriane felt tears running down her face. "Take me with you."

"That is not possible," the pack leader said. *"The mistwolf belongs with her own kind."*

Adriane felt numb. How could she stand in the way of her friend discovering the most important thing in her life? If Storm left, she'd feel deserted by her best friend. If she made Storm stay, she'd feel worse. She braced herself—Storm went to stand by the pack leader.

"Remember." Storm's golden eyes gazed warmly at Adriane. *"You found me once. You will always find me."*

Without a backward glance, all the wolves drifted into mist and swept through the portal. The portal swirled closed behind them, and vanished. Adriane let the pain wash over her as she howled in the empty field, alone.

3

"*A*RE YOU SURE there are no snakes here?" Heather's voice trembled as the redhead gingerly picked her way down the trail.

"Maybe there's pythons!" Joey ran up behind Molly and pretended to choke her. "They sneak up and crush you to pieces!"

"Ewwww. Stop that, Joey!" Molly squealed and ducked behind Kara, knocking into their blond tour guide.

"Dude." Marcus laughed. "Pythons only live in, like, South America."

"The Ravenswood Wildlife Preserve is home to many different species of animals, but we haven't seen any snakes." Kara Davies' voice carried over the group as they made their way from the Mist Trail into Wolf Run Pass. Kara's friends, Heather, Tiffany, Molly, Joey, and Marcus, followed their intrepid tour guide through the lush forest.

"Where's the dinosaur bush?" Joey asked.

Marcus mock-punched his friend. "Dude, that might be too scary for you."

Kara scanned the map that folded out from her notebook. "The hedge animals are in the topiary gardens."

"You should have, like, bear wrestling," Joey suggested.

"Man, I'd pay to see that!" Marcus jostled Joey as he roared like a bear.

"You are so immature," Tiffany scolded. "There's no more bears here."

A growl from the deep, dense forests answered back.

"What was that?" Heather nervously looked around.

"Well, this *is* an animal preserve," Kara said slyly. "If we're lucky, we'll see some wild animals through Wolf Run Pass."

"Are you sure this is safe?" Molly moved close behind Tiffany and Heather as the group entered a wide glade surrounded by large, moss-covered rocks and trees on either side.

"Ravenswood is a natural habitat for animals." Kara waved her arms and called out dramatically, "You never know what might drop in!"

Her friends looked at each other, puzzled.

"Aerobics?" Tiffany asked.

Heather shrugged.

"Ooo, I think I hear something," Kara carefully called out again.

Suddenly a shadow passed overhead as a large, flying creature circled the group.

"What's that?" Molly squealed.

"It's a bird—" Joey started

"It's a plane—" Marcus continued.

Heather crossed her arms. "It's an owl, you morons."

Ariel gently landed on Kara's outstretched arm, her wing feathers shimmering with purple-and-turquoise sparkles.

"A great snow owl. Hi, Ariel," Kara, beaming, said to the owl. "These are my friends that have come to meet you."

The owl surveyed the group with huge turquoise eyes. "Hoo doo yooo doo."

"Hey, that owl almost sounds like it talks," Joey said.

"You are so silly. Animals don't talk," Tiffany scoffed.

"Yeah, pretty silly," Kara remarked, scratching Ariel's head.

"I was chasing a mouse."

"No eating during showtime," Kara whispered, quickly nuzzling her cheek on the owl before gently releasing Ariel to fly away.

The group pressed forward down the trail.

"What other mighty creatures of the forests might be out here?" Kara asked dramatically.

A ferocious roar split the air.

Molly jumped. "What was that?"

"Shhh, look!" Kara whispered, pointing.

Before the group, perched on a large pile of rocks, was a big, spotted cat. Her lustrous fur shone orange with black spots.

"It's the leopard!" Heather yelped.

"Run!" Joey shouted, taking a step backward.

Kara stepped forward. "If we all stay real quiet, I think I can pet her."

"Are you crazy?!" Molly whispered.

The big cat jumped down to stand in front of Kara as she slowly reached out and moved closer.

"Kara, be careful . . ." Heather bit her lip.

Over her shoulder, Kara whispered to her friends. "If I just act friendly, maybe she won't eat me . . . I hope." She winked at Lyra. The big cat winked back.

"Kara! This is *so* not funny!" Tiffany called out, stamping her foot.

As Kara approached, the wild animal crouched low and gave a fierce growl.

"Ahhhhh!" Everyone screamed, falling over one another as they tried to run away.

With her back to her friends, Kara bent over, inspecting the cat's fur. "You need a bath," she said, examining the cat's ears.

"I do not. I smell like wildflowers," Lyra replied casually.

She gave the cat a quick kiss. "You got the wild part right."

"It's beauty and the beast," Marcus cracked as the cat scrambled up the rocks and back into the woods.

"Hey, that's a good one, Marcus." Kara quickly scribbled in her notebook.

"You scared us half to death!" Tiffany pouted.

"C'mon," Kara laughed. "I'll show you the lawn behind the manor where we're planning the benefit concert."

"Great tour, Kara!" Joey said, grinning.

"Ka-ra! Ka-ra! Ka-ra!" they chanted, heading down the trail.

A mournful howl stopped their chant. It came from behind a vine-covered opening between the trees.

"All right! A bear!" Marcus said excitedly.

Joey mock-punched his friend again.

The cry rose again.

"Oo, oo, me, me, my turn," Tiffany yelled. "I want to pet the animals, too." She skipped over to the vines.

"Hey, that's not part of the tour," Kara muttered, checking her notes.

"Here I am, cute thing." Tiffany slowly pulled the leaves aside and screamed.

Adriane stood, eyes glazed, dirt streaked and smeared across her face. From her hiking boots to her black jeans and up to her pullover sweater and forest-green vest, she was covered in mud, leaves, and grass stains.

"Oh, it's just you," Tiffany said.

Adriane eyed the group from behind straggly, damp black hair.

"What happened, you fall in a marsh bog?" Joey called out, walking over.

"Leave me alone," Adriane snarled, stumbling away.

The boy stepped back. "Hey, easy. I was only trying to help."

"She is sooo weird," Tiffany whispered to Heather.

"Yeah, even weirder than normal," Heather agreed.

Kara walked over to Adriane. "What's up?" She eyed Adriane more closely. "You look awful."

"Leave me alone," Adriane repeated and turned away.

"Hey, is she okay?" Marcus asked as Kara's friends moved in closer for a better look.

Suddenly, Ariel dove from the sky to land on Adriane's arm. The owl leaned into Adriane's neck, cooing softly and nuzzling her cheek.

"What's the matter with her?" Molly asked.

"Cat's got her tongue?" Heather quipped.

With a loud hiss, Lyra jumped to Adriane's side, standing protectively close.

"Keep away from her," the cat growled.

Kara's friends understood the cat's actions perfectly, even if they couldn't hear the words.

"Okay, okay, everyone back off," Kara ordered. "Head back to the main road. I'll be there in a minute."

When her friends had moved out of earshot, Kara turned quickly to Lyra. "What is it? What's wrong?"

"Stormbringer is gone," Lyra told her.

"Oh, that wolf is always wandering around," Kara laughed, picking leaves and twigs from Adriane's hair. "She'll probably be back in a few hours."

"No, the mistwolf is gone," the cat repeated.

Kara searched Adriane's eyes. They were red and puffy, streaked with tears.

"What do you mean, gone?" Kara asked.

Adriane pressed the owl and the cat close to her. "She's gone," she stated simply.

"Lyra," Kara said to the cat, "take her to Emily. I'll join you as fast as I can."

She gripped Adriane's arms and looked in her eyes. "Adriane, go with Lyra and Ariel. Okay?"

"Come on, Adriane, just hold on to me," Lyra said, leading Adriane down the path to the manor house. Adriane stumbled after her, silently calling for Storm and hearing nothing.

Emily Fletcher blew a loose auburn curl off her face and clicked on the icon to open the Ravenswood mailbox. She turned from her computer to a second workstation set up on a table next to her desk.

"Mail call," she announced. "It's from Meilin."

Ozzie, a golden brown ferret, sat on three pillows pecking away on the keyboard. Ronif, a quiffle, sat behind him as Balthazar, a pegasus, stood watching carefully. They were busy working on their secret database of magic and magical animals. After all, they actually had firsthand knowledge of these creatures, being magical themselves! Although technically an elf, Ozzie was determined that just because he was stuck in a ferret body, it didn't mean he had to act like one. At least not in front of his friends.

"Don't forget to include that they have bad breath," Ronif commented, flapping his rubbery beak over Ozzie's shoulder.

"Pe-yew! Believe you me" Ozzie remarked, "when there's a kobold in the neighborhood, you know it!"

Emily smiled proudly at her team. She turned back and opened the email.

Meilin lived in Shanghai, China. She and Emily had become good friends in the past month, trading emails and info about animals and legends. Meilin's father was an archeologist who used to tell her stories of great and powerful dragons. Meilin wanted to know whether Emily believed in dragons.

"Well, team magic," Emily asked her animal friends. "Dragons, real or myth?"

"Real, of course. Why wouldn't they be?" Balthazar answered.

After all the magical animals they'd seen here at Ravenswood, a dragon wouldn't be that far-fetched. Emily thought of Phelonius, a creature so magical he couldn't survive on Earth. He'd helped her find the courage to use her healing magic. He was the most amazing creature she had ever seen. And if she hadn't seen him with her own two eyes, she never would've believed *he* was real. So why couldn't dragons be real, too?

"You've seen one then?" Emily asked.

"*I* haven't, personally." Ozzie gestured with his furry paws. "But Cousin Schmoot had this friend who knew this troll whose brother-in-law had this neighbor whose cousin was a warlock who used to go to school with this dwarf whose grandmother swore on her deathbed that one time when she was little she had seen a real, live dragon!"

"I see . . ." Emily laughed. "How could I ever have doubted it?"

"Dragons are very rare and powerful magical creatures," Balthazar said. "They have long been extinct on Aldenmor." He looked up suddenly. "Lyra's here."

"How's Kara's tour go—" Ronif started to ask.

Lyra padded in, nudging Adriane along as if she were a rag doll.

"Adriane! What happened?" Emily was across the room and by her friend's side in an instant. "Ozzie! Get me some damp towels!"

Ozzie dropped to the floor and scampered off as Emily led her friend to a leather couch and sat her down.

Adriane was covered in caked mud and sticky leaves.

"Are you all right? Are you hurt?" Emily asked, eyes full of concern.

Fresh tears ran down Adriane's cheeks.

"What happened?" Emily repeated.

"Here, Adriane." Ronif handed her a water bottle.

Adriane took a long drink. "Thank you."

Ozzie returned with the cool, damp towels and Emily carefully wiped the dried mud and leaves from her friend's face, checking for bruises or cuts.

"Feeling better?"

"No." Adriane then launched into a breathless recap of what had happened out in the field, sobbing as her emotions overwhelmed her.

"She's gone, Emily!" Adriane finished, blinking away her tears.

"But Storm is the last mistwolf," Balthazar said, puzzled.

"Storm always thought she was the last of her kind. Can you imagine what she felt like, learning there were others?" Ozzie said.

"I know," Adriane sniffled. "But it's not safe there! I shouldn't have let her go."

"It wasn't your choice to make, Adriane," Emily said gently.

"We've been practicing to see how far away we could talk to each other. If I could use my wolf stone, maybe I could talk to her."

"But she's in Aldenmor," Emily said. "How could you—you're not thinking of opening the portal?"

"I have to know that she's all right."

"We've never been able to open it on command," Emily reminded her.

"Somehow Storm and I made it work."

"Sounds like it was opened from the other side," Balthazar pointed out

"There's got to be a way," Adriane insisted.

"I don't know . . ."

"Hey, kids! What's all the drama?" Kara walked into the library, pulling her golden hair back in a ponytail.

Ozzie regarded Kara. "There might be a way to open the portal," he said slowly.

The others all followed his gaze.

Kara stopped, a suspicious look crossing her face. "What?"

4

"MAGIC ATTRACTS MAGIC." Ozzie was pacing in the grass, reviewing the plan. "And we know the dragonflies have different magic. They pop in and out without a portal, and they wove Kara's hair into the dreamcatcher. Ergo, the dragonflies may be able to open it!" Ozzie opened his forepaws triumphantly, as if waiting for applause.

Adriane, Emily, and Kara stood in the empty field, listening.

"It seems like the safest way to open the portal. Let the dragonflies do it," Emily agreed.

Kara was not thrilled with this plan. She looked around furtively and shuddered, remembering her *hair-owing* experience not so long ago with the tiny dragons.

They adored Kara, but she'd finally managed to convince the pesky things to stop driving her crazy by popping in and out all over the place. Well, if she had to do this, at least Heather, Molly, Tiffany, Joey, and Marcus weren't here to witness it. Her school friends had gone home. They didn't know about the magic, yet.

"If the portal opens," Emily said to Adriane, "try to use your stone to make contact with Storm."

Adriane looked determined. "Ready."

Emily and Adriane stood on either side of Kara and held up their wrists. Kara always made the other girls' magic stronger when she helped them. Now she extended her arms, touching Emily and Adriane's gemstones.

Emily's rainbow jewel and Adriane's wolf stone began to glow. Halos of blue-green and amber light danced around Kara's fingers then jumped up her arms, swirling around her body.

"Okay, Kara, call the dragonflies," Emily prompted.

"Do I have to?" Kara complained.

The others looked at her.

"All right, all right." Kara took a deep breath, sighed, and called out in a singsong voice, "Yoo-hoo! Dragonflies! Barney, Goldie, Fred, Fiona, Blaze, where are you? Ollie ollie oxen free!"

"'Ollie ollie oxen free?' Ozzie was stumped. "I haven't heard that magical spell before."

"Picture them in your minds," Emily instructed.

Kara closed her eyes and pictured the bird-sized dragons. "Come out, come out, wherever you are!" she called.

Suddenly the air began to sparkle.

Pop! Pop! Pop! Pop! Pop!

Multicolored bubbles burst like small fireworks as a swarm of dragonflies popped in. The girls dropped their arms and stepped back.

"Kaaraa!" a golden dragonfly called out, swooping down to land on Kara's shoulder.

"Watch the hair!" she yelled.

Barney, the purple one, landed belly down on Ozzie's head, hanging over to stare into the startled ferret's face. "Oozzook!"

"Gah! Get away, you!"

"Shh, Ozzie, don't scare them," Emily warned.

The mini dragons flitted around Kara, jabbering excitedly, all angling to get closest to her.

"Yes, yes, you found me," Kara said. "Hooray for you." Purple Barney, red Fiona, yellow Goldie, blue Fred, and orange Blaze all began to dive and spin around the girls, pinwheeling and squeaking.

"Kara, get them under control!" Adriane said impatiently.

"I'm trying!" Kara batted the pesky creatures away.

"Try a gentler approach," Emily suggested.

"Hey!" Kara yelled. "Listen up!"

"Ooo!" The dragonflies stopped in mid-twirl, hovering in front of her.

"Instead of playing our regular 'Throw the Shoe at the Dragonflies' game that you all love so much, I have a special *new* game for us to play." The dragonflies twittered in anticipation. "It's called the 'Open the Portal' game! Yay!" The dragonflies twirled and squealed.

"We want to see the beautiful web you made for us," Emily told them.

"Ooo, Emee." Fiona nuzzled Emily's hair.

"Show us the web, Goldie. You remember." Kara pointed to her blond hair in front of the hovering golden dragonfly. "The web you made from my hair."

The five dragonflies buzzed into action. Forming a circle, they locked tiny claws together and began to spin. They spun faster, filling the air with colorful bursts of light.

"That's it!" Adriane exclaimed.

Faster and faster they spun as hundreds of bubbles popped like fireworks. Wind began to whip through the field as the air churned, boiling with color.

"Something's happening!" Emily called out.

Suddenly the bubbles all merged. The girls and Ozzie shielded their eyes as intense light filled the field. The light faded, revealing a circle of shimmering stars hanging just off the ground—the portal.

In front of the portal hung the sparkling dreamcatcher. It was just the way they had left it: rainbow-colored strands of Kara's hair still woven into a large, glistening web of protection—a dreamcatcher, designed to block evil magic from entering Ravenswood.

"They did it!" Ozzie yelled triumphantly.

"Hurry, before it closes!" Emily urged Adriane.

Adriane gazed at the huge dreamcatcher hanging in the sky. She held up her wolf stone and pictured Storm in her mind. "Storm . . . can you hear me?" she whispered. She concentrated harder. "Stormbringer?"

"Anything?" Emily asked.

"No, I can't get through."

"Try again," Kara said.

"Storm? It's me, Adriane!"

The web trembled, but she still couldn't feel anything. "It's not working!" she cried, frustrated.

"The dreamcatcher may be interfering with reception," Ozzie ventured.

Adriane quickly turned to Kara. "Get the dragonflies to open it."

"I don't know if that's such a good idea," Ozzie said.

"Please!" Adriane pleaded.

Emily nodded at Kara.

"D-flies, listen up!" Kara called. The dragonflies all zoomed over to hover around Kara. "We need you to open the web, okay? On your mark . . . Get set . . . Go!"

The dragonflies immediately flew to the top of the dreamcatcher, grabbing strands of webbing in their beaks.

"What are they doing?" Emily asked.

"How should I know?" Kara shrugged. "I'm amazed they understand anything I say at all."

Each holding a strand of hair, the dragonflies pulled the dreamcatcher down, making it spin end over end. It whirled hypnotically before the misty portal.

Adriane held up her stone and focused. This time she sensed a faint glimmer—a connection. Storm? "I felt something!" Adriane said excitedly.

"I think that's amplifying the signal," Ozzie observed.

The dragonflies began to slow down and Adriane's connection faded.

"Keep the dragonflies spinning!" she called out.

"How am I supposed to do that?" Kara asked.

"Hurry, the portal is closing!" Ozzie waved his paws in the air.

Adriane saw the tunnel swirling into a tighter spiral, drawing the edges of the portal toward the center.

Kara eyed the dragonflies' formation carefully. Bobbing her head in time with their motions, she watched the moving strands sweep over the ground and past her. She used to be really good at this game.

With one swift leap Kara jumped into the throng of dragonflies and start skipping over the moving strands.

The dragonflies all squealed with delight at this new game and began spinning faster, around and around.

Adriane felt the magic connection again, stronger—

—*Flash!*—

432

Crystal towers loomed over scorched earth, pulsing green—

—Flash!—

A dark dungeon filled with sick animals—

Adriane leaned in closer . . .

—Flash!—

A lone mistwolf crying for its lost human.

Adriane gasped. "Storm?"

"You are always in my heart." The voice was so faint it might have been a whisper. It might have been the wind.

It was hard to stay focused with all the commotion going on, with the web spinning, dragonflies buzzing around, and Kara singing, "Miss Mary Mack, Mack, Mack! All dressed in black, black, black! With silver buttons, buttons, buttons! All down her back, back, back!"

Adriane tried to ignore all the distractions and concentrate the way Storm had taught her: to focus on what she was trying to accomplish—to control the magic, get it to do exactly what she wanted. And what Adriane wanted more than anything at this moment was Storm by her side. She squeezed her eyes tightly shut. *"Stormbringer!"*

The starry lights of the portal dimmed with an eerie glow.

Tendrils of magic touched her mind, tentatively probing.

The dreamcatcher whipped around and around Kara, who jumped and ducked and did everything she could to keep from getting tagged.

The connection pulled at Adriane's magic, coaxing her. She reached out, grasping for some clarity, fighting to hold it, and felt . . . an animal? A human? She was confused. The magic suddenly locked tight as a vise.

"Agh!" Adriane recoiled in pain.

"Adriane?" Emily called out.

The dreamcatcher was trembling violently. Kara frantically jump-roped as if her life depended on it.

Adriane was jerked forward with a tremendous force. "Ahh!"

"Adriane! What is it?" Emily's voice sounded so far away.

"I'm being pulled in!" Something had latched onto the magic of Adriane's jewel and was dragging her toward the center of the portal.

"Whatever you're doing, Kara, cut it out!" she screamed, trying to calm her growing fear by focusing on a far more familiar emotion: being annoyed at Kara. "Call off the dragonflies!"

"Pook?"

Kara had jumped free. All the dragonflies clustered around her. They were no longer holding on to the dreamcatcher. "Uh-oh."

The web was spinning on its own, vibrating wildly at odd angles.

Sproing! One by one, the strands began to snap.

"This can't be good," Ozzie said.

Emily grabbed Adriane by the waist, trying to hold her back. "Help!" she screamed as her sneakers slid through the soft grass.

"Emily!" Ozzie yelled, hopping up and down.

Adriane felt the wind whip at her back as two large wings flapped behind her. Lyra had her front paws wrapped around Emily, her golden wings unfurled and beating against the force that pulled them forward.

Ozzie grabbed the cat's tail and pulled with all his might.

"Kookie!"

The dragonflies darted behind Ozzie. Goldie grabbed one of Ozzie's rear paws in her beak, pulling the ferret up in the air. Fred grabbed onto Goldie's tail. Each dragonfly pulled on the tail of the one before it, forming a line, their little wings beating furiously.

"Go, go, go!" Kara jumped up and down, cheering them on.

"Pull!" Emily yelled.

Suddenly, long strands of hair sprang out in all directions as the dreamcatcher unraveled. A blinding sunburst filled the field as the strands were sucked into the portal and disappeared.

Emily, Ozzie, Lyra and the dragonflies all tumbled backward, piling on top of Kara.

Adriane went tumbling forward, headfirst.

"Get off me!" Kara pushed the pile of animals away and scrambled to her feet.

The field was quiet. The portal was gone. Everything was back to normal . . . except for one thing.

Kara and Emily looked at each other in shock, speaking at the same time.

"Where's Adriane?"

5

*I*T WASN'T SO much a sensation of falling. It was more like flying, drifting in a dream. Adriane was surrounded by a golden glow, as if she were inside a bubble of light. She couldn't tell which way was up. Through the glow, she could make out what looked like rivers of stars.

Shapes came into focus. She was skimming over a cratered surface. Then she saw trees, a forest landscape.

"Humm-hamm-hamuckamuck!"

The strange sound rose in the distance.

"Hamma-doo-wark!"

Someone was singing, or at least trying to sing. It sounded more like a bullfrog croaking. She squinted, straining to make out any shapes through the golden light.

"Humm-dumm-dokkarrood!"

The singing was getting louder.

Adriane fell with a stomach-lurching drop and hit the ground—

"SPLAAGfooF!" The singing stopped.

—hard.

Well, not that hard. Something soft and mushy had broken her fall. The golden light faded, leaving a faint afterglow, matching the glow from her wolf stone.

The sky above was a milky gray. All was still.

She sat up and surveyed her surroundings. Maybe she didn't fall through the portal after all. Wide-open woods spread around her, not too different from Ravenswood. But as her eyes adjusted to the gray light, she realized that the trees—what few were still standing—were covered in a thick, tar-like muck. What looked like hanging moss at first was, upon closer inspection, rubbery, moldy, black seaweed choking the trees. The ground was damp with not a blade of grass in sight. Not a *color* in sight! Unless you count gray as a color. She shivered as it hit her: she *had* fallen through the portal. She was not on Earth anymore, and she was totally alone.

"Mmmmfff!"

Something cold and clammy was squirming in the mud right underneath her! Adriane screamed and leaped to her feet.

Something kicked its way out of the soft dirt.

"Who is you that rained on me?" the creature sniveled, shaking off dirt and mud like a dog.

"Huh?" She must've fallen out of the sky right on top of this creature. Adriane stood with her wrist raised, breathing fast. The wolf stone pulsed with golden light, reacting to her distress.

The thing began feeling around in the dirt, searching for something as its large round eyes found Adriane and widened in terror. "A witch!" It fell back over its own big feet and groveled in the dirt. "I am only humble Scorge. Do not turn me to stone, O Witch!" it wailed.

"I'm not a witch. I'm sorry. You frightened me," Adriane said, watching the creature warily.

"I frightened you?" The creature smiled, showing rows of little pointy teeth. "Must be very poor witch."

It stood up. It was sort of apelike in appearance, hunched, with long arms. Its short orange fur on those parts that weren't covered in mud made it look like a deranged orangutan.

"Uh . . . I'm sorry I landed on you, um, sir. My name's Adriane. Are you all right?"

"No! Me is not '*All right!*' Me is Scorge." The creature began frantically looking around again.

"You made Scorge lose big magic stone." He stopped, seeing Adriane's jewel. "Soooo . . ." The creature pointed a stubby finger at her wrist. "That means you must give Scorge magic stone."

Adriane's gem was softly pulsing with light. "I don't think so."

"You not from around here . . ." Scorge moved toward Adriane and her jewel.

"No, I'm from . . . over the rainbow," Adriane said, backing away.

"Where is this rainbow place, near Moorgroves perhaps?" it asked slyly.

"Uh, maybe. You just stay away from me now."

"Scorge need magic stone!" The creature charged at Adriane.

Before Adriane could react, her jewel exploded with power. A beam of searing gold light shot out at Scorge, knocking the creature fifteen feet in the air.

"Oooowahhh!"

"Oh, I'm so sorry!" Adriane ran over to the downed creature. She hadn't meant to use such force—the jewel had just reacted. "Are you okay?"

"No! No! No! Me Scorge!" He shook his furry head. "Me thinks Scorge don't want that jewel."

He got up, hanging his orange head in defeat.

This was not the best way to make friends in a brand-new world, Adriane thought. "Maybe I can help you find your stone," she suggested.

"Must find stone!" Scorge lifted his head, his big eyes lighting up. "Get big reward!"

"I think it might have rolled that way." Adriane pointed to a shallow gully in the dirt that traveled up and over a hill behind them . . . although she was fairly certain a rock didn't roll uphill.

Scorge scurried up the hill in the direction his "magic stone" had rolled, desperate to catch up to it. "Scorge get big reward for big stone!" He glowered back at Adriane, then tripped over his big feet and fell over the ridge, disappearing down the other side.

A great big magic stone? Adriane thought to herself, tapping her own stone in the bracelet on her wrist. Could this Scorge really have a giant-sized magic stone? She had to be careful. The magic seemed much more powerful here, and dangerous.

"GaooahooHoo!"

Scorge's cry came from over the hill. Adriane looked around. If no one had heard Scorge's horrendous screaming by now, there probably wasn't anyone else nearby. Sighing, she carefully walked up the hill.

Adriane peeked cautiously over and saw an empty riverbed. Scorge's dilemma became all too clear: the riverbed was filled with hundreds of identical muddy, gray rocks. She was startled as Scorge suddenly burst out sobbing uncontrollably.

"Oh, me face! Baddest luck finded Scorge!" he bawled. "Me, me, me!"

He was so pathetic. Despite how rude he'd been to her, Adriane felt sorry for him.

She got an idea. "Hey, maybe I can help you find it," she called out, walking down toward him.

Scorge looked up, wary, but still crying.

Stepping into the riverbed, Adriane held out her gem-stone, moving it carefully over the large rocks. She didn't even know if this would work, but as Ozzie had told them, magic attracts magic.

Adriane's wolf stone was beginning to pulse. She continued to wave it across the muddy riverbed when suddenly one of the many gray rocks began to pulse a dull, dirty light. "Look, Scorge!"

Scorge ceased his crying. "Ooo!"

He lumbered over and gleefully bent, kissing the big stone over and over again. Adriane flinched as she watched him kiss a rock covered in dried mud and goo.

"So, now that I helped you, maybe you can help me, huh?" Adriane hoped she wasn't pressing her luck.

Scorge stopped in mid-smooch. "What witch want from Scorge?" He gazed suspiciously at her and hugged the rock close.

"Where am I?" Adriane asked. "What is this place?"

"Pooowa." He spit out some dirt. "You never heard of the Shadowlands?"

Adriane gasped. The Shadowlands. This was a place of terrible danger. This was where Lyra escaped from that sorceress. The cat had been burned by the Black Fire poison here. This was where the manticore came from! She shivered. This was not good at all. Was Storm somewhere in the Shadowlands, too? Or had the mistwolf ended up somewhere else?

"GraaaK!!" Scorge was trying to lift the rock, but it wouldn't budge. He toppled over it instead. He got up and tried again, and fell over the immobile stone. This time he got up and kicked it with his big toe.

"OOhhhAAAA!"

That didn't work. That rock wasn't moving.

"What you do to magic stone?" Scorge yelled, hopping around, holding a swollen toe.

"I didn't do anything."

"Rock schtuck!"

Adriane gazed out at the desolate landscape beyond the riverbed. "How do I get out of here? Which way do I go?"

"Me don't care what way witch goes!" Scorge said angrily. "Me go get imps. They move stone with big magic. Make bad witch disappear!"

Imps? What are those? She shuddered.

Before Adriane could stop him, Scorge scampered off down the ravine without looking back and was gone.

A wave of fear swept over Adriane. Steady, she told herself. As much as she didn't want to, she knew she had to move. Although there was no sign of the glowing green poison that was called Black Fire, she knew it was here. All around her, the landscape was harsh, bleak, completely barren. Dark patterns instead of clouds swirled eerily in the sky, constantly in motion. It felt to Adriane like the land itself was trying to breathe, gasping for air. She had to find Storm and get out of here.

But Storm could be anywhere! She felt panic rising.

"Calm down!" she said aloud. She hugged herself, then exhaled deeply. One hand found the wolf stone on her wrist, and she instantly felt better. It was probably a good idea to go in the opposite direction from Scorge. Whatever imps were, she didn't want to wait around and find out.

Adriane held the wolf stone out, and, as if in response, a glow ignited, slowly swirling in its center. Gazing into the amber light, Adriane concentrated as hard as she could on Storm. She imagined leaning against Storm's soft fur. She relived, in her mind, the quiet moments they had spent together.

"Storm, where are you?"

The wolf stone suddenly flashed. A burning white-gold light washed out Adriane's vision completely. She felt as if she were being pulled through some kind of tunnel at a breakneck speed, zooming past hazy images she could not decipher. Cloudy shapes began to form in front of her. Dozens of figures slowly came into view, all four-legged creatures, silhouetted on a lush green hillside.

Lush green? Adriane hazily became aware that she was looking upon a forested, mountain landscape, when a moment before all around her had been barren and gray. Mistwolves paced back and forth. She could smell them and hear them. And she was among them. She was one of them!

Storm?

Where was Stormbringer? Adriane looked carefully at each mistwolf. None was familiar. Suddenly she recognized the big, black wolf she had seen in the portal—Moonshadow, the pack leader. He sniffed the air, then turned sharp golden eyes on her.

Adriane gasped.

The huge wolf spoke directly to her. *"Stormbringer! Let the human go."*

Stormbringer! He had called *her* Stormbringer! No, Adriane realized, she was seeing through Storm's eyes!

Suddenly the connection was cut off, as if someone had just hung up the phone.

The searing glow of Adriane's jewel faded, and the greenery around her gave way to gray. Adriane was again standing in the same muddy riverbed where Scorge had left her.

She had been in Storm's mind—seen through her eyes and saw that Storm had her real family now. Even so, Adriane refused to believe that Storm would ever turn her back on her.

Adriane squinted. More gray forests, rolling into hills . . . and, in the distance, she could make out snow-covered peaks of a mountain range.

That was where she had to go—she could only trust in the magic to guide her.

Adriane walked out of the riverbed in the direction of the mountains. They had to be a good ten miles away.

Something *clunked* behind her.

Adriane whirled around. But all was quiet.

She turned back and took a few steps, when she heard a clattering in the rocks.

She turned again, her senses on high alert. "Who's there?" She scanned the riverbed. "Scorge?" No answer.

Then she heard it again.

"Whoever you are, I know you're there! Show yourself!"

Adriane's heart pounded in her throat. She flashed on the nightmare vision of the manticore. That monster had terrorized the animals at Ravenswood until she, Emily, and Kara had sent it back through the portal—maybe right back here.

She heard a short rattle and froze. Then one large, oval rock, the size of a beach ball, shook back and forth.

"Huh?"

The mud-crusted rock teetered among the other gray rocks . . . and fell over. It wobbled and then slowly began to roll *itself!*

Adriane's jaw dropped. She watched in amazement as the rock gingerly toddled toward her and came to a stop at her feet.

"Hello," Adriane said awkwardly. "Great. I'm talking to a rock."

The rock rattled and shook and settled back at her feet.

"So you're, like, just a rock?" The rock said nothing. "Well, I'd love to stay and chat, but I've got to roll."

Adriane turned and began to walk away. The rock rolled after her. She stopped. The rock stopped. "I guess you didn't like Scorge, either," she said over her shoulder. The rock said nothing.

She started walking away again. This time she was pretty sure what to expect. She smiled when she heard the gravelly rattle behind her. Without looking back, she said conversationally, "Well, it is a nice day for a stroll—er, roll? You from around here? I'm just visiting."

Adriane began the long hike from the riverbed up into the desolate forest. She realized she was actually grateful for the company of the rock, and found it comforting, even. I guess this must be a pet rock, she chuckled to herself.

"Is that what you are, Rocky? A pet rock?" She leaned down and rubbed the rock playfully. It rolled in a happy little figure eight around Adriane's feet. "Yes, you are! Who's a good widdle pet rock? You! That's who!" If the rock had a tail, she was sure it'd be wagging it right now. Just wait until she showed it to the others—a pang of homesickness swept over her.

Adriane had been trying not to think about that. She wasn't exactly sure how she was going to get home. And what if she was *never* able to get home? No, don't even go there! Panicking wouldn't do her—or Storm—any good. She had to stay focused on the task at hand, as Storm had taught her.

"I have a friend here. I'm on my way to find her,"

Adriane explained as they continued to walk past dark and forbidding woods. "She's my best friend in the world—my world, anyway. You ever have a friend like that?"

The rock shuddered and rolled on top of her foot.

Adriane stopped and looked down. "Well, you have one now."

The rock rolled around Adriane's feet.

She brushed brambles out of their way as she pushed through small patches of fog, winding around dead trees, following the soft, golden halo of the wolf stone. Finally Adriane realized they were leaving the vicinity of the gray forest. Green grass was beginning to show in patches. Cold wind swept her hair as they crested a steep incline and looked at a series of mist-covered valleys before them. Adriane could see the tops of rocky cliffs, then foothills, and beyond them loomed the crystalline mountains.

"This is not the way I imaged Aldenmor to be," she mused. "Ravenswood is so beautiful. This is such a cold and frightening place."

The rock rolled silently by her feet.

"You're a really good listener, you know that?" Adriane was glad to have the rocky hitchhiker along for the journey. With it by her side, she felt a little less alone in this strange and scary world.

She didn't see the giant flying creature and its rider circling overhead, watching her every move.

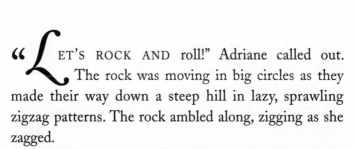

6

"LET'S ROCK AND roll!" Adriane called out. The rock was moving in big circles as they made their way down a steep hill in lazy, sprawling zigzag patterns. The rock ambled along, zigging as she zagged.

"Hey, you're pretty good." Adriane laughed as the rock twirled past like a graceful skater. "C'mon! Race ya to the top!" She took off up the next hill.

The rock spun around and with a burst of speed, plowed straight past her, right to the crest of the hill.

"No fair!" Adriane called out. "You rocked *and* rolled!" She laughed.

The rock stood frozen in place at the top of the hill.

Then it began shaking, spun around, and rolled back to Adriane, hiding behind her legs. It was quivering in fear.

Adriane's guard went up. "What's wrong? What is it?" But the rock wouldn't stop shaking.

"Hey, it's okay," she said. But something told her it wasn't.

She carefully made her way to the top of the hill and looked down the other side. Her heart thudded.

Below lay a wide, deep valley, covered in shifting mists. And through the flowing mist, Adriane caught glimpses of the valley floor. Deep gashes ran like open wounds ripped through the earth. They glowed with a sickly green. Black Fire.

"Oh, no!" Adriane gasped. The green glowed menacingly, moving in rivers through the valley, reaching for the mountains beyond.

She had seen the poison in the animals at Ravenswood. She had seen it dripping like venom from the manticore, but nothing could have prepared her for the magnitude of what lay before her.

Fear crept up her back. Nothing could survive the onslaught of such horrendous evil. She looked out at the mountains beyond. She had to cross this valley. They would have to skirt around the green rivers of poison.

She took a deep breath. "Come on. This way."

Mist crept down over the hillside. The rock took a tentative roll beside her, and stopped again. Adriane looked over and saw large shapes partially hidden in the fog. When they didn't move, she stepped closer. The shapes lay spread out upon the sloping hillside. She gingerly stepped closer and the mist parted to reveal bodies.

Adriane cried out, her hand covering her mouth.

They were huge animals. They reminded her of the wooly mammoths she had seen on a Discovery Channel special. What once had been an entire herd now lay still in the field. They were dead, all of them, covered in glowing green poison, horribly burned by the Black Fire.

Adriane fought back nausea. Tears ran down her face as she walked by the silent graveyard. The rock rolled right at her heels, not leaving her side.

What kind of world is this that would let such magnificent animals be slaughtered?

"Come on, Rocky, there's nothing we can do for them."

Adriane led the rock past the horrendous scene and entered the valley below, keeping a sharp eye out for the rivers of green poison. The air seemed to crackle with unsettling electricity. More and more, she felt as if she were being watched. She looked at the surrounding hills. Through the mist, she caught sight of something moving in the grass down the hill right toward them. Blue sparks of light flashed as it moved. And it was fast. Suddenly she saw more moving through the grass and down the hill to her left. She turned to look at the other side and saw dozens more racing toward them. Arcing blue flashes of electricity ignited sparks in the air as they moved.

Her wolf stone was pulsing with deep orange light.

"Rocky, we have to run!"

Adriane took off, her legs making long strides across the valley floor. Rocky rolled behind her, trying to keep up. She risked a glance over her shoulder and saw her pursuers moving faster.

Whatever they were, they were small—small enough to be hidden in the tall grass.

She didn't like this at all. She had to be careful not to run into the deep gashes of poison. And the flowing mist was making it very difficult to see.

She turned back and peered into the fog. Something screamed and lunged straight for her. She had a split second to register that it was jet-black with blazing red eyes before it knocked into her, sending her flying. Twisting as she fell, she folded her body into a tuck and rolled back up into a fighting stance. But there was nothing there. Whatever it was had vanished back into the mist.

More high-pitched screams erupted around her, surrounding her.

"Rocky? Where are you?"

Sharp pain lanced into her neck as something jumped her from behind. She screamed and whipped around, tossing the creature to the ground. The thing was instantly back on its feet. It looked like an inkblot in the shape of a small man with bright red eyes. A spark of electrical energy raced through its body with a snap.

It attacked again. This time, Adriane swung her arm,

and a blazing stream of fire whipped from her jewel. She turned, stepped to the side, and swept the fire upward, smacking the creature back into the mist. Four more came at her. Incredibly fast, they were on her before she knew it. Two went for her legs as the other two leaped for her head. Adriane jumped and kicked, knocking the lower ones against one another. She spun in a circle to shield her head as the other two screeched wildly, grabbing for her hair and eyes. Adriane screamed as magic fire exploded from her gem. Black ink splattered as the two creatures were ripped to pieces. Droplets rained to the ground, sparking and pulsing. Adriane watched in horror as the drops of black slowly moved together and rose up. The creatures began to re-form.

She dropped down, swiping her hair off her face, frantically searching for Rocky as she waited for the next attack.

To her right, the mist parted, and she saw a dozen of the inky things circling the rock, trying to keep it penned in the middle. Silver-blue sparks of electricity shot through the rock as they tried to trap it. She swung her arm, whipping out a long trail of magic and let it fly. Golden fire crashed into the creatures, splattering them into pools of black.

"Rocky! Over here!"

Before the things could re-form, the rock dashed past them to Adriane's side.

"Run!" she screamed.

They took off across the valley, streaking headlong

into mist—and stopped short. Across their path lay a glowing gash of Black Fire. It was too wide to jump.

Breathing hard, Adriane whirled around. The monsters had regrouped. Dozens were running toward them, screeching like mad spirits out of a nightmare.

Adriane looked back at the river of poison. It stretched into the distance both right and left. There was no way to run around it. They were trapped. The creatures were closing in fast. Rocky suddenly took off, rolling right at them.

"No! Rocky!"

The rock rolled into them like a bowling ball. The inky monsters went flying.

There was a rush of air, and dust and dirt swirled around her. Adriane fell to her knees, covering her eyes and mouth to keep from choking. Through her fingers, she saw a winged creature hovering above her. It had the body of a lion and the head of a giant bird. Its wings were enormous, spanning a good twelve feet. A hand suddenly reached down and grabbed her arm, pulling her up and tossing her onto the flying creature's back. Someone was sitting in front of her.

"I hate imps," the figure said simply, turning around to look at Adriane. Her jaw dropped. Adriane was pretty sure it was a human boy.

"Hang on!" he shouted, turning back to spur his mount. The creature's wings flapped and it rose into the air. Adriane twisted around to see Rocky still on the ground, toppling over as it desperately tried to jump.

"No! Wait! Let me go!" Adriane screamed. She bucked and struggled.

"Stop that! What are you doing?" the boy yelled, reaching back to try and keep her seated.

"Let me go!"

With a fierce push, Adriane flung herself off the flying creature. Grabbing its leg, she hung on, sending it careening into a dizzying spin. The surprised beast gave a loud squawk as it tried to shake loose its swinging baggage. Adriane hung on, forcing it toward the ground. Letting go, she dropped. She landed, rolled and sprang back up to her feet.

"Rocky!" she yelled.

The rock quickly rolled over to her and she bent to lift it. It was heavy! Adriane didn't know what to do. The imps were going to be on them in seconds.

"Hurry, pass it here!"

The boy was leaning over the side of the flying creature as it beat its powerful wings to stay in the air. She had no choice. She lugged the rock up to the boy, grabbed his other arm, and swung back up behind him. The imps swarmed, climbing on top of one another, madly grabbing at the flying creature's legs, igniting a flurry of sparks. The flying beast lashed out with sharp claws, splattering and toppling the pile of imps. Adriane hung on for her life as the mighty winged creature swept up into the sky.

7

ADRIANE WIPED HER eyes, coughing from the dust and grime. The valley below was a speeding blur of greens and browns. Ahead lay the mountains, their base draped in thick, swirling fog. The boy had wedged the rock securely between himself and Adriane.

She flinched as the boy reached down, retrieving something from an embroidered saddle bag. "Here, drink this." He handed her a soft pouch over his shoulder.

Very carefully, she let go of his waist with one hand and took the pouch. She flipped open the lid and took a careful sip. It was water. Warm, but it tasted clean and pure. She took long gulps. And she felt better.

"Thank you." She handed it back.

She studied the boy in front of her. He was maybe

fourteen or fifteen years old. His hair was sandy brown with blond streaks, long but not unkempt. His skin was bronzed, although Adriane saw no sun in the sky. He seemed healthy enough. He wore a loose-fitting white shirt with half the long sleeves ripped off, cloth pants stitched up the sides, and leather-like sandals.

"What kind of magic was that?" he asked.

"I've never seen creatures like those," Adriane replied.

The boy shook his head. "Not the imps, *your* magic."

She didn't know how much to tell this boy. "Uh . . . I have a gemstone. It controls magic, but I'm not very good at it."

"Not good?" The boy laughed. "You fought off two dozen imps!"

"You were watching me?"

"We've been watching you since you entered the valley."

"Nice timing," Adriane grumbled.

"What were you doing down there?" he pressed.

"I . . . I got lost."

"Lost? Where were you going?"

"I need to get to those mountains. I . . . uh . . . I'm looking for . . . my friend."

The boy spun around to face her, folding his leg beneath him, perfectly balanced on the winged animal's back. Eyeing Adriane curiously, he poked at her cheek and tugged her hair.

"Ow! Quit it! That hurts!" She knocked his hand

away, then quickly gripped his arm, as she tilted out over the swiftly moving ground far below.

"Are you human?" he asked.

"You know, I might ask you the same thing," she answered, pulling away.

"Are you?" the boy asked again.

"Yes. What else would I be?"

The boy shrugged. "You use magic—you could be anything."

Adriane was starting to get a little annoyed.

"What's with the rock?" He gestured with his chin, letting his long hair fly over his face.

"What about it?" she asked stiffly.

"You risked your life for it. Magic?"

"I don't know. I think so . . ." She hugged the motionless, silent rock.

The boy looked at her sharply. "Where did you come from?"

"Over the rainbow," she answered.

"How old are you?"

"One hundred and fifty."

His eyes opened wide. That shut him up.

"Look, who are you?" she asked impatiently.

"My name is Zachariah—Zach. This is Wind Dancer. I'm human. He's a griffin."

The griffin snorted a hello.

"I'm Adriane. Thank you for rescuing us."

"What are you doing out in the Shadowlands?"

"What are *you* doing here?"

"That's a stupid question."

"*Your* questions are stupid. You'd think you never saw another human before."

"I haven't," he answered.

That shut her up. What was he talking about?

Wind Dancer turned his head to Zach and gave a few angry squawks.

The boy looked up with a quick glance. "Hang on, we've got company." He swung back into his riding position.

Adriane twisted around. Behind them she could make out about a dozen figures soaring through the air, coming at them fast.

"Your little magic show has attracted a lot of attention," Zach said.

"What are those?"

"Can't tell yet. Too big for gremlins, maybe gargoyles. Nasty things."

"Worse than a manticore?"

The boy stiffened. His eyes narrowed suspiciously. "What do you know about manticores?"

"Nothing really. I . . . my friends and I met one once." Should she trust this boy or not? He *had* saved her life. He sure didn't seem to trust her much.

"Must be some friends," he grunted.

"They're gaining on us," Adriane yelled, looking over her shoulder.

"We can't outrun them, so we'll have to lose them," Zach told her calmly. "Hold your legs tight against Windy. When we turn, lean into the wind with us, keep your weight centered and hang on. Got that?"

"I think so." She told herself not to look down as she tightened her grip on the boy's waist.

Zach patted the griffin's neck, then wrapped his fingers in the big ruff of lion's mane that grew along the neck below the eagle head. "Okay, Windy, let's go."

With a beat of his strong wings, the griffin angled off to the right and dove straight down. The ground twisted, careening by at a dizzying speed. Adriane saw something white flashing on the mountaintops. When the mountains turned upside down, she closed her eyes and hung on tight as Windy dropped like a cannonball into the thick fog at the base of the foothills.

But even with hardly any visibility, Windy flew fast and sure.

"Whatever you do, don't use your magic," Zach shouted over his shoulder.

"Why not?"

Howls pierced the mist, echoing off the cliff walls behind them.

"They're magic trackers. Duck!"

Adriane obeyed—a second before a jagged rock flew just inches above her head. They were flying perilously close to the sheer cliff face. "Next time can I have *two* seconds?"

"Okay . . . duck!"

Windy dove under a wide arch that bridged a gap between mountains. They were flying through a narrow gorge, surrounded on both sides by long spikes of rocks that jutted out like rows of gigantic teeth.

Adriane looked down at a sheer drop into nothingness.

Windy gave a hissing snort.

"Are you using magic?" Zach accused.

"No!"

"They're still on us."

Windy gave the boy a few squawks. Zach was thinking, trying to make a decision.

"Windy thinks you're okay," he said finally. "Animals have a strong intuition."

"I wouldn't know," Adriane replied bitterly, thinking of Storm.

"We're going inside."

"How can Windy see anything through this mist?" she yelled.

"He knows these mountains cold." Zach laughed. The boy was actually enjoying himself. "Windy could find a craven's nest in an ice storm."

"I'll remember that the next time I need a craven."

"Besides, we've flown the Serpent's Teeth before . . . just never in the mist."

Windy dove and twisted, narrowly avoiding the spires and spikes that seemed to loom out of nowhere before disappearing back into the mist. Whatever creatures were trailing them weren't faring as well. Tremendous crashes were followed by painful howls that echoed over the gorges.

"Ooo, I bet that hurt." Zach chuckled.

Windy squawked, banked to the left, and flew straight for the mountainside.

"Where are we going?" Adriane asked, eyes wide.

"In there." Zach pointed directly ahead to the sheer rock cliff.

At the last minute, Adriane made out a thin vertical break in the cliff wall. Windy turned on his wing tip and slipped through the crevice. Adriane hung on tight and closed her eyes. They broke through the cliff wall, emerging into a wide canyon completely surrounded by mountains. The griffin straightened out and glided, perfectly balanced atop swift currents of cool air.

"Ha! Let those demons try *that!*" the boy whooped, hugging the griffin. "Good flying, Windy!"

The griffin spat back a response, reminding them how he felt about demons.

Adriane felt a pang of jealousy, thinking of the close moments she'd shared with Stormbringer. If Zach felt that way about Windy, he couldn't be so bad, could he?

The mists vanished as the griffin descended in slow circles. Below was a wide plateau crisscrossed with gorges. On the far side, the mountains rose, towering against swirling purple skies.

They dropped into a deep gorge. Adriane made out a swift-moving river at the bottom. Spindly trees dotted the scrub grass and ran up a slope to a series of caves cut into the rock wall. The griffin landed on the far banks of the running waters.

The boy slid from Windy's back and leaped to the ground. "We can stay here until everything calms down."

Clutching Rocky in her arms, Adriane slid to the ground. Her legs felt like rubber, and she could barely stand up. She gently dropped the rock and it rolled over to the riverbank, coming to a stop, then sitting motionless and silent.

Zach gave Windy a firm pat. With a snort and a shake of his eagle head, the griffin took off into the air. Adriane watched him fly away. "Where's he going?"

"To hunt. Don't worry, he'll keep an eye out for trouble." The boy turned and began walking up the slope toward the caves.

"Where are you going?" Adriane called.

"I have some dried fruits in the cave." He pointed to the river. The water runs down from the mountains—it's fresh and clean."

Adriane watched him walk away. A real human boy in Aldenmor—the *only* human, according to him. It was amazing. Then again, being in a magical world was amazing. So far it had been one shock after another.

What was it about him that bothered her? Should she

trust him? He seemed friendly, but there was something . . . secretive about him that made her feel uncertain.

She plopped down on the bank of the river. Light seemed to reflect evenly off the canyon walls although there was no direct sunlight. She could have been sitting at the bottom of the Grand Canyon, except that the rock strata were layered with pastel green and orange instead of the rusty sand colors of Arizona.

Adriane untied her hiking boots, took them off along with her socks, and put her feet in the water. It was cold and *sooo* refreshing. She bent over and splashed some on her face and neck. Then she checked the rock.

"Having a good time?" she asked.

Leaning over, she rolled the large rock toward her feet. "You need a bath."

Adriane splashed water over its crusted surface, peeling away layers of mud and dirt. She was a bit surprised at how much had built up. She stopped and inspected it. A patch of yellow had appeared under the layers of grime. Blue speckles seemed to shift against the yellow. "Wow! Are you an ugly duckling?" She started scrubbing harder and more layers of dirt and mud fell away. Adriane's eyes widened. "Look at you."

Underneath the muck, the rock was shiny smooth, its surface a pretty yellow, dotted with purple, blue, and orange speckles. The colors were moving, melting in and out of one another, reminding her of a mood ring.

"You are the most beautiful rock I have ever seen!" Adriane announced.

The rock beamed as the shifting colors shone even more brilliantly.

"That's not a rock."

Zach was standing behind her. He handed her a small slab of granite, a plate filled with dried apples, dates, and raisins. Adriane's mouth started to water.

"Go ahead. It's not poison." Zach popped a date into his mouth to demonstrate.

Adriane practically grabbed the slab away from him. She had never been so hungry in her life! "Thank you," she said, stuffing two dates into her mouth. Not bad, she thought, although right about now even a craven would taste good.

Zach was inspecting the now-clean rock, carefully touching it here and there with long, sure fingers. Looking worried, he bent over and put his ear to it. Then he pushed sandy hair from his face, and focused intense green eyes on Adriane. "It's an egg."

Adriane stopped in mid-chew. An egg? "How do you know—sorry." She finished chewing and swallowed. "I've never seen an egg like that."

"See this section?" He pointed to a shifting splotch of blues. She bent over to look, self-consciously aware of how close her face was to Zach's.

"The shell is thinner there," he explained. "And

warmer. Whatever's in there, it's alive, applying constant pressure to the weaker sections of shell."

Adriane sat back. *Alive!* It wasn't a rock after all. But then . . . what kind of egg was it?

"What do we do? Sit on it?" She smiled at her joke.

Zach broke out laughing. "No, I don't think it's a chicken." He fell over backward, holding his sides. Adriane laughed along with him—mostly out of relief that she was still alive.

"Nothing we can do." Zach chuckled, wiping a tear from his eye. "These kinds of eggs hatch when they're ready."

"These kinds?"

"Magic," the boy replied matter-of-factly.

Adriane tried to figure him out. It was time for some answers.

"What are you doing here—I mean here in Aldenmor?" she asked.

"I told you, I live—"

"But how did you *get* here? Did you fall through a portal also?" Adriane was suddenly terrified that if he did, he'd never found a way back.

"I was born here."

"Where are your parents?"

"Dead."

"Oh . . . I'm sorry . . ."

"I don't remember them," Zach explained. "They died when I was really little."

"How did you manage? I mean, how did you—"

"I was raised by . . . um . . ." The boy turned away. " . . . animals."

Adriane's eyes opened wide. "And you've never seen another human?"

"There are no other humans in this world, that I know of."

Adriane suddenly felt awkward. She didn't exactly consider herself the finest example of human society to meet the only boy from another world.

"I'm going to find Windy." Zach got to his feet.

"Then what?"

"I'll take you to the mountains. You said you had a friend there," Zach reminded her.

"Yes . . . I'm not sure where she is, exactly."

"The sooner you find a way to get home the better."

She looked at him uncertainly.

"This is a dangerous place," he explained.

"Oh, really. I hadn't noticed."

Zach's eyes twinkled and he smiled.

Adriane's eyes were downcast, but she smiled as well. "What do we do with our egg?"

Zach shrugged. "It likes you. Take it with you."

Great, a pet whatsit! That's all she needed. She slipped into her socks and laced up her boots, watching Zach deftly climb the steep slope above the cave opening. How could a human boy, hardly older than she was, have survived on his own here for so long? What wasn't he telling her?

She stood up and stretched her legs, watching the river wind its way around a bend in the gorge. She had crossed the valley and had made it past the foothills. Was she close enough to reach Storm?

She held up her wolf stone and concentrated, picturing the silver mistwolf. She began to turn slowly, gazing into the golden center of her gem.

"Storm," she called out. "Where are you?"

The light around the canyon grew brighter, reflecting off the water, until it suddenly flared out, washing her entire field of vision in pure white. She closed her eyes and felt herself once again race through a tunnel. Images flickered at the edges of her sight. She opened her eyes and looked at the mistwolf pack.

"Storm, can you hear me?"

"Yes. I am here."

The voice in her mind startled her. "Are you all right?" She could hear the other wolves. They were agitated, angry.

"Yes. Stay strong, warrior."

"Stormbringer!" Moonshadow stood in front of Storm, snarling. Adriane watched him through Storm's eyes. The great black wolf held Adriane in his golden eyes. Was he looking at her, or at Storm—or both?

"Was it not bad enough that a human killed our pack mother? Your human will only put you in danger. The pack must be protected. There will be no contact with humans! Never again."

Adriane cringed. She would never do anything to put Storm in danger. She could feel Storm's despair. Her best friend was torn between her new wolf pack and the human with whom she'd bonded.

Fog quickly gathered at their feet, and rose until it obscured Adriane's view. The mistwolves vanished—and Adriane was thrown violently out of Storm's mind.

She blinked, watching the sparkling river cut its path through the base of the ancient gorge. A human had killed the pack mother. But the only other human here was Zach.

8

"*W*HAT WERE YOU doing?"

Zach's voice startled Adriane and she whirled around to see him sliding off Windy's back. Windy's large, brown bird eyes studied her sharply. She hadn't even heard them approach.

"I was . . . trying to find my friend," she said, covering the wolf stone with her hand.

"I told you not to use magic!"

Adriane felt her face redden. "It's not like there's no other magic in this world."

"This is not some game," Zach continued angrily. "You and your friends can't just show up here and start doing anything you want. Your actions have consequences."

"I know that." She crossed her arms defiantly. "But if my friend's in trouble, I have to help."

"The one in trouble right now is you. And us," he added, his gesture including the griffin, "now that we've helped you."

Adriane felt a stab of guilt. She didn't want them to get in trouble because of her.

Zach started pacing back and forth, brow furrowed. "Those creatures are not going to give up."

Pop!

"The last thing we need around here is more magic!"

Adriane looked around. That sound . . . it was so familiar.

Zach stopped pacing. "Who knows what horrible monsters will show up next!"

"Ooooo . . ." A red dragonfly head peeked over the boy's shoulder.

Adriane's eyes went wide.

Zach followed her gaze. "What the . . . !" He jumped back, swatting at the bat-sized dragon.

"Pweek!" The mini dragon leaped into the air, flapping shiny red wings, and hovered in front of Adriane.

"Fred!" she cried.

"Uh-uh . . ." The dragonfly shook its head.

"Uh . . . Barney?" Adriane guessed.

"Pweoooo!" the dragonfly said, angrily releasing a small spark.

"Fiona?"

"Deedee!" The red dragonfly landed happily on Adriane's shoulder, nuzzling her neck, her round jewel eyes sparkling.

Zach slapped his forehead. "What did I just say about magic?"

Pop! Pop! Pop! Pop!

Four more dragonflies, all different colors, popped in, chittering and flying around Adriane. She was never so happy to see anything in her life.

"Ooooo!" The dragonflies spotted the egg and zipped over, nudging one another aside for a chance to land on it.

"What are you doing here?" Adriane asked happily.

A yellow dragonfly—Goldie, she remembered—fluttered up to her, golden-faceted eyes twirling. Clearing her throat with a quick spark, she spoke carefully, "Kaaraa skeep a peep peep."

"What?"

Purple Barney jumped up, nudging Goldie away. "Kee-kee deedee!"

"What are they saying?" Adriane asked.

"How should I know?" Zach scanned the skies, as if a horde of monsters might drop in any second.

Windy stuck his head next to Adriane and let out a loud, deep squawk that startled everyone.

The little dragons screeched and hid behind Adriane. Fiona poked her nose up over Adriane's shoulder. "Poot!" she yelled back at Windy.

Windy turned to Zach and squawked again, a little more softly this time.

"Windy says they have a message from your friends at Ravenswood," Zach translated, checking out the blue dragonfly that had landed on his shoulder.

"What?" Adriane felt like dancing. "Well, why didn't you say so!"

The dragonflies all jumped back up and flew happily around Adriane.

"What's Ravenswood?" Zach asked her. "Is that where you live?"

"Yes. It's a wildlife preserve and my friends and I are guides there," she explained.

"I like the name."

The dragonflies all twirled and spun in a circle around Adriane. Fred dropped a small roll of paper into her hand.

"What's this?" She carefully unrolled the paper, turning it this way and that, studying the drawing scribbled on it. "Some kind of map?"

"Let me see that!" Zach grabbed the paper. As he examined it, his eyes narrowed.

"Where does it lead?" Adriane asked excitedly.

Zach looked up, astonished. "The Fairy Glen," he said as if he couldn't believe it.

"Yes!" Adriane almost jumped for joy. Ozzie must have drawn her a map and sent it with the dragonflies. "Why, that little ferret! The Fairimentals will help me find Storm!"

"Storm?"

"Um . . . the friend I'm looking for," she said, avoiding the boy's eyes.

Zach ripped the paper to shreds.

Adriane's hand flew to her mouth. "No, wait! What are you doing?"

"This must be destroyed."

"That was from my friends!" Adriane yelled. "It wasn't for you! You had no right!" Adriane felt like crying, but stopped.

Zach's face had gone ashen. "Who sent this?" he asked accusingly.

"Ozzie. He's an elf."

"An elf?"

"The Fairimentals sent him to Earth to find . . . humans," Adriane said.

"The Fairy Glen is the heart of this world!" Zach was clearly distressed. "What if the witch found this?" He threw the tiny scraps of paper into the river.

"You mean the Dark Sorceress?" asked Adriane.

Zach swung to face her. "She is using magic to destroy this world!"

Adriane's heart ached remembering the giant creatures lying dead across the hillside.

"First your stone, then these . . ." Zach started to say.

Fred sat on his arm and cocked his little blue head, smiling.

"Dragonflies," Adriane said.

"Yeah . . ." he went on. "She's probably got half the planet looking for us by now."

"Maybe that's the point," Adriane said slowly.

"You think she's after you?" Zach asked.

"She wants magical animals."

"Goook!" The dragonflies leaped into the air, bumped into one another, and popped out.

"Well, I think we can rule them out," Zach said. "And it's not Windy. There's no other magical anim—" He stopped.

The egg! It was sitting still, colors shifting boldly across its surface.

"She's after the egg!" Adriane concluded.

"Yeah, whatever it is, it's magical, all right. Windy even sensed it. I thought it was *your* magic attracting all the attention. It's that egg."

Zach stood still, as if he were listening hard to something. Ominous shadows moved slowly across the river as the sky darkened.

The griffin had stood up, his sharp bird eyes scanning the skies.

"What is it?" Adriane asked nervously. Something didn't feel right. She checked her wrist. Her stone was pulsing with bursts of amber light.

The griffin spread his wings, squawking and spitting loudly.

Adriane didn't have to ask what the spitting sound meant.

"We have to get out here . . . fast!" Zach leaped onto Windy's back.

Something streaked across the sky, smacked into the canyon wall with a *boom*, and ricocheted off like a flaming pinball. A tree exploded in flames, sending shards of wood flying everywhere.

Adriane ducked in terror, covering her head. Fireballs began to rain down into the canyon.

The griffin screeched up at the skies.

"Let's go!" Zach yelled at her.

Adriane skidded over to the egg, grabbed it, and hoisted it up to Zach. He stared at it for a moment, then took it, and reached for Adriane. Gripping his hand, she threw her leg over the back of the griffin and pulled herself up behind Zach.

Explosions rocked the riverbank as fire rained around them.

With a ferocious beat of his wings, the griffin was off the ground, Adriane barely holding on. Windy rose into the sky and stopped, hovering in place.

A dozen winged creatures had swarmed into a line across the top of the gorge, blocking their escape.

"Gargoyles!" Zach breathed.

Adriane could make out what at first looked like big, hairy, flying apes. Then she saw pointed leathery wings flap in the air, and wicked-looking bony horns that ran down their arms, backs, and legs. She could see their fierce, blazing eyes bearing down on them.

Windy circled. There was no way out.

The monsters advanced, flying slowly into the gorge.

Zach was desperately searching for an alternate escape route. "We can't get through them!"

A booming voice cut through the air. It was loud and gravelly and completely undecipherable.

Windy squawked.

Zach told Adriane, "You were right. They want the egg. They want us to hand it over and they'll let us pass."

Adriane hugged the egg close. "This is your world. What do you want to do?"

The boy sighed. "I'm open to suggestions."

Adriane scanned the ridgeline along the top of the gorge. She saw boulders balanced precariously along the edges. "Take us close to that wall," she said, pointing to the far side of the canyon.

"We'll be trapped over there!"

"I'm going to try and loosen those rocks on the ledge above," she told him.

"With what?"

"With this," she said, raising her wrist. The wolf stone pulsed with power. "If we can break their line, Windy can fly through the opening and we run like lightning."

"That's crazy!" Zach exclaimed.

"That's my suggestion."

The boy looked at the egg for a moment, then looked back at Windy. The griffin snorted his vote.

"Okay, let's do it."

Zach guided Windy toward the far wall of the canyon. The strata reminded Adriane of sand sculptures, layered with pastel shades of green, red, and purple.

Adriane scanned the ridgeline. Huge boulders lined the lip, hanging over the drop. Remembering how she had used the power of her stone to move objects before, she focused on the largest of the rocks. In her mind, she saw it moving, breaking free of its ancient bed.

The gargoyles had turned their line toward them, advancing like flying nightmares. Green fire sizzled between them, forming into a fireball that danced over their heads.

Adriane concentrated harder and felt a familiar sensation, like she was pushing through water. But it was too thick, too hard to break through. A drop of sweat ran down her nose.

Zach glanced at her and up at the rocks above them. "Go for the small one." He pointed to a spot below the boulder. "See? It's wedged just under the cliff line."

Adriane switched her focus to concentrate on the smaller rock . . . the water barrier felt thinner, and she pushed harder. The rock began to shake.

One gargoyle had flown forward in front of the others.

The green fireball flew across them and landed in the leader's claws.

"Hurry!" Zach yelled.

With a grunt, Adriane felt herself break through—and the rock came free, tumbling out over the gorge. It landed on the head of the lead gargoyle—and bounced off harmlessly.

Zach's face fell and his shoulders slumped.

The gargoyles closed in, making harsh guttural sounds. They were laughing. They knew their prey was trapped.

A sudden, sharp grating sound echoed above them, stone against stone. Thunder reverberated across the canyon as the entire ridgeline crumbled, sending truck-sized boulders falling into the gorge. Before the gargoyles could react, their line was torn apart, crushed by the impact of the two-ton rocks. The six in the middle were swept away and vanished instantly. The others chaotically scattered in surprise. The fireball exploded, sending the leader and two others smashing into the canyon walls.

With a fierce yell, Zach spurred Windy forward. The griffin didn't need any encouragement. He reared up and shot between the gargoyles, straight toward the top of the gorge.

The monsters were confused long enough for the griffin to break what remained of their line. But the last four were quick. They fell on Windy, tearing at the griffin's wings with sharp claws. The griffin screeched in pain.

Adriane was suddenly surrounded by the beating of leathery wings. She tried to shield her face, but long, sharp claws grabbed at the egg, trying to pry it loose from her arms. She gasped as wings beat around her head. One monster was on Zach; another had a stranglehold on the griffin's neck, trying to drag him down. Adriane's stomach lurched as the canyon walls tilted, the ground far below sweeping past at impossible angles.

A glint of steel flashed through the air. The gargoyle on Zach fell away, howling, one wing sliced from its body.

Windy was struggling to stay airborne as the other gargoyles swarmed over his head, trying to avoid the killing wrath of the boy's sword.

Adriane kicked out, knocking the creatures away from her, and freeing her arm. Another dove at the egg, wrapping its claws around it. Blazing red eyes blinded her as razor teeth tried to snap at her neck. She screamed and golden fire exploded from her gemstone. The force threw the gargoyle off. The other swooped in and grabbed Adriane's arms, pinning her gem against her waist. She couldn't move her arm. She watched in horror as the monster unhinged its jaws, opening a mouth full of razor teeth. The creature leaned into her face—and suddenly its head was gone, removed from its body with one cleave of the boy's sword. The monster's body fell back, green gore spurting from its neck as it fell into the gorge.

The last monster came at them, flying in fast. With all of her might, Adriane swept her stone into an arc and whipped out a blaze of fire. The power smashed into the gargoyle, sending it careening into the canyon wall. With a shriek, it fell and vanished.

The griffin soared out of the canyon.

"You all right?" Zach called back.

Adriane was shaking so hard, she was sure she'd lose her grip. Yet, through her sweat and tears, she still clutched the egg, holding it tight.

Windy dove into open desert, gliding low and fast.

Adriane watched, as if in a dream, as Zach pulled a small container from the griffin's collar. He bit off the lid, and poured dark, thick liquid onto Windy's side. It was then that she saw deep gouges had been ripped through his flesh—leaving ragged green lines of glowing poison. Black Fire.

The griffin gave a violent squawk, sharp eyes now glazed with pain. The dark liquid covered the worst of the wounds.

"Is he okay?" Adriane asked worriedly.

"He's hurt bad. I have to get him down before the poison reaches his heart."

"I'm so sorry!" she cried out. "It's all my fault!"

"Stop it!" the boy yelled. "Pull yourself together! We would have all been killed if you hadn't done that trick!"

Adriane bent over the egg, sobbing, wishing Emily were here to heal the brave griffin.

They coasted over a stretch of wide-open desert pocked with huge craters like the surface of the moon. The mountains towered in front of them as Zach guided Windy toward a pass between two of the tallest peaks.

"I've never seen creatures attack like that!" Zach said. "Whatever this thing is, it's important enough to risk a full-scale war."

"What do we do now?" Adriane asked.

"We have no choice. We're going to the Fairy Glen."

"But you tore up the map. How are we supposed to find the Fairimentals now?"

"I know where they are."

Adriane's eyes widened. What was Zack leading her into? She had no choice now but to trust his judgment.

She hugged the egg close, feeling the pulse of the new life within as they flew deeper into a world Adriane never could have imagined.

9

THE DESERT QUICKLY gave way to tree-covered foothills. Ahead, rivers fueled by melting snow flowed through a labyrinth of fjords that divided the upper mountain range. They were soon flying over fast-moving water, following rough, white-frothed rapids through twisting and turning ravines.

The griffin dipped suddenly, then regained his balance, snorting and gasping for air. Holding tight to the boy's shirt, Adriane looked at Windy's wounds. They were bad. Glowing green pulsed along thin arteries, fanning into the griffin's wings. Whatever the boy had poured over them must only have dulled the pain. Adriane knew the courageous creature would never give up until his heart burst— and hers along with it.

Zach leaned low, calming the animal, whispering soothingly. Adriane couldn't hear what he was saying, but she could see his hand stroking Windy's neck.

"How much farther?" she asked worriedly.

The boy straightened up. "The Anvil's just up ahead. It's not an ideal entry, but it's fast."

They were flying low enough to feel the spray from the rapids tumbling and rolling beneath them. Adriane tried to release the tension in her shoulders and focused on the strange sword now sitting quietly in its leather sheath by the boy's side. The intricately carved hilt was set with small, shimmering stones.

"I've never seen a sword like that," she noted.

"It's an Elven spirit sword."

"Are you a warrior?"

"I fight when I need to."

Adriane shuddered. "I hate it here. So many awful things. How can you fight for this?"

"That's not what I fight for," he said quietly.

The roar of rumbling water suddenly filled her ears as they crested the edge of a tremendous gorge. Beneath them was a cavernous opening in the earth completely surrounded by colossal waterfalls. It looked as if the gigantic circle of thundering water served as a drain for the entire world. Adriane gasped. These were the most awesome waterfalls she had ever seen.

She knew now why this place was called the Anvil.

Water hammered ten stories down, crashing into an inferno of white mist far below.

Zach gently ran his hand over the griffin's neck. "Which one, Windy?"

The griffin nodded his eagle head toward the largest of the mighty falls.

"Hang on. This is going to get a little bumpy," Zach called back to Adriane.

"Where are we going?" Adriane screamed over the deafening noise.

"That one," he yelled, pointing straight ahead.

Rainbows arced in the air, sparkling off spray from the booming falls. Behind, thousands of tons of water plummeted straight down, crashing into the abyss.

"We're going around that?" Adriane cried in astonishment.

"No."

"Oh." She sighed with relief.

"We're going through it."

The griffin dove toward the center of the falls.

Before Adriane could question the sanity of this action, she was rocked violently forward as water thundered over them. For an instant, she felt the pounding pressure would pulverize them like tiny bugs. But nothing happened.

She slowly opened one eye. Then the other—and gasped.

Below were forests. Dense verdant forests that

stretched forever under a brilliant sun. There were no waterfalls, no mountains.

"What happened?" she asked, her heart beating wildly.

"We took a shortcut," he answered.

She looked down and her eyes opened wide at the sight of beautiful rolling hills and—farmlands? Villages? "You said there were no other people here!" she exclaimed.

"No other humans," Zach corrected. "We're over the Moorgroves, near Arapaho Wells. This is elf country."

"Elves?" Adriane repeated in amazement. Ozzie had always insisted he was really an elf trapped in a ferret's body, but the reality of it had never hit her—until now. There was a thriving civilization here, while death and horror threatened not a few moments away. Adriane shaded her eyes to block the sun, and saw mountains way off in the distance. She had no idea how far they had come.

"How did we get here?"

"Through a portal," Zach said. "Aldenmor is riddled with them, if you know where to look. Probably like your world. In ancient times, some connected the worlds."

"Some still do," she said.

They had left the populated area and were above forests so thick Adriane couldn't make out individual trees. Windy's breathing was labored, and he wobbled dangerously, trying to keep airborne.

"We have to get him help!" Adriane yelled.

Zach wiped sweat from his eyes as he peered down at the trees below. "There, Windy," he commanded, leaning over and pointing.

The griffin dove into green and everything went gray. They were in a blinding mist. Where had *that* come from? There had been no sign of it from above.

The jolt shook Adriane as Windy landed hard. Zach was off the griffin in a flash, checking his wounds.

Adriane slipped down to cool, moist earth and gently placed the egg on the ground. She recognized the place instantly. The magic glade at Ravenswood! She was home!

Then she realized that this was not the place she knew after all. It only looked like it. This glade was much larger. A deep-blue lake lay before her, its surface broken by sparkles of sunlight, twinkling like diamonds. Along the shoreline, willows swept delicate branches across the water. Tall trees surrounded the glade like a wall. And the meadows around them were filled with the rainbow flowers that had been brought to Earth by the great fairy creature, Phelonius.

"This is amazing!" She turned about in awe—and stopped, her breath catching in her throat.

Windy lay on the ground. He wasn't moving. Zach was kneeling quietly by his side, gently wiping dirt away from the griffin's eagle head. The creature's once sharp, clear bird eyes were closed and he wasn't breathing.

"Oh no!" Adriane cried out.

The boy looked up, his cheeks stained with tears. "He's gone."

"But these flowers have healing magic!" She swept her arm over the field of rainbow flowers. "They can help him!"

Zach shook his head. "It's too late. The strain to get us here was too much."

Adriane ran to the griffin, forcing her magic stone to pulse with healing light. "Please," she called in a hoarse whisper. "Emily, tell me what to do!"

But there was no answer. The griffin was gone and her wolf stone could not call on the power of Emily's healing jewel.

"No!" She fell to her knees, crying.

A sound like tinkling bells drifted over her. Then it became a voice. "We are sorry."

Adriane turned. A thin veil of mist lingered in the center of the lake, lit from behind by a single shaft of sunlight. She blinked. Through her tears, Adriane saw a girl standing about ten feet from shore—*on* the water. The figure was made of water, flowing blue and green, swirling up from the lake itself.

"The griffin was a brave warrior," the watery figure said. The clear, pure water caught glints of sunlight as if the magic within sparkled.

Dust and dirt swirled behind Adriane. She covered her eyes. When she opened them, another figure stood next to her. It looked like tumbleweed woven together with twigs and leaves. Small branches stuck out at weird angles. "Sometimes magic can bring great loss," the creature said in a rustling voice.

"Who are you?" Adriane asked, looking at the fantastical creatures.

"I am Gwigg, an Earth Fairimental," the pile of twigs said, bits of leaves flying off it.

"I am Marina, a Water Fairimental," the water girl said, gracefully gliding to the shore's edge.

"You have come a long way." A light, airy breeze brushed past Adriane. She caught the translucent shape of something moving, flowing and hovering near her. "I am Ambia, an Air Fairimental," the breezy shape said.

Zach stood up and approached the Fairimentals. "Windy died to get us here!" he yelled angrily. "Why couldn't you help him?"

"The spirit of the griffin has come back to the magic," Marina said, her voice like silky chimes.

"Spirits of the past will always guide us into our future," Ambia whispered like the wind.

"Why did Windy have to die?" Zach cried, wiping tears from his face.

"We will weep with you," the Fairimentals gently answered together, combining their voices into a melody that drifted into a breeze blowing across the Fairy Glen. The willows swayed, releasing hundreds of tiny flowers upon the crystal waters.

"It was my fault," Adriane said, looking down at her

boots, dark hair falling over her face. "If he and Zach hadn't rescued me, Windy would still be alive."

"Why did you send an elf to her planet?" Zach asked the Fairimentals, trying to make sense of what was happening.

"For her," Marina answered.

"What's so special about her?"

"We need human magic users," Gwigg rustled.

"*I'm* human. I—" Zach kicked at the dirt. "I could learn magic, too!"

Ambia hovered around the boy. Adriane could just make out her shimmering shape. With a soft breeze, the Air Fairimental dried the tears on Zach's face.

"There are many levels of magic," Ambia said, her translucent shape glittering in the light.

Marina's sparkling eyes focused on Adriane. "She has the ability to become a mage."

A mage? Ozzie had used that word. A mage was a human who used magic.

"Only through the bond with a magical animal can magic be mastered completely," Marina sparkled.

"And now my friend is gone." Zach's shoulders slumped.

"You have brought us the Drake," Gwigg said, his strange shape of twigs and leaves reforming as he spoke.

Adriane looked at the egg sitting silently by her feet. "The Drake?"

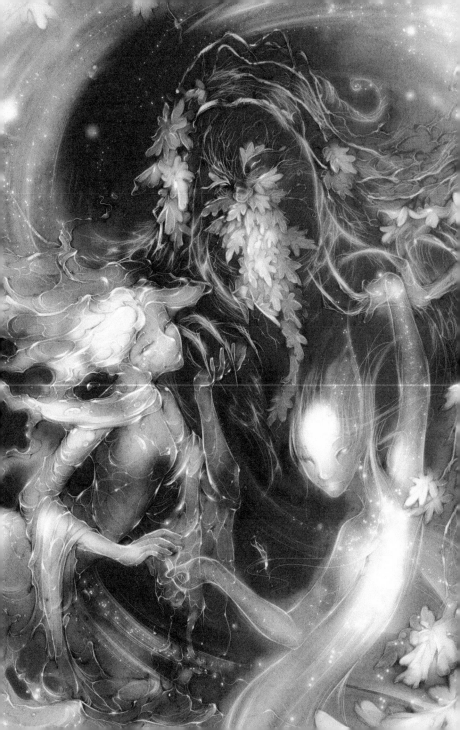

"If the sorceress had gotten the Drake, the balance of power would have shifted."

"The sorceress must be stopped," Marina's watery voice chimed.

"Aldenmor must be healed," Ambia whispered.

"What is . . . the Drake?" Adriane carefully asked.

"A dragon," Ambia breathed.

"A red crystal dragon," Marina added, magic sparkling through her watery shape. "They hatch once every thousand years."

"A *dragon?*" The boy looked horrified. "Windy died to bring a *dragon* here? They are vicious and horrible creatures!"

"The Drake is a very powerful creature. When dragons hatch, they imprint, bond deeply, with the first person they see. The sorceress intended the hatchling to imprint on her, giving her magic of unimaginable power." Gwigg shuddered, bits of sticks and dirt falling to the ground.

"That's why the sorceress wants magical animals?" Adriane asked.

"Yes."

"The unicorn would have fallen if not for the blazing star." Ambia swirled around Adriane.

Adriane thought of Kara. She'd give anything to see that bright smile right now, even though, only a day ago, she would have been happier to wipe it off that smug face. She felt a sharp sting of homesickness. She missed her friends. "Can you send me home?" she asked the Fairimentals.

"Yes."

Adriane's heart leaped.

"Your destiny is clear, Adriane," Marina said.

"How do you know me?"

"You wear the wolf stone. You have made it yours."

"Wolf stone? That's a wolf stone?" the boy asked.

"My friend . . . that I'm looking for, is not exactly human," Adriane said to him.

"What is she?" he asked, his hands balled into fists.

"A mistwolf."

Zach's ruddy complexion reddened and his eyes blazed with anger. "A mistwolf!" he spat and stalked away.

Adriane, confused and hurt, looked to the Fairimentals.

"Zachariah was raised by mistwolves." Ambia's voice blew like cool wind.

This time it was Adriane's turn to feel shock. Moonshadow had said a human had been responsible for killing the pack mother.

Adriane ran after the boy. The time had come for secrets to be revealed.

10

WILDFLOWERS SWIRLED AROUND Adriane as she walked down the lush path in pursuit of Zach. Wide, lustrous leaves of purple, pink, and blue sprouted everywhere, lending the glade a gleam of rainbow brilliance. She wished she could explore this extraordinary place, and she had about a million questions for the Fairimentals. But she had to find Storm—and get home. Her Gran was used to her going off on her own, but she would certainly worry before too long. Hopefully, Emily and Kara were covering for her.

The path led to a grassy meadow. In the center stood an enormous tree, giant branches stretching out in all directions from a trunk as thick as a house. In fact, it *was* a house—a tree house. Wooden platforms were cleverly hidden amidst the green boughs. They were connected by natural stairways made of branches and covered by foliage thick enough to keep out any rain or cold—although she wondered if there was really ever any bad weather here.

Zach was sitting on a platform two levels up, gazing out over the Fairy Glen.

"Hi," Adriane said shyly as she approached.

The boy remained silent.

"Can I come up and sit with you a while?"

"Suit yourself."

Adriane climbed up to join him. The platform formed the floor of a large room. Branches had grown around and through the floor, forming tree chairs and even a tree bed, with a mattress piled thick with soft leaves. Thinner branches hung down the sides, like green curtains.

"This is an amazing tree!" she exclaimed.

"This is Okawa," he told her.

She looked around. She didn't see anyone.

She pointed to the tree questioningly. Zach nodded.

She studied the enormous tree. Gran had always spoken about nature spirits but Adriane refused to believe her, shrugging it off as just plain weird. Yet this tree was very much alive. She could feel it.

Adriane politely bowed. "Hello, Okawa. I am honored to meet you."

The great tree rustled, and a few of the smaller branches seemed to bend in toward Adriane, enfolding her in the fresh green scent of leaves.

"He likes you," the boy observed.

"I like him, too." Adriane sat next to Zach and looked out at the lake. "I feel so protected here, so safe."

He cracked open a hard-shelled fruit that looked like a small red coconut and handed her half. "Okawa has taken care of me for a long time."

Adriane took the shell and drank the milky liquid inside. It was sweet and delicious.

"Thank you," she said.

"You can also eat the stuff inside, it's good."

As they ate, Adriane noticed an old steamer trunk next to them. It was open and she could see clothes, some old books, a spyglass, and a few assorted tools.

"What's all this?" she asked, pointing to the trunk.

"It belonged to my parents."

She reached in and picked up a photograph set in a brass frame. Two smiling, proud parents holding a laughing baby in their arms looked out at her.

"That's me," Zach said.

"The baby, I take it." She smiled.

The corner of Zach's mouth twitched slightly upward.

Adriane noticed an old pocket watch. "May I?"

He nodded.

She examined the watch. It was engraved in script lettering: "To Alexander, always yours, Graziela."

"A gift to my father from my mother," he explained.

"It's beautiful." She put it down and studied the boy. "How old are you, Zach?"

"I don't know."

"When was your last birthday?"

"What do you mean?"

"You know, birthdays . . . with birthday parties?"

Zach looked puzzled.

"You've never had a birthday party?"

"No."

"Well, it's fun. You wear silly hats and your friends give you gifts."

"My friend is dead."

"I'm really sorry . . ." Adriane felt her eyes brim with tears and quickly wiped them away.

"It wasn't your fault," Zach said.

They sat watching the sunlight play across the lake.

"Zach . . . tell me about the mistwolves."

"No!" Anger raged, threatening to boil over within the boy. He jumped up and walked away.

"Please, Zach. My friend is still alive. Won't you help me find her?"

Zach walked to Okawa's massive trunk, reaching for its strength.

"My parents were magic users," he said into the tree.

Adriane's eyes opened wide.

"They were killed when I was a baby. I was found by the mistwolves." He turned around, leaning his back against Okawa. "The pack mother, Silver Eyes, took me in and raised me. She taught me to run with the pack and to sing the wolfsong . . ." His eyes were dark with

sadness. "She loved me, and I loved her like my mother."

Adriane sat quietly, hardly breathing.

"I was the runt and my pack brother did not trust me. Now he is the pack leader."

Adriane flashed on the black wolf that had taken Storm . . . Moonshadow.

"A witch had begun using magic in terrible ways. We knew she was once human. Moonshadow believed humans did nothing but bring sadness and destruction. He thought I would bring ruin and death to the pack . . . and one day I did."

He slid to the floor, knees raised to cover his face.

"More than anything, I wanted to find the monster that had killed my human parents. I became obsessed with hunting it down. I thought that if I could prove my courage, Moonshadow would accept me in the pack . . ." He paused to steady his breathing.

"I was hunting in the Shadowlands with several of the pack when I found the creature. I was so full of hate, I thought of nothing for my packmates. Instead of avenging my parents, I . . . I led the wolves into a trap . . ." He faltered.

"What happened to them?" Adriane asked after a few seconds.

"I was the only one who escaped." The boy buried his head in his knees.

"One of the fallen wolves was Silver Eyes . . . my wolf

mother."

Adriane sat quietly.

Zach took a deep breath, calming himself. "Moonshadow sent me away. He said I would never be a wolf brother. I wandered for a long time until I met the elves. They took me in and fed me and brought me here, to the Fairimentals. I began my work for them, scouting, acting as their eyes and ears. When I found Windy, he was just a pup, caught in a trap. His parents had been killed, also. We've been together ever since . . . until today."

Adriane slowly rocked back and forth, hugging herself. "I never see my parents," she told Zach. "They might as well be dead. If it wasn't for Storm, I don't know what I'd do. And now, she's gone. She left me to run with the pack."

The boy sat watching her. "So we're both alone," he finally said.

"What's happened here, Zach? To Aldenmor."

"There was some kind of explosion in the Shadowlands. Since then the Black Fire has been spreading." He rose suddenly and walked to the edge of the platform, gazing out over the Fairy Glen. "Everything's changing so fast. Aldenmor is in terrible danger."

"Those poor animals I saw in the valley," Adriane whispered.

"Wilderbeasts. They once roamed all over that area, herds of them. Not anymore. And more animals are going to die if she is not stopped." His eyes blazed. "That is what I fight for."

Adriane stood up and joined him. "The Fairimentals must be proud of you."

"No. That's why they need you." He looked down. "I'm not good with magic."

"People have different ways of using magic," Adriane said. "My friend Kara, back on Earth, she doesn't have a gemstone, and she makes all kinds of magic just by being who she is—our magic just works better when she's around."

Zach listened intently.

"The way the Fairimentals treat you, the way Okawa cares for you . . . the way the Elven sword comes to life in your hands. Zach, everything about you is magic."

"No. You heard the Fairimentals. *You* have the gift, not me."

"Zach," Adriane said, searching his eyes. "I saw the way you were with Windy. You loved him. As much as I love Storm. I may not know much, but I have learned this: magic always starts here." She placed her hand on the boy's heart.

He looked at her hand, then into her eyes.

"I'm so sorry Windy is gone," Adriane continued. "But you have to go on. The Fairimentals need you . . . I need you."

"You . . . do?" he asked, eyes wide.

Adriane looked away. "You're everything I've always dreamed of being. Strong, confident, independent." She turned to him again. "And you understand what's going on around here. How are we supposed to figure this all out without your help?"

"I'm not going back to the mistwolves."

"But it wasn't your fault. It was a horrible accident."

"You don't know that!"

Adriane took his hands in hers. "You could come back to Earth with me. You'd meet lots of friends and you could go to school and learn all kinds of things."

"You think I could fit in there?" he asked uncertainly.

Adriane smiled at him. "If I can, you sure can."

Zach didn't return the smile. He dropped her hand, turned, and walked to the branch stairway. "I'm going to take care of Wind Dancer."

"Can I help?"

"No," he answered sharply, then his voice softened. "I want to say good-bye alone."

Adriane understood and respected his wish. She watched as he started down. "Zach," she called after him.

He stopped.

"I'm going to find Storm."

"I know," he said, and walked away.

THE BRIGHT SPECKLED egg sat on the sandy shores patiently waiting as Adriane walked back to the lake. Colors swirled through the shell as she approached. She knelt down and patted it.

"It's time for me to go," she explained.

The egg quivered slightly.

"You have to stay here. The Fairimentals will take care of you now."

Deep blues and purples moved across the shell as the egg learned into Adriane's arms.

"C'mon, now don't get like that. You're going to make me all sad again." But she was already crying. She hugged the egg. "Thank you, Drake," she said softly.

From the corner of her eye, she caught the flutter of air. She could just make out the hovering, translucent shape of Ambia.

"You have many questions," the Air Fairimental said.

"Was the wolf stone meant for me?" Adriane asked, sniffling as she got to her feet.

"Nothing that happens is truly random." Ambia's cool voice brushed against Adriane.

"Why did you choose me?" Adriane asked.

"You are a warrior."

"No, I'm not. I'm scared all the time," she said angrily. "What kind of warrior is that?"

"The heart of a warrior is not measured by how strong you fight." Marina rose in tinkling chimes out of the crystal blue waters. "It is your spirit that connects you to the magic."

"Why me? The magic . . . I mean, don't I get a choice?"

"Why did you come to Aldenmor?" Gwigg's scratchy

voice asked from the ungainly mass of twigs and dirt nearby.

"To find Stormbringer," Adriane said quietly.

"That is a choice of the heart." Ambia smiled. "That is why you have been chosen to find Avalon."

Avalon. It always came back to that mysterious place of legendary magic.

"What is Avalon?" Adriane asked.

"Everything around you . . . the sky, the earth beneath your feet, the magic itself—all are the forces of nature, of life. All are connected to Avalon," Gwigg spoke. "We have called on you to help us find it. To make the magic new again."

"If *you* can't find it, how are we supposed to?" Adriane asked.

"We are elemental spirits of this world," Ambia said. "We are bound to Aldenmor."

Gwigg swept around Adriane. "Three will be tested," the rough voice said. "One will follow her heart. One will see in darkness. And one will change, utterly and completely. This is the Prophecy of Three."

Ambia swirled across the grass. "It will take three—a healer, a warrior, and a blazing star—to find Avalon and heal the sadness. Only after each has met their challenge will you be ready."

"I don't know how to help." Adriane hung her head. "You need a knight, a hero, like Zach."

"This is *your* journey, Adriane," Ambia told her. "Even if you do not know, you know what is right."

"I can't do it without Storm."

"The mistwolves must find their own destiny." Gwigg spun close to Adriane and stopped. The Fairimental parted a thicket of leaves. A small, shining orb dangling from a metallic chain glistened.

"Give this to Moonshadow," the Earth Fairimental said. "It is a gift to help the mistwolves find their way."

Adriane took the sparkling orb from Gwigg and slipped it in her vest pocket.

"You must continue your path and follow your heart." Ambia swirled around Adriane.

A flash of light caught her eye. It glowed between two giant trees that surrounded the glade.

The Fairimentals' voices all blended together in a strange but beautiful harmony. "The magic is with you, now and forever."

Adriane looked at the Fairy Glen. It was so beautiful, so peaceful. She wanted to just sit by the water and feel the magic of the Fairimentals wash over her. To answer all her questions. Instead, she turned and walked away, toward the twinkling light hovering gently between twin towering trees. Adriane felt her wrist for the wolf stone and summoned her courage. She stepped into the light . . . and vanished.

11

THE SUDDEN BRIGHTNESS of snow-capped peaks
made her shield her eyes. Temporarily disoriented,
Adriane stood still, trying to get her bearings. She was on
a hilltop near the base of the upper mountain ranges. To
her right, great peaks rose above. To her left was the plateau
that led to the smaller ranges. She could see the crisscross
of gorges that ran like a ragged patchwork. She wondered
which gorge Windy had hidden them in, and felt a stab
of loss for the magnificent griffin.

She looked behind her, where she'd just been, and saw
nothing unusual. Not even mist. The Fairimentals would
take no chances that anything uninvited might find a way
into the Fairy Glen. There would be no evidence, no signs,
no clues to follow.

She zipped up her vest as a cool wind sent a chill through her. She felt something in her pocket. Startled for a second, she took out the sparkling orb given to her by the Fairimentals. Tiny stars twinkled in the small ball. It looked like a smaller version of the fairy map given to Kara by Phel; the map the girls had lost to the dark witch's manticore. Was this the same thing? Maybe the mistwolves would know, if she could find them. She slipped the gift back into her pocket.

The landscape was sparsely scattered with rocks, wiry brush, and short, wind-twisted trees. Ahead lay hidden valleys, covered in shifting, thick fog. This was a harsh environment. Suddenly Adriane thought she might have been a bit hasty leaving the Fairy Glen so soon.

Stay focused, she reminded herself. If the Fairimentals sent her here, the mistwolves must be close by. She had no choice but to use the wolf stone to contact Storm. She would have to chance any magic trackers. She couldn't just wander around without some direction.

She held up her wrist and concentrated, forming an image of Storm in her mind. Immediately, the gemstone pulsed with golden light.

"Stormbringer," she called softly. "Where are you?"

Adriane stretched out, reaching harder.

The smell of earth filled her senses. Cool grass cushioned her feet. She felt dizzy suddenly as the landscape moved past her. Gray shapes came into focus in front of her eyes—in front of Storm's eyes.

"Storm!"

She was running up a hill with several other wolves.

"I am here."

Adriane's heart leaped at the sound of the familiar voice in her head. "Where are you?"

"The pack is on the move."

Through Storm's eyes, Adriane saw them. Several hundred mistwolves, adults and pups, cresting the hill before her. The smell of the pack filled her nose and she longed to run with them. Storm howled, and the pack howled in return. The wolfsong filled her heart. Adriane threw back her head and howled with them.

"Stormbringer!" a different wolf growled.

Moonshadow stood before her, eyes blazing. *"The human will not join the pack."*

"I have brought something for you from the Fairimentals," Adriane said eagerly.

"Is this some human trick?"

"She is my packmate," Storm growled as she faced the pack leader.

The wolves circled around Storm.

Adriane felt her own lips pull back into a snarl. She growled—or was it Storm?

"Human," Moonshadow said to her.

With a start, Adriane realized the pack leader was talking to her.

"We are moving, seeking a new pack home far away from here. The pack must be protected. We need Storm now."

"The Fairimentals want you to have this gift," Adriane said. "I think it might help you find your new home."

Moonshadow snarled. *"I will give you until the two moons rise in the sky to bring this gift to me. If you are not with us in that time, so be it."*

The wolves began to disappear into mist.

"Storm, how do I find you?" Adriane asked quickly.

"The magic is with you," Storm's voice echoed through the mist and disappeared.

Adriane blinked. Sparse, empty hills stood before her. The sensation of sharing the wolf's mind, of being a wolf, had filled her heart with joy. To be separated from that made her feel so empty. She shivered.

The pack was leaving, migrating to a place far away. She had until Aldenmor's two moons rose over the valley to find them. Reaching out, she spun slowly in a circle, silently calling Storm. When she faced the hills to her right, the wolf stone glowed. Dusting herself off, she headed down into a valley of shadows.

The valley was thick with trees. But these woods were not inviting like the lush forests of the Moorgroves. Here the trees seemed to twist and bend, fighting against one another, struggling for a foothold in the rocky earth.

She wound her way around giant, gnarled roots and misshapen logs until she came to a dirt path. The going was easier, with better visibility, so she could see if anything was coming—which also meant that whatever she saw could see her, too.

She tried not to think about that and focused instead on what she had learned from the Fairimentals.

Three will be tested. One will follow her heart, one will see in darkness, and one will change utterly and completely.

What did that mean? She wished Emily and Ozzie were here to help figure it out—they were much better with riddles.

Were they each being tested in some way? Emily had learned to be a healer and had healed the animals at Ravenswood. Kara had saved the unicorn. Now was it *her* turn?

Three will find Avalon and heal the sadness. Heal Aldenmor? She should have asked the Fairimentals more, but she had a feeling they didn't have all the answers either. What was happening on Aldenmor was only the tip of the iceberg. If this sorceress—this witch—was not stopped here, Aldenmor, Earth, and the web—even Avalon itself—would not be safe. What would happen then? She shuddered. She had spent most of her life learning to live with loneliness, but she had never felt more alone than she did right at this minute.

Crunch!

Adriane spun around, ready to defend herself.

Nothing.

A dry branch cracked nearby. Then another. Behind her. She turned, but saw only gnarled trees, thick with thorns.

Searching for a good place to hide, she spotted some

large rocks partway up the side of a gully. Rivulets of melted snow formed splotches of water, some running into small streams, some lying stagnant. She tried to avoid splashing in the puddles as she scrambled up the ravine and ducked behind the rocks.

She waited. Her heart was beating fast, and she took deep breaths, willing herself to calm down.

A loud snap behind her made her jump. Something was pushing through the dense undergrowth, coming right toward her. Adriane gasped, thinking of the small, agile imps. She looked left and right. She had made a strategic error. The rocks she thought would hide her were boxing her in.

Adriane stood, back to the rocks, and held her gemstone out before her, its golden light pulsing . . . and waited.

Nothing happened. Cautiously, she stepped forward and parted the thick brush, slowly opening the vines and bramble. There was something there all right—

"Ahhh!" Adriane fell backward as the big speckled egg, bright colors swirling happily, rolled out on top of her.

"What the . . . ?" she exclaimed.

The egg tilted over and lay on her.

Adriane sat up, cradling the egg in her lap. "What are you doing here? You're supposed to be back in the Fairy Glen! Bad egg!"

The egg's colors shifted to blues and purples, and it quivered. Adriane rolled it to the ground and got to her feet, shaking her finger. "Oh, no!" Don't give me that. You are a very bad egg!"

The egg shyly leaned into Adriane's legs, shaking.

Adriane looked down and sighed. "Okay, okay. I didn't mean it. You just surprised me." She knelt down and hugged the egg. "I'm glad to see you, too. I missed you."

The egg beamed with bright colors.

"Do the Fairimentals know you followed me? You know I'm going to have to take you back to the Fairy Glen—if I knew where that was. But I don't. So I guess you'll have to come with me to meet the mistwolves."

Bright colors swirled over the surface of the egg as it bounced up and down.

"But *then* I'm taking you back."

Adriane climbed down from the rocks and started on the dirt path again. The egg rolled after her.

"Say, you didn't happen to bring any of those red co-conuts? No? Just wondering. And I like your name, Drake. It's so smooth, like a rock star." Adriane laughed. "Rock star, get it?"

The egg tagged along right by her side, glowing brightly.

"Never mind."

They continued across the valley floor. The trees began to thin out. The rivulets became streams, and the ground started becoming rockier. Several times Adriane had to help the Drake over fallen trees and jutting stones.

"Okay, let's take five," Adriane said as they came upon a deep gully. A small stream ran though it. She was thirsty, but she dared not drink the water, which might not be safe. She slid down the hill to the stream and sat down against a tree. The Drake rolled down and leaned into her.

"I wonder how much farther it is." She huddled close, arm around the Drake. "Looks like we're almost across the valley. I just need to rest for a bit . . ."

Something shook Adriane awake. She opened her eyes. How long had she been sleeping? The Drake sat silently shaking next to her, ribbons of bright red swirling. Adriane looked closer. Two reptilian eyes opened just under the surface of the shell.

Adriane gasped. Something tickled at her mind. She fell over as the ground trembled. What was that? She barely had time to look around before another shock wave hit, sending vibrations up and down her spine. Her wolf stone was pulsing with a strong, amber light. She recognized the pulse immediately as a signal of danger. She heard the sounds of monstrous feet slamming into the ground. Something was coming—something big!

12

*A*DRIANE PUSHED THE heavy egg up the sloping side of the ravine. It was fiery red and warm to the touch. She glanced over her shoulder. Whatever was coming was getting closer. If she had to fight it, she wanted the advantage of height.

"C'mon, Drake." She pushed the egg over the top of the slope as a tree fell over, smashing to the ground behind her.

Adriane whirled around and gasped.

It stood at least ten feet tall, massive with muscle. It had the head of a pig, with long curved teeth protruding from its bottom lip. Slightly hunched, its arms were like tree trunks. One giant hand held a double-headed ax, the other a gigantic round shield. Its beady, black eyes looked up at her and the egg. Its mouth turned in a vicious grin. The thing grunted something unintelligible and stepped forward, enormous feet with pointed claws hitting the ground, making it tremble.

Adriane scrambled over the top of the gully and stood protectively in front of the egg. She raised her gemstone, hoping it was powerful enough to stop this monster. The thing raised its ax. She braced herself as it stomped up the ravine.

Something flew through the air, swinging in on a vine—and crashed into the giant. Eyes widening in astonishment, the huge thing toppled over and fell back down. The ground shook as it hit bottom. Adriane carefully peered over the hillock—someone jumped up, knocking her back.

"Are you okay?" Zach looked down at her.

"No!" Adriane yelled. "What are you doing here?"

"Rescuing you." He grabbed her hand and hoisted her to her feet.

Adriane ran to the egg and struggled to lift it. "Nice of you to drop in."

"I thought so." He edged her aside and hefted the egg in his arms. Together, they took off, running along the ridgeline. Zach searched for a place to hide.

"Couldn't live without me, huh?" Adriane called after him.

"More like the Drake here couldn't live without you," Zach replied.

They leaped across a small chasm to a dusty ridge. The cliff wall below was filled with rounded caves.

"We'll have to borrow one of these caves. We can't fight them"

"Them? As in more than one?"

"They're in a patrol, six of them."

He placed the egg down and carefully leaned over to examine the caves.

"Six?!" One was horrible enough. "What are they?"

"Orcs. Disgusting." He spit on the ground, reminding Adriane of something Windy would have done. "We'll have to hide out and hope they pass us by."

"And if they don't?"

"Orcs aren't too bright. You'll think of something," Zach said.

"Thanks for the vote of confidence."

She watched Zach slide down the hill and begin sweeping branches and debris aside, uncovering a large opening in the ravine wall. His Elven sword was strapped to his back.

"This one looks empty," he announced. "Come on." He held out his arm and helped Adriane slide the egg into the hole. She followed, hoping they weren't disturbing anything too nasty inside.

It was dark and musty, but from the opening they could see all the way to the valley floor below. Adriane placed the Drake near the back of the cave while Zach quickly pulled back the brush and branches to cover the opening. They could just see through the debris, which acted like a screen.

Zach turned to Adriane. "Here." He took out three small red coconuts from his pocket.

Adriane smiled. "You came all the way here to bring me coconuts?"

"I thought you'd be hungry."

"Well, I am. Thank you." She put two in the deep vest pocket next to the orb, and cracked open the other, gratefully drinking the delicious milk inside.

"Actually, the Fairimentals sent me to bring back you-know-who." He gestured with his thumb and turned to look through the screen of brambles. "Orcs aren't great magic trackers but they can sense the Drake."

"What do we do if they come?" she asked.

"You'll have to create a distraction."

"Good idea. I'll just run around and they can chase me for a while."

"I was thinking of something a bit more magical," he said, looking at her wolf stone.

Adriane followed his eyes. "Oh. I can do that."

Zach crawled back to examine the egg. "What's with the Drake? It's all hot. I can barely touch it."

"I know. And it's all red."

The boy's eyes met hers. "I have to get it back before—" His face grew pale.

"Before what?"

Zach blinked. "You think those orcs are monsters? You

have no idea what a dragon is. It's mean, and vicious and, and—horrible!"

"How do you know that?"

"Because."

"Because why? Have you ever met a dragon before?"

"Well, no . . ."

Adriane crossed her arms. "So you're just assuming it's a horrible monster."

Zach turned away and crawled back to the opening. "Everyone knows it's true."

"Well, I don't. And no one is going to harm this egg!"

The ground outside trembled. The orcs were approaching.

Adriane tossed her empty coconut shell aside and kneeled next to the boy, peering out.

"They're coming this way," he said.

"I'm going to try something." She held up her stone and concentrated, focusing on the trees across the ravine. She pictured them shaking and rattling.

Suddenly orcs came into view, their ugly pig snouts opening and closing, drooling over fearsome boar's teeth. Some carried axes, some wielded spears.

Adriane concentrated harder and across the gully two trees shook. Maybe she could fool them by sending a ghost image of the egg and placing it behind the shaking trees.

The orc leader stopped and sniffed at the air. It looked at the far side of the gully and moved in the direction of the trees.

"It's working," Zach whispered. "As soon as they cross that stream, we'll make a break and run."

"Where?"

Zach looked at her. "I go back with the egg, and you . . . go where you have to."

"You could come with me," Adriane suggested.

"No way. Even if I wanted to, I couldn't bring the egg to the pack. Trackers would be all over them."

Adriane hadn't considered that. She could be putting the entire pack in danger by bringing the egg there. "But the Fairimentals want me to give this to Moon-shadow." She held out the sparkling orb on its chain for Zach to see.

"They gave you that?" he breathed, eyes wide.

"Yes, what is it?"

"A fairy map," he told her.

So it *was* like the gift Phelonius had tried to give Kara. "What is a fairy map?"

"A map of portals."

"So the mistwolves can leave," Adriane realized sadly.

"So they can leave *safely*," he corrected. "Hey, don't forget your mistwolf abandoned you to fend for yourself here."

"What's that supposed to mean?" Adriane shot back in anger, slipping the orb back into her pocket. The pack might have treated Zach callously, but Storm would never treat Adriane that way! Would she?

"Just that the pack leader has his own agenda. And the pack will follow him."

"So you're saying Storm isn't coming back."

Zach's eyes filled with compassion. "I don't know, Adriane. Things change."

He turned to look back outside. "Get ready to move—they're across the stream.

"Be very quiet."

Craaack!

Adriane jumped. "What was that?"

"It wasn't me," Zach said.

"Well, it wasn't me, either."

A high-pitched screech filled the cave.

The orcs had stopped and were looking around suspiciously.

Adriane and Zach exchanged stares.

"If it wasn't me or you . . ." Zach began as they both turned to look behind them.

The egg had a big crack right down the center.

"Oh, no!" Zach scrambled over to check it out. The egg writhed suddenly, its sides splitting into a dozen smaller cracks. Zach watched in horror as shards of shell crumbled. A low whine began to emanate from within. The egg was starting to hatch!

The boy's eyes widened in terror. "Make it stop!"

"What?! Are you crazy?"

With a screech, a single hideous claw broke through the shell.

"We've got to get out of here!" Zach kicked away the brambles covering the cave opening.

Adriane had a sinking feeling that the Drake might not be what she expected. The creature inside the egg was screeching like a banshee. A second clawed foot kicked out another section of egg. Two red reptilian eyes opened and peered out at her. As Adriane stared into those eyes, something flashed in her mind.

Zach grabbed her shoulder, whirling her around. "Let's go! Now!"

Adriane didn't know what to do. What if whatever was hatching was worse than what was waiting outside? She was trapped between an egg and a hard place.

13

ADRIANE STUCK HER head out of the cave. The giant orcs were stomping across the gully . . . right toward them. She looked back at the hatching dragon egg. "What do we do?"

"We run!" Zach grabbed Adriane's hand and yanked her out through the opening. They skirted the top of the ravine, making for the next valley. Zach was determined to put as much distance as possible between themselves and whatever monsters were behind them.

Adriane couldn't get those eyes out of her head. It was as if the dragon were calling to her, connected to her.

"Wait!" she yelled, pulling Zach to a stop. "I can't leave

Drake. I'm going back!" Adriane whirled around and ran back atop the ridge.

"I was supposed to bring back an egg," Zach shouted after her. "Not a live dragon!"

Adriane leaped over the ridgeline, sliding and skidding down toward the cave.

Bent low, she scrambled inside. All that remained were goo-covered shell fragments. Whatever had hatched was gone.

Zach tentatively peeked into the cave. "Well?"

"It's not here!" Adriane shouted.

"Oh, great." Zach slumped, head in hands, trying to figure out what to do.

Adriane spotted something out of the corner of her eye. Something in a shell fragment. She bent, pulled it free, and looked at it. It was a stone—rough-hewn but definitely some kind of crystal.

"Come on, Adriane!" Zach yelled in to her.

She slipped the stone into her breast pocket and climbed outside. "Which way?" she asked.

The ominous booming sound of marching feet resounded from the gully below.

"Not that way," Zach said, pointing.

Adriane's breath caught in her throat. Six orcs crashed through the trees, grinding rocks and logs into dust under their heavy feet. They brandished mismatched, battle-worn swords, spears and shields, some chipped and stained from other bloody battles.

She heard a swish and caught sight of a glint of steel. Zach had drawn his sword. A hint of fire licked up and down the finely honed edges, as if it were hungry for battle.

Adriane frantically scanned the area for anything that might have just recently hatched.

Ching!

A giant spear appeared in the wall not a foot away, sending clods of dirt flying in all directions. Adriane jumped back in shock and felt the loose earth beneath her feet give way. She was slipping. "Zach!" she called, desperately scrabbling for a handhold.

He grabbed for her arm but the hillside slipped down into the ravine, Adriane along with it.

"Ahhgh!" She landed hard on the gully floor.

Six orcs crashed across the steam, barreling down on her. She jumped to her feet, raising her wrist. The magic flowed from the stone like amber fire, swirling up and around her arm.

The orcs grunted and slowed at the sight, obviously aware of magic fire.

Zach landed in front of her, sword raised and glowing with fierce power. "Go for their legs," he yelled over his shoulder. "The hamstring just behind the ankle!"

The orc leader snorted, long upturned teeth moving on both sides of its pig snout. Beady, black eyes filled with rage, it roared, lunging at them with battle-ax raised—and suddenly stopped. The others stumbled as they barreled into him. The orc leader held his thick arm out to the side, its beady eyes now full of total terror.

"That's right, we're bad!" Zach taunted.

Adriane watched in amazement as the orcs started to shuffle backward. Then, squealing like pigs, they broke rank and ran away.

"Ha! Guess we showed them!" Zach turned around with a grin . . . which suddenly twisted into a horrified grimace.

"What?" Adriane had only to look at the gaped-mouth expression on Zach's face to know that whatever had really scared those orcs away was standing right behind her.

"Maamaa!"

Adriane turned at the cry ringing through her mind. She had never seen anything like it. It was a dragon all right or at least what she thought a dragon looked like! It was about the size of a really big dog. It sat back on two large feet. A rounded belly tapered off to a thinner chest with two arms and a long neck. It was covered with smooth scales in a variety of red colors, ending with a long, wagging tail, shaped into an arrowhead at the end. Its two silky wings shifted in colors, just like when it was still in its shell. It had a spiky ruff at the neck, not unlike a lion's mane, and two stubby, rounded horns jutting out from behind oversized, pointy ears that bent over at their tips. It actually reminded Adriane of a big puppy. Its long horse-like face had a wide mouth filled with tiny, sharp baby teeth.

This was the fearsome monster that everyone was so worried about? It was just a baby and it was crying—

"Maamaa!"

—for its mama. Uh-oh.

"Maaaaaama!"

The dragon lumbered toward her, tripping over feet much too big for its body. Joyfully, it bumped against Adriane. She hugged it. "Steady there," she said with a smile. She looked at Zach. "Look, Daddy. Baby's taken his first steps."

Realizing his mouth was still hanging open, the boy closed it, put his sword away, and stomped over. "I'm taking *baby* back to the Fairimentals right now."

The dragon buried its head behind Adriane, sweeping its body around and knocking its big tail into the boy. Zach went flying into the stream.

Drake sniffled, resting his long snout on top of Adriane's head. She wasn't afraid at all. She felt a bond, familiar and strong.

"Aww, it's okay, little guy," she cooed, scratching him under his chin. "You scared away those mean old monsters, didn't you? Yes, you did."

Zach stammered, tried to speak, but spat out water instead.

"You hungry, Drake?" Adriane reached into her pocket

and pulled out a coconut. She cracked it open and held it up to the dragon's mouth.

Drake stuck his snout in the coconut and happily lapped up the milk with his forked tongue.

"There, good baby," she cooed.

Zach had begun to pace back and forth in the gully, arms waving. "This is just great!"

"What's with you?"

"I'll tell you what's with me. The dragon has imprinted on you! He'll never let me take him back now. And I can't take him to the mistwolves. You're going to have to come back with me to the Fairy Glen."

"I can't. I only have until the moons rise. I'll never get to Storm in time."

"Well, we can't sit here!" Zach turned to look downstream. "Those orcs are dumb, but once they realize it's a *baby* dragon, they'll be back. Then what do we do?"

"UrRRRrp!" Drake belched a small fireball.

"Ahhh!" Zach's butt was suddenly crisped with black soot. He jumped up and down rubbing his smoking rear and yelling, "You big dummy! I'm not an orc!"

Drake lowered his head, cowering behind Adriane, one wide eye watching the boy dance around.

"I told you! That thing is dangerous!" Zach yelled.

"He didn't mean it." Adriane scratched behind the dragon's ears. The scales were amazingly soft. "Shhh, it's okay. Good dragon."

Her face was suddenly covered in sloppy wet dragon licks. Adriane giggled.

Zach walked over, brushing off soot. "You're still gonna have to come back with me."

"Drake, now you have to listen to me," Adriane told the baby dragon.

Drake sat, panting like a big puppy.

"I can't take you with me. You have to go with Zach to the Fairy Glen. Do you understand?"

Drake cocked his head and eyed Zach.

Zach forced a big smile over his face.

"See? He's okay," Adriane said.

She started to walk away. "Good dragon. Now stay with Zach. Stay."

She had gone only a few yards when Drake leaped up and ran to her, big feet clomping in the dirt. *"Maamaa!"*

"No, no. You have to stay with Zach! Ohhh . . ."

Panting happily, Drake reached out and gave her a big hug, slobbering all over her head.

"Oh, it's no use," Zach said in dismay.

A terrifying roar split the air. Followed by the thundering boom of feet.

Zach turned, whipping his sword free from its sheath. "They're coming back."

"Let's get out of here!" Adriane yelled.

"Good idea."

They ran down the gully, following the stream. Zach

was out in front, and Drake clumped behind Adriane. The ravine was getting deeper and narrower. Soon this stream would be a river and Adriane knew where that would eventually empty out. They ducked under logs that had fallen over the ravine like bridges.

The sound of marching feet echoed behind them. Those orcs were persistent.

"Let's get out of this ravine!" Zach shouted.

The sides of the ravine now rose up into muddy hillocks. They started up, but Drake was having trouble climbing, his feet sliding back in the mud.

"Get Drake over that hill," Zach said. "I'll hold them off."

"Wait." Adriane held his arm. "You're stronger than I am. You push him up, I'll hold them off."

Zach bit his lower lip, and then agreed. "Okay. But as soon as we're over, you'd better be right behind us."

Adriane faced Drake, looking deep into the dragon's eyes. "Now you listen to me. You go with Zach. I'll be with you very soon."

The dragon seemed to sense what she was saying and allowed Zach to push him up the steep side of the ravine wall.

Adriane slid back to the flat ground. With a crash, the trees ripped away and the orcs broke into the gully. She was suddenly facing six giants armed with extremely unpleasant weapons.

She glanced over her shoulder and saw Zach shoving

Drake toward the top of the hill. The dragon's head was craning back on its sinewy neck trying to see her.

Turning back, she whirled her arm in a circle, releasing a wave of golden fire, spinning it out like a lasso. Crouched in a fighting stance, she braced herself for the attack. She didn't have to wait long.

The orc leader, this time ready for magic fire, raised its shield and lunged forward.

Adriane swirled the fire around her. She threw out her arms and released the ring, sending it spinning out like a huge flaming Frisbee. It slammed into the orc, but its shield fractured the magic, sending it sparking into the trees.

Whoosh!

Spears flew at her. She dove, tucking and rolling away. The spears flew past her as Adriane landed in the shallow water of the running stream.

The orcs were forcing her out into the open so they could surround her.

She heard a whine in her head. *"Maamaa!"*

Oh, no. She whirled around to see Drake leap from the hill. He opened his new wings, but they weren't strong enough to hold him. His belly smacked in the mud with a *thwack!*

The orcs stopped uncertainly.

Drake rose up on his hind legs and roared. A lick of flame escaped his lips.

The orcs backed away. The dragon took a step forward and promptly tripped over his feet, falling flat on his nose.

The orcs snorted with laughter and raced forward.

"No!" Adriane threw herself in front of the dragon, diving to the ground and firing a stream of magic. The fire whipped out and wrapped around the ankles of two orcs. Adriane rolled, sprang to her feet, pulling her fist down sharply. The fire tightened, and the orcs went down, thundering into the water. Adriane leaped away as an ax split the air, cleaving into a boulder, sending splinters of stone flying. She danced and twirled, her gemstone exploding into blinding light that crisscrossed around her, creating a shield. Shards of rock bounced away.

White-hot pain pounded into her shoulder and she flew across the gully, landing face first into the water. She got groggily to her feet, hair streaked and dripping. Drake lumbered over to her, shaking with fear. The orc that had hit her towered over them as the others advanced. There were too many.

The orc raised its ax and swiped—but only the wooden handle came down, plowing into the muddy bank. It watched in surprise as the blade went flying into the trees.

Zach was standing on a natural bridge formed by a dead tree that had fallen across the ravine. His sword was out and ready. The orc threw away the ax handle, roared, and reached out with enormous hands to crush Zach like a fly. But the boy was too quick. The stunned orc looked down at the sword plunged deep into its chest. Its rib

cage opened with one terrible swipe. The boy kicked the bewildered monster back, and it crashed into the others like dead weight.

"Grab my hand!" Zach screamed. He had shimmied down and stretched out to grab Adriane.

"Hurry!" Zach leaned over farther.

Adriane looked at the regrouping orcs and then at Drake. Zach could save only one of them.

She reached into her vest pocket and raised her arm.

Zach slid lower, grabbing at her hand. Adriane slid her hand into his, but instead of grabbing on, she slipped the chained orb into the surprised boy's outstretched fingers.

She looked into Zach's eyes. "Take the Drake," she said, and pushed the dragon's tail into the boy's hand.

A look of shock registered on Zach's face. But he pulled with all his strength and yanked the startled dragon up beside him on the tree bridge. Then he leaped to his feet and ran, pushing the crying dragon away from the ravine.

Adriane threw back her soaking hair and stood facing the orcs. On her wrist, the golden wolf stone pulsed like the heartbeat of a warrior.

"Is that the best you can do?" she yelled.

"Adriane!"

Adriane looked back and saw the boy standing next to Drake at the crest of the hill. They were safe. She smiled. And everything went black.

14

A BUMP SHOOK Adriane awake. She opened her eyes to darkness. The creaking of wheels and the hard floor bouncing beneath told her she was in some kind of wagon, rattling on a very bumpy road. She was all scrunched up, trapped in some kind of sack. She had no idea how long she'd been there, but the ache in her muscles felt like it had been a while.

"Hummmrr doo raahh . . ."

Someone was humming. It sounded awful . . . and awfully familiar.

"Hummmahuma Wahh wahh."

She tried to move, but the sharp pain in her shoulder made her stop. Carefully she reached around the back of her neck and felt a tender spot. She winced. Definitely a bruise, a big one. She flashed on a giant monster swatting her with a fist the size of a chair.

She moved her wrist in front of her face and focused on the wolf stone. Its soft light was weak, but enough to see she was in a large, black sack.

She heard sounds of sniffing and quickly covered her wrist, dousing the magic like a small flame.

"Ooo, you feel that?" the voice outside said. "Magic rock! Scorge is gonna get big reward. LaLaaaa!"

Scorge! That was why the humming sounded so familiar. It was that pesky orange . . . thing. And he thought *she* was a magic rock.

"Magic rock all right." He patted the bag as he happily hummed.

Adriane heard the sound of wheels on stone as the road smoothed. Suddenly, the wagon came to a creaky stop.

The sounds of shuffling and scuffling closed in about her. She braced herself. A door on the wagon opened and she was dragged out, still in the sack, and dumped onto a hard surface.

"Be careful of rock!" Scorge complained.

Heavy doors opened and she felt herself being dragged across sandy ground. The sound of the doors slamming shut echoed behind her. She had a bad feeling in the pit of her stomach as the ground tilted. She was going downhill.

Soon the ground leveled out. The echoing of footsteps and voices suggested she was in a large, enclosed space.

Something hit the floor next to her.

"Great Queenie, I have traveled long and far to bring you this great magic."

It was Scorge and he was groveling on the floor next to the sack. Adriane felt something cold press in around her, probing with the touch of magic. She stifled a gasp as ice stung at her wrist.

A voice, sharp as a razor, hissed, "You have brought what I seek?"

"Oh, yes! Great magic that has slept for thousand years," Scorge said between his constant thumping. He must be groveling up a storm.

"From another world, Your Mightiness," he continued. "Reward should only be as gigantic as Royal Highness thinks humble servant deserves."

"Show me this great magic," the cold voice ordered.

Adriane heard Scorge scamper to his feet. "M'lady . . . your magic rock!"

Adriane was jarred as the sack was lifted up, ripped open, and turned upside down.

She spilled out onto a cold, smooth floor.

Her muscles spasmed painfully as she tried to uncoil. Flashes sparked in her eyes in reaction to the sudden rush of light. She heard voices around the room snickering.

She could see Scorge's back. He was facing another figure. Long, flowing dark robes glided silently across the cold floor, moving closer.

"You!" the figure said.

"Me, me!" Scorge squealed and danced in delight—then saw that the tall figure was looking past him.

He turned and practically choked. *"You!"* Scorge sputtered, leaning down to press his dirty orange head into Adriane's face.

Adriane's thoughts were hazy. She could barely catch her breath.

"What you do with Scorge's rock—*graagah!*"

Scorge was swept away with a flick of the figure's wrist. He dropped to his knees, and pointed at Adriane. "That witch stole rock!" He began bowing and groveling again, shaking with fear.

Snickers turned to laughter.

"Silence!" The chamber fell deathly quiet at the icy command.

Adriane's mind cleared as her eyes adjusted to the light. At first, she thought she was in some kind of cathedral. The vast chamber rose to a high vaulted ceiling hidden in darkness. Then she realized those weren't stained glass windows; they were crystals imbedded in walls as if the entire place had been carved out of a mine.

She looked up at the robed figure in front of her. A hooded cloak shielded the features from view. Adriane knew who it was. The same terrifying figure that she,

Emily, and Kara had once seen at Ravenswood—at the portal. The Dark Sorceress.

"Where is my dragon?" the sorceress asked with a deadly calm.

"Um . . . dragon?" Scorge croaked.

She turned on him. "The dragon egg, you imbecile!"

"Er . . . dragon egg?"

"That *rock* is an egg! Or . . ." she turned to Adriane. " . . . it was an egg." She raised an arm in the air.

With a jolt, Adriane was forced to her feet. She tried to resist but couldn't control her own body. The sorceress looked her over carefully. She moved her arm, and like a puppet on a string, Adriane lifted her own arm, exposing the wolf stone.

"Interesting," the sorceress said.

"Very . . ." Scorge groveled. " . . . interesting!" He bowed some more. "Smaller rock, smaller reward . . ." he muttered.

The sorceress's sleeve slipped down her raised arm, revealing a hand with slender fingers tipped with long, sharp nails. She flexed, and the sharp claws slid back into her flesh.

Two figures moved behind Scorge. They were as tall as the sorceress, serpent like, with snake heads, and long, scaly bodies. They carried staffs that sparked with power.

"Take our guest and make sure he gets . . . what he deserves."

Scorge looked right and left, eyes widening. "Um . . .

Scorge change mind, don't need no rewar*ghhh!*" A fist had grabbed Scorge by his throat. And then the guards were gone as quickly as they had appeared, Scorge with them.

The sorceress pulled back her hood and advanced toward Adriane. Strikingly beautiful, she had alabaster skin like a porcelain doll, rich red lips, and long, white-blond hair streaked with blazing bolts of silver lightning. Then Adriane looked into her eyes. They were not human, they were the eyes of an animal—no—some creature—slit by vertical pupils, cold, dark, and pure evil.

"So it was you I felt at the portal," the sorceress said.

Adriane choked, sweat running down her face.

"Come, come, child, I know you can speak."

"Please . . . let . . . me go," Adriane managed to sputter.

"Oh, I'm sorry. Was I hurting you?"

As if the string holding her had snapped, Adriane fell to the ground with a moan.

"Humans are such fragile things. Is that better?"

Adriane wiped spit from her mouth as she sat up. She rubbed her arms and legs to get the circulation moving. "Thank you."

"So polite." The sorceress circled Adriane, her silky robes rustling lightly as she moved. "Do you know any-thing about magic? No. How could you? No one to train you. Such a waste." She smiled and Adriane caught a glimpse of vampire fangs. "Now . . ." The smile faded and her eyes flashed like cold steel. "Where is my dragon?"

"I don't know," Adriane answered truthfully.

The eyes sparked dangerously. "Are you trying to make me upset? Is that what you want?" She flexed her hand, and the long, sharp claws slid out from her fingertips.

"I don't know where the dragon is." Adriane wobbled unsteadily to her feet, eyes carefully trained on the razor claws.

The sorceress continued to circle Adriane. "I have tracked the magic of the egg and I know it hatched. Then it just disappeared. Vanished . . . like mist." Her breath was cold as ice against Adriane's face. "Odd, don't you think?"

"I don't know."

The sorceress pointed a claw at her wolf stone. "Pity. Your stone is useless to me. It's been tuned to you. Just as the dragon has already imprinted on . . . whom?"

Adriane remained silent.

"But you are already bonded to a mistwolf, aren't you?"

Adriane said nothing.

"Aren't you?" The sorceress's eyes blazed into Adriane's.

"Yes," Adriane answered meekly. She couldn't turn away from those hypnotic eyes.

"Do you know that once a magical animal and a human are bonded, the bond is for life? One without the other is death to both. Did you know that?"

"Why—why are you telling me this?" Adriane stammered.

"So you know the truth. The animals are a burden and make you weak. Look at you now, you can barely stand up. All because you could not resist following the cry of the wolf."

Adriane stiffened.

"You think you are the first human magic user to try and help those pathetic Fairimentals by bonding with animals?" the sorceress said scornfully. "There have been many, and all have failed. The *truth* is the Fairimentals will use and manipulate you. And when you are used up, they will tell you how your spirit will be joined to the greater good of . . . Avalon."

She leaned in and hissed like a snake. "Avalon is not what you think it is."

She stepped back, her claws gleaming dangerously. "You are afraid to be here. You think this is all some per-version of the precious magic that binds you to these ani-mals. Now amplify that fear a thousand fold and you have a small sense of what Avalon truly is. The only chance you have of actually entering Avalon is by work-ing with me." Feral eyes blinded as a sly smile escaped her lips. "Give me what I need—what we need—to open the gates."

Adriane could feel the sorceress reach out her icy touch.

"Call the mistwolves. Bring them to me."

"No!"

"I wonder. Just how strong is your bond? Will your

mistwolf come for you? Or will she stand alone and watch you die?" She smiled evilly. "Let's see."

Instantly, Adriane was surrounded by serpent guards.

"Take her," the sorceress commanded, robes flying as she turned away.

Strong hands pulled Adriane toward a doorway. "I will never call the mistwolves!" she yelled.

"Then you will die," the sorceress said simply, then turned to her again. "Oh, how is your friend, Kara? I'm looking forward to meeting her again."

The sorceress's words echoed eerily as Adriane was dragged down a damp and musty tunnel. They passed open rooms, huge cavernous spaces cut into the earth, where dark figures worked on large crystals, sparks of fire flaring from the stones. The tunnel turned and twisted, going down into the earth. Adriane's heart pounded in her ears and her mind raced. These passageways all looked the same. She would never be able to find her way out of this place. The guards finally deposited Adriane in a wide room and she collapsed against a dank wall. Glints of light flashed off rock and crystal. She could feel energy flowing through the walls, pulsing like blood.

Adriane shivered, pulling her knees into her chest. She could hear moans in the darkness around her.

She got to her feet and held up her wolf stone, willing it to glow. Cutting a swatch of golden light in front of her, she saw rough crystal shapes jutting from the ceilings and cave floors. It was as if the entire place had formed right out of the earth itself. The light fell over a creature lying in the corner. Adriane moved closer and saw it was a pegasus, a winged pony, like the ones hidden at Ravenswood. This one was covered with ragged scars. Its wings were torn, green-glowing ooze on its back, sides, and legs. Black Fire.

Adriane edged closer and knelt before it, the light of her gem jittering.

The creature half opened its eyes. "Magic user . . ." It struggled to move.

"Shh, it's all right." Adriane tried to calm the creature, but she was shaking.

"Corintha . . ." it breathed.

"What?"

"Corintha . . . where is she?" It nodded weakly across the room.

Adriane got up and looked around, trying to steady the light as it swept across the room. It settled over the still body of another pegasus. There was no need to get any closer. She turned back. "I'm . . . sorry . . ."

The pegasus slumped. Tears ran from its eyes.

Something shuffled behind her. Other animals were slowly creeping out of the darkness. Adriane stifled a cry as her heart filled with anguish. There were dozens of creatures, some she recognized, like quiffles and jeeran, and some she didn't. The glint of golden cat eyes flashed as two big spotted cats emerged. They looked like Lyra—

before Emily had healed her. All the animals had the deathly glow of the Black Fire.

Adriane felt dizzy. Her stomach twisted into a knot. She felt as if she were suffocating.

"You are human."

She whirled around, and the light of her gemstone landed on a silver duck-like creature. It was a quiffle.

"Ye . . . yes."

"A human magic user!" another of the animals exclaimed.

Adriane heard the whispers from one to another as the word spread. A human was here among them. And she carried magic!

More animals crowded into the room.

Adriane didn't know what to do.

She felt in her pocket for the last of the coconuts. She took it out. These creatures were starving—how was this going to help?

Trying to control her shaking, she carefully broke the coconut into small pieces and began handing them out.

"I'm sorry, it's all I have," she said miserably. She was desperately fighting to keep herself from breaking down and losing it completely.

"Packmate . . ." a soft voice said in her mind.

Adriane jumped. The light of her gem began to pulse. She strained to hear the voice.

"You are not alone."

It was a mistwolf. Adriane knew it instinctively.

And the wolf was somewhere close, calling from the shadows of the prison.

She held up her gem and scanned the dark corners.

"Is there a mistwolf here?" she asked the animals, her voice trembling.

"Yes," one of the quiffles said. "She is dying."

"Take me to her. Please!" Adriane pleaded.

While the rest of the animals shared the small coconut, Adriane followed the quiffle under a low archway into another chamber. In the center was a clear box. As Adriane got closer, she saw it was a cage made completely of glass. And inside, curled on the floor, lay a silver mistwolf.

Adriane ran to the cage and placed her hands on the glass. Her stone flared wildly.

The wolf was ragged and weak, her rib cage sharply outlined through her skin. Patches of her once lustrous fur were gone, revealing burnt flesh crisscrossed with ugly green lines. As the light of Adriane's gem flashed over her, the wolf weakly raised her head, eyes half opened.

"It is good to see you."

Adriane's heart felt like it was being ripped apart. Anger welled, surging inside with the force of a hurricane. Filled with rage, she pounded her fist, spilling golden fire onto the glass.

The glass cracked, but held.

She turned to see the other animals watching her.

The animals huddled together and moved closer. She felt the weakness within them, overcome by the dark force of Black Fire. It ran through them, infecting their magic.

Still, she drew whatever strength they could offer.

Adriane screamed as a wave of green light swept from the animals and into her jewel. She threw the power at the glass. It shattered.

Crossing the scattered shards, she knelt and carefully lifted the wolf's head into her lap, gently stroking the mottled fur.

Everything she had experienced—the loss of the griffin, the dead wilderbeasts on the hill, the rivers of poison tearing across the land, the monstrous creatures, and now, these animals, alone and lost, dying—came pouring out at once.

Adriane's tears fell like rain as she hugged the mistwolf.

She thought about Storm, strong, vibrant, and full of life. She knew she couldn't call her. She could never bear to have Storm end up here. And suddenly Adriane realized why she had come all this way. Why she had risked everything to find her friend. All she wanted, needed, was the chance to say I love you . . . and to say good-bye.

Adriane cried until there were no more tears left.

"Your mistwolf loves you very much," the gentle voice said in her head.

Adriane gazed into her soft silvery blue eyes.

Although the wolf's body was wracked with poison, her eyes were clear and full of compassion.

"I miss her so much," Adriane sniffled.

"Shh, little one. No matter how far, she is always in your heart, as you are in hers."

Adriane curled into the mistwolf's side, snuggling close. She saw her wolf stone sparking from gold to green and knew that the poison was starting to spread through her own body as well. She refused to remove it. If this was the end, this was how she wanted to go.

"My name is Adriane," she said to the wolf.

"I am Silver Eyes."

Suddenly the air began to sparkle. Then she heard that unmistakable sound.

Pop! Pop! Pop! Pop! Pop!

15

FIVE BRIGHTLY COLORED dragonflies popped into the cave, red, orange, blue, yellow, and purple. They took one look at Adriane and the other animals, gave a chorus of shrieks, and immediately disappeared.

"Wait!" Adriane called out after them. "Come back . . . ohhh."

She couldn't blame them. She was among dozens of sick animals, a dying mistwolf by her side, and she could feel the Black Fire moving at a deadly pace through her body.

"Silver Eyes," she said to the mistwolf, "we thought you were dead."

She heard a soft bark, which Adriane recognized as a wolf laugh. *"Not yet."*

"Zachariah thinks so, too."

"Zachariah?" The wolf's eyes opened wide. *"Little Wolf?"*

"Little Wolf?" Adriane asked. "A human boy, he was raised—"

The wolf struggled to sit up. *"Is he all right?"*

"Yes, the last time I saw him."

"You saw my human son?" Her voice was full of wonder.

"Yes."

The wolf lay her head back down in Adriane's arms. *"Little Wolf is all right . . ."* She repeated over and over.

"He thinks it was his fault," Adriane told her.

"It was not his fault."

"Moonshadow thinks so."

"Moonshadow is the most stubborn creature in Aldenmor!" Adriane smiled.

"He could never accept the boy as his pack brother."

"Moonshadow is taking the pack somewhere safe," Adriane said. "My friend, Stormbringer, is with them. She thought she was the last mistwolf. Then we found the others."

"A wolf is bound to protect the pack," Silver Eyes said. *"But that does not mean she has abandoned you."*

"Then why did she leave?"

"Sometimes you have to leave to find your way home."

Pop! Pop! Pop! Pop! Pop!

The dragonflies were back, this time huddled together in a tight ball, shaking and squeaking.

Adriane slowly got to her feet and extended her arms. "It's all right. Don't be afraid."

Fiona broke away and landed, trembling, on Adriane's arm. "Ooo, Deedee!" Fiona's little red eyes swirled with distress.

"It's okay, Fiona. Did you bring me another message?"

She leaped into the air and chirped at the others. There was some confusing dragonfly chitter, and a few angry squeaks. Then they linked front wing claws together and started to spin in a colorful circle.

"Too Kaaraa!" Goldie squeaked.

Suddenly the area inside their circle began to sparkle.

The dragonflies had made a window about the size of a dinner plate—they had opened a small portal! Adriane peeked in and saw a hairy nose and a few whiskers.

She stepped back, confused.

Then she heard a familiar voice.

"I can't tell if this is working or not! Dooh! Those pesky things!" It was Ozzie!

"Ozzie!" she called out.

"Huh?" The hairy face pulled back and she could see Ozzie's whole ferret head. His little brown eyes opened wide in astonishment.

"Adriane!" He started hopping up and down, yelling over his shoulder. "I've got her! Hurry!"

Adriane couldn't believe it. She was looking through a window into the library at Ravenswood Manor. She heard the sounds of shuffling and running.

"Adriane!" It was Emily!

"Emily!" Adriane cried out, fresh tears streaming down her face. "I'm here!"

Ozzie's snout was pushed aside as Emily's face filled the little window.

Adriane was filled with joy. "It's my friends," she called out to the other animals.

Emily's face lit up, then changed to shock. "Adriane, what happened to you?"

Suddenly Kara's blond head pressed in tight against Emily's auburn curls. "You look terrible!"

"I missed you, too." Adriane didn't know whether to laugh or cry, so she did both.

The dragonflies' circle began weaving about as they argued among themselves. The window ghosted and flickered like a bad television signal.

"Oh, no," Adriane cried.

"Hey! Keep spinning!" Kara yelled at the dragonflies.

"OOoooOO!" Instantly the dragonflies stopped arguing and returned to spinning in a synchronized circle. The picture cleared.

Emily and Kara were looking at Adriane. Ozzie was jumping up and down on the desk, trying to get a look as Lyra paced behind them. Adriane could not remember ever feeling so happy. "How is Gran?" she asked.

"Fine," Kara said. "We told her you were staying at the Pet Palace helping Dr. Fletcher."

"Adriane, where are you?" Emily's face was full of concern. "What's happened to you?"

Adriane could only imagine what she must look like. She was filthy, her hair straggly and matted, the left side of her neck, purpled with welts. She could feel the Black Fire slowly creeping through her.

"Okay now, don't freak out . . ."

Her friends all held their breath.

"I'm in the sorceress's dungeon."

"What?" Kara and Emily looked at each other. Lyra growled behind them. Ozzie fell off the desk with a loud crash.

"There are a lot of sick animals here, and there's a mist-wolf. She's hurt so bad . . ."

"What about you?" Emily asked, cutting her off.

Adriane lowered her head. "The poison is in me too."

"GAHaaaah!" She heard Ozzie scream.

"What do we do?" Kara yelled, grabbing Emily.

Lyra yowled and Ozzie began leaping like a frog. The dragonflies squealed—and their circle began to flutter apart.

"Stop it!" Emily's voice cut through the commotion. "Chill! Everyone! Let me think!"

She turned to Kara. "Keep those dragonflies spinning!"

Kara yelled into the window, "Listen up!"

"Ooo!"

"Keep this window open no matter what! Got it?"

"Ookies, Kaaraa," Goldie squeaked.

"Adriane, let me see your wolf stone," Emily said.

Adriane held up her stone and Emily gasped. The once-bright gold and amber tiger's eye now glowed with a sickly green hue.

"Kara, Lyra, over here! Now!" Emily raised her rainbow jewel. Lyra and Kara were at her side in a flash.

"You, too, Ozzie."

The ferret leaped onto the big cat's head.

"Stand still, Adriane!"

Emily held up her jewel and concentrated. It flashed with cool blue light. "Kara, give me your hand," she said.

Emily and Kara joined hands as Lyra and Ozzie crowded in even closer.

"Concentrate on healing . . . feel Adriane's heartbeat and lock it on your own. Steady, strong, until our hearts beat as one."

The dragonflies squeaked softly, but kept spinning their magic window in front of Adriane.

"Now!"

Blue fire shot from Emily's jewel right through the window and slammed into Adriane's wolf stone. Adriane was thrown back. The dragonflies shrieked and broke their circle. The picture in the window sputtered, blinking in and out.

"Keep spinning!" Kara commanded.

Goldie sparked a golden flame and yelled at the others. They clasped wing claws again and spun. The window cleared.

Adriane's stone pulsed erratically, blinking from green to gold and back to green.

"Again!" Emily yelled.

Everyone concentrated and the magic leaped from the rainbow jewel, through the window, blazing into the wolf stone. Waves of blue light ran up and down Adriane's arms and began to spread, bathing her in pure healing magic.

Emily jerked back her arm and the blue light of the jewel faded.

Adriane stood, her arm raised, the wolf stone flashing golden light. "It's gone! You did it!"

A cheer went up from the animals in the dark cave.

Squealing with joy, the dragonflies started dancing and swooping, breaking their circle—causing the window to flicker and fall apart.

"Hey!" Kara yelled. "Not you! Keep spinning!"

"Ooop!" The dragonflies jumped back together and spun.

"Okay, Kara, can you move the dragonflies around the room so I can see the animals?" Emily asked.

"You heard her—start moving. Slowly!" Kara called out.

With a few squeaks, the dragonflies slowly spun their window over the animals.

Adriane quickly rounded up the wounded creatures in the dungeon, separating them according to how serious their injuries were. When the dragonflies flew over Silver Eyes, Emily studied the mistwolf closely.

Emily raised her rainbow jewel in the air. "Okay. She's

first. Just like before. I need everyone's help. Stay close and focused."

"Right!" Kara, Ozzie, and Lyra stood ready.

"Adriane, are you ready?" Emily asked.

"Let's do it!" Adriane said, her wolf stone raised

"A walk in the park," Emily raised her jewel. "Here we go . . . Now!"

Blue-white magic exploded out of Emily's rainbow jewel and shot straight through the window, wrapping the wolf in a cocoon of light.

Golden fire flew from Adriane's stone and enveloped the blue. With all her might, she willed the wolf to heal. Blue and gold lights flared brighter and brighter until they were a blinding white glow.

"Enough!" Emily shouted.

They lowered their gems and the light slowly faded from the wolf.

Adriane helped Silver Eyes to her feet. The wolf was still weak and thin, her fur still mottled, but there was no trace of the Black Fire anywhere on her body! Adriane's heart soared as she knelt to hug the wolf. "You're going to be all right."

Another cheer went up from the animals as Adriane turned to them, smiling. Tears of joy ran down her cheeks. "We have to hurry before the sorceress feels this magic," she said.

"I will use my magic to shield us," Silver Eyes said, as she slowly evaporated into mist.

AVALON: WEB OF MAGIC

One by one, Emily, Adriane, and Kara healed each animal through the dragonflies' spinning window. The process went faster and faster as the healthy animals added their pure magic to the healing. Others too weak to walk were carried in. Soon, every animal in the dungeon was healed.

Adriane's eyes shone as she looked at her friends through the dragonflies' window. "We did it!" she cried.

"Can you get everyone out of there?" Emily asked.

"It's an underground maze," a doglike creature said. "No one's ever gotten out of here."

The animals fell silent.

"I have." Lyra was looking into the window.

"Lyra?" a voice called from the crowd of animals.

"Rynda?" Lyra began scanning the animals.

A large, spotted cat stepped forward.

"My sister!" Lyra yowled. *"Where is Olinde?"*

Another cat pushed through the group. *"I'm here."*

"I thought you were lost," Lyra said.

"And now we are found," the cats mewed.

"Can you help us get out?" a quiffle asked Lyra.

"I escaped the dungeons. Listen to my thoughts, Rynda."

Rynda closed her cat eyes.

"Look into my mind. Can you see the path I took?"

"Yes, sister," the cat said.

She turned to the animals. *"This way,"* Rynda directed, and led them out of the chamber and into the dark tunnels.

Adriane saw her friends in the window back at Ravenswood.

Kara, Emily, Lyra, and Ozzie all stared back.

"Keep the faith," she said to them. "I will come home!"

With a quick series of *pops,* the dragonflies vanished.

"We love you, Adriane!" her friends called out as the window faded. And they were gone.

"I love you, too," Adriane said and followed the animals.

With Rynda in the lead, the entire group moved up through the tunnels. Adriane ran alongside, senses on high alert. As they passed a small cave, she heard a moan.

She ducked into the opening, golden gem held high.

Scorge lay chained to a wall. He looked even more wretched and pathetic than usual. "Scorge is so doomed. Oh, me, me," he moaned.

Despite what he had done to her, Adriane couldn't leave him here. She flung out a stream of magic and broke open the old rusty chains with one swipe. Scorge's eyes opened wide and he fell to his knees, groveling.

"Oh, thank you, thank you. You are good witch. Scorge is humble servant . . ."

"You're on your own now. Good luck." She turned and ran after the others.

Tunnel after tunnel, twist after turn, the group followed Rynda upward, toward the surface. Occasionally they had to sneak by large caverns occupied with workers, but nothing stopped them. No one expected the prisoners to ever attempt an escape.

Finally the floor leveled out and the tunnel ended at a large set of doors.

Adriane held her hand up to silence everyone. Then, slowly, she pushed open the doors. Outside was an open, stone-paved yard, and beyond it, the barren gray landscape of the Shadowlands. Night had fallen, and she could see the twin moons rising into the starry sky.

Four serpent guards marched back and forth across the yard.

Adriane walked out right between them. "Say, is this where the bus stops for Stonehill?"

The guards turned on her at once, staffs raised. Green fire licked from the tips, and they charged.

Suddenly they skidded to a stop, shock on their serpentine faces. Behind Adriane thirty animals came charging out the door. Adriane whipped out golden fire and yanked the staffs into the air as the animals raced forward, barreling over the surprised guards.

Adriane led the triumphant group across the yard and onto a stretch of flat, sandy ground. Behind them, several small volcanoes were rising from the desert. There were doors at the bases of each. She wondered briefly if she had come out the same place she'd gone in.

All around them lay the forbidding Shadowlands. Adriane held her wolf stone out in front of her. Which way should she go? They needed to get as far away as fast as they could. It would not be long before the sorceress learned of their escape.

"Follow my voice!"

Adriane's heart soared. "Storm!"

"I am with you." The voice of the mistwolf rang clear and true in her mind.

Adriane saw a line of dunes ahead, dark against the night sky.

"This way!" she yelled, herding the group toward the distant dunes.

Under the bright light of two moons, the animals fled across the parched sands. Adriane was out front, her wolf stone flashing in the night, a beacon to lead them.

"Storm!" she called.

Suddenly her gemstone flashed, and Adriane's mind whirled. Once again she was being pulled into the mind of the wolf. She breathed in fresh night air, felt sand beneath her padded feet, but saw no pack. Instead, only the image of a single figure. Slowly it came into focus. It was human. It was . . . *her!* Adriane was looking through Storm's eyes and seeing *herself*.

She blinked and saw a lone wolf standing strong, silhouetted by the light of the rising moons.

"Stormbringer!" Adriane cried. She ran to her friend and hugged her hard, as if she'd never let go.

The mistwolf licked her face. *"You found me."*

The light of the moons suddenly went dark, then brightened. A large shadow flew across the sky. Adriane felt her stone pulse with danger.

The animals began cowering and whispering. They felt it, too. Something was coming . . .

With a sound like thunder, the ground shook.

Something was here.

Behind the animals, a shape stood, unfurling immense bat wings, each with pointed razor tips. The demon's huge muscles rippled along a body covered in thick leather armor. Its eyes blazed red. Green venom dripped from its set of long razor teeth as it smiled.

A vision out of her worst nightmare stepped forward and Adriane's heart sank.

The manticore roared and leaped straight for them.

16

THE ANIMALS SCREAMED and scattered as the manticore landed with a ground-shaking *crunch* not ten feet in front of them and straightened to its full height. Armored in dark leather, its lower body looked like a mutated lion; the upper part resembled some bizarre ape-beast, with arms muscled like steel cords. A thick tail, tipped with iron spikes, swayed dangerously behind it.

"We meet again." The monster's guttural voice grated like shards of metal. "What magic do you have for me this time?" it challenged.

Adriane realized it was toying with them, reminding her that it had attacked once before, at Ravenswood, and had stolen the fairy map. It had taken the magic of the three girls working together to send the monster back through the portal.

Now she faced it alone.

No! She was not alone. Storm stood by her side, the bond between them strong and true. And her friends, Emily, Kara, Ozzie, and Lyra—they were with her, always.

"Let us go!" she yelled.

The demon snarled. "I was told to bring you back alive. But accidents happen."

"Stay away from us!"

The manticore stepped forward.

Adriane raised her wolf stone high, her other hand gripping the thick fur of Storm's ruff. The silver wolf snarled, teeth bared. Golden fire flared from Adriane's fist, spiraling down her arm, and covering her entire body. She and Storm stood bright as flames in the desert darkness and sent a beam of white-gold magic flying into the manticore.

The power slammed into the creature hard, forcing it back. The manticore roared. Together, Adriane and Storm whipped the magic around the manticore, wrapping the monster in fire.

The beast stood in the magical inferno—and smiled. Then it opened its blood-red mouth and took a long, deep breath. A ribbon of gold snaked its way into the manticore's mouth. It was inhaling the magic!

Adriane was suddenly jerked forward.

"Storm!"

The mistwolf leaped in front of Adriane and snapped at the manticore, looking for an opening to attack.

The manticore opened its mouth wider and began swallowing the magic. Adriane was being pulled in. She tried to resist but it was too strong.

Golden light flew wildly into the creature's nose, its mouth, and its ears. Then, with its chest fully expanded, the manticore heaved, spewing sickly green light back at Adriane.

From the corner of her eye, she saw all the animals closing in, trying to give her what magic they had.

"No!" she called to them. "Stay away!"

Like a bullet, Storm streaked for the manticore's back, hitting it from behind. Teeth imbedded in leather and flesh, the wolf violently shook its head. The monster roared and twisted around, trying to dislodge its attacker.

It was enough of a distraction. Adriane pushed back, trying to keep the green fire from flowing into her gem. The beam of light warped, angling sharply into the air. She twisted her wrist, trying to cut off the flow. With all her strength, Adriane smacked the beam down hard, cutting a smoking rift into the ground. Sand and rocks went flying as the magic burst apart, shooting sparks of lightning into the air. Her stone free from the creature's grip, Adriane tumbled backward.

With a flap of its dark wings, the manticore suddenly rose into the air, throwing Storm to the ground. With a booming thud, the creature landed behind the frightened animals.

The animals went running in chaos and confusion over to Adriane and Storm.

The manticore slowly looked over the huddled, shaking group.

"Healthy animals for the mistress to begin her work again. You did well." Its eyes focused on Adriane. "She cannot use your stone. But I can. You will have no use for it back in the dungeons."

The manticore closed its wings to reveal a regiment of armored serpent guards, one hundred strong, marching across the sands. The animals gasped and cried as the serpents fanned out into a line as they approached, and then came to a halt. The thudding sound of a hundred staffs pounding the ground echoed across the terrified group. Each serpent held its staff in front of them, pointed at the sky. Green sparks leaped into the night from the tips.

"Your magic is strong, but you cannot win," the manticore said.

The animals pressed tightly around Adriane and Storm, trembling, eyes darting about nervously.

Adriane leaned against Storm, wrapping both arms around the mistwolf. She was drained. She felt as if everything was slipping away, out of reach—except for one thing. The thing that mattered most.

"Storm," she said softly, her face buried in the wolf's neck. "You came for me. You risked everything for me."

"You did the same for me."

"Moonshadow was right. I have only brought you danger. Go. Please!" she begged. "Save yourself."

The wolf nuzzled Adriane's cheek. *"I would not be able to go on without you."*

"Really?"

"Yes."

"I love you, Storm."

"And I love you, Adriane."

An eerie howl split the night, echoing across the desert.

Adriane's eyes widened.

Another howl, then another swept over them like a ghostly chorus of ancient spirits.

Suddenly Storm raised her head to the moons and howled in response. Standing up, Adriane threw back her head and howled alongside her friend.

One by one, the animals added their voices, sending the wolfsong over the desert and back into the night.

The booming roar of thunder rolled over them, washing out the cries.

A huge thundercloud, black and gray, was moving down the dunes toward them. The cloud spilled across the sand and began to form into individual shapes— wolves. The entire pack racing straight for them.

And behind them, Adriane saw something else.

It was Zach, his Elven sword drawn to protect the big red baby dragon that lumbered beside him. The dragon craned his neck, straining to push forward, looking for something.

"They come!" The manticore roared to his serpent troops. "Tonight we will finish this. Ready!"

As one, the serpents raised their staffs high and pointed at the oncoming wolves. Green fire sparked from one tip to the next, racing across the line of weapons and joining into a single web of roiling fire.

Adriane looked in horror from the wolves back to the serpents as the truth suddenly hit her.

It was a trap! She had brought the mistwolves and the dragon to the sorceress. She was responsible.

No wonder it had been so easy to escape the dungeons. The sorceress needed *live* bait.

"Remember, we want them undamaged!" the manticore's voice boomed.

"No! Go back!" Adriane screamed at the charging wolves. She whirled to Storm. "Tell them!"

But it was too late. The serpent army stepped forward . . . and fired.

Green lightning lit the night skies as the fiery net flew forward from the line of staffs. As the wolves drew nearer, the net spread wide, ready to engulf the onrushing pack.

The manticore's eyes blazed with triumph. "Yes!"

The net fell to the sandy ground in a haze of sparks.

The manticore's eyes flew open in rage as the serpents began looking around frantically. Thirty animals and a hundred mistwolves had just suddenly vanished from sight.

From under the misty veil, Adriane knew exactly what had happened. At the last moment, the entire pack had dissolved into mist. The magic of the mistwolves had settled over the animals, making them invisible to anyone outside.

"Maamaa!"

The Drake bounded into Adriane's arms, covering her face in warm, wet dragon licks.

"Drake!" she cried happily. "I'm so glad you're okay."

"Find them!" the manticore screamed. Through the cloud, Adriane could see the manticore stomping around, enraged. It was searching for them, sweeping the sand into clouds with its huge wings.

"Hurry!" The voices of the wolves filled the veil. *"We must move quickly."*

Under the magic mist of the wolves, the animals huddled close behind Adriane, Storm, and the Drake, and began to move away.

Green flashes erupted around them as the serpents fired random blasts at the ground.

Adriane held up her stone and focused on the light at its center. Yellow-gold flashed. Concentrating hard, she sent a ghost image of her gemstone to a spot on the far side of the guards.

"Over there!" one yelled, as a gold light sparked in the

distance. They started running toward the false magic signal—away from their prey.

The manticore sniffed at the air and turned its head. Slit demon eyes looked directly at the place where Adriane and the others were hidden. Adriane held her breath. With a low growl, the manticore started for them—but stopped.

Adriane saw Zach standing in front of the monster, sword out and ready.

"We can't leave without Zach!" she cried.

The manticore snarled and grabbed for the boy. Silver steel stung the beast's arm and it roared in pain, lashing out. Zach leaped out of the way. Spinning around, he sliced into the manticore's leg, sword flashing. The creature swung its body, plowing giant arms at the boy's head. Zach ducked, but he was slammed to the ground by the beast's iron-spiked tail. The boy shook his head, pushed himself up, and tried to get to his feet.

The monster raised a giant foot and roared. "I will kill you as easily as I killed your parents, boy!"

"Then you will have to kill me as well."

A large shape materialized in the air as it flew at the monster, knocking it back and taking it down. It was a wolf, huge and black. The manticore fell with a booming crash as it tried to throw the wolf off. But the wolf was too stubborn and held on, raking its claws down the creature's chest, locking teeth into its neck.

Adriane saw a sparkling orb dangling from the black wolf's neck. It was Moonshadow.

The manticore writhed and struggled, pulling at the wolf with massive hands. It ripped the wolf free and threw him to the ground. The monster twisted to its knees and raised a giant fist—but Zach was much faster. He lunged forward, plunging the sword deep into the manticore's side.

The monster screamed as green blood burst from the wound.

Wolf and boy stood side by side, watching the monster stagger to its feet, open its wings, and lift into the sky, trying to stem its lifeblood from spilling out into the sands.

Zach stepped forward, eager to finish the monster, but Moonshadow stopped him.

"Another time, brother," the wolf said. *"We must protect the others."*

Zach looked at his wolf brother, sheathed his sword, and gave a short nod. Together they ran toward Adriane and the animals and entered the cloud of mist.

"Move. Now!" Moonshadow commanded.

Once again, the group started walking into the desert.

Zach ran to Adriane's side, his face full of concern. "Adriane, are you all right?"

"Yes." She smiled. "You rescued me again."

He smiled back, and his face blushed bright red. Then his eyes opened wide as he looked past her.

A wolf stepped forward from the group of animals. Silver Eyes.

Zach and Moonshadow started toward her at the same time, then the pack leader nodded his head, and the boy ran to embrace his wolf mother.

"I thought I'd never see you again," he cried into her fur.

"And I, too, Little Wolf, my son."

They raised their heads and looked to Moonshadow. The great black wolf stepped close and touched his nose to Silver Eyes' cheek.

"My heart soars with happiness, my wolf mother."

"As does mine, Moonshadow, my son."

Adriane looked on happily, Storm on one side of her, the Drake on the other.

Moonshadow and Zach, Silver Eyes between them, stepped forward to lead the group. Everyone followed, moving quickly between the dunes.

"How do we find our way?" Adriane asked.

"The gift from the Fairimentals will show us," Moonshadow told her.

Adriane saw the sparkling lights of the orb that hung from the pack leader's neck. He led the entire group into a shallow ravine beyond the far side of the dunes. The mist-covered group entered the hidden portal and vanished in a blinding white light.

17

"**H**OLD STILL!" ADRIANE said, tying a vine under the wolf's chin. She adjusted the big, bright blue leaf in place atop Storm's head.

"Why do I have to wear this silly thing?" the wolf complained.

"Because it's a party. We all wear them." She grinned at the thought of the lovely lavender leaf draped over her head at a rakish angle. Even Kara would be impressed at this Fairy Glen fashion statement.

Adriane and Storm sat together by the shores of the sparkling blue lake. It was a beautiful morning and Adriane felt clean and refreshed, having spent practically two hours scrubbing every inch of her body in the cool, clean waters.

"Storm . . ."

"Yes."

"I was hurt when you left . . ." Glints of sunlight played across the crystal waters. "But I understand why you had to come here." She gazed at her friend. "What the mist-wolves can do here, helping the Fairimentals and everyone in Aldenmor, is so much more important than . . . well, what I'm trying to say is . . ." She cast her eyes down and tried to be strong. "If you want to stay here, I want you to, also."

Storm nudged Adriane's cheek with her nose and licked the girl's face. *"Warrior,"* the wolf said. *"Thank you. Let us see what the pack decides."*

"Okay." Adriane smiled. Grabbing an armful of leaves, she got to her feet. "Come on."

The sun shone brightly through the trees as they walked down a path to an open meadow.

Rainbow sparkles spiraled in the air. Adriane watched the Drake open his beautiful red wings. They shimmered in colors. With a great flap, the dragon succeeded in lifting himself off the ground for a few seconds, then crashed, playfully rolling in the heather. A moment later, he popped up again like a giant red kitten, trying to grab a gleefully singing breeze that hovered just out of his reach. The Air Fairimental giggled as she danced around the dragon.

"Yeah! Stretch your wings. That's it." Zach circled, watching the Drake intently. "That's really good."

The dragon hopped up and down excitedly and promptly rolled over on his back. Zach plopped down and rubbed his round belly. The dragon crooned happily, his big legs running in the air.

Adriane had her hand over her mouth, trying to hold back her laughter.

Zach looked up at her. "What? He likes his tummy rubbed."

Adriane smiled. "You two were meant for each other, you know that?"

Zach smiled back. "He belches louder than I do."

Adriane sighed as she and Storm walked over. "Here, put this on." She carefully tied a big, floppy yellow leaf onto Zach's head.

"Do I have to?"

"Yes!" She wagged a finger at him. "Don't make me mad, now!"

The Drake gazed hopefully at her with his big, puppy-dog eyes.

"One for you, too." She tied a purple leaf between his horns.

A wet forked tongue licked her forehead.

She stepped back and admired the three of them, Storm, Zach, and Drake. "Perfect. C'mon, let's go."

As they headed down the path, Adriane moved up behind Zach and covered his eyes.

"Hey!"

"Shhh, it's a *surprise* party." She giggled.

Only when they entered Okawa's meadow did she take her hands away.

Under the giant branches of the huge tree, all the animals had gathered. Cats, quiffles, pegasi, even two small wilderbeasts. They cheered as Zach stood, his mouth open in surprise. Ambia hovered next to Gwigg beside a wooden platform piled high with fruits, coconuts, and a tall layer cake that sparkled with tiny, sugary lights.

A pegasus pony with blue-and-white wings stepped forward. "It was the most daring rescue ever in the history of Aldenmor!" it exclaimed.

"This day will be remembered always," a hamster-sized dog said.

"We will compose many songs for you, warrior," a rubbery-beaked quiffle said to Adriane.

Adriane smiled. "Well, in the meantime, do you remember the one I taught you?"

"Sort of."

"Okay, then, all together now . . ." She raised her arms to conduct the animal chorus. They all sang out as best they could, a cacophony of animal voices—hoots and neighs, growls and chirps, hollers and hums.

"Happy birth today you, happy you to birth, too, happy day haay, hey you hoot, happy birthday to you, too!"

The animals stopped and waited expectantly. Zach looked happily bemused.

Adriane clapped, laughing. "Wonderful!"

Cheers filled the meadow.

Zach bowed graciously. "Thank you, all."

Adriane stood in front of him and held out a bright package wrapped in yellow and pink leaves.

"What's that?" he asked.

"It's your birthday present."

"Say, how do you know it's really my birthday?"

"Because I said so. Here, open it."

Zach took the small package and looked at it. He held it to his ear and shook it.

Adriane rolled her eyes.

He smiled and unwrapped the carefully folded leaves. His eyes widened as he took out a red stone. It was round and rough-edged, but the tiny, faceted crystals in the center flowed with red fire. "It's . . . it's . . ."

"I found it in the Drake's egg. The Fairimentals confirmed it. It's a dragon stone."

"I can't take this!" he whispered in wonder and sudden fear.

"Yes you can, Zach." She put her hands on his and closed them over the dragon stone. It pulsed with red light. At her wrist, the wolf stone sparkled in response. "Make it yours," she smiled.

Zach broke out in a wide grin. He held the stone up high so everyone could see. "It's a dragon stone!"

Everyone cheered.

"Tummy rubb!"

"Huh?" Zach stared at Drake in amazement. The

dragon was lying on his back, gazing at Zach expectantly. "What did you say?"

"Tickle, Zaaakk!"

"Hey, I can hear him!" He grinned at Adriane. "This is the best present ever!"

She looked past him. "Zach . . ."

He turned around and saw Moonshadow and Silver Eyes standing with Ambia and Gwigg. He walked over to join them.

"You have a leaf on your head," Moonshadow observed.

Zach blushed. "It's my birthday."

The black wolf cocked his head curiously.

"Happy birthday, son," Silver Eyes said.

Adriane and Storm joined them.

Moonshadow lightly pawed the ground and then spoke. *"It has been decided."* The black wolf's keen eyes moved from the Fairimentals to the animals.

Everyone waited.

"With the safe return of our pack mother to guide us, we will put aside our differences. The mistwolves will stay and work with the Fairimentals."

The animals gave a resounding cheer.

"What about Storm?" Adriane asked, her heart suddenly beating faster.

"The choice is hers," Moonshadow's gaze settled on Storm.

Storm stepped forward and addressed the wolves. *"Since I was a pup I have dreamed of running with the pack.*

But the bond I made with my human packmate makes me who I am. My heart beats with hers." The wolf stepped to Adriane's side. *"I belong with her."*

Joy filled Adriane's heart.

"You are always welcome here, packmate," Silver Eyes said to Storm, and then looked at Adriane. *"As are you . . . wolf sister."*

Silver Eyes turned to Moonshadow. The black wolf pawed the ground then lifted his head to Adriane. *"You honor us, warrior."*

Adriane smiled and bowed to the pack leader. "The honor is mine."

"There is much to be done." Ambia hovered by Adriane's side. "You must continue your work with your friends. The magic web is full of mysteries and the search for Avalon must continue."

"We will continue our work to protect Aldenmor," Gwigg said. "Together."

Moonshadow nodded to Zach. *"My brother's fight is my fight."*

"Good, then you'll need this." Zach quickly pulled a giant pink leaf hat over Moonshadow's head.

The black wolf snarled, shaking his head. *"I am not wearing that!"*

"Oh, yes you are!"

The boy tussled with the wolf, trying to pull the hat onto his head.

"Oh, no, I am not!"

Moonshadow pulled the boy down and they rolled around in the grass, struggling with the leaf.

Silver Eyes looked at Adriane with a twinkle in her eyes. *"Boys, what can you do?"*

"Adriane," Ambia said, her fresh voice cool and breezy. "You have proved yourself far beyond what we could have hoped for."

"Close your eyes and picture what you want most," Gwigg rumbled.

Adriane closed her eyes.

A gust of wind blew across the meadow, filling it with soft, twinkly lights. The lights swirled into a glowing circle that expanded before them. Everyone looked in wonder as a picture formed inside. It was a grassy field. Two girls, a large cat, and a small furry creature stood there waiting.

"Emily, Kara, Ozzie, Lyra!" Adriane called out, waving.

"Adriane!" Emily yelled, looking back through the portal.

"Gahhh! It's the Fairy Glen!" Ozzie started hopping about excitedly.

Zach peered into the portal curiously.

"Who's that?" Kara asked, tilting her blond head forward to get a better look.

"Are you all right?" Emily asked.

"Who is that?" Kara persisted.

"This is my friend, Zach," Adriane said.

"Hello."

"Helllooo," Kara called out. "Nice souvenir, girl!"

Adriane turned to Zach. "You could come with me . . ." she said.

"No, I belong here. This is my home." He hugged her. "Thank you, Adriane."

"Hey, remember me?" Ozzie was jumping up and down.

"Ozymandius," Ambia called to him. "The things you do for us do not go unnoticed."

"Well, that's nice, but I itch!"

Ambia fluttered over Adriane. "Adriane, what is it you most desire?"

With one hand on Storm, she turned to her friends at Ravenswood. "I just want to go home."

Together, Adriane and Storm stepped through the portal and went over the rainbow.

BESTIARY
& CREATURE GUIDE

*I*F YOUR HEART is in the right place and if a magical animal deems you capable of loving and caring for another creature, you might be gifted with the special friendship of these animals. When your magical animal befriends you, it will speak to you. Once a connection is made, the bond remains forever.

Stormbringer

AFFILIATION: Good

Storm is a mistwolf that has bonded with Adriane. Mistwolves are shape-shifters, able to change to shadowy fog and clouds, becoming practically invisible.

Storm's bloodline goes back thousands of years, enabling her to tap into memories and visions of the past. Noble, courageous, and true of heart, Storm is a true warrior, always ready to protect her friends.

JEERAN

AFFILIATION: NEUTRAL

Jeeran are beautiful deer-like animals with long ears, purple eyes, and soft green-striped fur. Agile and fast, Jeeran are originally from the hills and forests of the Moorgroves, but have found their way into many of the forested regions across all of Aldenmor. They are thought to be sentient but keep to themselves.

PEGASUS

AFFILIATION: Good

*P*egasi are magnificent winged steeds, intelligent creatures, shy and wild and not easily tamed. When they do bond, they serve their friends with absolute faithfulness.

QUIFFLE

AFFILIATION: Good

Silver duck-like creatures that flourish throughout the lakes and wetlands of Aldenmor.

Quiffles are intelligent and fun-loving with strong family bonds. They are also loyal friends and allies to the other good animals of Aldenmor.

Lyra, Magic Cat

Affiliation: Good

Lyra is an exotic leopard-like magical winged cat. Only those with magic can see her magnificent wings. The magic cats of Aldenmor vary in size and coloring and possess a keen intelligence, sharp intuitive senses, and deep empathy for others.

Unicorn

AFFILIATION: Good

*U*nicorns are the most legendary and powerful of all magical animals—highly sought after and coveted by those seeking magic. Fast as lightning, unicorns can run upon the magic web itself, transporting themselves and their rider anywhere on the web without the need of a portal.

DRAGONFLY

AFFILIATION: NEUTRAL

𝒟ragonflies are miniature dragons originally bred in the Fairy Realms. Their magic derives from fairy magic, giving them unique abilities. They can pop anywhere without the need of a portal and can communicate between worlds. Being fairy in nature, dragonflies are fun-loving and playful. Wild dragonflies basically spread magic seeds and rarely ever bond with humans.

Water Fairimental

Affiliation: Good

$\mathcal{F}$airimentals are elemental beings, protectors of the good magic of Aldenmor. They take form and shape from one of four elements: air, water, earth, and fire. Fairimental magic is tied to Aldenmor, and they can appear only for very short amounts of time on Earth.

DRAGON
AFFILIATION: NEUTRAL

*A*n ancient, winged reptilian race known and feared for their size, physical prowess, and powerful magic. Fast and sleek, there are few creatures that can keep up with a dragon in flight. Dragons usually only associate with other dragons, but the rare mage that bonds with one finds exceptional empathic understanding and fierce loyalty.

Dragons are thought to be extinct on Aldenmor, but it is rumored they have hidden themselves in Dragon Home, located in an isolated place on the web.

GRIFFIN

AFFILIATION: Good

*H*alf-lion, half-eagle, griffins are ferocious avian carnivores. Though not as fast or sleek as other fly-ers, a griffin's muscled lion's body allows exceptional endurance and stamina for long distances.

Keen eagle eyesight and sense of smell make griffins excellent trackers.

Griffins are brave and very loyal to those mages lucky enough to bond with one.

İMPS

AFFILIATION: EVIL

*D*iminutive members of the Demon class, imps are formed by twisted, electrical magical currents that hold their oily jet black forms together. If injured, they can re-form themselves or merge together into larger forms. Imps have no individual thought, they act as a unit and follow one group prerogative.

GARGOYLE

AFFILIATION: EVIL

𝒲inged medium size member of the Demon class, gargoyles are vicious monster predators. Unlike imps, gargoyles are cunning and ruthless hunters, using their terrifying and nightmarish looks to their advantage.

OZZIE
IN THE SPOTLIGHT

MEET THE FUZZY STAR FROM AVALON—WEB OF MAGIC

HOT ON THE heels, or paws, of the best-selling book series, "Avalon—Web of Magic," a new star has emerged. The plucky ferret, who is actually an elf stuck in a ferret's body, has found fans all over the world as a starring character in the popular book series. Ozzie recently took a break to answer questions from his fans about what it's like to be a ferret superstar.

Is it fun being in a book series?
Tons. Cousin Schmoot is so proud! He and the other elves are going to be the first in line at the Barns and Acorn in Dingly Dell for the latest release!

How's the adventure going?
It's wild. I never know what's going to happen next. One day I was an elf doing my thing in the Moorgroves and the next, I'm a ferret involved in a great magical quest.

We're helping all the animals that have come to the Ravenswood Preserve and I think it's always a good thing to help animals. Especially now that I know what's it like being fuzzy!

What kind of magic do you have?
Well, none that I know of, but the Fairimentals turned me into a ferret, that's something. Emily thinks there's magic in me that I haven't discovered yet.

Do you think everyone has magic inside of them?
Absolutely. I like the idea of discovering magic inside ourselves. Anyone can feel good about that. Each day if you do something nice for someone else, that's magic because it creates a magical feeling. Calling a friend, or hugging your animal best friend is magical, 'cause it feels good inside.

Do you think you'll ever get back your old body?
One day I think so. But I've got a lot of work to do with

the mages and I realize that the Fairimentals wanted me to have a good disguise. A bear would have been nice. But being a ferret has its advantages.

Like what?
Well, for one, I can climb and run and bake. My paws are very dexterous for using computers and eating.

What's next for Ozzie?
I'm thinking spin-off, "The Amazing Adventures of Ozzie."

When's your birthday?
Why, you got a cake?

What is your real height and weight?
I'm 4 foot 6" 100 pounds

Really? Are you on a diet?
Very funny.

STAR STATS

NAME: Ozymandius

NICKNAME: Ozzie

BIRTHPLACE: Farthingdale

CURRENT RESIDENCE: Ravenswood Preserve, Stonehill, Pennsylvania

HOBBIES: very good with computers, wigjig dancing

FASCINATING FACT: will eat any kind of cookie; orders all the supplies for the Pet Palace

Ozzie's Fred-X Home

Dear Mother Elf,

I don't know if you will ever get this letter. We're trying out a new Fred-X transweb delivery service and it's not like I'm in the Moorgroves. In fact, I'm nowhere near home. I'm on a place called Earth. I know you told me not to wander past Dumble Downs, but the Fairimentals called me. That's right, your little elf actually met Fairimentals! You should have seen them: powerful fairies made of earth, air, and water—amazing!

They told me Aldenmor is in danger. Elder Elf Rowthgar was right. There is a poison called Black Fire spreading across our world and it's hurting a lot of creatures. Don't you worry, though—the Fairimentals are protecting Farthingdale with their magic. They sent me here to find three human mages: a healer, a warrior, and a blazing star. (Check with Auntie Ishris—she knows the stories about humans). Anyway, I found three girls. They hardly know anything about magic so I'm trying to teach them, guide them as best I can. If they can ever work together, they might just learn something. I'll say one thing, they're full of surprises. They've been helping the hurt animals that managed to get here from Aldenmor and I think, given time, they can learn to help the Fairimentals . . . and all of us.

I fear I have a long journey ahead of me before I'll ever see our beautiful elf hills again or enter a prize turnip at the Applecrab Festival. The Fairimentals need to find this place—a place of pure magic, maybe even the source of all magic, Avalon. How can the Fairimentals expect these girls to find such a place? I don't mind telling you I am worried. But if there's anything you taught me, it's that there is nothing you cannot do if you truly believe.

I have no idea where this journey will lead me, but wherever I wander, no matter how far I may be, my heart is with you. Give my regards to Uncle Plith and cousins Schmoot and Tonin. I hope I can make you all proud of me.

Take care and love to all,
Your loving elf,
Ozymandius

P.S. One more thing. Remember you're always saying
how you've always wanted a cute, furry pet? Well, if I
ever get home, I think you're gonna get one.

Rachel Roberts on Writing, Best Friends, and Elephants

"AVALON—WEB OF MAGIC" is Rachel Roberts' first series of novels. She says most ideas for her stories and characters come on long hikes with her best friend, Ensign, a silver white husky. She carries a small notepad for jotting down thoughts and discussing with Ensign. Then at home she expands on the ideas with cat pals, Attila and Raider.

Rachel is an avid campaigner for animal rights. "My secret wish: I'd love to adopt an elephant, but I know wild animals need to be in their natural environment or in the proper care of professionals for the animal's own best interests—and probably my neighbors'. Oh well, elephants are still cool."

Rachel Roberts
on Making Magic

*E*MILY, ADRIANE AND KARA started out by helping a handful of animals, then saved the Ravenswood Preserve, and are now on a quest to save the entire Magic Web. Even if you don't have a herd of magical animals or a portal, there's still so much you can do to help. Remembering to turn off lights to save energy, planting a tree, or donating old blankets to an animal shelter are small acts that have a big impact.

My greatest hope for Avalon readers is that these stories will help you discover the magic waiting for you in your own backyard. Once you find it, you'll do everything you can to make it flourish, and your friends will want to get involved, too. One spark of magic can ripple out and make a huge difference, like circles in the stream.

—RACHEL ROBERTS, March, 2008

The magic of Avalon comes to manga for the very first time!

AVALON

THE WARLOCK DIARIES

Experience a whole new level of fun, excitement, and mage magic as Adriane, Emily, Kara, Ozzie, and the entire Avalon gang begin a brand new illustrated adventure written by Rachel Roberts, with visually dynamic manga-style artwork!